SHATTERED GUILT

KATHLEEN J ROBISON

ISBN: 978-1-951839-24-6

Celebrate Lit Publishing

304 S. Jones Blvd #754

Las Vegas, NV, 89107

http://www.celebratelitpublishing.com/

To my family. All of them. My love, my husband, Bruce; My beautiful children, and their families. David and Tomo, Titus, Felicity, Silas, and Baby due September '21; Jonathan and Maki, Aki, Leon, Hugo, Rhea; Jennifer and Kevin, Aliyah, Eli and Adah; Daniel and Shannon, Brucie, and Peter; Julie and Darren, Avalynn, and Isla; Sam and Jocelyn, Harper, and Baby due September '21; Josh and Tess, and Asher; Joanna. Your love, support, and affirmation mean everything to me. Thanks for following Jesus. Next to Him, you are my most treasured gifts. You are the love of Christ in action, and you bring God's purpose of existence to my life. Not to mention you are a ton of fun! I love you all.

IN MEMORY OF

My cousin Joni Hawe, whose voicemail expressed how much she loved my book and told me to keep up the good work. I didn't know that would be the last time I would hear her voice. I miss you so much, Joni. Thanks for the pep talk and always pointing me to Jesus. I'm jealous that you're with Him, our glorious Savior, but you fought the good fight, dear cousin, and I'm so glad you claimed your reward in heaven. See you soon, and very soon. That's a promise.

CHAPTER 1

A pile of unpaid bills lay on Melanie's desk, and her chest felt the weight of a burden that she couldn't fix. Quaint Affairs, her pride and joy. The wedding business her father had helped her launch. They'd procured a grant in Bay Town, Mississippi, a little old southern town sitting on the Gulf of Mexico. The shop was her dream. And she was about to lose it all.

Gazing around, her eyes stopped on her prized piece of furniture, a Maitland Smith dining table. Set with goblets, china, and linen napkins. The rich wood glistened beneath the lace runner. Her eyes followed the intricate carvings along the bordering ledge surrounding the tabletop. The smooth walnut finish warmed her heart. It even made her smile, but it didn't last. The Maitland Table was an investment piece.

A loud-sounding pop jolted her. A creaking came from the front door. Stepping around from the back of her desk, she peeked through the candelabras. The broad, muscular back of a tall man fought to push the old door closed.

"Sorry," he said, "I guess it sticks."

"Yes, I've got to get that fixed." Melanie took a deep breath. A strikingly handsome face stood before her. "Good morning, Pastor Brooks. What brings you into Quaint Affairs?"

Desmond Brooks, the pastor of Bay Town Community Church, removed his sunglasses. He glanced around. "Good morning. I came to talk to you about a wedding." His dark eyes sparkled.

Melanie's smile faded, and her heart raced. Everyone knew he was a widower and the most eligible bachelor in town, and she was certain she wasn't a candidate for anything in his future. Still, she sighed.

"Congratulations. When's your big day?"

"What?" Pastor Brooks drew his shoulders back. "No. Not me. Someone called about getting married in our church." His laugh was friendly.

"Oh. I see." A silly grin rose on her lips, and Melanie chuckled. She babbled on about church venues not being trendy anymore and prattled that other venues were much more in vogue these days. She crossed her arms and squeezed.

"Our church gets a few calls now and then asking about booking it for a wedding, so I guess I could use a coordinator."

"Oh, well, you've come to the right place then. Have a seat." Melanie waved at a Louis XIV reproduction. The chair covered in a classic gold-striped fabric appeared too elegant to sit in. Dollar signs rose in her mind—another investment piece.

Melanie took a seat behind her desk. "Well, I'm the coordinator," she said, pointing to herself. "Me. The planner. I do all the weddings." A nervous giggle escaped.

The pastor smiled and nodded.

Melanie sunk into her chair. *He thinks I'm an idiot.* They'd only ever spoken at church and church events, so this was a first. They were both newcomers to Bay Town when they'd met a year or so ago, and secretly, she wanted to get to know him better, but it hadn't happened. Melanie shuffled a few papers, picked up and set down her pen, and folded her hands.

His kind eyes stared back, and she felt herself flush.

He broke his gaze. "So, there's a young couple who needs help with their wedding. But I'm afraid they don't have much in their budget."

Melanie's heart dropped. Budget. That meant almost for free, and that was no way to grow a business. A struggling business. She stared. Thick, dark hair, piercing eyes, and chiseled jaw. Heck, he even had the dimple. Why not? Melanie sighed again. Maybe, just this once.

He looked around her shop, and Melanie followed his gaze. Polished silver and crystal pieces glinted. A replica Ming vase filled with fresh white roses rested in the center of an English rosewood tea table. He squirmed and leaned forward taking a brochure. It read, "Quaint Affairs ~ Creating Unforgettable Memories for a Lifetime."

"That's a big order to fill." He smiled.

"Oh, you know, that's just marketing." She winced. A year ago, she believed in creating unforgettable memories. It was her dream. Now, the certainty wasn't there. Now it was survival.

He looked away, searching the room again, and his brow furrowed a bit. A sizable mantle held an array of champagne flutes, wedding favors, and a basket filled with engraved invitations. Most things boasted elegance and extravagance.

Melanie could only guess what he was thinking and blurted out, "I only look expensive."

He turned back to her. "What?"

"The shop, everything looks pricey, right? But I can work within any budget." She wished she hadn't expressed that but banished the thought. "I'd love to help. I started out doing budget weddings, you know? Before moving here, I did weddings out of my apartment back in California. And believe me, most of my clients had practically no budget."

Melanie smiled. She recalled the last big wedding in Malibu. That was what she dreamed would put her on the map, and here she was struggling again.

"I see. Did your husband help with the business back there?"

Melanie's smile faded. "My husband?" Her face wrinkled. "How do you know him?" Besides one close neighbor, Melanie had never spoken of her ex-husband, and surprisingly, no one asked.

"Oh. I'm so sorry. I just assumed. I mean … your daughter and …"

Melanie shrugged. "Oh, no worries." Her eyes darted back and forth. "Shhh, I'm divorced." Once the words escaped, she could sense how terrible he felt. "I'm kidding. Hey, this is the new millennium, Pastor. Divorce isn't a dirty word anymore." Melanie joked, but her throat tightened at the thought of her own failed marriage.

She blinked long and sighed. "Bad joke. You know, Bible belt and all."

He chuckled. "Well, I apologize if anyone in the church has said anything. I know with some people, it's still a sensitive subject. And I'm sorry if I gave that impression."

Melanie felt terrible for putting the poor man on the defensive. "Oh, you didn't. I'm fine with it. My daughter, Lacey, and I started out living with my parents, and they helped me out. It was my father that pushed me into getting this business going."

He seemed to be interested.

"So, Lacey's father and I were married for barely a year. He wasn't even there when she was born. He came back once, but we got divorced before her first birthday."

"Doesn't sound like such a great guy." His eyes grew wide. "Oh. I'm sorry again. I didn't mean to judge. I don't even know the guy." He removed the sunglasses resting on the top

of his head and attempted to shove them in his front shirt pocket. Twice.

Melanie laughed. "Actually, he was a great guy, just a terrible husband. I made some foolish choices back then. But God blessed me with a wonderful daughter."

"Yes, Lacey's pretty special. She sure brightens up the church on Sunday mornings."

Hearing him say her daughter's name warmed her heart and made something spark. A sigh escaped. "So, let's make an appointment for this couple."

Flipping through her planner, Melanie glanced up and caught him smiling at her. His eyes seemed to shine from behind his dark lashes, and she felt the heat rising in her cheeks again. She dropped her head and, without looking up, asked, "Okay. So, when is the wedding day?"

They discussed the date and some other minor details and planned to meet with the couple soon.

Pastor Brooks stood. "Well, thanks. I'll be looking forward to working with you. I know you'll be a big help to them and to me, too." He extended his hand.

As she shook it, the mere touch of his hand tingled her fingers. She felt like a teenager with a first crush.

He moved to the front of the shop and waved as he left.

Melanie followed but stopped at the door. She leaned out, watching him walk down the sidewalk, and something fell from his back pocket. She ran and picked it up.

"Hey, Pastor Brooks?" Melanie waved her wedding brochure in his direction.

Turning, he strode back and reached to take it, but with a gust of wind, the brochure fluttered to the ground. Both Melanie and Desmond bent to retrieve it and knocked their heads together. Laughing, they reached out, and their hands touched. With a jolt, both released the brochure, and it floated down once again.

He put up his hand. "I got it." He bent, gripped the paper,

and straightening back up, he nodded. "I'll pass this on. See you in church, Mrs. Thompson."

Melanie frowned.

He stopped and turned again. "Hey, are you going to the church softball game tomorrow night?"

Melanie bit her lip and blurted out, "Please, Pastor Brooks, it's Melanie or Mel, anything but Mrs. Thompson."

He laughed. "Okay, Melanie, and please call me Desmond."

Desmond? This is a first, thought Melanie. "Deal. So, what's this about a game?"

"Well, it was in the church bulletin that nobody reads." He shrugged. "But we have a friendly game against Our Lady of the Gulf Parish. It's an annual event, but my first."

Bay Town Community Church was the first place Melanie and her daughter had connected when they arrived a year ago. Grieving the loss of both her parents, the small-town community was just what they needed. Family.

"Oh, well, maybe. Are you going?" Melanie rolled her eyes. "Yes, of course, you're going."

"Oh, yeah." He stared back at her for a little too long and finally spoke. "I, uh, I just thought if you and your daughter weren't doing anything, you could stop by. It should be a lot of fun." Desmond glanced at his watch. "Well, I better go. Hope you can make it."

Melanie's stomach fluttered, and something inside her stirred. Something she hadn't felt in a very long time.

The elation was short-lived as she walked into her shop and the desk phone rang. It went to voicemail, and it was the bank vice president asking for her to return his call. Her heart dropped.

Her house. The business. Her livelihood. Her dream. Her father would have led her to prayer in times past, but she didn't feel like praying now. Not without him. Closing her

eyes, the ache in her shoulders returned. *Daddy, what would you do?* Melanie rubbed her temples and picked up a pen.

Option #1 Sell everything in the shop.

Option #2 Sell the house.

Her wrist rested on the desk, her pen poised above a floral line notepad.

Option #3 Chris.

Her flakey ex-husband. She hated to bring him into this, but she didn't have much choice. He did well for himself. A real estate broker with multiple licenses so he could work in different states. He always seemed to be rolling in the dough, but he was forever hit and miss with child-support. And Melanie had been okay with that—until now. She had always prided herself on not depending on him. But with her parents gone, where could she turn?

Folding her hands, Melanie rested her forehead on her knuckles. The last thing she wanted to do was depend on Chris. But he said he might have a referral for her. A huge one. The bank was about to foreclose on her house, rent on the shop was months late, and only one wedding was on her calendar. Well, maybe two. She thought of Desmond. And perhaps just this once Chris might come through, too. She looked up. *Thank You, God!*

CHAPTER 2

Melanie pushed aside her problems, and instead of waiting for Chris's call, she went to work on the event before her, the wedding on Sunday. It would be an extravagant, opulent affair at a beautiful local venue in town—the Barn. Although the family was from New Orleans, the bride had contracted Melanie when she still lived in California. Sunday's wedding would be a spectacular showcase. It might be the only one left on her books, but it could be the steppingstone to launching her business in the South. With New Orleans money right next door, who knew what the possibilities were? Her heart dropped a little. Deep inside, she wasn't putting all her eggs in that basket like she did with the Malibu wedding.

She had only a few loose ends that needed tying up. Organizing, implementing, and executing were her strengths, and her storefront shop on Main Street allowed her to do that well. So far, this shop had fared well compared to her last venture in California. Despite the debt she owed, at least the building was still standing. Melanie shivered at the memory of the arson fire that had engulfed the bridal shop in California.

Quaint Affairs was so much different. Most importantly, it wasn't a bridal gown store but a showcase for her wedding

consultant services. When customers walked into Quaint Affairs, they often gasped. Melanie knew it took their breath away. She'd planned it that way. When guests opened the antique door, they were greeted with twinkling lights, the melodious background of violins, and the sweet smell of fresh roses. The magical setting whisked her potential clients into the heart of a fairy tale. And they loved it.

The phone rang, and glancing at the caller ID, she rolled her eyes. Her ex-husband. Forcing herself to smile, she answered. "Hey, Chris. What's up?"

"Wow. I love you, too, babe."

She stopped and forced another smile. "So, you got that referral for me?"

"Yeah. Yeah. Listen, about that wedding gig. It's not a good idea."

Melanie placed a palm down and rose from her desk. "What do you mean, it's not a good idea? Chris, I was counting on you. I mean it."

"I know. Just hold your horses, Mel. I got a funny feeling about it. I work for the bride's father, and I'm not feeling it. In fact, after a year of closing deals for him, I just quit. Something's not clean about the guy."

"Since when were you the judge of what's clean?" Melanie winced. That was mean.

"Ouch. Well, don't you think if *I* have an awful feeling, it must be pretty bad? Considering what you think of my moral markers."

He had a point, but she needed the work. And how bad could it be? It wasn't like Chris worked for the mafia. "Listen, Chris, why don't you let me be the judge. Just give me the number. I'll meet with the bride and go from there."

"No. I'm telling you, the dad is a big gun in New Orleans. I'm not even sure if the name of his company is legit. Much less the company itself. I don't know exactly what he does, but he sits up in that One Shell Tower Plaza penthouse in New Orleans and calls all the shots."

Melanie's eyes widened. That was the most impressive building in New Orleans. He had to be somebody big. Her palms began to sweat.

"Did you say One Shell Tower Plaza? The Penthouse?" Her pen flew across her pad.

"Nah. Not doing it, Mel. Listen, I'll dig up some more business, and as soon as I close a few deals, I can help you out."

Melanie felt a fire burning inside and seethed. "I don't need your help. I just need a referral. Chris, I'm good at what I do. People pay me good money to make their dreams come true." Melanie bit her lip, wishing she could take the words back. Sounding desperate and self-promoting wasn't her.

Chris's laughing didn't help. "Dreams come true? Yeah, baby, you sure made my dreams come—"

Click. Melanie hung up.

Incorrigible. What did she see in him in the first place? He was nothing but a self-absorbed player. She shook her head. A good-looking, charming, sweet-talking, self-absorbed player.

Crossing her arms, Melanie looked around. The wood antiques almost spoke to her. Begging her not to sell. What other choice did she have? Selling them off piece by piece might cover the rent one month at a time, and the income from the upcoming wedding would buy her a little time. But then there was the house mortgage. Her eyes widened. The bank manager! Picking up her cell, she tapped the numbers.

"Mr. Woodley? This is Melanie Thompson...I'm fine... And you? Good...May I come in and speak with you this morning?"

Locking up, Melanie walked down to the far end of Main Street. The largest brick building on the block housed Gulf Bank. A small, family-owned bank, and they'd treated her as such, until lately.

Mr. Woodley sat in his office waiting for her. He stood when she arrived.

"Hello, Mrs. Thompson. I am sorry for the notice of default. You know I had no choice." His thick southern drawl was soothing even when delivering disheartening news. He sat in his big, cushy, leather chair, much like a gentle, old grandfather.

"Of course, Mr. Woodley. But I have a wedding this weekend, and I plan on paying a month's—"

"I'm sorry, but you're three months behind." He clasped his hands.

"I know. I know." Melanie raised her palms. "Just hear me out. I'm on the verge of landing a wedding referral for a family in New Orleans. A pretty prominent client, from what I understand." Her body tensed. "If I get the contract, I'll get a retainer, and I'll be able to catch up. Please, Mr. Woodley. Just a little more time."

He tugged at his bow tie and pushed up his thick frames. The genuineness of his face and the kindness in his eyes made her hate herself for stretching the truth.

"Mrs. Thompson—"

"The potential client occupies the penthouse in One Shell Tower Plaza in New Orleans."

He removed his glasses. "Oh my. That could be quite a lucrative contract. How potential?" He leaned forward.

"Very potential. My husband, uh, my ex-husband, works for the client. He's referring me for his daughter's wedding." Melanie's gut wrenched, and her hands sweat. It was just a little white lie, wasn't it?

Tapping his glasses on his desk, he looked up. "Mrs. Thompson, please call me with an update in a few days. I'll grant you one month to show me a contract. We may be able to negotiate the default at that time."

Melanie stood swiftly. Her chair scraped across the old wood flooring. Mr. Woodley seemed to be trying to stifle a smile. She reached over the desk, took both his hands, and shook them, pumping his arms vigorously.

"Oh, thank you, sir! You won't regret it. I promise!"

Her insides felt like Jell-O. Just like the state of the dealings she'd promised. Thanking Mr. Woodley, she hit the sidewalk, hoping for some sunshine to warm her shaking body. Instead, the breeze blew, and her hands clasped her tunic sweater tightly around her thin frame. One down. One to go. Max was next. The landlord of her shop building.

Max owned the florist shop a few doors down, The Pink Rosette. Melanie breathed deep when she entered. The scent of sweet flowers filled the air. He came out around the counter to greet her. His round, wire-rimmed glasses and flowing, thin, white hair made him look like an old rock star. The smeared green and brown stains on his apron almost covered the signature single pink rosette embroidered on the bib.

Melanie smiled. The thought of a "Max" being the owner of a sweet flower shop always made her chuckle. He had been a gardener for the local cemetery. He had a touching story behind the opening of the flower shop with his life savings. It was his and his wife's dream. Melanie loved it. Another endearing Bay Town personality. When Max's wife had passed, he sold their home, and coupled with her life insurance policy, he bought a couple buildings on Main Street. He dedicated himself to developing the downtown charm of Bay Town. Melanie rented one of those buildings from him.

"Hello, my dear. What can I get for you?" Max's proper British accent always lifted Melanie's spirits. It was lovely, just like his flowers. Holding up a bouquet of baby pink roses, he raised his brows.

"They're beautiful." Melanie tried to smile. "Max, I wish I had better news. I'll be able to make this month's rent, but not the back …" Before she could finish, he raised a hand.

"No need to explain, dear. All in God's timing. You bring

me the rent when you're able. I trust you. And besides"—he winked—"I know where to find you."

"Well, thank you for your patience. I'm sorry. Things just didn't work out here as I expected." Her shoulders dropped. "Maybe I should have stayed in California."

"Now, now, dear. We're family here, aren't we?" He patted her arm.

Melanie nodded, and the thought of her mom and dad caused her eyes to water. Charlene, her only sibling, lived in Washington, D.C. "Yes, yes, we are."

Pulling out a pink rosette from the bunch, Max handed it to her. "On the house. Dry your tears. Sweeter days are always ahead." Max winked and directed Melanie to the door.

She nodded and stepped out, sniffing the pink rosette, but the spicy smell of men's cologne and tobacco overpowered.

A tall, slender man, well-dressed, blocked her path. His foot crushed a cigarette beneath expensive shoes.

"Excuse me, ma'am."

His voice sounded friendly enough, but his smile was a bit alarming. He didn't move, so Melanie stepped around him.

"Ma'am, I'm sorry to bother you, but I'm looking for Melanie Thompson, the owner of Quaint Affairs?" He raised a hand to smooth his already slicked-back hair. "I drove by the shop, but the closed sign hung in the window."

Melanie stopped in her tracks. Tourists and strangers were frequent on Main Street, but there was something about this guy. She couldn't place her finger on it, but she shrugged. Never look a gift horse in the mouth, her father used to say. But the gifts he referred to were often those sent by God.

"Oh, well, that's me. I'm Melanie Thompson." Desperation threw caution to the wind. "What can I do for you?"

"Well, ma'am, my employer's daughter is getting married, and they would like to book your services for the wedding."

"Your employer? How did he hear about me?"

"Why, it was Chris Thompson that referred you."

Melanie scrunched her brow. "What?! Who?" Melanie couldn't believe her ears.

Max stepped out of his shop. "Everything all right out here?"

She nodded.

"Chris Thompson's, your husband, right?" said the man.

Did Chris change his mind? "He's my ex-husband. Divorced long ago." She rolled her eyes. "Listen, my shop is just a few doors down. Why don't you follow me there and we can discuss the wedding?"

The stranger pulled a business card from his pocket. "No need. Here, ma'am. Call the number. The secretary will take care of you. Have a pleasant day." He tipped a hand to his forehead.

Melanie stared at the card. It read *One Shell Tower Plaza, Penthouse Suite, New Orleans*. A phone number was the only other print. By the time she looked up, the man had disappeared. "So, what do you make of that, Max?"

"Not sure, dearie. Not sure. Your husband? Is he still around?"

Melanie shook her head. "He's my ex, and we haven't been married in forever. And no, he's not still around. Rarely."

A wind blew up, and Max pushed the hair off his forehead. He patted Melanie's hand and retreated inside.

What a morning! Her first thought was to call Chris and ask him why he had a change of heart. She glanced at the card again and chuckled. This guy must be bigger than Elvis. He didn't even need a first name! Melanie deposited the card in her purse and peeked into Max's shop. "Hey, I'm going to Mockingbird Café. Can I get you a cup of coffee?"

"No, thanks, my dear. Had my cup this morning."

"So did I, but I need a double shot!" Melanie fluttered her lips.

CHAPTER 3

After leaving Melanie's shop, Desmond drove to the church office and parked. Stepping out of his car, the fresh lemony-citrus scent of white magnolia blossoms greeted. A rustle in the trees drew his attention upwards, and he watched sheets of white wisps blow across the sky. His feet crunched across the gravel parking lot. With the picture of Melanie Thompson still in his head, he walked a little lighter.

Stepping into his office, he threw his keys on the desk. Desmond emptied his pockets and pulled out the folded Quaint Affairs brochure. Turning it over, the back of the pamphlet had a picture of Melanie. *What is it about you, Ms. Thompson?*

Chuckling, he dropped the brochure atop a stack of papers and turned to retrieve his phone messages. Staring back at him, sat a silver-framed photograph of Emily.

Sweet, Emily. They were only married five short years before she died. He stared at the photograph and studied her image. Blonde hair, a pixie cut, and large, doe-like, brown eyes. Her full lips smiled back at him, and his heart ached. He picked up Emily, the photograph. So full of life and love, so full of dreams and purpose. His meant-to-be partner in the

Lord's work, but now gone. Painfully gone. He laid down the frame.

Something stirred inside him again. That suffocating, stifling weight on his chest. Pinching the space between his eyes, he tried to block out the painful memory of how he'd failed her. He eased down into the desk chair, staring at another picture of the two of them. He in his Navy Seal uniform. One of the few pieces of memorabilia of his stint in the armed forces. If he hadn't been off on a mission, he would have been there when she needed him. Propping up his elbows on the padded armchair, he folded his hands and rested his chin. Silence screamed back at him. How he longed for Emily. Longed for her presence and her love. Glancing outside, he gazed at the beautiful white clouds. Emily. She loved beautiful skies.

The shrill ring of the phone shattered his thoughts. "Hello. Pastor Brooks here."

"Hello, Desmond. It's Professor Locke, just checking in on you."

Desmond's mind drifted to a phone call just a year and a half ago when the Professor called to present him with a pastoral position. A church in a small town in Mississippi sought a solid, Bible-preaching pastor. That's what the church wanted. Nobody political, not divisive, an adept teacher of the Word, and a good shepherd for the flock.

The professor had proposed that it might be just what Desmond needed. And the church needed someone like him. He'd graduated from seminary and served there as a teacher for a few years following Emily's death. When he had faltered on his decision to apply for the position, the professor reminded Desmond that Emily would have wanted this for him.

An invisible fist squeezed his heart.

"Things are going well, sir. This was a good move for me. It's a friendly group of people. A little set in their ways, but that's to be expected." Desmond stared at Emily's photograph.

"Yes. All transitions come with their problems. They've probably never had a pastor under the age of fifty, much less barely forty!" He laughed, then paused. "So, Desmond, have you met anyone new down there?" Professor Locke's voice sounded optimistic.

"I don't know what you mean, sir. I've met a lot of new people here." His eyes shifted over to Melanie's brochure.

"You know what I mean, Desmond. You're too young to remain single. The right wife could help you out a lot."

Desmond laughed. Not really what most women were looking for in marriage these days. Still, that was Emily. She couldn't wait for them to serve in ministry together. When Desmond had found God, he'd wanted to attend seminary, but she died before he could do that. And he wasn't there to assure her he would do it anyway.

"Yes, sir. But I'm not looking. You know, Emily is a hard act to follow." Desmond sighed. Breathing deep, he realized the way Melanie made him feel. How could he betray Emily? "Anyway, I'm not sure this congregation is ready for their pastor to get married."

"The right woman will win them over. Anyway, if you need help, not with women, of course—I couldn't be much help in that area." He paused. "On the other hand, my wife …"

"No, sir. I'm doing fine on my own for now. I appreciate the offer, though. And thanks for checking on me."

"Look, Desmond, I know how much you miss Emily."

Desmond closed his eyes. He never wanted to forget her, but the guilt he felt for not being there when cancer took hold hung over him. He could have come home, but his call of duty overruled his heart of compassion. And his false optimism had told him she had plenty of time. She didn't.

"I'm fine, professor. I'll never forget her. But I'm fine."

They said their goodbyes, and Desmond switched on the computer, trying to focus on sermon prep when he heard a knock.

"Come in."

A thin, frail man stood in the doorway. Desmond stifled his surprise. "Well, good afternoon, Mr. Copeland. What brings you to church today?" He winced at the poor choice of words. "What I meant was—"

"I know what you meant. I don't need your stammering and stuttering apology." Richard Copeland continued, "Fact is, I'm not here for me. I left because you came. I'm here today for my wife."

Mr. Copeland appeared aged and weathered, although it had only been five months since he'd left. His hair seemed a little thinner, his clothes hung a little looser, and his thin lips didn't do much to enhance his sad, smile-less expression. Months ago, Richard hadn't left the church amicably.

"Deena? How is she doing, Richard?"

Though risky, Desmond used their first names, hoping to reduce the friction between them. He never worried about that with Deena, Richard's wife. Though they only stayed on a month after he arrived, she proved to be the most helpful and kind person he'd ever met in Bay Town.

Richard shuffled a bit at Desmond's question regarding Deena. He looked up, and his lips disappeared as he pressed them tightly together. "Deena is … Deena is in the hospital in Gulf Port. She had an unpleasant episode." He clasped his hands, and his whole body shook. "Fact is, she had a heart attack just yesterday."

Desmond drew a breath. He sighed, remembering sweet Deena Copeland. Her tall frame always stooped with the extra weight she carried, so she always walked with a little limp. Her dyed-blonde and graying hair, forever wind-blown, added to her sweet smile from behind her bright pink lips. Deena loved the church, cared for everyone, and helped at every function.

Desmond missed Deena's kindness. In some ways, she reminded him of Emily. If Emily would have lived that long.

Richard's body shook, and Desmond stood, moving him to the small sofa. Richard gripped his folded hands together so tightly that his bony knuckles turned white. He took a deep breath and continued, "The hospital said the damage was significant, and my wife is not expected to—"

"May I come to visit her?" Desmond interrupted.

Richard looked up, and his eyes drooped. "That would be nice. Deena would like that. Can you come tomorrow morning?" His eyebrows rose.

"I can come right now if you'd like."

Richard straightened and unfolded his hands. "No. She's having some procedures and tests run today. You can't help until tomorrow."

"Sure, Richard, I'll be there in the morning, first thing."

"No. Not first thing—changing of the nurses' shifts and doctor's rounds. You'll be in the way."

Desmond prayed silently. *Lord, please bring him to surrender his pride and trust You.*

"What time would you like me to come, Richard?"

"Not me. It's not me that wants you to come. Deena wants it … well, she didn't ask, but I know … look, come at nine o'clock or ten o'clock."

"Great, I'll be there."

Reaching into his pocket, Desmond pulled out his wallet and removed a business card. He handed it to Richard, who hesitated.

"If you … I mean, if Deena needs me sooner, please call me. Richard, can I pray for you now?"

Richard shook his head and looked away.

Desmond nodded. "I'll keep you in my prayers."

After shaking hands, Richard shuffled away, his shoulders stooped with the weight of the world.

"For my burden is light, and my yoke is easy." Desmond

whispered, "Give it up, Rich… you won't make it if you don't." He spoke from his own painful experience.

The coffee shop was quiet, and the morning rush was over. Melanie ordered a double latte and searched the cozy store for a seat. Her eyes stopped on a blonde sitting across the room by herself. Earbuds seem to make her oblivious to the surroundings as her fingers scrolled her phone. Melanie walked over and bent to peer into the teen's face.

"Virginia?"

She jumped, and tousled curls fell across her face. Pulling out her earbuds, she stood. "Oh, hi, Miz Thompson! What are you doing here?" She pushed back the hair off her forehead.

"Well, I should ask you that question. Shouldn't you be in school this morning?"

Virginia dropped back into her seat. Large blue eyes rolled, and she bit her lip. A smudge of red lipstick streaked her front teeth.

"I missed the bus."

"I can give you a ride." Melanie looked at her watch. "You'll be in time for third period."

Virginia shook her head. Curls fell forward again, and she tugged at the oversized sweater falling off her shoulder. "The kids are all haters there, and they already counted me absent, anyway."

"Even Lacey?" Melanie gave Virginia a sideways glance.

"No, your daughter's nice. But we don't have any classes together."

The sweet teenager was in Special Ed, and the program at Bay High was lacking. Lacey, Melanie's daughter, had brought Virginia home a few times after school and tried to help her with her homework. She'd also brought her to church once, but Virginia wanted no part of it. She said it was boring. Still, Melanie's heart went out to her. Virginia's upbringing was unknown to Melanie, but it was evident that a nurturing home life was lacking.

Virginia took a quick look out the window and smiled at Melanie. She grabbed her paisley print hobo bag and stood. Her tight, ripped jeans showed a little too much skin. So did the loosely knit tunic.

"My ride's here, anyway! See you, Miz Thompson." Virginia ran out the door.

Melanie watched as a light blue sedan waited. She stepped closer to the café window and stared at the driver's slightly opened window. Sunglasses shaded his eyes, and though she couldn't make out his face, there was a familiarity about the driver. He winked at Virginia and held out a little wrapped gift. She made some jumping gyrations, grabbed the box, and ran to the passenger side. And just like that, they drove off.

Not liking the sinking feeling in the pit of her stomach over whom and what she'd just witnessed, Melanie picked up her cup and headed back to the shop.

CHAPTER 4

The morning and afternoon sped by, and Melanie finished up most of the upcoming wedding details. She had difficulty concentrating with all that had happened that day. Closing her desk planner, she dug her fingers into the back of her neck. The knot was back. Time to go home, but something gnawed at her. It was Virginia. Skipping school was a big deal to Melanie.

Driving over to Virginia's house, she prayed for strength and courage to face the aunt, Virginia's guardian. Melanie had never spoken to her and had seen her only once at the grocery store. Virginia had been with her. Otherwise, Melanie would have never noticed. A pang hit her heart. She parked in front of the address and stepped out. Before starting up the steps, she heard a voice.

"What'cha want?"

Melanie turned.

Hilly walked toward her down the cracked sidewalk. She gripped a plastic grocery bag hanging by her side.

A wind funnel stirred up, and Melanie shivered. Not so much at the breeze but at Hilly's appearance. A light t-shirt, leggings, and sandals provided no warmth, her thin, frizzy hair hung limply, and the smell of tobacco and slight body odor lingered. Hilly shoved past Melanie and trudged toward her house.

"Hi. It's Hilly, right? Virginia's aunt?"

Hilly stopped but said nothing.

Melanie cleared her throat. "I'm Lacey's mom."

"I know who you are."

Gripping the shoulder strap of her tote, Melanie smiled. "I saw Virginia this morning."

Still nothing.

"Anyway." Melanie was at a loss. Taking a deep breath, she gushed, "Hilly, can I buy you a cup of coffee?"

Hilly turned and narrowed her eyes. "No. I don't need no coffee. I don't need no food or clothes. We're good."

"I'm sorry, I thought maybe …"

"Listen, Miz Melanie, thanks for being nice to Virginia." Hilly looked down. "But I'm good. I don't need no help."

"Oh, I wasn't implying …"

Her head bobbed, and Hilly looked up, then her eyes glazed past Melanie.

Melanie turned. Nothing was behind her. As the wind whipped up, Melanie's mind went into a whirlwind. What to do?

"I know what you want. I been to shelters all my life. They're nice people. Always telling me Jesus is the answer." Her eyes focused on Melanie now. "But what I've done, and my life now? He can't help me. He don't want me." She turned back toward the house. "But Virginia, if you can help her, I'd sure appreciate it. Bye, Miz Melanie."

Melanie drew a deep breath and stepped behind her. She tapped Hilly's shoulder and felt her body jerk. "I'm sorry, Hilly, please. I will help Virginia, but you need to know." Melanie's voice lowered. "Jesus does want you. He loves you, Hilly. He cares about you, and He is the answer. Why if it wasn't for Him, I wouldn't have—"

Hilly laughed and turned. "You don't have no idea, do ya?"

Melanie stared. The laugh that escaped from Hilly wasn't happy. It matched her eyes and her countenance. It held no animosity, only joyless defeat.

Still, Melanie's head lowered, and her stomach roiled. How could she even mention her own trials compared to Hilly's? That's not what she intended. She'd only wanted to give hope and help. She felt ashamed and nodded. "I'm sorry." Her eyes pooled.

Suddenly, a hint of a smile crossed the woman's lips—a genuine turning up at the corners and a glimmer of something brightened in her eyes.

"Thank you." She looked down. "I said a prayer once. That prayer all you Christians want people to pray." She looked up, her eyes stoic. "I said it, but it didn't change my life one bit."

Melanie's mind reeled, trying to think of scripture verses. Pleading silently for the words to say. Words of encouragement but understanding. She came up blank.

Hilly shrugged. "But I still believe it. What else can I believe? I'm just not so sure His promise of heaven includes me, though."

Melanie let her tote slip to the ground. "Hilly, can I pray with you?" She didn't know what else to do.

Silence.

Melanie reached to take Hilly's hand, and the woman didn't withdraw. *Thank You, Lord.* They closed their eyes, and Melanie asked God to let Hilly know and experience the height, depth, and width of His love for her. She felt Hilly's hand tremor, but a firm squeeze followed Melanie's "Amen."

"He loves you, Hilly. Don't ever forget that." Melanie smiled as she pulled Hilly close. Although Hilly didn't hug her back. Melanie embraced the thin, frail woman. "If you need anything at all …"

Shoving Melanie off, Hilly straightened. "I told you, just take care of Virginia. Don't let nobody hurt her."

She walked up the front steps to a porch in need of repair. Peeling paint and broken railings revealed rotting wood. She turned. "I done what I could with her. It ain't much. But with nice folks like you, maybe she's got a chance." She nodded. "Thanks, Miz Melanie. Bye."

Melanie sunk into her car and drove toward Beach Road. Toward home. It was a humbling, helpless feeling knowing she could do nothing more for Hilly. Nothing but pray. Her heart lifted a little. *That's the most I can do.*

The sun bounced off the gulf, and God's brightness warmed her. Tension floated, and her thoughts turned to the pleasant part of her day. Desmond. But a pang of guilt knifed her—guilt for feeling a joy of her own.

When she arrived home, she entered her house through the kitchen entrance. "Hey, Lacey, I'm home." She kicked off her shoes and dropped her tote.

Lacey sauntered into the kitchen, hugging her mom. "Hey, Mom. What's for dinner? I'm starved."

"Lacey, I just walked in the door."

"Just kidding. I'm taking you out! I've got some birthday money saved up and nothing to spend it on."

A smile broke across Melanie's face. Her daughter. Her pride and joy. Somehow Lacey had avoided the teenage angst. Maybe because of being raised the last fifteen years by both a mom and grandparents. Lacey had an innocent and joyful outlook on life and people. Unlike Melanie, she hadn't made any brainless choices yet. And Melanie made it her job to make sure Lacey didn't make the same mistakes.

Melanie kissed her daughter's cheek. "Save your money. My treat, you pick."

The same green eyes and shiny chestnut hair mirrored back at her. Melanie stared at her daughter's long, wild mane. The unruly waves came from her dad, but Lacey inherited her mother's lean body type. With Melanie's youthful genes, some people had mistaken them for sisters. It thrilled Melanie, but Lacey, not so much.

"I sure wish they had In-n-Out Burger here. I think, next to Grandma and Grandpa, that's what I miss most about California. But I guess Fat Boyz will do."

Melanie stopped and turned. "Are you serious? I was hoping for something a little healthier."

Melanie drove as Lacey relaxed in the passenger seat, staring at the gulf on the way to the Land's End Fat Boyz. The burgers were the best in town and the closest thing to California's In-n-Out Burger, but Melanie often avoided burgers and fries. Glancing at Lacey, she smiled. If it made Lacey happy, good. She deserved it. Her daughter had never given her any trouble. Other than the occasional lazy or stubborn attitude, Lacey gave no cause for concern. Melanie thought of Virginia.

"Lacey, was Virginia at school today?"

"Nope."

"How about later in the day?"

"I don't think so. I know she wasn't at her stop, and Big Joe waited a long time for her."

Big Joe was the bus driver, and he took excellent care of all the kids on the bus. He was one of Melanie and Lacey's favorite people. He also attended the same church. Melanie thought of Pastor Desmond Brooks and changed subjects, keeping the morning's Virginia incident to herself as well as her visit to see Hilly.

"So, guess who stopped by the shop today?" Melanie glanced at Lacey.

"Mom, come on. Just tell me." She lounged in the front seat but suddenly squealed. "I know! Oh my goodness. It was

Pastor Brooks, right?'"

Melanie felt herself flush.

Lacey shook her mom's shoulder. "It was! Wasn't it? I knew it. I could tell he liked you at church!"

"That's crazy." Sitting taller, she avoided glancing at her daughter. "He just came by to talk about a wedding."

"Did he ask you out?" Lacey asked.

"Of course not. He had some questions about doing weddings at the church. But ... oh, never mind."

"Wait. What? Come on. You can't stop there." She pulled at her mom's arm.

"Well, Desmond ..."

"Desmond?" Lacey's voice dropped. "You called him Desmond?" She kicked her feet, laughing.

Melanie ignored her. "Pastor Brooks invited ... I mean, he asked if we, you and I, were going to the church softball game tomorrow night." Melanie scrunched her shoulders.

"And you said yes?"

Lacey enjoyed Desmond's company. Ever since they started attending church, Sundays were her favorite day. The kindness Desmond extended to Melanie's daughter made Sundays even more special. Lacey often remarked that he was just the nicest person in Bay Town. Excited at his singleness, she often teased her mom.

"I knew this was coming!"

"Well, I didn't say we would go to the game, but—"

"Well, we are going to the game, and that's final." Lacey clapped.

After finishing their meals, they left Land's End, the tiny town next door to Bay Town. Less population, less beach, but no less charm. Although Melanie loved the small cities along the gulf, Bay Town was by far her favorite. Arriving on Main

Street, Melanie parked. The girls loved to stroll down charming, picturesque Main Street, admiring the French Quarter architecture of some of the quaint old structures. The eclectic mix of some of the new shops integrated well with the old brick buildings. Melanie glanced up at the wrought-iron balconies and hanging flower baskets above.

Stopping at Lacey's favorite shop, Melanie smiled. "Want to go in?"

The thrift store, Second Chances, was more like a small, upscale vintage boutique. Carol, the owner, created stunning outdoor displays. A wooden tea cart lined with crocheted doilies held a porcelain teapot and a few delicate china cups. Tiny silver spoons scattered about complemented the flowered, decoupage wood grain on the cart. Off to the side stood an old dressmaker's form, fitted with a vintage floral print apron.

The owner came out to greet them. "Hey there, Mel. Hey, Lacey. I just got some new spreads and linens in. They're in the back." Carol waved for Lacey and Melanie to follow her.

"Lacey, you're going to love these textiles! I can't wait to see them in your designs." Carol stopped and turned. "You are still designing, ain't ya?"

Shrugging, Lacey smiled. "Sketching, yes."

Melanie gave a sideways glance and hugged her daughter. "And designing. I can't wait for her to start designing wedding dresses. Someday, we'll expand Quaint Affairs to a bridal shop, too." Melanie frowned. She had no idea why she said that after her failed shop back in California.

"Now, that's what I'm talking about! You go, Lacey girl. We women can do anything we set our minds to."

A brass butterfly hair clip held back Carol's long, faded-red hair. Loose streaks of gray escaped and floated about her face. Her teal, paisley-print maxi skirt, and a pashmina shawl completed the boho chic outfit. Add to that a surplus of

bangles and dangling jewelry that tingled like music accompanying a belly dancer.

As Carol led the girls to the fabrics, Melanie stopped and shuddered. A man stood partially hidden behind a curtain. The flimsy barrier, meant to close off the shop's working part, did little to conceal him.

Melanie shot a glance at her daughter.

Lacey shrugged, mouthing, "Creepy."

Carol yelled out. "Come on, girls. Look at my new treasures."

The man moved the curtain aside as the corners of his wrinkled mouth curled up. It was more of a sneer than a smile. Melanie pivoted, bumping into Carol.

"Whoa there, Mel." Carol leaned around her. "Grady. What's the matter with you? You scared the daylights out of these girls."

"Sorry, sugar."

His sneer disappeared. Leaning against a wall, he shoved one hand into the front pocket of his faded jeans. A blue plaid shirt, half-way unbuttoned, revealed a plain, white tee underneath. His sleek gray-blonde hair pulled back into a thinly braided ponytail, hung down his back. He leered at Lacey, and Melanie fumed.

"Carol, you know, it's a school night, and I think Lacey still has some homework." Melanie took Lacey's arm.

"Oh, come on, girls. Grady don't bite. Mel, Lacey, this is Grady Mitchell. My ... uh, my new friend."

Carol was friendly with the men and dated a lot. That was putting it mildly. She was never shy in talking about her life and relationships. Sadly, she seemed much like many other desperate women. Lonely and thinking a man was the answer to all their problems. Melanie knew. She'd been in that same place when she was young, and if it weren't for God, she might still be there.

Melanie had invited Carol to church a few times, and the woman attended once. After that, there was always an excuse.

"Hello, Grady. Nice to meet you." Melanie offered her hand.

Lacey's jaw dropped as her mother nudged her.

"Hi," Lacey mumbled.

"Nice to meet you, ladies." Grady winked, with a lingering hold on Melanie's hand.

"So, Grady. Are you from Bay Town?" She slid her hand away.

"No, he's from Jack—"

"I'm, uh, from Alabama," interrupted Grady.

"Alabama?" Carol squealed. "You said you was from Jackson."

"Yeah, sweetie, Jackson, Alabama," Grady said with clipped words.

"Oh." Melanie nodded. "Well, we need to run, Carol."

Melanie took Lacey's arm. She heard Carol's voice behind them.

"Grady! Knock it off. You're scaring my customers away."

The girls left the shop and stepped out onto the street. Melanie breathed a sigh of relief, and chuckled when Lacey did the same.

"Hey, Mel. Hey, Lacey!" A booming drawl came from across the street, followed by squeals of giggling and little footsteps.

"Watch it, little children. We's crossing the street here."

Dragging his son and daughter behind him, Big Joe Cunningham, the school bus driver, ambled over and stretched out his hands. His massive body engulfed them both.

"So, what you gals doin' down here? We's havin' dinner over there if you wants to join us. My wife Lyla's awaiting for our reservation." Joe nodded at a restaurant across the street.

"Oh, thank you, but we already ate," said Melanie.

Suddenly her brow furrowed. "So, Joe, Virginia missed the bus this morning?"

When he shrugged, his entire massive body moved. "I waited, but she never showed. Usually, she comes running out all flustered. Today it was like she wasn't even home."

"I don't think she was. I saw her at the Mockingbird Café this morning."

"Mmm, mmm. I don't like to think what might become of that girl." He continued expressing his concerns about Virginia's life and future, and Melanie sullenly agreed.

Lacey teased and tickled Joe's kids as they ran in and out of the adults' legs.

Joe stopped talking and fixed his eyes across the street. Melanie followed his gaze and stared at two men in black hoodies leaning against a white van.

"Hey, wasn't that van behind us this morning?" asked Lacey.

Melanie and Joe turned and stared at her.

"When I got on the bus this morning, I saw them parked down the street."

Joe clenched his fists. "You saw them, too?"

"Uh-huh. No big deal, right?" Lacey shrugged.

Melanie signaled a silent head shake.

He nodded back. "Yeah, no big deal."

"Joe? Come on now. They's calling our name." Lyla yelled from the diner. "Oh, hey, Mel! Hey, Lacey!" She waved with both hands high in the air.

Lacey grabbed the children's hands and asked, "Can I take them across?"

"Sure, go right ahead, honey." Joe waved to Lyla and turned to Melanie. "No big deal?" He huffed. "I don't got a good feeling about those guys. They followed the bus all the way to school, then took off." He stared. "You ever seen them around these parts?"

Melanie pulled her denim jacket tight and shook her head. "Where do you think they're from?"

Joe shook his dark, bald head and continued staring. "Don't know. But I's going to keep my eyes out for them."

"Joe! Come on, we going to lose our reservation." Lyla called again.

"Lyla, go on in. I'll be there in a minute." He yelled so loud that the men turned.

Joe walked toward the van, and the men laughed, throwing bottles into the gutter. Joe kept walking. His frame lumbered toward them. As he approached, they scrambled and jumped into the vehicle. A loud roar erupted from the engine, and the van peeled down the road. Joe turned and waved at Lacey and Melanie. He threw up his arms and emitted a deep belly laugh.

"Cowards!"

CHAPTER 5

Virginia stepped off the city transit at the bus stop and wobbled toward the Bayou Bar. At the end of Main Street sat the eyesore of downtown. A dumpy establishment. Every town had one, or one like it.

Virginia didn't think about the trouble she might encounter for sneaking a shot of vodka at home. It gave her courage. Her aunt had planted the seeds of temptation for fun and attention. She'd told Virginia about the Bayou Bar, and Virginia wanted some of the action. She had left her aunt passed out on the sofa at home.

A feathery, white wrap blew around her shoulders in the light breeze of the evening. Stopping under a streetlight, Virginia took out a small, silver compact mirror and lipstick, reapplying and lavishing on yet another dense layer of red color. She'd watched too many old movies with her aunt. Approaching the Bayou Bar, she pulled down her short, tight skirt, finger fluffed her wavy hair, and stepped inside.

Virginia's circumstances made her a target for all kinds of abuse. No one cared about her. She was a haplessly discarded burden, and her special needs placed her at a disadvantage. A feeble mind and vulnerable spirit crippled her. Her path held no promise. With promiscuity so easily plated before her, she walked the road headed to misery and despair like many other adolescent girls.

Virginia's beauty was her curse, and her limited mental capabilities brought more than her share of problems. Yet to her, it seemed her looks were the only thing that got her what she thought she wanted—love and attention, and the numbing false security of a warm touch. Often though, whether solicited or not, the experience turned out to be rough, cold, and harsh. Virginia naively convinced herself those incidents wouldn't be repeated. They always did.

Opening the door, the blaring music stifled her grand entrance. She pouted as she walked to the bar. A few men sat hunched over the glass-ridden counter. Glancing over, one caught her eye and smiled. Leering, he nudged the man next to him, and so on down the bar it went. Many heads turned, eyes rolled, and snickering clicked around the dark, noisy room.

She craved the attention. Their jeering somehow gave Virginia a false sense of worth. They made her feel pretty, wanted, and desired despite her being different.

"Hey, gorgeous!"

"I'll buy ya a drink, beautiful!"

Virginia turned and flashed a coy smile. A few of the men approached her, and the flirting commenced.

The female bartender heard the obnoxious hooting and glared. Servicing the bar, she pushed back her bright purple hair that hung loosely over her colorfully tattooed shoulders. "Honey, go on. Get out. Ain't no way you're old enough to be in here. Git, before I call the police."

Virginia protested, but the bartender waved a dishrag toward the front door. Virginia turned and said, "Hey, where's your bathroom?"

Bursts of hoarse laughter broke out, and the bartender shook her head, nodding at the restroom sign. Virginia started toward the back of the building. She saw the exit sign instead

and winked. The men stared after her, and she pointed to the back door.

Outside, the pulsating beat from the bar spilled into the alley. She danced and sang along with the familiar words to the song, gyrating to the pounding beat, oblivious to the men's lewd innuendos. Soon the men were shoving and tugging at her, and a fight broke out. Virginia screamed like a scared child.

Stepping from the shadows, a well-dressed man appeared. "Boys? Best you moved on. Leave the little lady alone."

They turned around to face him and laughed.

Underneath the lamplight, he opened his suit coat. A gun flashed in a shoulder holster under his arm.

"What the heck? Are you serious, man? She came on to us."

Virginia shoved the man closest to her and pulled her wrap over her shoulders. Moving to join the man with the gun, she tripped and broke the heel of one of her shoes. They laughed again.

A car passed by, and the men quieted down. The vehicle backed up, blocking the alley driveway. The man with the gun hid his weapon.

The car window slid down. "Virginia? Is that you?" the passenger called out.

"Hey, come join the party!" the drunks yelled.

The well-dressed man glared at them and patted his hand against the concealed weapon. "Party's over, boys. Go inside."

Raising their arms in surrender, they complied and ran inside, stumbling over one another.

Virginia peered down the alley. "Lacey? Is that you?"

Lacey called out from the car window. "Yes. We're on our way home. Come on, we'll give you a ride."

"I don't need no ride." Virginia pouted, hanging on to the arm of her rescuer.

"But it's late, and we have school tomorrow," said Lacey.

The man patted Virginia's arm. "No worries, ladies. Ginny is with me."

"Yeah, he's my daddy." Virginia laughed and added, "Sort of."

"Shut up, Virginia." the man seethed.

She squirmed and frowned.

Melanie stepped out, approaching the alley.

The man stepped back. He yanked Virginia, slinking into the shadows. "We're just headed home ourselves. Have a wonderful night, ladies."

Melanie stepped back to the driver's side and jumped into the car and Virginia heard Lacey scream, "Mom. How can you leave her?"

Before she could hear Melanie's response, Virginia felt a tug and the man pulled open the passenger door of a parked car, and shoved her in the front seat.

"Hey. You hurt me." She slurred.

"Do you think I care?" he yelled. "What the heck are you doing here, and where'd you get the alcohol?" His pent-up rage spewed. "You took your Aunt Hilly's bottle, didn't you? You stupid girl."

She cowered in her seat. Tears stung Virginia's eyes as she covered her ears and sunk down. *No! Not again!*

He often terrorized her with rants and ravings over her bizarre behavior. Then later, he lavished her with gifts that soothed her simple spirit. Virginia embraced his gestures, mistaking them for love. It helped her to stuff down the painful memories that caused so much hurt.

Virginia sat, fraught with absolute stillness, never knowing what to expect when he got into one of his moods. He often became like a ranting character in a horror movie. Lifting her knees to her chest, she hugged herself. She attempted to stifle her tears for fear of enraging him more.

He slid down the window and lit a cigarette. "What am I gonna do with you, girl?"

It seemed a genuine question, and Virginia stole a swift glance at him. Out of the corner of her eye, she saw him raise his hand. Instinctively her arms flew up, covering her face.

He laughed and said, "There, there, you silly girl. Here, wipe your tears, darling." Handing her a linen embroidered handkerchief, his voice deepened, and he asked, "Virginia, what in the world were you doing here?"

She took the handkerchief and blew her nose. "I just wanted to have some fun. You know, just be happy sometimes."

"Now, darling. Happiness is not a possession to be prized. It is a quality of thought. You know, a state of mind."

Virginia scrunched her face. "Huh?"

The man laughed mockingly. Taking the handkerchief, he gently wiped the running mascara from her cheek. Suddenly, he pulled back and clapped his hands once.

Startled, Virginia jerked, hitting her head on the window.

"Hey, girl? I got something for ya'."

Her eyes lit up, and her fearful panic subsided as quickly as his anger.

"Oooh. What is it? Can I have it now?"

He reached over the back seat and pulled out a little package. "Here you go, darling. Go on, open it."

Ripping the pretty, papered package, Virginia squealed, holding up the bundle of bracelets. She slipped them on and shook her wrists, delighting at the tingling sounds they made. The sparkling gold and gemstones glittered in the lamplight shining through the windows. She smiled and reached over, hugging her benefactor.

He peeled her fingers away from his neck. "All right. All right. We're good now, right?"

Virginia's happiness displayed joy, much like a child on

Christmas morning. Her innocence at forgiveness held the same childlike quality.

Further down Main Street, off a side street, Desmond sat in Miss Ellie's house, one of his housebound church members. He breathed deep. The house still smelled of onions and savory beef.

"Miss Ellie, you're a great cook. Can you bring that to the next potluck?" He winked.

She waved him off and smiled. "Why, sure. Just for you, Pastor."

Desmond leaned forward. "Well, I better get going. Anything I can pray about for you?"

Miss Ellie stroked the arms of her wheelchair and smiled. "The Lord's been good, but if you'll pray for my loneliness." Her lips pressed together. "I gotta confess, I throw myself a pity party once in a while."

Desmond patted her hand. "No harm there. The important thing is that you turn it into a praise party when you're done."

"I always do, Pastor. Just like King David in the Psalms." Her eyes disappeared as a big grin wrinkled across her dark face.

Desmond glanced around the darkened room, and his eyes rested on a picture of a nice-looking young man. She'd mentioned him before. "Have you heard from your grandson lately?"

After a big sigh, Miss Ellie stuck out her tongue and rolled her eyes. "Trevor? Why, ever since my daughter died, God rest her soul, that boy's been living up north. Took on his white Daddy's fancy ways up there." She shrugged. "He calls me every holiday, but he don't come visit me no more."

"How long has it been?" Desmond asked.

After a long sigh, Miss Ellie scratched her head. "Well, he's pretty near twenty-four years old. So, I'm guessing it's been 5 years since he's been back." Miss Ellie's head dropped to her chest.

"I imagine you must miss him a lot." Desmond touched her clasped hands.

"I do. But I gave him up to the Lord a long time ago. Why wouldn't he like that life up there? It's a lot more exciting than this here gulf life he grew up with. His daddy put him through law school, and he never come back."

"Well, I'll be praying for him." Desmond took both of her hands. "How about it? Shall we pray?"

"I'd sure like that."

After a moment of seeking God, Desmond stood. He planted a friendly kiss on Miss Ellie's cheek and headed for the door. She waved goodbye from her wheelchair.

Closing her bold-red front door, he stroked the glossy, painted surface and smiled. It reflected the only bright spot on the dull street. He strolled to the corner with his head down and hands stuffed in his pockets. As he attempted to step off the curb, a vehicle screeched to a halt at the stop sign. He stepped back but squinted, trying to see in. "Lacey? Lacey Thompson, is that you?"

Jumping at the sound of his voice, Lacey fumbled with the door handle and fell out of the car.

Desmond loped forward and caught her by the shoulders. He peered in. "Mel?" Joy, at the sight of her, instinctively turned to concern. "Are you two alright?"

Lacey interrupted. "No! Virginia's down at the bar."

"What? What were you doing there?"

"We were on our way home," said Melanie.

He listened as the incident with Virginia unfolded—the men in the alley, the stranger. Melanie stopped mid-sentence, and her eyes widened.

"Melanie? What's wrong? What happened?"

"I think I saw that man this morning. He was picking up Virginia." She looked at Lacey. "Maybe it was just her father? Or a relative?"

"No, Virginia doesn't have one. No dad." Lacey shook her head.

"I'll run over there. It's just a block back. Call the police chief and tell him to meet me there. Take Lacey home, and I'll call you later, Mel."

Desmond helped Lacey back into the car and Melanie drove off. His long stride made the easy run down the block. He turned into the alley just as a car started up. As it eased down the to the driveway, Desmond jumped in front, hands raised. The driver stomped on the brake, causing the vehicle to jolt to a stop. Desmond slammed his open palms on the hood of the gleaming blue sedan.

"Whoa!" a voice yelled.

Desmond heard the car shift into park, and with the car still idling, a man stepped out.

"Are you crazy?" he yelled. "What in the heck are you doing?" The man glared.

Desmond threw his hand in the air like a captured prisoner. "Sorry, man. I heard a young woman, a girl named Virginia, was in trouble here, and I came to help."

He stepped back and covered his eyes, the headlights blinding him. Still, he made out the figure of a young woman bouncing to the loud music emanating from inside the vehicle.

"Trouble?" The man sneered and narrowed his eyes. "Who told you that, Mr. ..."

"Brooks. Desmond Brooks. Look, I just want to make sure the girl's okay." Trying to stall until the chief arrived, Desmond rambled. "Is she okay? She's way too young to be here, isn't she? I heard someone was bothering her."

"Bothering her? That's a joke." The man laughed. "Yeah. I got her under control. We don't need your help. Just git out of the way. I need to get her home."

The man retreated inside the car, but Desmond didn't move.

Standing up again, the man leaned out, holding onto the car door. He growled, "Are you deaf or just dumb? I said move."

Desmond wiped his hand over his face. He knew if he moved out of the way, he'd lose her. If he stayed put, this guy would run him over.

"You know, Mr. ..."

"Mr. None of your business. You got a death wish or something?"

"Hey. Okay, look. I'm Pastor Desmond from Bay Town Community Church. Just trying to help here." He had to buy time. "I know it's hard raising teenagers. I'm a pastor. I have resources. I can help."

Sirens rose in the distance.

The man ignored them. "I don't care if you're the pope. Get out of my way." The man pulled back his suit coat just as a squad car squealed to a stop, blocking the driveway. Red and blue swirling lights lit up the alley. The man covered his holstered gun.

Desmond breathed a sigh of relief. Turning around, he leaned back on the shiny, blue car.

"Great. Just great," hissed the man.

The chief of police of Bay Town, Alberto Hidlago, stepped out of the squad car. He was tall, on the heavy side, but muscular and made for an imposing figure. Ignoring Desmond, he walked over to the driver and pointed a flashlight straight at the man's face. "License and registration."

Raising his arms to cover the glare, the man turned his face aside. "Hey, Officer. My daughter snuck out, and I found her down here. You know teenagers. But we're headed home now."

"I said license and registration," Chief Bert repeated.

Desmond watched as the man eased back into his car.

Virginia slid down her window, leaning out as the man rifled through the glove box. He thrust the requested documents toward the chief.

"I'll be back." Stopping to look at Desmond, who still leaned against the hood, he asked, "So, you attached to that car or something?" the chief chuckled.

Desmond straightened up and glanced over at the man, who leered back.

Chief Bert shook his head and continued walking. He called over his shoulder, "Step aside, Pastor."

Desmond waited quietly off to the side, trying to pray for Virginia, but struggling to maintain concentration. Chief Bert sat in his car for what seemed like forever. Finally, he emerged. As he walked by Desmond, he whispered, "Something does not jive."

"Well, Mr. Will Boudreaux, we have a problem. Your driver's license here says you live in New Orleans. Your car registration address is in Jackson, Mississippi. But I understand your daughter goes to Bay High right here in our little town. So, what's the story?"

Before Boudreaux could answer, Virginia giggled and yelled from the passenger seat, "He's my daddy, Mr. Policeman, sir."

Annoyance covered the chief's face as he glanced between the two. "Okay, little lady. So, where do you live?"

"I live with Auntie." Virginia giggled again.

"Where?"

"Over there." She pointed in an obscure direction.

The chief shook his head, and his eyes bored into Boudreaux. "Okay. And you? What's your story?"

"I travel a lot because of my business, so my sister takes care of her." He tapped the top of his car door. "Look, we best be heading home now. Ginny will be staying with me in New Orleans for the weekend."

Desmond interrupted, "But it's Thursday. Virginia's got school in the morning."

Both Boudreaux and the chief turned in his direction and gave him a look.

"Uh, yeah, sorry about that. I'll just be over here when you need me." Desmond stepped back under the lamplight.

"Yeah. What about school, Mr. Boudreaux?" Chief Bert asked.

"We're just making our trip a little extended weekend."

"Well, I think we'll take a visit to Auntie first. Give me the address, and I'll follow you there."

"Yes, sir, Chief." Boudreaux sneered.

Chief Bert walked over to Desmond. With his back turned from Boudreaux, he asked, "Hey, so you didn't pull that 'religious card,' did you? I mean, the pastor thing?"

Shrugging his shoulders, Desmond nodded.

Chief Bert clicked his tongue and said, "Okay, Pastor, I don't know what you're doing here at the Bayou Bar ..."

Desmond started to explain, but the chief raised both hands to stop him. "I don't know, and I don't care." He took a step but stopped. "Hey, hop in the squad car with me. You can fill me in, and I'll give you a ride back to your car after I get this little lady home and figure out what's going on with her."

Desmond wasn't about to argue. "Sure glad you showed up when you did, Chief."

"Yeah, well, you didn't do so bad yourself, Pastor."

CHAPTER 6

They soon arrived at a dilapidated house on the sketchier side of town. Desmond glanced between Boudreaux's fancy car and the gloomy structure. "Sure doesn't match up," he said.

"Nope, sure doesn't." The chief shook his head and stepped out of the vehicle.

A full moon illuminated the shadows of junk scattered across the lawn. Garden weeds entwined the chain-link fence like grotesque fingers stretching to reach every inch of the perimeter. A couch slumped on the front porch. Dust particles floated around the backdrop of a glaring naked bulb as a fluttering moth flitted back and forth.

Barefooted, Virginia ran up to the torn screen door. Her broken heels dangled from her fingers as she slipped past the woman leaning on the door jamb.

Lines accented the woman's sunken eyes, and the wrinkles on her haggard face didn't seem to belong to her age. A long robe covering flannel pajamas hung to her knees. One bare foot rested over the other.

"What's the problem?" She fidgeted with a cigarette between her fingers.

Boudreaux spoke first. "Virginia snuck out again. You

didn't even know she was missin', did ya?" He spat the words at her. "I was just taking her home when the officer here stopped to question us." He narrowed his eyes. "Listen, Hilly, like I told the chief, Virginia and I are headed to New Orleans tonight, so get her things."

He turned to the chief. "Thanks again, Officer. You can see we're okay. Just teenage girl problems, you know? Nothing I can't handle."

Desmond stiffened and glanced up. A light upstairs flickered, and Virginia stood by the window.

Chief Bert took off his hat and pushed up his thick, black frames. "Mr. Boudreaux, it's late, and unless you want to produce some ID that shows Virginia here is your daughter, I suggest she not miss school tomorrow. I can't hold you here, but I will check on Virginia, and I've got your information. I know where you live."

The chief stared at Hilly. "I'll check Virginia's attendance at Bay High in the morning. She better be there."

Hilly nodded. Her hands shook as she lifted the cigarette to her lips.

Boudreaux glared. "If you don't mind, I'm saying goodnight to my daughter." He started up the front steps.

"Night, sir. Night, ma'am." Bert replaced his hat and tipped it toward Hilly. Sauntering back to his car, he motioned for Desmond to follow and opened the door. He turned. "Mr. Boudreaux?"

The man stopped and glanced over his shoulder.

"I have a very competent and very capable officer out on patrol tonight. You'd be smart to keep things calm around here if you know what I mean."

The chief turned back and slid into the squad car. As he drove away, Desmond asked, "So, what do you think, Chief?"

The chief stared straight ahead. "Man, this makes my blood boil. I hate to think what his plans are for that kid."

"I don't even want to guess. We need to pray a lot on this one."

Chief Bert giggled, a laugh unbefitting the chief of police. "That's your job, Pastor."

Desmond glanced at Bert. "Maybe, but we can all pray."

"Yeah. Yeah. Okay, where to, Pastor? Back to the bar?" The chief laughed. "I can't quite figure out why all you church people hang out down there. Mrs. Thompson, her daughter, and you? But, hey, I'm not judging."

Desmond pointed. "Yes, well, you can drop me off on the corner of First and Main. I'm parked near there."

When he reached the destination, Chief Bert raised his eyebrow. "So, you don't live around here, do you Pastor? I mean, I know clergy don't make much, but the church can do you better than this, can't they?"

Desmond exited the car but leaned in. "No. I don't live here. I was visiting one of our senior church members, the widow, Ellie. You know her?"

Chief Bert shifted and scratched his head. "No, can't say that I do."

"Yes, well, Miss Ellie uses a wheelchair, so it's difficult for her to get around." Desmond widened his eyes. "Hey, why don't you pick her up this Sunday and bring her to church?"

Chief Bert squirmed. "Uh, yeah. Maybe, we'll see." He coughed, clearing his throat. "Anyway, Pastor, thanks for your help. I'll call you if I have any questions. This Boudreaux guy has got me bugged."

"Yes. Sure wish we could do more for that poor girl." He stepped back and waved.

A fog rolled in as Chief Bert pulled away from the curb. Desmond stared at the mist crawling toward him. The damp air closed in, as did thoughts of Virginia, and he bowed his head.

The moon shadowed through translucent clouds blowing over the old house on Oleander Drive. The victims inside were oblivious to what awaited them.

Will Boudreaux ranted and screamed, and his arms flailed. "Hilly, what in the heck is the matter with you? You can't even control this lame child!"

Hilly trembled and stepped backward toward the sagging sofa.

Virginia stood at the top of the stairs and screamed, "I am not lame!"

Grabbing an ashtray, Boudreaux hurled it up the stairs, and Virginia ducked, hitting her head on the railing. Crouching, she slumped down and cried.

"You stupid girl! 'Cause of you, you're stuck in this rat hole for the weekend."

Hilly stepped to the stairs, but Boudreaux's raised arm stayed her position.

"Hush up, both of ya! Quit your whining. Virginia, you get to bed now."

Virginia stood and scrambled down the hallway to her room.

Boudreaux paced. He drew a breath and laced his fingers behind his head. Spinning around, he glared at Hilly.

"You listen to me. That girl will be in New Orleans this weekend. And you ain't got no say in it."

Long ago, Boudreaux had tried to prostitute Hilly. But her anorexic appearance, coupled with the tracks on her arms, rendered her a useless commodity. He now looked to beautiful, fresh Virginia for his future.

Dropping onto the sofa, Hilly's lit cigarette fell from her mouth, and she glanced down. The gray ash crushed into the stained carpet under her bare foot.

Hilly looked up. "But why now, Will?" Her voice shook. "That girl ain't ready yet. Can't you let her finish high school

first?" Hilly's eyes filled with tears. "Maybe give her a chance?"

A long, guttural laugh rolled from Boudreaux. "Not ready? Why she's parading herself all over town. You expect me to support you both until graduation? You're not worth a red cent. But that pretty little girl, she can earn her keep real good now." Boudreaux sneered. "Yeah, that little darlin's got a chance all right, and it's with me." He stepped toward the door. "I'll be staying at the Edgewater Hotel tonight, but I'll be back tomorrow after school's out."

"What about me?" Hilly whined. "You heard the chief. He's gonna be patrolling the street. He'll haul my butt to jail if Virginia goes missing."

"Just stay put tonight. Virginia will be at school tomorrow, and after that, we'll be in New Orleans."

Boudreaux stared off. He was not Virginia's father, though he was Hilly's cousin. Even still, he lied, and deception was a tool of his trade. When he sweet-talked young girls, he gained their confidence. And he was good at it. He'd thought about branching out on his own. He'd even had a low budget operation before, but now, he worked as the go-between for a huge New Orleans global trafficking hub. The lucrative industry depended on the likes of many Will Boudreaux's to keep their demand for girls met. And although they paid a hefty sum, they harassed him to no end for a steady supply of pretty young girls.

Boudreaux shook his head and lit a cigarette. He scrunched his face and stared through Hilly. *How did this mess begin?* He spoke out loud. "What was that woman doing there tonight?"

Hilly sat up straight. "What woman, Will?"

Boudreaux shook his head. "Do you know that Melanie Thompson woman? The one who owns the wedding shop on Main Street?"

"Is her daughter Lacey?"

His eyes narrowed. "I think that's what Virginia called her."

Hilly nodded. "She always invites Virginia over to her house and church and stuff. Why, Will?"

Boudreaux recalled approaching Melanie in the morning, and he didn't like the unexpected encounter with her again in the evening. His job with the ring had gotten complicated. Now they wanted him to kidnap Melanie Thompson's daughter and not for trafficking. Something about her ex-husband not cooperating with the big boss. A little insurance, he was told. Still, he didn't like it, so he hired some parolees to handle her.

"That Lacey's one of the good girls, always trying to be Virginia's friend," Hilly pleaded.

"Virginia don't need no friends. She's got me." Boudreaux jabbed his chest.

He loved what he did. Besides the money, he loved the game of enticement. It urged him forward with no regard for the girls. Will Boudreaux wasn't a "kidnapper," per se. Not his style. He worked slower and thrived on the manipulation. He wooed the girls or their guardians, found their weaknesses, and weaseled himself into their lives. Most often, lonely, unmarried women with daughters were where he found his niche. When he gained their trust, he lured the girls from their homes or schools with promises of modeling. They'd run away with him, and he'd sell them to the ring. Reasonably uncomplicated. It was the nature of the women he dealt with. Lonely and with little family support. He stared at Hilly. *Like her*, he thought.

Hilly fidgeted. "Will, maybe Virginia could just live normal like? These people are nice to her." Hilly interrupted his thoughts as she sat peeling layers off her jagged fingernails.

"Nice to her? Why, Virginia hates school. She doesn't fit in. Why do you think she was at the bar?"

Hilly looked up at Boudreaux, her eyes sad. "Will, Virginia ain't right in the head, you know that. It ain't fair."

Virginia's mother had been an addict and never stopped using throughout her pregnancy. Hilly loved the sweet-faced baby and tried to raise her alone, but as an addict herself, her difficulties led her to seek out Boudreaux. He could care less for the sob story but used it to his advantage. Knowing Hilly's love for her niece, he pretended to take care of them. Virginia was all Hilly had left of the family. Her and Will.

Family or no family, Boudreaux had plans of his own for Virginia. Her striking beauty made her a candidate to sell to the trafficking ring. Still, her disability made her difficult to control. Not a marketable trait. With Virginia's mental challenges, Boudreaux needed Hilly to look after her, although he had his doubts there, too. He had been considering the pornography industry. He could definitely use Virginia and other teens to launch the feeder industry to trafficking. He nodded at the possibility without a second thought.

"Hilly, we made a deal." Boudreaux glared. "You best be sure the girl is at school in the morning. I'll come by in the afternoon. Be ready to go, ya hear?"

She picked the fuzz off a worn cushion. Her hands shook, and she nodded. Without looking up, Hilly whispered, "Where we gonna live, Will?"

A low, guttural laugh flooded out, and he spun around. Sweeping his arms wide, he bellowed. "Live? Why? You gonna miss your little ole home-sweet-home here? Why that's a joke! This place is a dump. You can't even keep up the house I provide for you."

She sat, defenselessly beaten. Her eyes riveted to a stash of needles and white powder on the end table, and she stared, offering him no response.

Boudreaux stepped to the end table and blocked her gaze. He needed her coherent. Tomorrow was important. He needed Hilly's help to get Virginia out of town. Or did he? He

stared at the sad woman before him, blaming her for the evening's fiasco. It wouldn't have happened if she was sober. Virginia wouldn't have left the house. His eyes narrowed again. A smile turned up the corner of his mouth.

"Well, Hilly? You just gotta trust me." He crooned, "You know I've always taken care of you and Virginia, haven't I? Wasn't it me that took you in when you was hurtin' real bad? I even set you up here in this nice, little ole Bay Town." Boudreaux eased into his smooth talk as if he were beguiling his next victim. "I got a nice old hotel that my employer just purchased. To him, it's just a holding joint, but for me, well, you can help me fix it up real nice." He followed with a lie. "Maybe we'll get into the movie business. Why, Virginia's a natural. We can live real comfortable there. Make it a fancy studio, you know?" He winked as the grandiose plot unfurled in his mind.

He stepped aside, and Hilly stared again at the end table. She squeezed her arm and blinked—her eyes begging and pleading.

"Okay, darlin'." He prepared three times her usual dose and filled the vial.

Like a child offered candy, Hilly grabbed the syringe hungrily. She jabbed her arm, and within seconds, her limp body slumped back onto the sofa.

Boudreaux lifted her feet and turned her body, then covered her with a thin, worn blanket. He picked up the remote and turned on the TV. "Sweet dreams, cousin."

CHAPTER 7

Walking in the door, Lacey's shoulders slouched.

"Lacey, Pastor Brooks will call us. Virginia will be okay." Melanie crossed her arms, stopping herself from flinching, wanting to believe her own words.

"Yeah, I know. I'm just feeling a little guilty. We had such a great time tonight, well, most of it, anyway. Then poor Virginia ..."

"We'll keep Virginia in our prayers, okay? Why don't you go change, and then we'll do that?"

"Sure, Mom." Lacey left for her room.

A growing knot in Melanie's stomach gave way to anxious doubt. The incident at the Bayou Bar made her shiver. Melanie walked into her bathroom and slipped on her night-clothes. She stared at herself in the mirror, looking past the light lines on her forehead.

"God, what is going on with that poor Virginia? Why couldn't I do more?"

Seeing a movement out of the corner of her eye, Melanie turned. Lacey stood leaning against the doorway, wearing a dark blue sweatshirt with Huntington Beach, Surf City, emblazoned across the chest. Melanie's Dad's hometown. It somehow comforted her.

"You okay, Mom?" Lacey leaned against the door jamb.

"Yes. Fine."

"I'm worried about Virginia."

"I know, me too, sweetie."

Taking Lacey's hand, Melanie pulled her to the bedside. The small master bedroom provided Melanie a pleasant haven of rest. The monochromatic color scheme of white-on-white emitted peace and serenity. Jasmine scented, wood wick candles flickered, and her small, tan Bible lay open atop a stack of books. Melanie looked forward to bedtime each night. With down pillows enveloped in Battenberg lace shams leaning against her headboard, her comfy bed called to her at the end of each day. The blush tone of the pale pink walls purposed to soothe her soul. But not tonight.

"Mom? Why didn't we stay and help Virginia?"

Melanie pulled back. "What could we have done? The man looked like he had a gun."

"Exactly. We should have made Virginia come with us."

"Lacey, you can't make someone do something if they don't want to." Melanie finished quietly, "Believe me, I know, I've tried." Her mind drifted.

Lacey stared at her mom and raised her brows. "Mom, we're not talking about my dad. This is about Virginia. She doesn't know how to make good choices."

Melanie thought how alike her ex-husband and some teenage girls were when it came to impulse decisions and the consequences that resulted.

"Neither does Chris," Melanie whispered. She rolled her eyes, and a smile escaped her lips. It didn't go unnoticed.

"Mom!" Lacey yelled and hit her in the shoulder. The mood lightened somewhat.

"I know, I know. But you brought him up." Melanie nudged her. "Lacey, we couldn't have done anything tonight." She paused and looked at her daughter. "How about we pray for Virginia?"

A loud vibration rattled the nightstand. Melanie reached for her cell, but it slipped from her fingers and fell between the bed and the wall. By the time she retrieved it, it had gone to voicemail. She clicked on.

"Hey, Mel, Desmond here. I just wanted you to know we got Virginia home safe tonight. Chief Bert will check things out in the morning. Glad you were there." A pause almost caused Melanie to click off, but the voice continued, "And Mel? You did the right thing. Good job."

Melanie pressed her forehead on the carpet and breathed, *Thank You, God.*

She lay still on the floor, but a digging in her side caused her to wince and turn over. Lacey's toes wiggled underneath her. Melanie suddenly moved, grabbing Lacey's ankle, and pulling her down. Lacey landed on top of her mother with a thud.

"Ugh." Melanie moaned.

"It's your own fault," Lacey said as she tickled her mom. They rolled and poked one another in a heap on the ground when Melanie finally flipped over and jumped up.

"Okay, done … I won." She ran for the bathroom, but not before Lacey tripped her, and Melanie fell across the bed. Lacey sprang up and raised her hands in victory.

"Oh yeah, my win." Plopping down, she threw the fluffy pillows to the ground.

Melanie's heart warmed. *God, I love her so much. Please don't let anything ever happen to her.* Her smile faded. Thoughts of her failing business and where they might end up if Chris's deal didn't come through flooded her mind. Then the concerns for Virginia rose again. She offered a palm to Lacey.

Lacey took her hand, and they bowed their heads to pray. Thanking God for Pastor Desmond, Chief Bert, and their safety, Melanie also asked for protection for Virginia, and she ended by expressing her gratefulness for her beautiful daughter. A tear escaped when she said, "Amen."

"Amen." Lacey looked up. "Mom? Who do you think he was? The one Virginia called Daddy?" Lacey shivered. "Eeeew."

"I don't know, Lacey, but I got a terrible feeling about him."

"Yeah, me too." Lacey looked down. "I mean, she called him daddy. You don't think he was, like, her boyfriend or something...A sugar daddy..."

"Lacey!" Melanie's eyes flew wide open.

"What? Come on, Mom, I go to public school, you know."

Melanie's heart dropped a little.

"Mom, seriously? I may be innocent, but I'm not naïve."

"And what does that mean, young lady?"

"Just because I know what's going on out there doesn't mean I'm going do it. I'm not that stupid."

Melanie closed her eyes and pursed her lips. Old snapshots of her young choices flashed before her.

Lacey clapped a hand over her mouth. "Oh, Mom. I'm sorry. You know I didn't mean you."

Melanie's shoulders dropped for a moment, but she straightened herself, rising tall. "I know what you meant, Lacey. You won't just run off with some cute guy who comes along and sweet talks you off your feet into marrying him."

"Wow, I never heard that version before. But you're right." Lacey paused. "At least I won't marry him."

Melanie's mouth dropped. "But, but ..." She shook her head and yelled, "Yeah, but I don't even want you to meet that kind of guy, much less marry him."

Lacey raised her eyebrows up and down one too many times.

Melanie grabbed the last pillow and chucked it.

"Missed!" Lacey jumped up and kissed her mom. "Night, Mom. I love you."

"Love you, too."

Melanie sat with hands clasped between her knees. She

couldn't help smiling, and her thoughts drifted to Desmond. *Maybe if I'd met him first, I wouldn't have made those mistakes.* She drew a breath and thought, *Lacey, is not a mistake.* Still, her stomach fluttered.

Walking into the bathroom, she reached for her cleanser but stopped. *God is in control. So why am I afraid?* Melanie shook her head. She'd given her life over to God a long time ago, but trust, guilt, and worthiness still played a tug-of-war in her spirit.

She closed her eyes and rested her elbows on the sink counter. Clasping her hands, her head sunk into her palms. After a few minutes of silence, her shoulders relaxed, and a gentle wave of calm washed over her. She stood, turned off the bathroom light, and walked straight toward the Bible on her nightstand. The bookmark nestled where she'd left off. Her eyes followed the scripture. *Thou dost keep him in perfect peace, whose mind is stayed on Thee because he trusts in Thee.* Melanie turned off the light, blew out the candle, and slept in her comfortable bed.

Outside, a white van crept by the quiet, little cottage across from the gulf.

CHAPTER 8

A crack of thunder awoke Melanie. She looked out her bedroom window at the heavy clouds. Snuggling down beneath her comforter, she glanced at the open Bible on the nightstand, and it reminded her of the reason for her sound sleep amid trials. Stretching her arms overhead, she groaned and pressed her eyes tightly, recalling the night before. *Virginia.* Melanie sat up straight and took a deep breath. *She's safe, for now.*

Her eyes fluttered open. Before she took the time to thank God, her mind flooded with what the day held. Grabbing her phone, she checked for Chris's return call. If he didn't call this morning, she would call One Shell Tower Plaza anyway. Her stomach turned, unease rose, but that tingle of warning went unheeded. The uncertainty in her life at present raised desperation that clouded common sense.

The thought of losing her house, and maybe even her business, weighed heavily on her chest. Her body rose just a little as her bed depressed under the weight of someone jumping. She felt arms tighten around her waist, and a head nuzzled her neck.

"Good morning, sleepyhead." Lacey planted a kiss on Melanie's cheek. "Bye, Mom. I have to go. Love you!" Lacey squeezed her mom and ran out of the room and the house. The front screen door slammed.

The warmth of Lacey's touch lingered, and Melanie relished it as she slid into her slippers and headed down the hall. She stopped in the kitchen and rolled her eyes at the brown lunch sack left sitting on the counter. She snatched it.

"Lacey!"

Melanie ran outside and waved at the school bus. She stood with her other arm lifted high, gripping the brown paper bag. Lacey never turned as she bounded up the bus steps. Big Joe, the bus driver, didn't notice Melanie either, and the folding double doors closed as the school bus drove away.

Raising a hand to her brow, she stared at the bay across the street. A peek of the sun shined off the Gulf of New Mexico. The clouds moved in, and Melanie stepped inside to change. She needed her run to clear her head this morning.

Stretching her legs and taking some deep breaths, Melanie crossed the street. She stared back at her white clapboard cottage, and the uneasiness in her stomach returned. Her house. Her home. For how long? Feeling like an Eeyore, she shook her head and counted her blessings instead. *I have a wedding this weekend. The bank gave me a month. Chris came through.* Melanie furrowed her brow. *Did he?* Shaking her head, she continued the count. *Desmond.* Melanie looked up, realizing once again she always had things for which to be thankful.

Her lean body suited her choice of fitness well. Treading lightly, she avoided puddles and occasional slimy creatures on the sidewalks. Reaching up, she tightened her ponytail and swept the loose brown strands back off her face. A familiar fisherman trolled by, and she waved. The small population of Bay Town, Mississippi, afforded the luxury of being acquainted with most people in the city. She slowed down to call out a friendly hey to some local homeowners hauling up their crab traps off little piers. The private landings were a sweet novelty all along the gulf.

Melanie stood on the corner, looking both ways before crossing. A cream-colored convertible pulled up to the curb, blocking one lane of the two-lane highway.

"Hey, Mellie," said the driver.

"Oh, hi, Tina. Where are you headed?"

"To the gym. Want to come? You're already dressed for it." She pointed. "Love the outfit!"

"No, thanks. Running clears my head." Melanie smiled.

A few years older than Melanie, Tina was Melanie's next-door neighbor. A gorgeous African-American woman with a full head of bouncy, ombre curls that framed her striking face. Large almond-shaped eyes peeked out from long, dark lashes, and high cheekbones graced her perfectly shaped lips. And to top it off, she had a positively effervescent personality that put everyone at ease. When Melanie and Lacey had moved to Bay Town the year before, they became fast friends with Tina. Tina's fun-loving nature proved to be the best medicine for Lacey's and Melanie's grieving hearts after her parents' death and the abrupt move to the south.

A horn honked, and a large, late-model sedan sat idling behind Tina's car. Melanie looked back at the driver. A frowning, gray-haired, well-coiffed older woman stretched her neck to see over the steering wheel. Tina looked in her rearview mirror and grinned. Sticking her hand out the window, her flashy polished fingernails fluttered a friendly hi, waving the woman forward.

Tina spoke through grinning teeth. "Should she even be driving?" Her curls bounced as she shook her head. "All right, Mel. See you later, then. Byeee."

Melanie jogged past more wooden and concrete pilings that rose up out of the water. Some supported new planked, wooden walkways that jutted out over the gulf. Some were remnants of the destruction from the last big hurricane that had ravaged every structure along Beach Road. Living across the street from the bay was a life most weren't willing to give up. After the big storm, some former residents moved away, but many returned.

Melanie recalled living there when she was young. Her father had taken a contract and moved the family to Bay Town. Melanie and her sister, Charlene, were school-age girls when her parents had rented a home on the gulf. She smiled, recalling the memory of fun times.

Melanie's cell rang, and, glancing at the screen, her heart warmed.

"Hello, Char. I was just thinking about you." She smiled and watched for cars before crossing the street.

"Good, sis. Did I catch you on your run?" asked Charlene.

"Yes, but I'm good. I'm slowing down to watch the locals pull up the crab traps," Melanie teased.

"I hate those traps. I always did. They ought to outlaw them all."

Melanie laughed. She missed the weathered boardwalks and the large, decades-old beach homes, now long gone. But she appreciated the affordability of some of the newer, smaller cottages—one of which she owned. They still maintained the small-town charm. Melanie waved to a homeowner fishing off the docks. She continued her jog, slowing a little so she could speak.

"Well, then you couldn't eat that crab salad you used to love so much, could you?"

"No, I couldn't, and I wouldn't. I don't eat crab anymore, or fish or chicken—"

"Oh, yeah, I forgot." Melanie had many friends who'd gone vegan nowadays. Still, her sister seemed to think that all of Melanie's friends were carnivores and couldn't care less about the environment. She didn't want to go down that road again.

A wind blew up, and Melanie raised a hand to cover her nose. A rank stench wafted up from the rocks—low tide. Years ago, she would often jump off these piers into the smelly gulf.

It was one of her favorite things to do. On the sweltering days, she and Charlene couldn't wait for school to be out so they could feel the tepid gulf waters swirl around their bodies. But the fishy odors made her anxious to take a shower after each dip.

Not her sister. Charlene loved the gulf waters. The smell never bothered her. It was the social injustice of people that troubled her. So, she became an activist, though she didn't like being identified as such. Charlene was several years older than Melanie, and the sisters agreed on most things but had plenty of room for argument in others. Still, they got along well. In the last year, they'd grown even closer.

"Okay, so what's up, Char?" The pause was too long. "Are you all right?"

"Don't you know what today is?"

Melanie's eyes widened, and she threw a hand up to her forehead. "Oh, my goodness! I had such a crazy day yesterday. I totally forgot. It's Mom and Dad's anniversary." Melanie groaned. "I'm sorry, Char, you're so good at remembering dates." Her shoulders slumped, and she felt a little guilty after all her parents had done for her.

"I can't believe they've been gone a year. It seems like forever," said Charlene. "They would have been married forty-six years. Go figure they died the same month as their anniversary." Charlene almost whispered.

Melanie stopped. Her suddenly heavy feet dragged. Nearing a bus bench, she sat and dropped her head in one hand. "I still think Mom died of a broken heart. Forty-five years with Dad, that's a long time. She couldn't think of living another day without him. It's like God took them together."

"She died of a massive stroke, Melanie. A hemorrhaging brain bleed in the base of her skull." Charlene sounded cold.

"A week later? One week after Dad passed? I'd say it was providence."

"And I'd say Mom had high blood pressure, and Dad had

heart disease. Anyway, I thought I should call." Charlene's voice went monotone.

"I'm glad you did." This time Melanie paused. "I miss them so much. Daddy should be here with me. In Bay Town."

"Come on, sis. If you really believe all that stuff that he's in a better place ..."

"I do. I mean, I don't doubt that. But this business. It was his dream, too."

Charlene sighed. "Yeah, he always wanted to be an entrepreneur. You live his dream for him, sis. And do a good job, will you?"

"I'll try." The odor arose again, and Melanie pinched her nose. "Oh man, the fishy gulf is churning up today."

Charlene laughed. "Yeah, remember how Mom loved that? I mean, she loved all the free crabs and lobsters, too. Well, sis, I wish I were there with you. We could have a drink together. Oh, wait, I could have a drink, and you could tee-toddle."

"Sparkling cider, Char. I'll have a glass for you tonight." Melanie stood. "So, what's going on in D.C.?"

"It's crazy. I'm working on a human trafficking case."

"Oh? I've read some things on the internet. We had a speaker at our church, too. A young woman who escaped. Her experience was heart-wrenching. But her faith was inspiring."

"Yeah, without faith, or something ... but that's good to hear. Escaping. You don't have too many happy endings to those," Charlene said.

"Well, yes, happy that she got out, but so sad the trauma she still suffers. It's awful." Melanie paused. "I'm not sure my faith would sustain me as hers does."

"Are you kidding me? Your faith is like a rock. Mom and Dad were so proud of you."

Melanie scrunched her face. Since her parents' deaths, she wasn't so sure. The guilt of past stupid choices early in life kept coming back to haunt her. Her parents had forgiven her and always reminded her that God had too, but had she forgiven herself? And now, the threat of losing her house and business shook her confidence.

"Mel? You there?"

"Yes. So, about your job. What about the case?"

"Did you hear about the missing girl from Jackson High?"

Melanie hadn't jogged a quarter mile but stopped again, her mouth falling open. Thoughts of that Grady guy at Carol's shop flooded her mind. "Jackson, Alabama, or Jackson, Mississippi?"

"There's a Jackson, Alabama?" Charlene blew out a breath. "Alabama, Mississippi? What is this a geography quiz?"

"Wait, when did this happen?" asked Melanie.

"What, are you living under a rock?" Charlene's voice rose. "It happened about a week ago." She sighed. "Do you think maybe Lacey knew her?"

Melanie rolled her eyes. "Of course not. Jackson is a good two-hour drive from here. I can't imagine how Lacey would know her," said Melanie.

"Oh. Isn't Jackson right next door?"

"No, Charlene. Mississippi is 48,000 square miles, and we don't all know each other. But what makes you think this has anything to do with human trafficking? Couldn't she be just another troubled runaway? Doesn't that happen a lot?"

"Just another? Listen, Mel. Those victims are the target. Most often, the runaways get caught up with human trafficking. We have a hunch that a huge ring has been operating in New Orleans for a while now. We got a tip from a girl who escaped from a hotel down there. Anyway, the ring is tight, and we've never been able to prove this was happening, but this is the break we needed."

"What if the missing girl just took off with a friend or relative or something?" Melanie bit her lip, thinking of Virginia and the man she called Daddy. "They wouldn't be trafficked, right?"

"Well, it does happen. Like with this case, this teen's mom had a boyfriend who skipped town right after she disappeared. He's a suspect."

Melanie raised a hand to push back some loose strands of hair off her face. She paced back and forth. Placing one hand on her hip, she squinted. "What's this about a boyfriend?"

"The girl's mom had a boyfriend. He disappeared, and now he's a person of interest. Anyway, her name is Acadia Perrin. Does the name sound familiar?"

All Melanie could think about was Grady. She had to talk to Carol. She had to speak with her before she told Charlene.

"So you think this girl … what's her name?" Melanie asked.

"Are you even listening?" Charlene huffed.

"I am. I'm sorry, go on."

"Acadia Perrin. She's only fifteen. But her social media profile picture made her look much older. She had on a ton of makeup and a skimpy top, but that makes no difference."

Just like Virginia, thought Melanie as she recalled the previous evening outside the Bayou Bar.

"Sis? You there?"

Melanie shook her arms by her side. Generations of families in the South stayed close together. She knew that. But she'd not lived here long enough to know the common names. "I've never heard of a Perrin family down here. We have a quiet little community. Not much happens, you know. That's why Dad applied for the grant for me to start my business down here. That and he loved living in Bay Town." She bit her lip.

"Yeah, I know. Well, I don't mean to raise alarm, but keep an eye on Lacey, okay?"

"What does that mean? Are the girls down here in any danger?" Melanie rubbed her forehead. *Virginia*.

"Well, anyone can be a victim. Human trafficking is on the rise for obvious reasons, and we uncovered evidence about that ring operating out of New Orleans. Anyway, I know Bay Town isn't far from there, so don't freak out. Just be careful, okay?" Charlene's tone softened.

"Is there anything we can do here? I mean to help?"

"Just get the word out. I think that girl speaking at your church is a good start. Most people are oblivious. And discredit the normalcy of pornography. R-rated movies, internet porn. Yuck! That feeds this industry. It's infuriating that it's even legal. Don't get me started!"

Melanie listened, and her skin crawled. "Listen, Charlene. We have had some stuff happening lately." Melanie stared down the road and cut her run short. She was only a half-mile from home. "Can I call you later and fill you in? It'll take a while, and I have to finish my run. I've got an appointment this morning."

"Stuff? What kind of stuff?" Charlene's voice rose.

"I'll call you later, okay?"

Charlene again protested to hear more, but Melanie said goodbye and clicked off. The noise from a beat-up fishing boat rang out across the water. The rusty, old thing chugged up the inlet with ropes, gaffing, and lines hanging all over it. It made so much noise and blew so much smoke, the vessel looked as if it could sink at any minute. Barely making out the name on the bow, through squinted eyes, she read *Fish Stalker*.

Shivering, she jogged for home. Running up the front steps of her cottage, she pulled out her keys. The gap of the slightly open door peeked back at her.

CHAPTER 9

B oudreaux had spent the night at a hotel in town and drove back in the morning. He parked his car across the street, a few doors down from Hilly's house, fixing his eyes on an old, yellow school bus idling. The driver honked.

Thumbing his fingers on the wheel, he twisted his wrist and glanced at his watch. Seven-thirty. The bus horn sounded a second time. Virginia stumbled out onto the front porch and ran down the walk. Her limp blonde hair hung in her face, and she hoisted a large tote over her shoulder as she hopped on the bus. An enormous smile gleamed across the face of the patient bus driver as he greeted Virginia.

Boudreaux blew out a sigh. If she wasn't such a pretty thing. His trade took a toll on the girls, and their short-lived productivity increased the constant demand. *Yup, I need her, alright. I need 'em all.*

The bus passed, and he stepped out, flicking his cigarette on the ground. He crossed the street and bounded up the front porch, finding the door partly open. He nodded, confident that in her rush, Virginia never noticed Hilly. He'd counted on that.

In the last ten hours, Hilly's body had grown cold. The dusty TV screen was blue except for a mundane, ever-rolling script, playing a redundant generic tune. He picked up the remote and clicked it off. Hilly lay still, covered with the blanket, her body turned to the back of the sofa just as Boudreaux left her the night before. Though he wondered at the lack of stench, other than the house's normal odor, he shrugged. Too soon, he surmised and stepped to her side, pulling the blanket slightly higher to cover the back of her head.

That idiot Chief, he'll just rule it another overdose, thought Boudreaux. Hilly's worthless life wouldn't warrant an investigation. He raised a hand to his brow and tipped an imaginary hat as he strolled out.

With hours to kill before Virginia got home, Boudreaux drove across the Bay Bridge to a casino, never giving another thought to his dead cousin. He pulled up to the casino entrance, smoothed back his hair, and threw the keys at the valet.

"Take good care of her," he called as he sauntered into the lobby.

The blaring music served as a backdrop to slot machines clanging and loud cheering from the gaming floor. Tourists and sleep-deprived retirees mingled about.

Boudreaux entered the men's room, and his phone rang. The screen ID caused him to utter a single expletive.

"Yes, sir. What can I do for you?" Boudreaux asked.

"We need to meet. I need an update," said Mr. Black, the liaison between the trafficking kingpin and Boudreaux.

"I'm at the Golden Slipper in Pass Christian. Meet me in the Cajun Bar."

"I'll be there in two hours."

"Sure thing, Mr. Black." *Figures, you'd make me waste my time.*

Boudreaux washed and dried his hands. He peered into the mirror, examining his image and smiled. Just before leaving, he swept a hand over his slicked-back hair and nodded.

The smell of a hot breakfast filled the air, and his eyes found the restaurant. His hunger for food was undiminished at the handling of his dead cousin's body earlier. He sat in a booth near the entrance and glanced around. Eyeing a cute, young waitress, he waved her over and ordered eggs, pancakes, bacon, sausage, and coffee.

"You got yourself quite an appetite there, sir," the young girl drawled.

"Yes, I sure do, sugar." He winked and leaned forward. "So, why is a sweet, young thing like you working in a place like this?"

She laughed. "Oh, I need the money, ya know." Leaning down to his eye level, she whispered, "I dropped out of high school. Got a fake ID, and this is the only job I could get." The messy bun atop her head framed her fresh face.

Boudreaux leaned back. "Anybody ever tell you you're pretty enough to be a model?" He rested his hand on hers.

Her large brown eyes widened, and her straight white teeth glistened. "Well, sir, I have been told …" She giggled.

"Well, well, looks like today is your lucky day. How would you like to join my agency?"

She squealed with delight.

Boudreaux sweet-talked her throughout breakfast and didn't leave until he felt confident that he had his next victim. He enjoyed every bite of his breakfast, wiped his mouth with the white napkin, and placed it on his plate. One last wink at the cute waitress and Boudreaux left a generous tip and his business card, positive she'd call.

Melanie stared at her front door. She was sure she'd locked it when she left for her run. She turned, looking up and down her street. Not a car. She fingered her house key then pushed in. Swiping the sweat from her brow, she swept back some loose strands falling across her face and stepped in, peeking around.

Everything was right where she'd left it. Except for a pillow on the floor, nothing was amiss. She ignored it, walking toward the kitchen. Passing the Victorian, marble-topped lampstand in the hallway, she stopped. There appeared to be a long scratch through the marble. It was an antique, but Melanie was sure it hadn't been there when she bought it. She shrugged. It was a garage sale treasure, so she wasn't too concerned. Heading toward her room, she threw off her clothes and jumped in the shower.

The warm water soothed her body, and after toweling off, she dressed for the storm whipping up outside. Grabbing her tote and her phone, she stopped. *Call Chris*, she told herself and dialed his number. It went straight to voicemail.

The side pocket of her tote held the business card, and she lifted it out. She tapped it on her phone a few times but stuffed it back and left the house.

Driving down Beach Road, Melanie flipped on her wipers, peering out at the beginning storm. Within minutes, she arrived downtown and stopped for coffee. She parked at the Mockingbird Café. The morning rain had dumped a lake of water. Puddles dotted the parking lot, so Melanie hopped, skipped, and jumped, maneuvering the little pools. She forged around the rivulets of water rolling in front of the entrance and pulled the door open.

A collective but quiet chuckle arose, and a few customers stared back as she entered. She nodded at the smiling faces and got in line. Her eyes shifted downward, checking her clothes for anything amiss.

"It's the dance you did outside," whispered a male voice behind her.

Turning, she rolled her head to one side and dropped her shoulders, glaring. The scathing look instantly converted to a smile.

"Oh, good morning, Desmond." She fingered her damp hair, twisting a strand.

"It was all that hopping and skipping in the parking lot. Kind of like a rain dance." He laughed in a friendly manner that should have put her at ease. It didn't.

"That noticeable, huh?" Biting her lip, she shrugged. "I didn't want to get my shoes wet."

"Don't blame you." He smiled down at her. "Hey, can I buy your coffee?" His dark eyes shined.

Melanie stared up at him as if she were in a trance. He was way too handsome for his own good.

"Uh, Melanie? Can I buy your coffee?" Desmond repeated.

Melanie's phone dinged, and she blinked. She shook herself, breaking her gaze. "Oh, no, thanks. I'll get it. You go ahead. I need to check my phone first, anyway."

Stepping aside, she checked, and her morning appointment asked to reschedule. Melanie confirmed and took a few more minutes to edit the change in her calendar app. She answered a few texts from the bride-to-be for Sunday's wedding, clicked off, and turned.

Desmond stood in front of her holding two steaming, hot cups. The earthy aroma of just ground coffee and freshly baked pastries finally hit her, and she breathed deep.

He smiled. "Took a chance you just might be a latte, no whip, no syrup kind of girl?"

"Presumptuous, wouldn't you say?" Melanie raised her eyebrows. "Or is it prophetic, Pastor?" Melanie giggled.

"Wow, I'm impressed."

"I don't always fall asleep in church, you know."

"Ouch." He winced and offered the coffee. "Can you sit for a minute?"

"Yes, I can. My morning appointment just got pushed back to this afternoon."

Desmond looked around. People streamed in, and the place was packed. He nodded and motioned to a corner. The only open spot was a loveseat by the window.

Once seated, Melanie sipped her coffee, but her brow furrowed. "Hey, that was so weird with Virginia last night, wasn't it? I mean, I'm sure glad you were there to help."

He nodded.

"What were you doing down there, anyway?" asked Melanie.

"Having dinner with Miss Ellie."

Melanie tried to hide a frown. "Oh, I don't think I know her."

"Well, she doesn't make it to church much. She's all alone. A widow."

A widow and he's a widower. Melanie forced a smile.

"She's a housebound senior, so we have dinner together once a week."

"Oh, that's so nice of you." A good feeling bubbled up, and she tried to squelch the relief she felt that Miss Ellie wasn't some sweet, young thing.

"Well, I think I get the better end of the deal. She's a good cook, even from her wheelchair." His brows furrowed. "But yes, that was a strange evening last night. You should have seen the house we took Virginia to afterward."

Melanie gulped and lowered her cup. "Yes. I was just there yesterday morning. I spoke with Virginia's aunt." Melanie leaned back and sighed. "She asked me to watch after Virginia."

"I'm not surprised with that Will Boudreaux around." Desmond shook his head.

"Is that his name? Virginia's dad?" Melanie shivered. "Lacey said he's not her father."

"Yeah, I don't think so either. The aunt was afraid of him. Chief Bert's on it, and we need to keep her in our prayers."

Melanie nodded. "So, what about you? Shouldn't you be stressing in your office about your sermon for Sunday?"

Desmond chuckled. "Yes, but I have a hospital visit to

make today. Some former church members. I don't know if you remember Richard and Deena Copeland."

He explained the situation with the elderly couple. Though Melanie tried to concentrate, Desmond proved too much of a distraction. His navy polo shirt and grey jacket deepened his eyes like a beautiful pool beneath a waterfall. And she was drowning. She fidgeted with the protector sleeve on her coffee cup and closed her eyes, trying to find some connection to who he was talking about. Her eyes fluttered open.

"Oh, yes. I do remember them. Deena was such a hard worker. She always seemed to make time to help everyone." She shrugged. "I hope I'm like her when I get to be her age."

Desmond's brow furrowed.

"Wait, I mean … she's not that old, right? I'm sorry. I …" Melanie fluttered her lips.

"She is older, and I know what you mean. My wife, Emily" —Desmond's eyes sparkled even brighter at the mention of his wife's name—"I thought Emily might have been like Deena one day." He paused. "If we had shared a longer life."

Melanie lowered her eyes.

"Emily was the best." He huffed. "I wished …" He stopped and shook his head. "You know, I just have to trust that God's plan for me didn't include us growing old together."

"Wow. That's a lot of trust," she replied.

"Yes, it's difficult, but trusting in Him means I know He's got something else for my future. I didn't always think that way. It's something Emily and I disagreed about a lot. The trusting in God thing." Desmond now fidgeted with his cup sleeve. "I'm afraid I realized it too late for Emily to see it. Anyway, my job now is to seek out God's plan for me and do it."

"Seems like you've got that figured out already. I mean, you're a pastor and all."

"Well, it was something Emily wanted to be a part of with me. But I didn't become a pastor until after she passed. She was always active in the church, but me, not so much." He leaned back, and his long legs stretched out to the side as he crossed his arms.

Melanie wrinkled her brows. *Sort of like me and Chris.* "So, how long has it been? I mean since your wife passed?" Melanie lowered her voice. "If you don't mind my asking?"

"Five years. She's been gone five years. And we were married for five. I was away a lot with the military." His words clipped out staccato-like.

"What branch?"

"Navy Seals."

Melanie's eyes flew open. "You were a Navy Seal?"

He nodded, and his eyes floated somewhere far away.

She waited. The silence stretched, but when he returned, his eyes suddenly widened.

He gazed at Melanie and smiled again. "Hey, would you like to join me in visiting Deena? It might lift her spirits to have someone else besides me visit from the church."

Melanie stuttered a bit and shook her head. "Oh, maybe not. I've never done that before."

"Oh, come on. Try it," Desmond coaxed.

She couldn't believe he was asking her. But the thought of a dying person made her think of her parents, and she didn't know if she was ready for that. After thinking about his invitation, though, she realized she had no good reason to decline. Her dad had always said, *If you see a need, fill it.*

"Do you think she'd mind?" Melanie sat up straight and smiled. "Whenever Deena was around, it was like … I don't know … like there was a holy presence or something."

"I think I know what you mean. Some people have that effect on us. Deena would love it if you came."

"But what about Mr. Copeland? I don't think he ever smiled at me even once, and I always got the feeling he didn't like me. I don't know why." Deep inside, Melanie thought it was the single mom thing. Whether her own guilt or an accurate perception of what people thought of her, she struggled with those conflicting feelings either way.

"I wouldn't worry about Mr. Copeland. That's just kind of how he rolls." Desmond's gentle eyes pleaded. "Join me?"

Melanie paused, then blurted out, "Sure. Why not?"

"Good!" He glanced at his watch. "Whoa, it's already eight-fifteen. I'd hoped to get some flowers first."

"I've got it covered," she assured him. "We can make a quick stop at Max's. It's just around the corner."

Inside the Pink Rosette, the cool, damp air made Melanie shiver. Max always left the top half of the Dutch door open, which let in the cool gulf breeze. She yanked at the collar of her thick sweater. Desmond helped as he unfolded the tucked-under cowl-neck. Though his hands didn't touch her skin, she felt warmer.

"Good morning, Pastor. Good morning, Mel."

"Hi, Max. Can you fix me up a quick bouquet? Maybe some pink peonies, white snapdragons, and greens?"

"Very well, Melanie." He brushed back his white hair and pushed up his glasses. "You know 'tis the fall season? You sure you want pink, dearie?"

Pink fluff filled her brain as she thought of Deena and her always brightly blushed pink cheeks. Baby pink, hot pink, bubble-gum pink. She wore the color all year round. "Yes, I'm sure."

Max went to work, and Melanie watched his hands gather and clip the stems.

"Wow. Those beat the generic, mixed garden bunch I would have bought," said Desmond.

When he finished, Max offered the short, square vase to Melanie.

"Max, you never cease to amaze me. It's gorgeous. Can you bill my account?"

"Of course," said Max.

"Oh, no." Desmond reached for his wallet. "This is on me. How much do I owe you?"

Max looked back and forth between the two of them and nodded. "You can take it up with the lady."

Desmond and Melanie were walking out of the shop, still arguing about the bill, when her cell phone rang. She handed Desmond the vase and mouthed, "Sorry." She turned and answered. "Chris, can I call you back?"

"Sure, babe. I'm just returning your call," said Chris on the other end.

"Chris!" Melanie yelled, catching Desmond's stare. "I'm not your babe," she whispered. "I'll call you this afternoon. Bye."

The blustery wind whipped up, and as Melanie turned, her scarf blew, tangling in her hair. She batted it about a few seconds before dropping her arms in defeat. She peeked at Desmond through the mess of wavy chestnut tresses covering her face. Her shoulders drooped.

"Melanie, if something's come up, it's fine." He pursed his lips. "I can go myself."

She stared at him. Was it the phone call? He seemed to not want her company anymore. For the first time in sixteen years, she'd let herself feel something for a man. A man way out of her league, or so she thought. And here was her ex, messing up her life again. Melanie shook her head and looked up, rolling her eyes. *Whatever. I'm not invested yet, anyway.* Her thoughts did little to convince her.

"Nothing's come up. Nothing at all." She fluttered her lips. "But go ahead. I'll get back to the office."

He narrowed his eyes and stared. "You don't want to go?"

She let her tote slip off her shoulder. Was it even worth it? It had been just her and Lacey for so long, Melanie wasn't sure if she had the energy for this. Or the confidence. A break in the black sky opened, and a sliver of sun shone on Desmond.

A laugh came from the shop. "Look at that! A promise of light," Max called from his shop.

Both Desmond and Melanie looked at Max. He leaned on the double-Dutch door and winked.

"Maybe the guy knows something?" Desmond laughed and took a step, staring at her with raised brows. "How about it? Are you coming, Mel?"

Melanie wasn't sure what Max meant, but it was enough incentive for her to lay aside her insecurities and go for it. "Sure, why not?" She wouldn't let Chris spoil this.

The drive to Gulf Port was a short twenty-five minutes. They remained quiet, listening to the mellow tunes on the radio as they crossed the Bay Bridge. Light from the sun danced across the water and somehow made Melanie feel a little calmer, and Desmond's presence somehow made her feel a little closer to God.

CHAPTER 10

W ill Boudreaux strolled past slot machines and roulette wheels. He stopped at the blackjack table, but too many hands later, he threw down his cards and left for the bar.

Looking at his watch, he signaled the bartender and ordered a plain orange juice. He wanted a keen mind for his meeting. Boudreaux looked around and noted his surroundings. He was always on the alert for local authorities who may have a lead on him. Yet, he was good at covering his tracks. He swept the room once more, and nothing caused him concern.

Raising his glass to his lips, he sipped but suddenly stopped. A wiry man sat at the far end of the bar. Something familiar caught his attention. Putting down his glass, he moved closer, resting on a stool, a single seat away. Boudreaux waited until the man turned. Their eyes locked, and with a startled jerk, the man knocked over his drink and attempted to sop up the mess.

"Hey there, do I know you?" Boudreaux squinted.

"Nope."

Nodding at the bartender, the man threw down a few bills and left. He loped with long, quick strides toward the casino.

Boudreaux stood up and followed but stopped at the bar

entrance. His eyes continued to follow the man when Mr. Black arrived.

Wearing an expensive, dark suit, a plain white shirt, and a thin-striped, black tie, he walked straight to Boudreaux. "Good afternoon." He extended his hand.

He refocused his attention on Boudreaux as they shook. Boudreaux had an uncanny knack of appearing calm under any circumstance.

"Trouble?" Mr. Black asked. He turned and looked toward the casino floor.

"No, no trouble. Just thought I recognized someone." He stood unmoved. "No worries."

"Someone who?"

"Someone, no one." Boudreaux made no move to sit. "So, what's the deal? I delivered last week. The package from Jackson ..." Boudreaux stopped. A switch flipped in his mind —the guy in the bar. *Jackson.* He continued. "I'm just about all caught up."

"We have a contract. The deadline is next week, and I'm here to ensure the deliveries happen."

"Don't you worry about a thing." Boudreaux smiled but detested being held in check. "Provided, of course, we don't have an unforeseeable hindrance." His rebellious spirit often challenged authority.

"And has anything been hindered?"

Adjusting his cuffs, Boudreaux tipped his head. "No, sir. Smooth as glass from here on."

He knew full well the pickup arrangements for the girls he held captive in New Orleans. The plans were always the same. The threat of discovery was imminent, but so far, every move had gone without incident.

Glancing at his Rolex, Boudreaux wrapped his knuckles on the counter. "Well, lookie here. I have to go. I got a package to pick up this afternoon," he lied.

"One more thing. Mrs. Thompson? She hasn't called yet."

"That ain't my problem. I delivered the message. I left the card."

"What about the daughter?" asked Mr. Black.

"What about her? My boys are on it. You say the word, and they'll take her."

Mr. Black nodded. "If Mrs. Thompson doesn't call soon, we'll give the order. The daughter is not to be harmed. We have no leverage with her father if she is."

"Seems to me a little harm can be good leverage." Boudreaux raised a brow. "What's the deal with this guy, anyway?"

"It's a need-to-know basis. Wait for my call and make sure you complete the deliveries. I'll be in touch."

"I'm sure you will," sneered Boudreaux.

"Good. I'm glad we understand each other."

Boudreaux waited, then followed a distance behind Mr. Black. Relieved to see him move in the opposite direction, Boudreaux strolled outside. He wrinkled his nose at the smell of cheap cigars coming from the busloads of weekend tourists. The chances were slim that he'd find the man from the bar. Still, he squinted and searched. Nothing.

Retrieving his Lincoln from the valet, he drove to the far end of a lot where the city transit was pulling out. In a back-seat, near a window, sat a man slouched down. His face was covered with a ball cap. Boudreaux followed.

Thirty minutes later, the bus pulled into the Main Street terminal in Bay Town. Boudreaux's blue Lincoln parked behind, and he watched as people filed off the bus. A man with a ball cap pulled down tight exited. He fidgeted as he glanced back and forth. Boudreaux's fingers paused above the ignition button, but the man walked across the street and entered a shop. Second Chances.

"What do we have here?" Boudreaux said aloud.

Somehow, this guy was connected to Acadia Perrin from Jackson, Mississippi. But how? And what did the guy know?

Boudreaux staged the Perrin girl with the others in the old hotel in New Orleans. He was set to get paid a generous fee for this group of girls, and he couldn't afford a so-called hindrance. And this man? He posed a potential threat.

"Grady!" A woman with long, red hair yelled from down the sidewalk.

The man with the ponytail emerged, and they spoke outside. Moments later, she walked away from the store.

"Thank you, ma'am. Grady, it is." A smile stretched across Boudreaux's face.

He now recalled that Grady was the boyfriend of the Acadia girl's mother. He'd seen them together at the house whenever he picked up or dropped off the daughter. Unlike Boudreaux, Grady and the mother were not so discreet. Boudreaux had gained the girl's confidence and promised her a modeling contract with his non-existent agency. She had kept their friendship a secret from her mother. So he was at a loss as to how Grady had recognized him in the bar. But the girl was the only connection they shared.

The news media had reported about a boyfriend that ran off after the girl's disappearance. Boudreaux narrowed his eyes and stared at Grady. Police had implicated the boyfriend's involvement, but without evidence, the story died. The mother's testimony did little to help. For the first two days after the girl went missing, the distraught woman appeared on all the local news channels, defending her boyfriend. The lead went cold, and the teen's odds of being classified as a runaway rose higher every day.

Pulling out a cigarette, he tapped it a few times. *If Grady gets taken into custody, he'll give me up in a hot second.* Boudreaux decided to get rid of him. But Hilly's death complicated matters. Two deaths in one week, in the same location? He lit his cigarette and slid down his window. His cell buzzed, but before he could answer it, a voice outside boomed.

"Well, well. If it isn't Will Boudreaux."

He turned in his seat and sneered. "Chief?"

Chief Bert pushed up his hat and rested his arm on the top of Boudreaux's car. "I thought you were leaving town last night?"

"Had to be sure my daughter got to school today." Boudreaux's jaw tightened.

Chief Bert leaned in. "Since you're here, I got some questions to ask you. That Bayou Bar isn't a place for teenagers."

"Is that a question?" Boudreaux seethed inside but remained unruffled.

"How did she get there?"

"She snuck out of the house, right under the nose of her Aunt Hilly. It won't happen again, and there ain't no cause to worry. She's my daughter." His fingers moved to the window control. "May I go now, sir?" Boudreaux knew the chief had no cause to detain him.

"Sure thing." Stepping back, he added, "So, what are you doing downtown?"

Boudreaux's eyes shifted to Grady across the street.

The chief turned to follow his gaze.

Clearing his throat loudly, Boudreaux's voice startled the chief's gaze back. "I told you. I'm taking care of family, and I just pulled over to answer a business call, is all."

"Okay, Mr. Boudreaux."

He nodded, sliding up his window. "Sure thing, Chief."

Boudreaux pulled onto Main Street and drove straight to the main highway. His knuckles turned white as he gripped the steering wheel. Thinking about Hilly and Grady, he realized he had too many loose ends. He drove toward Highway 10, hoping to deflect the chief. When satisfied that he wasn't being followed, he made a sharp turn and sped down country roads to Hilly's house. He bumped up the cracked driveway and through the rickety carport. Maneuvering the car through knee-high weeds in the backyard, Boudreaux parked behind the house, ensuring no one in the neighborhood saw him. He waited for Virginia's return.

Melanie and Desmond arrived at the hospital and approached the receptionist's desk.

"We're here to see Deena Copeland, please," said Desmond.

"Room 114." A girl with silky black hair looked up. "Oh, hi, Mrs. Thompson."

"Allie? I wasn't aware you worked here." Allie wore the vintage candy-striper uniform. "A volunteer, right?" Melanie asked.

"Yes, it helps my college transcripts." Her eyes widened, and she covered her mouth. "But that's not all. I am interested in health care. I mean, helping people and all."

"Well, they're very fortunate to have you here." Melanie chuckled.

Allie stared at Desmond. "Hi. You must be Lacey's dad. Chris, right? It's so nice to meet you. Lacey said you're a lot of fun."

Melanie went white, and Desmond turned red.

"Uh, no ... I'm—-"

"Allie Higa, this is Desmond Brooks. He's the pastor of the church Lacey and I attend. We're here to visit a church member," Melanie interrupted.

Desmond waved.

Allie tapped her forehead with an opened palm. "Oh, that's right. I attend the youth group on Wednesday nights sometimes. I am so sorry. I should have known. Lacey told me ..."

"It's okay." Melanie drew a breath between her teeth. *Chris again.* "We should go." She pushed Desmond ahead as her heels clicked down the quiet hallway.

"Allie Higa's great-grandmother lives on Beach Road. She's a neighbor and friend of ours." Melanie bit her lip. "Sometimes, the girls hang out." Stopping, her shoulders dropped as she faced Desmond. "Look. Lacey's dad, Chris? He's hardly ever here. I have no idea what Allie was thinking."

He put up his hands. "No worries." He then ushered her forward.

As they turned the corner, they walked through double doors and passed a quiet nurse's station. He pointed toward Room 114, and Melanie dragged behind.

Peeking in, she saw Richard Copeland sitting in a chair, with Deena's hands in his. He laid with his forehead resting on their clasped hands. As quiet as Desmond and Melanie were, Richard glanced up. His face was flushed and wet with tears.

Melanie stopped short. A gasp stuck in her throat. Deena's pale face, marred by her parted mouth and tongue resting on her lips, reminded her of her own mother. The picture of her last hours forever emblazoned in Melanie's head.

A wire ran from Deena's chest, and a tube from under her blankets was all that was visible. A slight gurgle emitted from her throat, and her labored breath caused her chest to rise and fall. But with her eyelids closed, she appeared to be resting peacefully.

Richard faced them. "She took a turn yesterday afternoon, and they moved her to this ward. They said it wouldn't be too much longer." His head hung low, and his wrinkled face held deep sorrow. "There's nothing more we can do."

"We can pray." Desmond went to Richard and touched his shoulder.

Deep lines formed on the sides of Richard's mouth as he pressed his lips and nodded. Desmond touched Deena's hand, and his words flowed as if he was merely talking. He asked for God's grace, peace, and mercy on Deena and for Richard's divine comfort.

When he finished praying, Desmond drew Richard into a

casual conversation. He expressed his thanks for Deena and spoke of her work and friendships at the church. When Desmond inquired about their life together, Richard sat a little straighter. A smile appeared, accompanied by a faraway stare, although he related the various facts about their life together as if read from an encyclopedia.

Melanie marveled at how effortlessly Desmond comforted him. She studied his actions. He reminded her a little of her dad. Kind, thoughtful. Daddy would have liked this Desmond Brooks. Melanie smiled. It would have thrilled her mom also that he was a pastor. Her heart warmed.

As she leaned against the door jamb, a long, loud gasp emitted from Deena. It made her jump. She soon heard footsteps behind her, and a nurse touched Melanie's arm and scooted past her.

The nurse checked Deena's pulse and glanced at Richard. "I'm so sorry," she whispered.

Melanie's heart broke as she watched the nurse record numbers and discreetly silenced the machines.

Richard's quiet cries escalated to painful sobs.

The kind nurse hugged him. "Take your time, Mr. Copeland." She typed on the computer in the corner and left.

Melanie stood frozen with the beautiful vase of flowers still in hand. Tears trickled down her face as she watched Desmond steady Richard's heaving shoulders.

They all stayed in their respective positions for what seemed like forever. When Richard's cries subsided, Desmond waved Melanie over. With her face red and her hands numb from clinging to the vase, the challenge was to make her feet move forward. He nodded for her again, and she stepped to the bedside.

Richard turned and stared at the flowers, and a slight smile formed on his lips. "Peonies. Those are Deena's favorite." He looked at Pastor Brooks. "Guess she's sleeping in them now, eh?"

"More like dancing in them, I'd say. Dancing with Jesus." Desmond breathed deep. "I'm so very sorry, Richard. I know how much you'll miss her."

A darkness settled over Desmond as he seemed to be struggling himself. Melanie couldn't watch. She set down the flowers and stepped out, leaving Desmond and Richard sitting huddled side by side.

Melanie roamed the hospital, staring at the few sparse paintings on the walls as she strolled through the wing. The deafening silence and the absence of visitors lent an eerie feel. Except for a woman hurrying through the hall, Melanie was all alone. As she looked around, she gasped. This was the hospice ward. She breathed deep and gulped at the memory of her mother in a ward like this. Her last painful memories.

Continuing her walk, Melanie stopped before a wide picture window. Behind it grew a full atrium with lush, thriving green plants. Droplets of water dotted the larger leaves, and smaller shoots pushed up underneath the mature plants, much like her mother's garden. Always sprouting new life. *And now, Deena has a new life.*

"Thank You, God," Melanie said aloud.

"He's a great God, isn't he?" Desmond's voice rose behind her.

Melanie's eyes widened, and she turned. "What? Oh, yes. Yes, he is." She bit her lip. "Mr. Copeland … do you need to stay with him? I can call an Uber."

"No, Deena's sister just arrived."

"Is there anything we can do?" Melanie choked a little. She couldn't help but think of how lost her mom was when her dad died first.

"He'll be okay. It will be rough, but the church is here for him. And Deena's faith was powerful. That's a significant source of strength, too." He spoke as if he knew.

Desmond offered his hand.

Confusion unsettled her, but she hesitatingly placed her

fingertips on his palm. His touch made her stomach flutter as his fingers closed around hers. He squeezed.

"You did fine, Mel. The flowers were perfect." Smile lines formed around his eyes. The squeeze of his hand so comforting. "You know, Richard never even remembered who you were. See, God works in mysterious ways." Desmond chuckled as he pulled her to standing and dropped her hand. As they walked toward the exit, he said, "You know, it's nice to have a woman's touch."

She felt her skin flush as they left the hospital. The clouds parted, the sun broke through, and Melanie stepped lighter with Pastor Desmond Brooks by her side.

CHAPTER 11

Joe Cunningham drove around the back to the maintenance yard. As he parked the yellow bus behind the school, he shuffled his large, oversized body sideways and out the door. He felt the gravel crunch beneath his feet. It was bus washing day, but he couldn't help wondering what those guys were doing in town last night. He thought he'd seen them again this morning, following the bus. But he wasn't sure. Either way, the kids at Bay High were his kids, and he wouldn't let anything happen to them. He pulled out his cell.

"Chief? Joe here. Listen, you gonna be around later? ... Okay, good. I'm stopping by."

Gazing at the blue skies, Joe smiled. He was thankful for the opportunities God gave him each day to help others. He felt it was his responsibility to stand up for those who wouldn't or couldn't defend themselves. He wasn't just their bus driver. He was their protector.

Joe grew up on the other side of the tracks, literally. Just as his parents and grandparents had. They were honest, hard-working, but poor. Conflict, strife, and petty crime were commonplace in their neighborhood. But Joe's family was a God-fearing bunch, and his parents and the church reverend guided him and his siblings to a higher calling. When Joe was young, he went to school in Bay Town when schools were already integrated. But here it was decades later in the south, and the discrimination remained. Yet, in the little borough of Bay Town, the tightly knit, God-fearing community had managed to progress more than most others.

Clipping his keys on his belt, he commenced the washing. Hours later, when finished, he climbed into his SUV. Pulling out onto the street, he paused and searched. Bay High was a small public school, so he was familiar with most of the cars that carried the kids not riding the bus. That white van was unfamiliar. Plain, unmarked, and without windows. Something was up. He just knew it as he drove to the Bay Town Police Station.

The Bay Town Police Station occupied an old, antiquated building, but it stood as a symbol of safety and authority. A glass panel on the door read, *Police Chief Alberto Hidalgo.* He'd held the office for three terms. The former police chief of Bay Town had tried to retire for years, but no one took him seriously until he opened a bait and tackle shop down on the gulf and turned in his resignation.

Joe pulled down on his shirt and turned the knob. He smiled at the jingling of the rusty bells, sounding as if he were in a general store in the wild west.

"I hate those bells," bellowed the chief.

Chief Bert, as many called him, hailed from New Mexico. In cooperation with the mayor, he had done an impressive job of cleaning up a small town riddled with crime. Illegal drug activity, prostitution, and auto theft were rampant, and he had implemented a firm but compassionate hand. A rare gift, but it paid off. Amid lots of publicity, Bert's popularity grew. Cities, both locally and in other states, sought him out, Bay Town included.

Chief Bert waved. "Hey, Big Joe, what's happening there, buddy? Church good last week? Did you stay awake, or did Pastor Brooks give a real snoozer?"

His funny laugh infected all who heard the silly giggle. Almost as big as Joe, but much more muscled and fit, Chief Bert exuded protection. Much like Joe. Most folks called him Bert, but for those who weren't that familiar, he was chief.

Joe walked through the little gate and eased himself into a too-small chair placed against the small wood railing that separated the desks from the lobby area. The little building had a pleasant, musty odor of worn leather and aged wood.

"Church is always good. Pastor Brooks, he's a good man," said Joe.

"That he is. I sure found that out last night."

"Why? What happened?" Joe leaned forward.

Waving a hand, Chief Bert swatted the air. "It's a long story. What's up? Why are you here?"

"We been missing ya, Chief. You ain't been to church lately." Joe furrowed his brow and gave the chief a sideways glance.

The chief shifted. "Hey, I go to church. Catalina takes me to the Catholic church." He scratched his head and squirmed. "Sometimes."

"Well, don't forget who brought ya to Bay Town." Joe widened his eyes and nodded.

"I know, I know. If it wasn't for those little old ladies over at Bay Town Community Church." The chief looked a little guilty.

Joe smiled at his friend, recalling how Bert came to Bay Town in the first place. One of the senior church members, Sally Trotman, always had her keen eyes and ears open. She'd seen the chief on a TV morning show when he received "Law Enforcement Officer of the Year" in New Mexico. Sally did her research and got the idea to bring him to Bay Town. She didn't have the money to pursue him, but Bethie Cooke did.

When given the authority, another senior member gladly agreed to lead the charge to search for a qualified appointment in her hometown.

"Yup. If it wasn't for all them women, you might never experienced our peaceful gulf-life." Joe attempted to lean back, but the chair was too tight. He wiggled about. "Ain't nothing like it here." He struggled more.

Sally, Bethie, and the women's ministry of Bay Town Community wielded much clout. Their philanthropic generosity had made a tremendous difference in the town. A couple years back, they had attended every Town Council Meeting, Chamber Mixer, and Community Event, campaigning for Chief Alberto and his wife, Catalina. Though the salary couldn't entice such a high-profile law enforcement individual, the quiet lifestyle of Bay Town did. The chief and his wife agreed.

"Anyway, I didn't come to judge ya, but I is anxious. Yesterday mornin', I sees a white van following my bus all the way to the school. Then, last night, I sees them again downtown on Main Street. They don't belong here, and I think they up to trouble." Joe's brows furrowed. "Those are my kids. I take care of 'em on the bus, and I don't like it."

Chief Bert nodded. "Is that all you got? A white van? Not much to go on." Chief Bert leaned back in his large swivel chair and scratched his thick, short hair. He frowned. "Seems like, all of a sudden, some action is picking up around here. You know there was that missing girl up in Jackson County about a week ago?"

"Yeah, I heard about that. Hey, ya think these guys got something to do with her, too?"

Chief Bert seemed to ignore the question and continued, "Hey, you heard of a girl named Virginia? Goes to Bay High? Older than most of the kids, and a little—"

"Yeah, I knows her. She rides my bus. Why, Bert? What's up?"

The chief sat up straight and stared at Joe. "Did Virginia ride the bus this morning?"

"Yeah, I's always havin' to wait at her house. This morning weren't no different. I had to honk three times before she come stumbling out. She looked bad this morning."

"I'm not surprised. I ran into Virginia and her father last night and—"

"Father?" Joe interrupted. "That girl ain't got nothin' but her aunt. And she's a sad woman. Virginia been on my bus route going on a year now. I's pretty sure there ain't no daddy."

"I had my suspicions, but her dad, or whoever …" The chief threw his hands up. "He said he was moving her to New Orleans this weekend."

"New Orleans?" Joe leaned toward Bert.

Bert waved him back down. "So, how about a Will Boudreaux? Ever heard of him?"

Joe eased back and thought a moment. "Nope, can't say that I have."

"Are you sure there's no dad?"

"Pretty sure. I told my wife about Virginia, how she always got picked on at school. You know my Lyla, she got a heart as big as the gulf and tried to reach out to that girl a couple times. Took some dessert over to her house and introduced herself to the aunt."

Bert settled back in his chair, knowing Joe's story could ramble.

"You know, invite the poor girl to church, youth group stuff. But that aunt, she was pretty unfriendly. Didn't want Lyla around. Can you imagine anyone not wantin' my wife's cookin?' I went with her once, too. If Virginia's got a daddy, he ain't nowhere around." Joe hardened his eyes, "What's up, Bert? You better clue me in." Standing, he leaned over Chief Bert's desk.

"Slow down, Joe. If she was on the bus this morning, it's

all good. Saves me a trip over there. I'll check it all out and get back to you."

"You better check it out." Joe pointed a finger.

"Hey, how's Lyla and the kids? I can't believe you're still chasing those little critters around. Geez, I got grandkids their age, and I'm a way younger dude than you." Bert gave Joe a punch in the arm, and they both bellowed loud enough for people on the street to hear.

"Don't you worry about me. I can chase my li'l ones all day." He winked. "And Lyla all night, too! My knees not shot like yours, you old lazy catcher."

Bert walked around his desk, taking a boxer-like pose, and Joe threw a friendly punch. Bert flinched, feigning his legs buckling on him. Old college baseball injuries plagued him from early in life.

They shook hands and gave one another a big bear hug.

"All right, all right, Big Joe. We'll keep an eye out for that white van, and you keep an eye on Virginia, will ya?"

"I's always do." Joe stood and ambled for the door. He turned before leaving and said, "Hey, I almost forgot, we's havin' a church softball game against Our Lady of the Gulf tonight. It's just a friendly game, and we sure could use a catcher."

Bert waved him off. "Are you kiddin' me? My catching days are over. Except for the bad guys. But I'll talk to my Lina. Maybe we'll stop by later."

"Shoot. I thought maybes I could get you to church somehow. Not even softball will do it, huh?"

"Hey, I told you, I go to church. Sometimes. Besides, my wife goes to two churches, one for each of us." The chief chuckled. "Where's it at, anyway?"

"Over at St. Stanislaus, the boys' high school across from the gulf. The fields is in the back. Look for the lights. We'll be warming up at six." Joe shuffled out as he called over his shoulder. "Bring your gear, ya hear?"

"I better. You sure don't look like you're going to be any help for tonight."

Joe waved him off, shaking his head as the rusty bells jingled.

After the hospital visit, Melanie declined Desmond's invitation to lunch because of her scheduled appointment with the photographer. Instead of retrieving her car at the Mockingbird Café, he dropped her off in front of her shop, just around the corner.

Standing outside Desmond's car with the door open, Melanie leaned in. "Thanks for taking me along." She shrugged. "And please call me if I can help Mr. Copeland in any way."

"Sure thing." Desmond stared back. "Hey, Melanie. I think I'll stop by Virginia's house after school today. She's been on my mind. Would you care to come along?" He raised his eyebrows. "I mean, it's a church visit?"

Melanie smiled back. His thoughtfulness warmed her heart. So unlike Chris. She shook her head, and replied, "I'd love to, but I can't. Will you keep me posted on how she's doing?"

"I will, and thanks again, Mel." He waved as he drove off.

She took a few steps to her shop, and with her hand on the doorknob, Melanie stopped. She turned and glanced down the sidewalk. Grady, Carol's new friend, stood outside Second Chances, just a few doors down. Leaning against the door jamb, he took a puff of a cigarette and blew the smoke in her direction.

She shivered a little and let herself into Quaint Affairs. Dropping everything, she slumped into the small chair behind her desk. She needed time to think. The last two days had been a rollercoaster. Thoughts of Desmond fresh in her mind made her smile. But then Charlene's phone call, the Grady thing, and Virginia and her "daddy." The smile faded, and a frown formed. Her lips twisted when her eyes rested on the pile of bills again.

Taking out her cell, she called Chris, but it went straight to voicemail. "Chris, call me." She would get that referral if she had to kill him! *Well, not literally,* she thought.

Melanie closed her eyes and rubbed her temples as if it would make her problems go poof. She switched on the aromatic oil diffuser and breathed the sweet scent of jasmine, lavender, and bergamot oils.

Desmond popped back into her head. What was this thing with Desmond? Was it a thing? She pushed out the thoughts, and went to work.

The appointment with the photographer had gone well. She promised to contract with him if she could just get another booking. Her day planner lay open on her desk, and Melanie entered some detailed notes. She returned a few phone calls, paid a few bills, and juggled the rest. But still, her unsettled mind kept going back to the latest hiccup. Grady.

Tapping her fingers lightly on her desk, she eyed a little devotional book. Picking it up, she thumbed through the pages and laid it open. *Be still,* she thought and closed her eyes while shifting in her seat. She clicked her pen for five agonizing minutes while drawing cleansing breaths. It wasn't helping.

Finally, she stood. *Chief Bert. I'll talk to him about Grady.* Pausing for a second, Melanie dropped back into her seat. *Carol. I owe it to her. I have to speak to her first.*

Melanie grabbed her purse and slipped out. Walking toward Second Chances, Grady still stood outside smoking. She waved weakly and shivered as he leered. She stepped into the shop and called, "Hey, Carol, it's me, Mel."

"Come on in. I'll be with ya in a minute."

Worried about Grady coming in, Melanie walked to the back, hoping to speak privately.

Pushing aside the sheer curtain in the back of the store, Carol wiped her hands on a hand towel and waved. "Hey, Mel. What's up, sweetie?"

Lowering her voice, Melanie asked, "Carol, what do you know about Grady?" She glanced at the front of the shop.

Carol squinted and gave a sideways glance, but a smile exploded across her face, and she laughed. "Oh, Mel, don't you worry about him." She waved the towel at her and continued, "Honey, look, Grady's a little different. Maybe even a little weird. But he's harmless. I met him at a cowboy bar in Gulf Port. He was a little drunk. But a pleasant drunk, and we got to talking and ... well, you know. He's hanging out here in town for a while."

Melanie lowered her head, feeling sad for Carol. "Where is he really from?"

"Why?" Her eyes narrowed. "Where's this coming from?"

"My sister told me something that went down in Jackson."

"Oh, Mel. Like I said, when I met Grady, he'd had a little too much to drink ... he said he came from Jackson—"

"Jackson, Mississippi, or Alabama? Which did he say?"

"Mississippi." Carol pursed her lips and added, "Hey, look here now. I know he said he was from Alabama last night, but who cares, right? I'm enjoying his company right now. It's not like he's moving in or anything." She raised her eyes to the ceiling and laughed nervously.

"Has he?" Melanie winced. "It's none of my business, but has he moved in?"

Carol flushed and dropped her head, gazing at the floor. "He doesn't have a place to stay right now. Said he had a girlfriend in Jackson that went all crazy on him, and he left. Something about a teenage daughter that ran a ..."

The conversation sounded all too familiar. *Jackson? A teenager running away, missing? Isn't that what Charlene said?* Melanie's head felt light, and she could feel her pulse in her temples.

"Mel, are you all right? Here, sweetie, sit down." Carol grabbed an old wooden stool and set it under Melanie's drooping frame.

Her forehead glistened, and her face paled, but Melanie drew a breath and spoke. "Did you even hear about the missing teenager in Jackson?"

Carol fidgeted. "No, I don't watch the news much ... Wait a minute. Mel. Come on. You don't think he had anything to do with that? That ain't Grady. I told you, he's harmless. I can boss that scrawny fella all over the place." She twisted her hands together, then threw them in the air and laughed. "Why, girl, that's why I brought him home from the bar. Kind of like a little lost puppy. He keeps me company." She wound a strand of hair around her finger.

"Don't you think it's worth checking into?"

Carol dropped atop an old antique steamer trunk and clasped her hands between her skirt folds. "Don't you ever get tired of being alone?"

Melanie paused. "Well, not really. I mean, I have Lacey." Only a tiny white lie.

"Well, I do. And at my age, the prospects are getting slim out there. I get lonely sometimes."

Lonely for a man, and for any man, it seemed. Melanie shook her head. A knot glitched in her throat. She hated the judgmental thought but wanted so much to convince Carol that a man wasn't the answer to all her problems. Discernment silenced the words.

"Yes, me too," Melanie admitted. "I do get lonely."

Carol looked up and patted Melanie's arm. "Well, you are lucky. You have Lacey." She swept back her hair with a flair and straightened. "But I'm good. And I'm not complaining. I can take care of myself."

Melanie's throat tightened. "Yes, you can. And, well, you should."

Carol peered intently into Melanie's eyes. "Grady didn't

do nothing, Mel. Why would he tell me about that mother and her runaway daughter in Jackson if he did something wrong? It's just a coincidence." Her voice rose. "Please don't say nothing to anybody. He's stupid, but he's not a criminal."

Staring, Melanie thought, *Are you sure about that?*

"Please, Mel. He doesn't need any trouble. He just hit some poor luck is all and needs a break. Besides, he makes my life a little fun right now."

Melanie sighed and squeezed Carol's hand. "Okay, but if anything turns up ..." Her voice trailed, and she got up to leave. "You know, you're a special woman. You don't need a man like that. None of us ..."

"A man like what?"

Melanie stiffened as she turned to see Grady.

Carol laughed and threw the towel at Grady, who had just walked in.

Afraid of what he'd heard, Melanie stood, steadied herself, then squeezed past him. "Bye, Carol."

CHAPTER 12

Boudreaux sat in the parked car behind Hilly's house, waiting for Virginia. The rumbling of a school bus sounded out front, and he entered the house through the back.

Virginia barged through the front door and slammed it. "I hate school! I hate the bus! I hate those mean kids!" Throwing down her bag, she ran to the stairs.

"Well, darlin', then you'll be happy to know that I'm taking you to New Orleans." Boudreaux smiled.

"New Orleans? Really?" Virginia jumped up and down. She stopped. "Wait, now?"

"Sure 'nuff, sweetie pie. Go get your things."

She ran over, hugged his neck, and hurried back to the stairs. She stopped and looked over at the couch. "What's the matter with Auntie? Auntie Hilly, you ok?" Virginia stammered. She scrunched her face and looked at Boudreaux. "She was like that this morning. It's like she hasn't moved."

"She's fine, sweetie. You know your Aunt Hilly. She overdid it again last night."

"But has she been sleeping all day?" Virginia took a step.

Placing his hands on her shoulders, he squared her to the stairs. "She'll be fine, sugar. Aunt Hilly's just sleeping it off," he lied. "Hurry on up now."

Boudreaux paced the room, and as he passed the front window, he stopped. A car pulled up and parked in front of the house. Moving back away from view, he squinted. Recognizing the man outside, he shook his head.

He moved to the front door and drew his gun. With his hand on the knob, he could feel the knock from the other side, and it vibrated through his hand. *Go about your business, Pastor. This ain't no concern of yours.* Boudreaux couldn't chance Pastor Brooks discovering their plans. This deal was getting more complicated with these nosy townspeople, and if he had to take care of the pastor, well then, he'd just have to take care of him.

Boudreaux cocked his gun and waited. Silence. Seconds later, he stepped to the front window. Pulling the drapes aside, he watched the pastor walk down the sidewalk to his car. Boudreaux shook his head as the car disappeared.

"Virginia? You ready?" he yelled up the stairs.

Re-holstering his gun, he growled, and taking two stairs at a time, he stormed down the hallway and stopped at Virginia's bedroom door. He placed both hands on the doorway and leaned in.

Gathering her things, she struggled to fit everything into her oversized tote bag. Makeup, hair tools, even clothing, and some shoes. It wouldn't all fit, but with arms loaded high, she scooted past Boudreaux and traipsed through the hallway, and started down the stairs. She almost reached the bottom but missed the last step. She went down hard, and everything tumbled out of her arms onto the filthy carpet. Scared, more than hurt, Virginia cried.

Boudreaux hovered over her and yelled obscenities. "Shut up!" He moved in her direction with his arm raised.

Lying beneath his feet, she screamed, "No! Auntie, help me." Tears flooded her face.

Boudreaux stared at the bay window, and moving to

silence her, he crooned softly instead. "There, there, Ginny, honey. Auntie's gonna join us in New Orleans later."

His jaw clenched as he picked up a few things to help her. He steered her to the backyard. Virginia attempted to turn back, but Boudreaux said, "Shhh. Go on now, sugar. Aunt Hilly needs her rest."

Slowly backing out of the yard and down the driveway, Boudreaux checked up and down the street. All clear.

Virginia inserted her earbuds, totally unaware of the "adventure" that awaited her in New Orleans.

The back route would take fifteen minutes longer, but with New Orleans only an hour's drive away, Boudreaux preferred the country roads. Soon out of town, the forests on either side of Highway 90 displayed a brilliant array of orange, red, and yellow leaves. He paid no attention to the beauty surrounding him.

Neither did Virginia. She continued listening to her music, eyes closed, humming, and moving to her tunes.

Leaving Mississippi behind, they crossed over into the wetlands of Louisiana. When he reached the Chef Mentaur Pass, a long, high bridge loomed before them. The bridge crossed over the Rigolets, a strait of water that connected the smaller Lake Catherine with the well-known Lake Ponchartrain. The long bridge drew a reaction from Virginia. Her eyes flew open, and she squealed with delight. Boudreaux chuckled as he internally mocked her childish excitement.

The bridge, about five football fields long, with high metal beams and arches riveted with huge bolts, gave a sense of security as they crossed over the strait. Pines, hardwoods, and dead cypress trees rose, spindly and high along the banks, their roots covered by tall grasses lining the waterway. Virginia pushed herself up, trying to look down into the river. Boudreaux reached over and yanked her down.

"Settle down there. It's not like you haven't seen a river before."

"That was a long time ago. When we moved to Bay Town." Virginia stared out the window.

"Only a year ago, Ginny. That was only a year ago." Boudreaux's arm hung on the steering wheel.

Arriving in New Orleans, Boudreaux drove straight to an old run-down hotel in the Lower Ninth District of New Orleans. It was one of the hardest-hit areas after the last devastating hurricane. The neighborhood saw little redevelopment, and most plans to rebuild had fallen through.

Many of the properties went up for auction, with listing prices as low as one hundred dollars. But the land and distressed structures were a deal only if you had the cash to renovate them. Banks weren't lending in the area, so those with liquid assets were in luck. Exploitation waiting to be had. Opportunists purchased the properties and did the minimal renovation, just enough to make it profitable. And since one could pay off a government inspection employee, a sign-off for permits didn't prove to be too difficult either.

Shadows cast an ugly hue over the buildings stained with watermarks from the storm surge a decade ago. Graffiti-splattered plywood boarded up most structures, but the new windows on a small two-story hotel posed a stark contrast. Boudreaux pulled into the driveway where the building stood sandwiched between taller buildings and set back from the street. It lay conveniently hidden from plain view.

Boudreaux couldn't claim ownership of the recently acquired building but had free rein of use if he delivered. Next week, the abducted girls housed in the hotel would be transferred to the ring. With the hotel vacant, Boudreaux was hatching plans of his own for the interim.

Opening the front passenger door, he beckoned Virginia out.

With earbuds still in place, she seemed oblivious until she saw the building. "Eeewww! I'm not going in there!"

He grabbed her shoulder and yanked her out, slamming the door. "Antoine! Get out here."

A large man with long, thick, wavy hair emerged. The sleeves of his Hawaiian print shirt stretched tight over his biceps. "Yeah, boss?"

"Antoine, this sweet thing is my Ginny. Hold off on giving her our usual welcome." Boudreaux sneered. "You can put her in the suite for now."

"The suite?" Virginia's innocent voice perked up. She tossed her head back, raised a limp wrist, and said, "Antoine, please get my bags." She giggled as she ran into the front lobby.

Boudreaux pointed to the car. "Take her stuff upstairs. Make sure she has something to eat and lock her in the suite."

He watched as Antoine nodded and loaded his arms with all Virginia's loose articles from the backseat. A scream emitted from the hotel, and he immediately ran for the lobby.

"Forget that!" he yelled.

Antoine followed close behind.

Virginia's nails dug into her cheeks. "Girl ... dragged ... through that hallway!" She pointed.

Boudreaux threw a nod at Antoine.

"There, there, sweetie, you most likely saw one of them homeless people. We're cleaning up this place, and they think they can just sneak in here anytime they want. Antoine will take care of it. Don't you worry your pretty little head."

"Auntie Hilly." Virginia sniffled. "I want Auntie."

Boudreaux growled. Virginia might prove harder to handle than he thought. He coaxed her into believing that Hilly would be here soon. Virginia asked many questions about the girl she saw, but Boudreaux's smooth talk did the trick. He dissuaded all her apprehensions. With promises to take her shopping soon, she settled down, and he walked her up the staircase.

The renovated suite boasted luxury and swank. It

contained all the eccentric amenities. A thick new carpet, yards of window draperies, and expensive furniture. A big, comfy bed with lots of pillows and an inviting thick, white down comforter graced the middle of the room. A mini but well-stocked refrigerator and baskets on the counter filled with snacks and fruit made for an inviting kitchenette.

Eyeing the chips and candy bars, Virginia smiled. She opened the fridge. "Oh, all for me?" she squealed as she grabbed a soda and popped it open.

"Yes, darlin', all for you. Now get your magazines out of your backpack and sit for a while. Here's the remote for the cable TV, too. Don't you go anywhere now. I'll be right back, ya hear?"

Boudreaux closed the door behind him and locked the deadbolt. He sauntered down the stairs and looked around. Stepping outside, Antoine bent over, retrieving all Virginia's things off the ground.

"Well?" Boudreaux hissed.

"Sorry, boss. One of the girls needed to use the bathroom. Matt roughed her up a bit. I took care of it. That Acadia girl."

"Shut up, Antoine! I told you, don't mention their names here. In a few more days, they're gone, so don't let Ginny see 'em. And you leave her alone. I'll be back to take care of her."

Antoine nodded.

Contemplating going to look for Grady in Bay Town, Boudreaux looked at his watch. Not much daylight left, but he couldn't risk the chance of another run-in with the chief of police. He also couldn't risk that loose end hanging around.

The casino was Boudreaux's option to kill time. He played a few hands at the blackjack tables, then checked the restaurant, hoping that pretty, little waitress might be there. He could build some rapport. No luck.

Loud noises across the casino floor hailed from the roulette table. Boudreaux joined them, and thirty minutes later, he fared well. He picked up his winnings and stepped out into the darkness.

Arriving in Bay Town, Boudreaux drove down Main Street and parked near the bus terminal across from Second Chances. Scooting down in his seat, he got comfortable and waited, but not for long. Grady stepped out, his long ponytail stuffed up under a baseball cap and the brim touching dark glasses that all but covered his face. A green flak jacket completed his odd ensemble. Boudreaux stepped out of his car and followed him. Picking up his pace, he rounded the front of the bus only to see Grady hop on.

He shouted an expletive as he looked around and saw a little ticket booth with one person inside. As he approached the window, he demanded, "Where's this bus headed?"

"Strand Beach, Gulf Port, Biloxi, Ocean Springs, Pascagoula. But it leaves in a few minutes. Wanna buy a ticket?" drawled the attendant.

"Where from there?" Boudreaux shot back. Looking back at the bus, he saw the doors close.

"What do ya mean?" asked the attendant.

"Where does it go from Pascagoula?" Boudreaux replied, patience waning.

"Why, it comes right back here. It's just a county line. Hits the major bus terminal in Pascagoula. Buses go from there to everywhere. Up north, Alabama, Georgia. Heck, you can even catch 'em to—"

Boudreaux left. The bus rattled down the road, and he ran to his car. Catching up, he drove close behind, stopping whenever the bus stopped at every little town along the way. Grady never got off. Not until Pascagoula.

Following Grady into the terminal, Boudreaux glanced around and got in the ticket line behind him. When he heard

Grady's intended destination, Boudreaux turned his back and kept his head down until Grady left the counter.

Leaning in, he asked his questions. Greyhound #90B would leave in two hours. He hoped Grady hadn't wandered too far as he ran outside and looked in both directions. Nothing. Boudreaux ran a hand over his slicked-back hair. Squeezing behind his neck, he went inside and searched the terminal. Slapping his leg, he seethed and strode to the men's room.

As a slender older man in a green jacket and baseball cap exited the bathroom, Boudreaux stepped aside. He pulled out his phone and pretended to speak. Sneaking a look back, he squinted. The man sported wire-rim glasses, a goatee, and was inches shorter than Grady.

"Shoot!" Boudreaux spun around, storming out of the building. The terminal was a busy place on a Friday night.

Boudreaux returned to his car, regretting that he lost Grady and dreading the long ride back to New Orleans. Before sliding into his car, he spotted a man leaning against a brick building a couple shops down. The man puffed on a cigarette straightened, then walked across the street. *Bingo!* Boudreaux followed and watched as Grady turned down a lane between two buildings.

Boudreaux followed on foot, hurrying to catch up. He turned the corner just in time to see Grady enter a bar halfway down a long, dimly lit street that dead-ended. Glancing at his watch, Boudreaux waited a few more minutes before leaving to retrieve his car.

He drove to the street housing the bar, maneuvered his car to the end, made a U-turn, and parked. Fog rolled in. Dampness settling on the street and sidewalk. Boudreaux flipped his wipers intermittently and waited. It was ninety minutes before Grady emerged. Boudreaux sneered as he watched Grady wobble from the bar.

Boudreaux started his engine. Grady staggered close to the

curb as he attempted to light a cigarette. Slipping, he tripped off the slick sidewalk and sprawled forward in a perpetual fall.

The ice-blue Lincoln roared to life and sped down the street. Grady's body flew like a rag doll, and Boudreaux never stopped.

CHAPTER 13

R ather than let her anxieties take over, Melanie forced the Grady and Carol thing out of her mind. She spent the rest of the afternoon tying up loose ends. Looking at the antique mantle clock, she called it a day.

As she drove home, she reached to change the radio station but stopped. She recognized the song from an old black and white movie.

The way you hold your knife
The way we danced until three
The way you changed my life
No, no, they can't take that away from me

She smiled and thought of Desmond as she pulled into her carport. Suddenly, Chris popped into her head as she recalled how they used to scream along to the radio in the car together. She turned off the engine and groaned.

"That good, huh?" Lacey stood at the back screen door.

Melanie felt the color rise on her neck. "What?"

"Your day?" Lacey asked again.

Melanie stepped out of her car. "You know, some of it was nice." Melanie smiled. "Yes, my morning rocked."

Lacey laughed and held the door open for her. Melanie stopped at the sound of a vehicle speeding down Beach Road.

She peered down her driveway and watched as a white streak sped by. Not giving it another thought, she walked in, dropped her purse on the kitchen table, and strolled to her room to change.

"Okay, Lace. It's my choice. Let's go to Starfish Grill. I'm in the mood for some good fish tacos," Melanie yelled from her room as she pulled off her tan slacks and slipped on her comfortable blue jeans. She pulled a plain, black, long-sleeved tee over her head and stepped out into the hallway.

Lacey walked out at the same time. She stared at her mom, then looked down at her own black tee and blue jeans. Her shoulders dropped. "Really, Mom. I wore it first."

Melanie laughed. "So, mother-daughter outfits. How quaint."

Lacey wasn't laughing. Just then, they heard the back door creak open. Both headed toward the kitchen. Shiny ombre curls peeked around the opened screen door.

"Hey, girls. Ohhh, mother-daughter outfits. I love it," Tina cooed, pointing a glittery, gold polished nail at the girls.

"Oh, no! Mom, you win. I'll change. Hey, Tina," Lacey yelled as she walked back into her room.

"Whatcha girls doin' tonight?" Tina asked.

"Well, it's our Friday night date and my pick. I'm in the mood for fish tacos." Melanie smiled. Slapping her hands, she rubbed them together.

"Yumm. Gotta go to Starfish Grill, eh?" Tina licked her glossy lips.

"No," said Lacey, strolling into the kitchen wearing a burgundy and white striped tee. "No healthy food, please. It's Friday, fast food night."

"Cute top." Tina pointed.

"Why, thank you." Lacey smiled.

"It's my pick tonight. Besides, you had that junk last night. You're just lucky you have a good metabolism," Melanie scolded as she winked at her daughter.

"She's right, dear. It'll catch up with you. It did me," Tina said, caressing her curvy thighs.

"Yeah, well, if I look like you when I'm your age, I'll keep on scarfing the junk food." Lacey laughed.

"Ouch. My age?" Tina pushed out her lip in a pout.

"Lacey!" Melanie glared.

"No worries. That's the splendid thing about my age. I don't care anymore … well, maybe not too much." She winked.

They all laughed, and Melanie, noticing the colorful paper Tina held, said, "What's that in your hand?".

"Oh. I almost forgot. When I visited your church last week, the bulletin announced the annual church softball game. It's tonight. Are you going? I bet that handsome Pastor Brooks is quite the athlete." Tina winked teasingly at Melanie.

"Oh, yeah. Yesterday Mom said Pastor Brooks invited her to the game." Lacey wore a silly grin.

"Whaaat? Details, girl. You didn't tell me. Come on! Dish it out, Mel."

"Well, he sort of invited us." Melanie's eyes sparkled. "Yesterday, he stopped in the shop for a chat. And that's when he told me about it. Then, this morning, we bumped into each other and had coffee and—"

"And? And there's more?" Tina interrupted.

"Mom?" Lacey's eyes widened. "You didn't tell me about this morning."

"Okay, okay, I didn't have a chance. Anyway, Desmond asked me to go to the hospital with him today to visit someone." Melanie's smile faded as she thought of Richard and Deena.

Neither of the other girls seemed to notice as they sang in unison, "Desmond?"

"I mean Pastor Brooks. Actually, it turned out to be a sad morning." Melanie told the girls about the hospital visit. "Anyway, it's been a busy day, and I'm ready to eat."

"Okay, let's go eat. Love those fish tacos! I'll get Rudy," said Tina. "He's been working on a big remodel this week. I can't wait till he pulls me in to decorate."

"No one's better than you, Tina." Melanie was happy to get the attention off her and Desmond.

"Tell Rudy that. Sometimes I think he'd still rather be on Wall Street. Then he wouldn't have to argue with me about color."

"Forget eating out. Let's go to the game. I can't wait to see Mom and Desmond all goo-goo-eyed."

"Lacey, it's Pastor Brooks! And since when do you care about baseball?"

"Softball, Mom. And since I don't want to go to Starfish Grill. Besides, we can eat at the snack bar." She glanced at Tina. "There will be a snack bar, right?"

"Of course, sweetie. Good thinking. I love those cheap hot dogs." Tina licked her lips. "And hey, Rudy wants to play, too. It's been a while, but he loves a good, friendly game. Come on, Mel, please, honey?"

Melanie blew out a sigh. "Oh, all right. But no hot dogs." Tina and Lacey pouted, but Melanie narrowed her eyes at them. "Oh, don't give me that. You know I'll give in."

Both Tina and Lacey jumped up and down and clapped like little schoolgirls. Tina sauntered toward the door as she hollered, "Call when you're ready to go. Can't wait to see Pastor Brooks in action, wink, wink." Turning around, Tina grinned from ear to ear.

"Tina. Stop it." Melanie smirked.

———

It seemed almost everyone in town showed up at St. Stanislaus High School, including some sketchy-looking characters. Melanie squinted. Were those the guys in the white van, down on Main Street? They wore black hoodies, partially covering their faces. A fearful feeling arose, and she questioned their attendance, but then it seemed reasonable for anybody to be there on a Friday night in Bay Town. There wasn't much else to do. Priests from the parish, wearing black shirts and cleric collars coupled with athletic pants and jeans, produced a comical sight. One would have thought the game was a professional championship with all the screaming and cheering going on.

The snack shack served a steady crowd as everyone ordered cokes and hot dogs. Melanie waved at the bleachers where Lacey saved some seats. As she waited, she noticed the two men in hoodies standing aside, waiting for their order. When they picked up their food and drinks, Melanie watched as they moved toward the back of the bleachers. They wolfed down their food, throwing wrappers on the ground, and disappearing under the stadium seating. Melanie shuddered and looked up to find Lacey once more. She nodded and waved again.

CHAPTER 14

B y the sixth inning, the scoreboard already showed 12-14 in St. Stanislaus's favor. To make matters worse, they couldn't have commissioned a worse umpire — a middle-aged, heavyset man from Hancock County Little League. Nobody particularly liked his umpiring skills, but he didn't seem to care. It was a typical case of giving the wrong guy a little too much power.

Desmond played shortstop and played it well. He and Rudy, Tina's husband, who played second base, turned some fantastic double plays. Unfortunately, the ump saw it differently. Big Joe, who played first base, threw down his glove whenever the ump called the runner safe. Chief Bert had agreed to play catcher on the Bay Town Community team, and rather than getting up and down from the crouch, he could throw guys out at second from his knees, which was quite a feat.

Chatter between the team and the spectators bantered back and forth, and wives teased their husbands, who threw out bravado claims before approaching the plate. Desmond couldn't help glancing up at Melanie, sitting with the women from Bay Town Community right above the dugout, every time he entered and exited the dugout. Catching her eye, he smiled and waved. Suddenly, Chief Bert's wife, Lina, put her fingers between her lips and let out a shrill whistle. Everyone covered their ears.

"Okay, Bertie, baby. You can do it, my man." Lina screamed.

Desmond's puzzled face matched the confusion of the other women around Lina

Lina smiled. "What? Chief Bert to you, but to me, he's my Bertie."

A sweet chorus of "Awww" rose from the group.

An inning later, thundering noise filled the stadium like a stampeding herd of horses. The crowd stamped their feet in rapid succession. Crunch time. In this annual match-up, the game was only seven innings long, not the standard nine. Everyone stood on their feet. It was the bottom of the seventh inning, Bay Town was the home team, and they were two runs behind with one out.

With Rudy on second and Principal Ladner on first, Desmond stood at home plate, taking practice swings. He could be the winning run. The first wild pitch by Father Ned hit the dirt, and the catcher, Father Hannigan, fumbled as he scrambled to retrieve the ball. Desmond never lifted the bat off his shoulder.

"Strike," the ump yelled.

Mouths dropped. Even Father Ned almost protested.

"Are you kidding me? That ball's got dirt all over it," screamed Tina. But when Rudy took off to steal third, Tina jumped up, spilling her coke, and shouted, "Go, honey, go!"

The crowds roared and clapped while the catcher panicked and made a wild throw. Rudy took off for the home plate. Desmond jumped out of the way, waving Rudy in, who did a magnificent pop-up slide, and gave Desmond a chest bump as they laughed and gave each other high fives.

Pointing to second base, Chief Bert yelled from the

dugout, "Lookee there. Principal Ladner made it to second. Not bad, Lad!"

Bay Town fans went crazy as Principal Ladner gave thumbs up. He was the tying run. The catcher finally threw the ball back to the pitcher, stopping the stealing taking place around the bases. A moment later, the pitcher let the next pitch fly.

"Ball," yelled the umpire.

The catcher had to jump out of the box to get it. Desmond shook his head and nodded to the ump. He flashed a wide grin accompanied by a raised brow. The next pitch was so high that Desmond just stood there.

"Strike two," yelled the ump.

Desmond spread his arms wide, blatantly questioning the call.

The chief yelled, "You're killing us, ump. That ball almost took your head off."

Desmond joined in, loud enough for all to hear. "Yeah, Don, come on. You can do better than that." Shaking his head, he stepped out of the batter's box.

The umpire took off his mask and yelled, "First warning, Pastor."

Desmond felt a rush of heat rise from his neck. The umpire motioned him to step back into the batter's box. Dropping his head, Desmond complied and swung the bat to his shoulders. The umpire pointed to the pitcher to commence, the game continued, and the count was now full. Three balls and two strikes. No one in the stands or anywhere else remained sitting. Desmond could be the walk-off winning run.

He stared down the pitcher, and Father Ned perspired even in the chilly night air. The wind-up, the pitch … another outside ball, missing the plate. Desmond smiled at the umpire as he flipped his bat and jogged for first base.

"Strike three, you're out!" the umpire yelled, doing that

umpire thing, yanking his fists in parallel but opposite directions.

Desmond stopped in his tracks, and Bay Town went silent. Our Lady of the Gulf screamed wildly out of control. As Desmond picked up the bat, he strolled back to home plate and shook his head. "Seems to me you're having a hard time calling those balls and strikes, Don."

The umpire took off his mask, and with an effort to move his stout body, he threw his hand, holding his facemask in the air, and screamed, "You're out of here, Pastor! Off the field."

Desmond kept walking, shaking his head the whole time. Dropping his bat in the dugout, he approached the stands, and Bay Town groaned as he faced the bleachers. His face flushed as his eyes locked with Melanie, who seemed to be stifling laughter. She waved.

As Desmond climbed the bleachers to join her, Lacey scooted way over, and Tina gave a sideways glance. They giggled and squeezed one another's hands. Desmond ignored their exchange.

"So, you had some words with the umpire, huh?" Melanie nudged Desmond.

"Yeah. I probably shouldn't have."

Melanie chuckled. "Well, I guess you're human, too." She nudged him.

"Oh, yeah."

They stared into one another's eyes, and Desmond almost forgot where he was.

Suddenly, Lyla gasped, and Desmond looked back at the field. Those around her hushed as she grabbed Lina's arm and yelled, "Sweet Jesus, Joe's up!"

Lina patted her arm and said, "No worries, my friend. He'll get on base, and my Bertie will hit them all in."

Lyla laughed and boomed, "I hope so, cause my Joe can't run worth a darn, and he's outta home runs!"

Everyone held their breath as Joe lumbered up to the

plate. He'd already hit two homers this game. No one expected another, but secretly they hoped for a miracle. Father Hannigan set up behind the plate as Father Ned went into the stretch.

Boom!

A crack of the bat and everyone stared upward as all eyes followed the ball out over the center-field fence. It sailed, not just over the wall, but over the trees. Cheers erupted, and the crowds jumped up. Desmond threw his arms around Melanie, celebrating the victory. She reciprocated his embrace, but seconds later, their bodies stiffened. They pulled away, and he wondered if he was as red as she had become.

Lacey grinned and flashed thumbs up. Desmond shoved his hands in his pockets, still feeling the heat rising inside.

The noise was deafening as Joe lumbered around the bases and stomped on home plate. The players rushed the field. Game over! Bottom of the seventh, 15-14, Bay Town won it. As the crowds dissipated, Desmond offered a hand to Melanie, helping her down the bleachers. With her planted securely on the ground, he nodded and turned to the approaching umpire.

"Hey, Don, sorry about all that. Thanks for your time." Desmond extended his hand.

Umpire Don beamed and answered, "Oh, yeah. No hard feelings, brother."

Desmond laughed, and they shook hands.

As everyone dispersed for their cars, Melanie's gaze lingered on Desmond. *Could he be any more perfect?*

"I was thinking the same thing." Tina sidled up next to her friend.

Melanie blushed. Did she say that out loud?

"He's simply perfect. For you, that is." Tina winked. "I'll

CHAPTER 15

Saturday morning, freshly-baked blueberry muffins filled the kitchen with yummy smells. Melanie removed them from the oven. She felt as good as they looked. Remembering the exciting rivalry and still impressed at Big Joe's three home runs, she laughed. But most of all, she relished Desmond's attention. It felt natural and comfortable.

"Mmm," Lacey yelled. "Smells good." She entered the kitchen and hugged Melanie. "I love Saturdays!" She grabbed a muffin. "Lemon-blueberry! The best."

Melanie and Lacey spent a leisurely morning eating the delicious muffins and sipping coffee, although Lacey's creamy drink contained more milk than coffee. Reaching for another muffin, Lacey smiled and mumbled her approval.

"So, what say you join me for an easy run?" said Melanie.

Lacey rolled her eyes. "Oh, all right. Since you made my favorite muffins. But you said an easy one." She sauntered to her room and returned with running shoes in hand.

Melanie and Lacey started a slow jog along the coast. Up the street, Mrs. Higa hoisted traps from the pier. The woman was an astonishing ninety-year-old wonder. Bent over, wearing long, thick gloves, she pulled out the lobsters. A big, floppy hat hid her face from the sun.

meet you and Lacey at the car. I'm going to go give Rudy a hero's kiss!" Tina scooted off, and Melanie suddenly realized that Lacey was nowhere to be seen. She scanned the area again and finally spotted her. Lacey had apparently headed for the restrooms across the school grounds. Two women coming from that direction waved at Lacey as she passed.

Melanie yelled as loud as she could, "Lacey, come back here!" Some around her turned at the booming voice that came from the slender woman.

Lacey turned and pointed toward dimly lit restrooms. Raising a finger, she signaled, *Just a minute.*

With an exaggerated shake of her head, Melanie ran to the grassy area. "Lacey, no!"

Dropping her shoulders, Lacey huffed, shuffling back to her mom. When Melanie urged her daughter back, she observed two shadows that she couldn't clearly make out on the side of the restrooms. As Lacey got close enough, Melanie placed an arm around her shoulders. A clatter and clang caused both Melanie and Lacey to jump. They turned and saw nothing but a metal trash can rolled a little ways before it stopped to rest on its side. Melanie peered into the darkness and watched the shadows disappear.

"What was that?" Lacey asked.

"Maybe raccoons?" said Melanie, convincing no one. She shivered and pulled at Lacey as she picked up their pace.

"I wonder where Allie is?" Lacey asked. "She's usually helping her grandmother."

"Maybe working. I saw her at the hospital on Friday. They're a hard-working family." *A wonderful family.* Melanie stopped to tie her shoelaces. Her eyes fixed on Mrs. Higa. "She amazes me. I don't think I'd have the courage to move to the South after being imprisoned in an internment camp. I can't believe she and her husband settled here in Bay Town after the war."

"Which war?" Lacey squinted.

"Seriously?" Melanie eyed Lacey. "Come on, let's go."

They jogged the rest of the way, slowing as they headed down the pier to greet Mrs. Higa.

"Watch that board!" Mrs. Higa pointed to a rotting plank. "I wish my husband were still alive. He'd have this whole pier replaced by now."

"With concrete, no doubt." Melanie smiled.

"You got it. Those engineers always have to keep up with the latest ideas. But I'm not complaining. If he hadn't been one of those nerdy guys, we wouldn't be here." Mrs. Higa chuckled.

"He was an engineer?" Lacey asked.

"Yes, a guard from Giza got him a job at his father's company in Biloxi."

"What's Giza?" Lacey's brows furrowed.

"Arizona." Mrs. Higa almost whispered. "Where we were interned."

Lacey looked confused, and Melanie placed a hand on her arm. It didn't stop her. "But I thought you were living in California?"

"That was our home, before the war. But they moved us to Arizona."

"I'm so sorry, Mrs. Higa." Lacey reached out, "Hey, let me help." She grabbed a trap.

"Here you go!" Mrs. Higa smiled as if she'd diffused these

memories and the sentiments that accompanied them many times over.

Melanie sighed. Her heart wrenched a little, but when Lacey picked up a lobster, shaking it in the air, Melanie screamed. Mrs. Higa's bright eyes shined, then disappeared behind her laughter.

Melanie cringed at how Lacey could handle those creatures and not even flinch. Just looking at them sent chills up her spine. All those legs, claws, and antennae wiggling about caused the sparse hair on her arms to rise.

Lacey helped load the lobsters into the coolers. Putting on the mesh lids, she pulled the wheeled-cooler up the pier, and Melanie followed to help just as Mrs. Higa's grandsons approached.

"Hey, Mrs. Thompson, hey, Lacey. We'll take it from here. Thanks for helping Grandma."

"What are you doing here?" Mrs. Higa asked. "I thought you were working out this morning? How you going to build your guns if you skip?" She raised her arms as if she pumped iron. Ironically, at her age, she still had muscle tone.

Lacey and Melanie laughed as the boys rolled their eyes. They both looked as if missing one day at the gym wouldn't hurt either of them. They were lean, well built, and strong. Taking the coolers, they thanked Lacey again and crossed Beach Road.

"I'll send some lobster over later." Mrs. Higa's wrinkled face beamed.

"That would be wonderful. Thanks!" Melanie waved, and she could almost taste the freshly caught seafood. She relished the thought of it as much as she did the memories of the Higa family.

When Melanie and Lacey arrived in Bay Town, the Higas helped make leaving California a smooth transition. Grief-stricken after her parents' deaths, Melanie prayed Lacey would find friends, and Allie, who volunteered at the hospital, was the first person that Lacey met when they arrived.

The summer before, the Higa kids had walked up to their great-grandmother's pier to set the traps. Seeing Lacey a ways down on the grassy knoll, they waved her over and introduced themselves, inviting her to join them. Lacey had a glorious summer with them, jumping off the pier, roasting marshmallows and hot dogs on the hibachi, and lying out on the dock late at night watching the stars. Then school started, and they attended separate high schools, Allie at St. Joseph's Girl's High School and her brothers at St. Stanislaus For Boys. Lacey attended the local public school. Still, she was thankful they lived close by and always kept in touch.

"You know, Mom, the Higas are a great family."

"I think you read my mind." Melanie sprinted. "Now keep up!"

They finally reached Pier One, where the harbor was. Lacey and Melanie slowed to a walk and stopped. The *Fish Stalker* sat docked. Nowhere in sight was the man she'd seen piloting it days ago. Melanie's eyes were riveted on the rickety old boat.

"So, Mom, what's the story? Drugs, right? It's an illegal drug operation?"

"Lacey, stop."

"I know, he's a kidnapper ... No, a murderer ... on that old piece of junk."

"Lace—"

"Ohhh," Lacey screamed, and Melanie jumped. "Blood. Is that blood on that giant fishhook?" Lacey grabbed her sides, laughing at her mom's reaction.

"Lacey, enough. I saw that boat chugging up the jetty the other day. That's all. But the man driving it—the captain, I think?—he's a little strange, you know? He just kind of stared off into space, not even looking at anything. Kind of checked out."

"Oooh, so it was the giant fishhook," Lacey teased.

Melanie turned around to run, stepped back, and screamed.

The man from the *Fish Stalker* faced her. Melanie drew a breath and stumbled. He reached out to steady her as she pulled back. "Oh, sorry, I didn't know you were there."

"He wasn't," whispered Lacey.

The man with the wild, matted hair didn't say a word. He was a mess, and he stunk to high heavens. Short in stature with a tanned and leathery face, his round glassy eyes stared. He brushed right past them and jumped onto his boat. Another seedy-looking character joined him, dragging an odd-shaped black bag. He slid it onto the weathered deck, and the man never looked back but started his engine, backing away from the pier.

"It's the body," Lacey hissed quietly and chuckled.

Melanie shot a glare at her daughter, recalling the conversation she had with Charlene the day before. She shook a little, waved Lacey on, and returned to her jog. Finishing their run half-way, they slowed by Bubba's Catch Shack, yelling a "hey" to the owner as they grabbed a cup of ice water from the water cooler outside on the window counter.

The smell of hot oil and seafood filled the air. With his enormous smile, Bubba yelled good-bye while wiping his palms on his greasy white apron. He waved a thick hand and stroked his long red beard. Melanie waved back. Gulf people, she loved them.

After they got home, Lacey spent the rest of the day sketching in her room. Melanie sat at the old kitchen table, finalizing the last-minute details of the wedding she was coordinating the next day. It had been on her books for over a year, and now everything was ready to go. She had to get more bookings. This was the last one.

She wrinkled her brow. *I hope it's not the last one.* Melanie reached for her purse and once again pulled out the business card. The plain white card felt slick and thick in her hand. Expensive paper. She pursed her lips and looked at her cell phone. Chris still hadn't called. She contemplated calling the number anyway. Shaking her head, she breathed deep and closed her eyes. *Lord, if You want me to do this, make it clear.* Waiting a few minutes, she looked around and rolled her eyes at no one. She shrugged and picked up her phone to call. The phone buzzed in her hand, and she glanced at the screen but didn't recognize the number.

"Hello? ... Who? ... Oh, yes ... Sure, let me get my planner."

The young couple that Desmond had referred couldn't wait for their appointment and peppered Melanie with questions. She loved their excitement and enthusiasm, and her heart fluttered just a little. It always did with young, first-time-married couples.

She'd done lots of weddings in California, and some were second marriages. Too many of those where the pair were living together, and a few who already had children. But it was this pure youthful love—first timers—that gave her the most joy, and especially so when they loved God and sought to put him first. She prayed for all her clients, but these young lovers gripped her heart. She thought of her Las Vegas wedding and shook her head. Not these guys. She shared in their joy.

"Great, I'll see you in two weeks. If you'd like to come in sooner, I'm available. Thanks so much for calling. Bye."

Melanie hung up and glanced upward. *Was that an answer to prayer?* She tucked the expensive business card back into her purse.

Melanie made a few phone calls and did some internet searches on her laptop, looking for more new venue ideas. She had to keep abreast of the trends, just in case. Her mind wandered, and she searched for the Bay Town Community Church website, then clicked on the photo gallery.

She attended every Sunday, but these pictures shed the

best light. It was a cute little building. Too bad church weddings weren't popular anymore.

As Melanie scrolled down, Desmond's picture popped up on the staff page. She stopped and stared. It wasn't just how handsome he was, but his compassionate faith was something she admired. His athletic build added a lot, too. Melanie chuckled. But then again, Chris had it in the physical realm as well. However, this attraction was not just the passion she'd felt when she met Chris. This went a lot deeper.

Recalling the hospital visit, she allowed herself to dream of how wonderful it would be working alongside Desmond. How nice it would be to do anything with him. Melanie leaned back in her chair and sighed.

Lacey walked into the kitchen. "Ooh, must be a hottie."

Melanie sat up and blinked. "Lacey!"

Lifting the plastic wrap off a plate of cookies, she peeked over Melanie's shoulder and laughed as she turned and ran down the hall.

Clicking off the church page, Melanie went back to searching. She'd explored yachts and boats before, but she unexpectedly typed in a search for *Fish Stalker* and scrolled down a few pages before her fingers stopped. The keyboard went silent. "*Fish Stalker* for Hire."

For what? Who would hire that old thing? Melanie shivered, thinking of the owner. She tried to find more info, but the generic website was just a listing. How in the world did he get money to advertise? Although the website wouldn't attract any decent clientele, the only contact was a phone number. No email, no address, nothing.

She glanced at her watch and realized the whole afternoon had sped by. Just as she pushed back the little ladder-back chair and stood, Lacey, walked into the kitchen again.

The doorbell rang, and Melanie flinched. She wasn't expecting anyone. She shrugged, and both she and Lacey

walked into the living room at the same time to see the front door push open. They'd forgotten to lock it. A head peeked in near the upper part of the door.

CHAPTER 16

"Chris!" Lacey ran for the door and jumped into his arms. Melanie stood, arms crossed, head tipped to one side, tapping her foot. "Lacey, he's your father, not Chris. And Chris, since when do you just walk in unannounced?"

"Unannounced? When did you get a butler? Hey, Jeeves, come announce me, will ya!" Chris laughed. "Maybe you shouldn't leave your door unlocked."

Melanie bristled, and Lacey put her arms out like a referee at a prizefight. "All right, all right, don't start already. I haven't seen Chris in like forever." Lacey punched his arm. "So, where have you been? The Caribbean is not that big for a year vacation."

"Lacey, he's your dad. You don't call your dad by his first name," Melanie scolded.

Lacey blurted out, "You always say that, but he's not a dad."

Melanie's eyes widened, and then she glared at Chris. He looked back, exaggerating a hurt expression.

"I mean," said Lacey, "he's my father but not my dad. Come on, Chris, really. I don't even remember you from when I was a kid. You don't do dad things. Not that much, anyway. You know you're my ... my biological father."

"Ouch." Chris grabbed his heart and feigned a pain there. "Okay, so call me Bio-Dad? How's that?" Dropping his arms by his sides, he smiled. "Besides, I do, too, do dad things. Just not that often. But, hey, I'm here now." He flung out his arms as if asking for another hug.

"Bio-Dad?" Lacey tapped her lip and raised an eyebrow. "Nah, I think, 'Father Chris' sounds good."

"Don't think I could handle that one, Lacey. And I don't think your mom could either. We never could agree to disagree on religious stuff."

Melanie shook her head and whispered under her breath, "Right on that one, Chris."

"So, I came to take my lovely ladies to dinner." Chris slapped his hands together, licked his lips, and smiled. "Well?"

Melanie stared at him. Chris was always charming, entertaining, good-looking, personable, generous to a point—whenever it suited him. But he was also unreliable, undependable, unpredictable, and very, very self-centered. Melanie's eyes became glassy, and her resolve to keep him out of her life waned.

When they first met, Chris's wild, party side attracted Melanie, and her sweet spirit attracted him. Flinging all caution aside, Melanie had fallen fast and furiously in love. A whole unfamiliar world opened for her, and her ordinarily quiet, controlled life gave way to a wild streak, much to her family's dismay.

"Mom? Mom!"

"Go get dressed, princess. I'll work your mom." Chris winked.

Lacey nodded and ran down the hallway.

Chris turned to face Melanie, his jovial self subdued and his eyes sad. "Hey, Mel, I'm sorry I didn't make it to the funerals. I ..."

Melanie held up a hand. "Chris, that was over a year ago."

He was always sorry after the fact. His "I'm sorry" lacked sincerity.

"Mel, I was out of town. I couldn't get back …" He went into a lengthy explanation, and she felt her eyes glass over.

Sixteen years ago, when she found out she was pregnant with Lacey, Chris wanted to marry her, and they ran off to Las Vegas. Within a few months, sick and lonely, she knew she'd made a huge mistake. She gave Chris his freedom, and he ran.

"Mel, please?"

Shaking her head, she stared at him. "Please what, Chris? You want something from me?" She jabbed her chest with her index finger.

Ruffling a hand through his hair, he stuttered. "I don't know. Please forgive me, I guess? I should have been there."

"No, you shouldn't have. My last days with Mom, before the stroke, were something you wouldn't understand. She read her Bible a lot, and we studied and prayed together. But Mom just missed Dad so much. She only wanted to be in heaven with him." Melanie looked at his blank face. "You wouldn't understand." Guilt gripped her heart, convicting her of her judging thoughts.

"Maybe not, but I know they were a great example of what a committed marriage should be. Too bad we didn't follow their example." He shoved his hands in his pockets.

"We, Chris? We? You ran before the ink was dry on our marriage certificate."

Chris's eyes brightened. "Did you want me to stick around?"

Melanie moaned and turned her back. When she finished counting to ten, she faced him and forced a smile.

"So. The big wedding referral in New Orleans?" Melanie raised her brows.

Chris shook his head. "Oh, no. I told you no, Mel. Uh-uh."

"But the man? He gave me a business card."

"What, man? What business card?"

"Thursday morning, right after we spoke. A man approached me on the street and told me to call the number on the card."

Chris clenched his fist and threw a punch in the air. "You took it? Are you kidding me?

What did the card say?"

"It just said One Shell Tower Plaza, New Orleans, and had a phone number." She thought to show him the card but decided against it. He might take it.

"You didn't call, did you?"

"Oh, so you afraid I'll smear your name or something? Don't think I can do the job? Look, Chris, I need this job." She winced, hoping he didn't catch her desperation.

"Mel, did you call?"

"I almost did. You never called me back."

Circling his hands out in front of him, Chris shook the air as if he were strangling someone. "Because the answer is no! Listen, Mel—" Lacey came running from the hallway. "So, let's go! How about The Manière Sisters Restaurant? All-you-can-eat pasta." Lacey clapped her hands together.

Melanie tried to put on a happy face, but Chris one-upped her.

He swung his arms wide and flashed a grin. "The sky's the limit, Lacey. And I love all-you-can-eat!"

"Oh, that sounds healthy. Can I at least change my clothes?" Melanie looked down. "Oh, never mind. Jeans are fine."

"And how great they look on you, baby." Chris winked.

Rolling her eyes, Melanie opened her mouth to speak, but Lacey interrupted.

"Don't you two start fighting again. I'm starving." She ran out the door and yelled, "Whoa!"

Melanie chased after her. Stopping short, she stared at the

shiny, black, sporty automobile sitting in her carport. Chris always had the best of everything. And this BMW 6 beat all. He must have closed more deals in the year since they'd last seen him. Chris always fell into good deals, and no wonder everyone loved him. Melanie breathed deep. She couldn't deny it. This job was perfect for him.

Chris flew and drove all over the country, wheeling and dealing real estate. Although she thought it an excuse for never seeing Lacey much, Melanie had to admit he was good at what he did. The landscape was always changing as well as the responsibilities, and Chris never seemed to mind dropping everything and leaving to go wherever he was needed. It was great for a single guy, but not for a family man. Another reminder he wasn't good for her.

"Like my car?" Chris spoke behind her.

"Yeah. Give me the keys." Melanie wriggled her fingers.

"Oh, no, you don't. Here, Lacey, you drive." Raising his arm with keys in hand, he aimed at Lacey but winked and pulled back his hand. Dashing to the car, he slipped into the driver's seat of the flashy convertible. Lacey started after him, but Melanie beat her to the passenger side, and with the top of the car down, she jumped over the closed door into the front seat, and Lacey scooted into the back.

As they drove down Beach Road, the wind blew, whipping Melanie's hair around her face.

"How cool is this," Lacey screamed.

Melanie glanced back and caught her daughter gazing at the illuminating red and purple hues coloring the horizon. White wisps blew across the spectacular view over the glassy water. The surreal scenery painted a picture almost as phony as the happy family in the convertible.

Chris pulled into the Manière Sisters Restaurant's paved driveway, and whiffs of seafood gumbo filled the air. Melanie remembered coming here as a child. In fact, every Friday night, when she lived in Mississippi, her dad brought the family there for dinner, but back then, there was no all-you-can-eat pasta.

Initially, the Manière Sisters were two young sisters who took over the family restaurant back in the 1960s. Currently, two middle-aged Manière cousins ran it, but they kept the nostalgia alive. Rushing about wearing '60s-style, print dresses swirling about their knees. Crinoline petticoats peeked out. They greeted every table with a smile as they pulled pads and pens from the patterned half-apron pockets, reminiscent of a time long ago.

Melanie smiled as they took their seats and ordered the pasta and salad. After filling their plates, Chris picked up his fork and dug in.

"Lacey, will you pray for our meal?" Melanie glanced at Chris.

He finished his mouthful, swallowed, and laid down his fork. He slumped forward and whispered, "Go for it, Lacey."

She prayed, and Melanie's heart wrenched a little when her daughter asked for God to bless her dad. The thorn in Melanie's heart needed pulling. She stared at her ex-husband, forcing a smile.

"So, Chris, how are things?"

He sat up straight and looked around. Licking his lips, he took a napkin and wiped his face. Chris pointed to himself. "Me? You're asking about me? Wow!"

Melanie rolled her eyes. "Oh, forget it." *I'll try later, God.* "So, Lacey, do you know anything about the girl that went missing? From Jackson High?"

"Jackson High? I don't know anyone from Jackson High." Lacey stopped a moment but quickly resumed slurping up the spaghetti noodles.

"Well, don't kids from all over come to the youth group? Even if they don't attend the church?" Melanie paused but received no answer. "Anyway, Charlene called me and thinks she was kidnapped by—"

"Kidnapped?" Chris gasped. "Did she think some fanatical right-wing radical is responsible?"

"Chris, stop it. Charlene is working on a case, and they discovered a human trafficking ring in New Orleans. It's infuriating. One girl escaped from the ring, and she said the missing girl from Jackson High School was abducted. It's kind of under wraps until they can get this escaped girl into secured safety," Melanie whispered.

"Why are we whispering?" Chris said under his breath.

Melanie shot a look that could kill. "Knock it off, Chris. This is serious. Anyway, I told Charlene I'd check around. Lacey, I want you to be careful. We don't know what's going on out there, and New Orleans is just down the bay."

"You said trafficking?" Lacey paused.

"They kidnap young girls, drug them, sell them to a human trafficking ring, and then use them for prostitution. Perverted, disgusting things happen, you know." Melanie spoke so passionately that customers turned their heads and stared.

"Hey, Mel, don't sugar coat it. Tell it like it is. She is already sixteen years old." He threw down his napkin. "Come on. Seriously?"

"Well, she needs to know that it's out there, so she can be careful."

"Oh, you mean sex trafficking." Lacey nodded. "Why didn't you say so?"

Chris and Melanie looked at one another and stared back at Lacey. Their mouths gaped.

Melanie threw up her arms. "Well, now it's here."

Lacey opened her eyes wide. "Wait a minute. Here? Come

on, Mom. Maybe Aunt Charlene is just overreacting and exaggerating. You know, like you do when you tell me stories about the old fisherman on the rickety boats out there on the gulf."

"She still does that?" Chris mumbled through a mouthful of pasta.

"Yup." Lacey scooted out of her chair. "I'm getting more breadsticks." Taking her plate, she left.

Melanie wiped her mouth with the linen napkin and replaced it onto her lap. She sat back and stared at Chris. "Why do you make it sound like you know so much about me? And about my sister? About my family?" She glanced at her daughter across the room. A nudge inside told her to stop, but she couldn't. "You've been around all of about sixteen days in sixteen years. You don't know a thing about me."

Lacey returned, and an awkward silence hovered.

Chris swallowed hard. "Right." He clapped his hands together. "Okay, let's go to the movies. Anyone want to see … *Taken?*" Chris knew how to avoid confrontation.

"Really, Dad? Isn't that about that girl that gets kidnapped, drugged, and sold? Oh my gosh! That's for real, isn't it?"

"Okay, that's enough. Forget I said anything. We'll talk later when … we'll just talk later." Melanie looked down and lifted one lettuce leaf with her fork.

"When your deadbeat dad isn't around, is what she meant to say." Chris blinked. "Okay, no worries. Let's just go to Land's End and get ice cream." He grinned and raised his hand. Lacey slapped it for a high five.

Melanie huffed. As much as she hated to admit it, Chris knew how to diffuse and put people at ease. If only she could let go.

"Banana splits?" asked Lacey.

"Anything for the princess."

"Great. I'll have to run three miles tomorrow." But Melanie smiled at the thought of Land's End's Fosters Freeze. Yummy, thick, creamy banana splits were a favorite since childhood.

After they finished their meal, Chris drove to Land's End. Their evening ended sitting atop a rickety, old, wooden picnic table savoring mounds of vanilla ice cream laced with strawberry preserves, chunks of pineapple, thick caramel syrup, bananas, real whipped cream, and maraschino cherries topped off to perfection. Melanie couldn't help but notice the smile on Lacey's face. They enjoyed a cool breeze as it brought a hint of fresh pinecone aroma from the nearby woods. Melanie felt a pang of guilt as she watched Lacey staring at Chris.

Chris's cell rang. When he looked at the screen, he rolled his eyes. "Excuse me, ladies, gotta take this."

Melanie watched as he walked aside and answered. "Hi, Stella. Honey. What's up, babe? … What? … No, no, not tomorrow … I thought that was next Saturday? … Where am I? Uh … sweetie, I'm on business in the gulf. Wait … no … but … I thought I told you I had some real estate to check out down here … No. I can't make it back tonight … No way, not tomorrow morning either. I'm sorry, honey, I could have sworn you said next Monday … wait … no … don't hang up …" Pulling his phone back from his ear, he yelled, "Come on!"

Chris moved to chuck his phone but stopped. Instead, he ran his fingers through his bushy hair and spun around.

Melanie glanced back as she led Lacey to his car. She tossed her unfinished ice cream in the trash. "Chriiis. Baby, sweetie, uh, we have to go … Now!" Melanie cooed loudly, rolling her eyes.

Lacey threw her hands up. "Guess it was too good to last."

Except for the blowing wind, it was a quiet ride home.

Upon arrival, Lacey reached over the seat and hugged her dad. Climbing out, she dragged herself into the house. Melanie sat in the front seat, looking straight ahead for a few moments.

Chris squirmed.

Glancing at her purse, her eyes rested on the business card peeking out of the side pocket, and she pulled it out. She wanted to throw it in his face, but as anger began to rise, she tucked the card away. Too late.

"Don't call them, Melanie. I'm telling you. I didn't send them. Let me at least check it out. I'll take care of you. Don't worry."

Melanie laughed, but looking at him with his shoulders slumped made her close her eyes. She smoothed down nonexistent creases in her jeans. "Listen, Chris, I can take care of myself and Lacey. As for you? Who you see and what you do is none of my business. I don't care. I stopped caring a long time ago, and I don't even remember when it used to hurt." It wasn't totally the truth, but she was trying. "As for Lacey? Well, we've never talked much about what you do, but I think you should keep that part of your life to yourself. Deal?"

He reached his arm out to touch Melanie's shoulder. "Mel, honey—"

"Are you kidding me?" She jerked away and threw open the car door. "Didn't you hear me? I don't care. But I care about Lacey, and obviously, you don't. So keep your honeys and sweeties to yourself."

Stopping herself from slamming the door, she pressed it closed instead. "Goodnight, Chris. We had fun tonight. Really, thanks." Tipping her head, she said, "See you in about six months." She ran for the back door.

"Hey, Mel, any chance the couch is—"

"Not a chance," she yelled over her shoulder as she let the screen door slam shut.

Before Chris backed out of the driveway, he yelled, "Can't blame a guy for trying."

Leaning against the door, Melanie laid back her head. "Oh, yes, I can."

CHAPTER 17

Sunday morning, Chris drove down Highway 12, getting an early jump in returning to California. Though he was tempted to stop and drop a few bucks in the casino on his way from Bay Town, he resisted. It wasn't worth the heat he'd be taking from his current girlfriend, Stella. Drumming his steering wheel with his thumb, he wished he hadn't taken her call when he was with Melanie and Lacey the night before.

With the top down on his BMW, the crisp air chilled his body, but the sun felt good, warming up his kinked neck. He'd had a good night's sleep. So good, he hadn't moved all night. It must have been the good, wholesome time he'd spent with his girls. He smiled. *My girls.* He liked the sound of that. Nothing exciting, but a relaxed, pleasant evening with no drama. Well, almost none.

Heaviness hung in his heart when he thought about how he'd walked out on Melanie so many years ago. How much he'd neglected Lacey as she'd grown up. He just wasn't the daddy type, he'd convinced himself. But teenagers? Maybe he could handle that stage. Make up for lost time. He glanced in his rearview mirror and touched the smile lines around his eyes. *I'm not getting any younger.*

He turned on the radio enjoying the tunes as the landscape of greenery whizzed by. An upbeat song helped to dissipate his guilty thoughts. His mind snapped back to Stella. Gorgeous Stella. Hopefully, she'd still be waiting for him back in California. He turned up the song on the radio and sang along.

But the song faded out, interrupted by the ringing phone. He glanced at the screen on his dash and rolled his eyes.

"Voicemail!" he yelled, and the radio began again. Instantly, another call came in. "What the heck?" The screen showed the same caller ID. No way. I'm done with you guys.

Chris ran a hand through his hair and seethed. He thought of his conversation with Melanie. Were these the guys bugging her? His boss's daughter was getting married. He'd only met the man a few times in all his dealings, but before he quit, he'd made a plug for Melanie, trying to get her the job. He told them she was a wedding planner. Chris slammed the steering wheel. Stupid.

But how did they find her? Glancing at his smart watch, there was no message left on the screen this time either. The radio returned, but he didn't sing along, and the warm sun slid behind a cloud. His body chilled with the cold breeze and the troubling thoughts about Melanie. Maybe he should return the call.

The end of his carefree ride came with the push of a button. The roof of his convertible rose up and over as it whizzed closed. An RV he'd passed earlier pulled up alongside and honked. Chris glared at the driver, who threw a thumb toward the rear of his RV. It sped up a bit, and Chris looked over. Kids in the back had their noses pressed against the window. They excitedly gave him thumbs up, pointing to his roof. They made frantic hand signal gyrations, and Chris laughed. Always the big kid, he complied. Pushing the button once more, his convertible top whizzed down. He couldn't hear them, but he knew they were hooting and hollering as he waved and sped off. Smiling to himself, he forgot why he'd raised his roof in the first place.

After driving over three hours, Chris tired of the green landscape and looked for a place to stop. He yawned while passing all the trees. So many trees. A few old barns, houses, and structures started popping up along the interstate. The quaint calmness of Bay Town had worn off, and his fast-paced life called again. Chris stopped at the next big city.

Coffee time. Finding a familiar shop, he pulled off and parked. He climbed out of his car and stretched his arms out wide, then cracked his neck.

"Hey, mister?" Some kids waved at him.

Looking their way, he furrowed his brow but nodded. Chris raised a hand to his head as if tipping a hat. Finally, recognizing them as the kids in the RV he passed hours ago on the highway, he gave them a thumbs up.

"Cool Transformer, you got there. He with the most toys wins, eh?" A friendly man about Chris's size and build waved. He pointed between his RV and Chris's snappy BMW. Chris wrinkled his face. The guy didn't look like the RV type or a family man, for that matter.

"Hey. Yeah, thanks." Not being around kids much, the thought of a Transformer had never crossed his mind. And his BMW a toy? … Well, maybe. Chris laughed as he nodded. "So, all those kids yours?" He pointed then frowned.

The kids were touching and smearing their little fingers all over his car.

"Yup. Wouldn't trade them for the world. Best toys of all." The dad chuckled.

A slim, tall woman appeared by his side. She slipped her arm around her husband's waist and hugged him. She wore her dark blonde hair pulled back in a ponytail with a baseball cap and sunglasses that shielded her face. Wearing simple jeans and a flannel shirt over a plain white tee, her persona somehow emanated with comfortable happiness. Nothing was striking about her, but certainly a feel-good presence. Happiness seemed to reign over their family, and the thought of Melanie and Lacey popped into his head. A pang of guilt returned. Chris waved to the happy family and turned to get coffee.

The short line allowed him to order quickly and use the restroom before returning to retrieve his drink. Pulling out his phone, he thought to call Stella. Although reluctant at what her response would be, he almost hit the call button. But, glancing at his phone, he opened his eyes wide—the calls.

Stepping outside, the bright sun blinded him, and he pulled his sunglasses down and walked around to stretch his legs a little before getting back in for the long drive. Punching his phone, he listened.

"Chris Thompson. Return this call. I have an offer I need you to write immediately. I'll need you to stay in the gulf. The property is in New Orleans." Click.

Chris's lips tightened as he squinted at his phone. He shook his head, staring into the sky. *Why me?* Last year, he'd quit. But then he'd caved in and wrote one more offer that recently closed. Chris spun around and scratched his neck. *How did he know I was in Bay Town? Did he know I was in Bay Town?*

Closing his eyes, he ran a hand over his bushy hair and stuffed his phone in his pocket. He'd handle it later. He climbed into his car and pushed the button that lowered the top. The engine roared, and he peeled back out onto the highway. The wind blew his hair, and he cranked up the radio. Surprised at the old song, he thought of Melanie and sang along.

The way you hold your knife
The way we danced until three
The way you changed my life
No, no, they can't take that away from me.

Melanie awoke Sunday morning with mixed feelings about going to church. She didn't want to miss it, but she had the wedding in the evening. She'd taken care of every detail, still the temptation to skip church and micro-manage hounded her. What was she thinking last night wasting time with Chris? She shook her head. Nope, he wasn't going to deter her from church. He'd done that long ago, but not anymore. She went to get dressed.

Pulling into the church parking lot, she stared at the building. Bay Town Community Church was a quaint little church, not unlike those always depicted in the movies. The quintessential white clapboard structure with a high steeple and a wide front porch with massive double doors opened to rows of beautiful wooden pews lining a center aisle. A polished wooden altar and a colorful stained-glass cross illuminated the sanctuary's front, completing the peaceful serenity.

So unlike the converted industrial warehouses and mega campuses that housed many of the large churches in California.

Pastor Desmond Brooks was a considerable change from the former pastor. He'd made some changes, but most everyone loved him. Melanie stared at him as he greeted members on the church veranda. Piano notes drifted out beautiful hymns. It was another of the changes. The church formerly had an old organ, and its removal was one thing that caused Pastor Brooks to lose some popularity among a few seniors. But he won them over with his solid teaching. Melanie thought she even saw Richard Copeland back. She breathed deep. Desmond's friendly manner made everyone want to be around him, including her.

"Well, hi, young lady. Don't you look nice this morning?" Desmond smiled.

"Hey, Pastor Brooks." Lacey gave him a side hug. "What

are you preaching on today? Self-control?" she teased. "What a game Friday night! You sure know how to handle those umpires."

Desmond grimaced. "Yes, well, actually, I thought I'd preach about women." He tugged her long brown hair playfully. "You know, how you're to have a gentle and quiet spirit and not be adorned by heavy jewelry and plaited hair. Something along those lines." He winked.

"Great, I'm glad I didn't plait my hair today, whatever that means." Lacey shrugged.

Melanie followed right behind. She greeted Desmond with a firm handshake. "Good morning, Des—uh, Pastor."

"It's still Desmond," he whispered as he squeezed her hand.

Melanie sighed. "Well, I better go in." Taking a step, she stopped and turned. "Oh, Desmond, did you have time to talk to Virginia on Friday? I forgot to ask."

Desmond frowned. "No. I stopped by, and nobody answered the door. But it sounded like someone was inside. I sure hope she showed up at school."

"I'll check with Lacey."

Searching, the church, Melanie spotted Lacey in the front row, grinning. She signaled thumbs-up, and as Melanie passed by Richard Copeland, she stopped to acknowledge him. Taking a step back, she placed a hand on his shoulder, and he stood. His eyes watered a little, and he extended a hand. Her heart lurched as she took his hand in both of hers and squeezed.

"Would you like to join my daughter and me?" Melanie pointed upfront.

He waved her off, shaking his head.

Joining Lacey in the front pew, Melanie mentally protested but quieted herself instead. She liked to sit in the back for a quick exit, but she resigned herself and scooted in next to Joe Cunningham. He looked so different when not in his bus uniform. Dressed in a neat, plain black suit, white shirt, and red striped tie, he resembled a Secret Service Agent. Melanie smiled. Fitting, she thought. He loved and cared for the kids at Bay High. It made her think of Virginia again. She turned to ask Lacey about her, but Lacey was chatting with someone else. Melanie touched Joe's arm.

"Hey, Joe? Was Virginia James at school on Friday?"

Joe nodded. "Yes, ma'am. She almost missed the bus. But she finally came a'straggling out the house like a wet cat."

"Good. Thanks, Joe."

Pastor Brooks walked to the front, everyone took their seats, and the singing began. Melanie loved to worship. One or more of the songs almost always made her cry. Her parents had taken her to church long before she could even remember. And now, the singing forever made her think of them. She smiled as an off-key note of some unknown voice in the back brought her back down to earth. But she never felt as close to God as during this time of praise.

Desmond preached on the scripture that he'd quoted to Lacey, but he emphasized the gentle and quiet spirit. Melanie couldn't help but think of Deena Copeland, then staring at Desmond, she thought of his Emily and lowered her eyes.

As the service ended, not everyone exited quickly. People lingered, hugging, talking, and enjoying one another's company. This was their community. Melanie loved that Lacey enjoyed it, too.

When they made it outside, Lacey gave Desmond another hug, and she grabbed Melanie.

"Hey, Pastor, why don't you come over for lunch today?" Lacey grinned.

Melanie's eyes widened, and her jaw dropped.

Tina stood by and turned to join the group. "Oh, why don't we all just go out for lunch?" She raised an eyebrow, winking at Lacey. "Pastor Brooks, how often do I get to Bay Town Community Church? It's a reason to celebrate. By the way, wonderful sermon. I needed it. I guess you wouldn't know it, but I have a little difficulty with the adorn thingy." Jingling her bracelets and twirling her dangling earrings, she laughed, and everyone else did too.

Desmond chuckled and added, "Well, thank you, Mrs. Paulson. And thank you for the invitation. Can I take a rain check?"

"Oh, Lacey, what were you thinking? I've got that wedding tonight. Today isn't a good day for us either. Maybe another time. Sorry, Pastor Brooks." Melanie tugged at Lacey.

"No problem. Next Sunday is potluck. Let's do lunch then," Desmond called after them and waved a friendly hand. "Goodbye, have a great afternoon."

Walking to her car, Melanie glanced back. Her eyes locked with Desmond's, and she couldn't help but recall their times together this week. Was it the start of something? She hadn't had a man in her life since…well, in an awfully long time.

Desmond turned to shake hands, and Lyla Cunningham stood by grinning. He turned as bright as the red ribbon on her white hat.

"Potluck? Mmm, mmm. Looks like that'll be your lucky day, Pastor. How about my jambalaya and sweet potato pie for dessert?" Lyla's beautiful grin spread wide.

"I can't wait, Lyla. Thanks for coming this morning. Keep belting out that praise, will you? You make Jesus happy up there." He pointed upwards.

"Why, Pastor Brooks, He ain't just up there." She gave him a nudge. "You knows He's always here with us."

"Hey. I had that first," little Joey Cunningham screeched as he and Jasmine, his little sister, fought over a giant pinecone that one of them had found on the church's front lawn.

"But it's my turn to hold it," Jasmine whined.

The arguing escalated until Lyla turned and glared at them both. Their pleas ceased.

"Does it matter who had it first?" Lyla drawled in a firm, hushed tone.

"No, ma'am," came a unison answer in sweet, high voices. The children lowered their eyes and hung their heads. Little Joey kicked at the dirt with his shiny, black church shoes.

"Good. Then let me have it. I thinks this would look mighty nice on Pastor Brooks's desk. Ain't that right, little Joe?" She eyed him as he gripped the pinecone.

"Yes, Mama," he answered, still clinging to his treasure.

"Well, 'yes, mama' don't mean nothing, 'less you give it to the man." Lyla stood, hands on her hips, with her red purse dangling from her elbow. "Well, go on."

Little Joey handed it reluctantly to Desmond. The latter hated taking it but dared not contradict a mother correcting her children.

"Why, thank you, Joey. You come by and play with it any time, you hear? And you too, Jasmine. I may even have some candy if it's ok with your mom?" Desmond winked at them both. They nodded their heads yes and ran off yelling.

"I'm gonna find another one, and you can't have it." Jasmine's high-pitched voice sang back.

Lyla just shook her head. "Gots to keep training those two. Children." She headed down the church steps after them. Turning, she called out, "Come on, Joe. We gots to go."

Big Joe held back. Desmond went to shake his hand, but Joe shifted his large body, hiding behind a wide wooden pillar covered by the old, thick wisteria vine crawling up the church veranda. As he leaned his shiny, bald head out, it seemed his gaze was riveted across the street.

"What's wrong, Joe?" Desmond asked.

"That white van across the street there. Don't look now. They can sees you but not me, so don't turn around."

Joe's eyes still fixed across the street. "Now, where's the

chief? He show up today, Pastor?" Without waiting for an answer, he continued. "Probably not, huh?"

"No. Not today. Maybe he hurt too much after the ball game." Desmond chuckled.

"Well, that white van across the street was at the school this week. Now what you suppose they's doing here? I don't like this at all. Mmm, mmm."

Joe's face wrinkled, and drawing up his shoulders, he stepped out from behind the wisteria. His demeanor changed, and he grabbed Desmond's hand, pumping it up and down. Lumbering down the front steps, he threw his head back, the rolls on his neck folding over. "Great sermon, Pastor. See ya next week."

"Sure. Thanks, Joe."

Desmond watched as Joe approached Lyla. Taking her hand, he said, "Lyla, let's go. I gots to go call Chief Bert."

Desmond replaced his sunglasses and turned to look at the parking lot across the street. He saw no white van, but just then, Melanie's sporty Mustang pulled out of the church parking lot. He turned to lock up but glanced over his shoulder as he heard an engine. He saw it. The white van pulled out into the lane.

He shrugged, debating whether to call Joe. Instead, he walked to his office, feeling a little uneasy but trusting that Joe was taking care of it. Whatever it was. His mind returned to the events of the past week. Maybe that's where his uneasiness stemmed. He thought of Virginia and the bar incident. Will Boudreaux and the aunt bothered him, too, and it bugged him that nobody answered the door on Friday afternoon at Virginia's house when he stopped by. Yet, he thought he heard some rustling upstairs. Desmond stopped on the gravel path to the rose garden and gazed upward.

"Lord? I could use some wisdom and discernment here." Continuing to his office, he entered, closed the door, removed his navy jacket, and sat down on the leather chair behind his desk. He took a deep breath and loosened his polka-dot tie. Leaning back, he spent the afternoon reading his Bible and thinking about the events happening in Bay Town. He bowed his head to pray, but his eyes rested on Emily's photograph smiling back at him.

"You'd know what to do, wouldn't you, Em?"

CHAPTER 18

Melanie approached her house when a van following close her inched up behind too closely. Trying to avoid being rear-ended, she turned sharply into her driveway. The van swerved recklessly behind her, narrowly missing. She hit the brakes and came close to crashing into the posts holding up the carport. Shoving the gear in park, she jumped from the car and ran to the street. The van had slowed down, and the passenger peered back, sticking his head out the window.

"Sorry, man," he yelled.

The van raced down Beach Road just as Lacey caught up with her mom.

"Come on, Mom. It's the Lord's day. Turn the other cheek."

Melanie stood with her hands on her hips. Sweat beaded on her forehead as she glared. "You're right. You're right, Lacey." But she didn't take her eyes off the road till the van was out of sight.

Walking back to the house, Lacey ran back to the car. Melanie turned to wait for her daughter, who was grabbing her Bible and bag.

"So, Mom?" Lacey caught up. "What's up with that?" Her voice sounded a little shaky.

"I'm not sure, Lacey." She shrugged. "Probably some crazy troublemakers from out of town." She wanted to soothe Lacey's fears but didn't believe her own words. She was certain they were the ones she'd seen downtown and maybe even at the softball game. She threw an arm around Lacey and pulled her close. "How about some healthy soup for lunch?"

"Soup sounds good. I don't know about the healthy part, though." Lacey scrunched her nose. "Brownies after?"

"Of course."

They changed, and Melanie heated a hearty vegetable soup for lunch. Chunks of thick-cut carrots, celery, potatoes, onions, and a mixture of other veggies in a spicy tomato broth. Lacey ate without complaint. Melanie smiled. Brownies were coming. They were the standard fare for Sunday afternoons.

Melanie didn't have much time before the wedding. After she got ready, Tina came over and stayed with Lacey for the evening. With butterflies in her stomach, Melanie prayed before leaving. She always felt this way before an event, and God always calmed her.

Standing in the kitchen, Tina held up an old black and white DVD. "I'm so glad your daughter loves the classics." She winked at Lacey.

Lacey gave a thumbs up. "You know we can rent those online? You don't have to use DVDs."

Tina threw a wave. "Oh, it's not the same." She turned and pointed at Melanie. "Don't you look gorgeous? Chic, but subdued. I like the look!"

"Thanks. Well, you two have fun. Say a prayer that all goes well. I need it."

"Mom, you'll knock them dead. You're the best." Lacey gave her a squeeze.

The attention to detail resulting in late nights and early mornings for Melanie proved her forte for the elegant affair. The arriving wedding guests marveled at the old barn venue. The bride, Summer, had booked it over a year ago before even hiring Melanie. She had become a friend and was partly responsible for Melanie moving to Bay Town. Or at the very least, she was one of God's instruments. Back in California, shortly after her parents' deaths, Melanie signed the contract to be Summer's wedding consultant, and it propelled the move to Bay Town. Building a clientele in the South took more time than she'd anticipated, but Melanie hoped this event would launch her reputation as a top consultant in the area. She wasn't staking that claim yet, as she'd put all her eggs in one basket before. God had other plans.

The 450-acre working farm oozed centuries-old warmth mixed with modern luxury. Breathtaking views of beautiful farmland were quite a contrast to the Bayou life on the water not far away.

After the ceremony, the barn doors opened to dining and dancing—tables and chairs placed inside and outside. Guests spilled out all over on the grounds. Melanie walked through the crowd, checking on details when Summer caught her eye from across the estate. She waved, and the bride blew her a kiss and mouthed, "Perfect."

The bride and groom came from generations-old southern families, and all the important community people were there. A local news reporter, a New Orleans society writer, and a journalist for Southern Bride Magazine were among the invited guests. Butterflies fluttered when they asked Melanie for an interview. She agreed after all the traditional activities took place.

She approached the table of reporters, smoothing down her black silk sheath. Her messy updo and loose tendrils softened her already sweet face. She sat, placing one knee over the other.

"Hi. I'm from the New Orleans Times." The woman pushed up her thick, dark glasses, looking the part of a typical reporter and not just for a society page. "So, how did you come about doing this wedding? It's quite an honor."

"Yes, it is. The referral came from a wedding I did back in California." Melanie twisted her small, diamond-stud earrings.

"Wow, that's quite a distance." A woman with close-cropped, jet-black hair and striking angular features widened her already large eyes. "Southern Bride Magazine." She smiled, reaching out to pat Melanie's hand. Her ebony skin popped against the taupe suit with a plunging white camisole underneath. "So, Melanie? Did you commute just for the wedding?" She leaned forward.

Before Melanie could answer, a casually dressed young woman spoke. "Clearly, you haven't done your homework." She tipped her head, and long side-swept bangs fell forward. The other side of her head was shaved, adding an edginess to her all-black ensemble.

Her condescending tone made the beautiful journalist laugh. "How's that?" Sparkling white teeth dazzled behind full matte, taupe-colored lips.

"Well, Ms. Thompson here, she owns a shop down on Main Street. Right here in Bay Town. Quaint Affairs has been in operation for about a year now." She beamed and pointed to herself. "Bay Town Gazette."

Melanie looked down, hiding a smile.

The New Orleans reporter asked, "Is that right, Mrs. Thompson?"

"Well, yes. I used to work on the west coast. I did a wedding in Malibu, California, and she"—Melanie pointed to the stunning bride on the dance floor—"Summer was the maid of honor at that wedding."

All the reporters drew back. Surprise expressed in subtle gasps and wide eyes.

"And you moved here to do this wedding?" The chic journalist from Southern Bride asked her.

"You might say it was providence. My father found a small business grant here in Bay Town and applied for me." Melanie chose not to mention that the bride's grandfather was the founder of the foundation offering the grant. "We lived here when I was younger, and my father had dreams of returning to the small-town life." Her eyes burned a little.

"Now that is the sweetest story." The Southern Bride journalist warmed.

"So, what's your next big event?" Bay Town Gazette asked.

Melanie smiled. "Well …"

"Ms. Thompson? Can I talk to you about the wedding for my employer at One Shell Tower Plaza?"

The reporters all turned their attention to a large, well-dressed man standing over Melanie. She turned and looked up. Her brows furrowing and her mind spinning.

"Excuse me?"

"The Penthouse? At One Shell Tower Plaza?" The New Orleans reporter narrowed her eyes. "And you are?"

Melanie caught the look and wondered what she knew.

"Just a liaison." The gentleman glanced at the dance floor. "I'm here as a representative of the family."

"Of course you are. All you big money people know each other," the local reporter clipped.

Melanie's stomach swirled, and she clasped her shaking hands. Chris had told her not to call. Had he changed his mind?

The Southern Bride Magazine journalist raised an eyebrow and tapped a pen to her full lips. She smiled and glanced from the man to Melanie. "No matter, our readers love the extravagance." She stared at Melanie. "And you, my dear, appear to have quite a booking coming up. Care to comment?"

Melanie's throat felt as if a vise was clamping it shut. She looked at the barn. "I'm sorry you must excuse me." She stood and wobbled on her strappy heels, wishing she'd worn sensible pumps. "It's almost time for the bride and groom's departure. Thank you, ladies. Maybe we can continue this later."

She left the man to the reporters, who peppered him with questions. Thinking she'd blown the publicity she needed from this wedding, Melanie continued walking away. Could she afford to refuse the New Orleans job now? Her reputation was on the line. A scoop about Quaint Affairs planning the biggest wedding in New Orleans was practically being written. She chewed on her lip as she entered the barn. Rubbing her temples, she thought, *He seemed calm and professional. Legit ... enough ... Maybe?*

Just before she reached the stage, someone called her name.

"Mrs. Thompson?"

Melanie turned. It was him again.

"This is a job you don't want to pass up. Please call." He extended another card.

Melanie's mind raced. She stared and thought of Chris. He'd said he had a bad feeling.

"If you'll call, I think you'll be pleased with the initial monthly retainers we'd like to offer you. You won't have to wait until the event happens for payment." He smiled.

I need this, she thought. Envisioning all her bills floating away, she nodded and reached for the card but stopped. Waving it off, she smiled. "I have one, thank you, Mr. ..." The man didn't offer his name, and she awkwardly continued. "Well, that's very generous. Thank you. I'll try and call tomorrow. If you'll excuse me, please." Melanie walked away but kept a sideways glance at the man.

He pulled a cell phone from his pocket.

Lacey and Tina watched the old black and white movie back at the house and munched on brownies.

"Who is that guy?" Lacey asked as she pointed to the screen. "He's a hottie!"

Tina burst out laughing. "Are you kidding me? That's John Wayne!" She squirmed on the couch, tucking her feet underneath her.

"Who's John Wayne?" Lacey asked.

"Why, just one of the most iconic actors in Hollywood! Well, he used to be. Now, I guess you'd say it's Denzel." Tina winked.

Staring back, Lacey shrugged.

"Leonardo? Brad Pitt?" Tina raised a brow.

Lacey frowned. "They're old."

"Ouch. Then who?" Tina asked.

"Timothee Chalamet? Ansel Elgort?"

"Never heard of them." Tina smirked.

"Scott Eastwood?"

"Oooh! Clint's son? Now that's what I'm talking about." Tina raised a hand, and Lacey slapped a high five.

"Listen, Rudy has a bunch of John Wayne DVDs. Do you want to watch another one?"

"Sure." Lacey shrugged.

Sliding off the couch, Tina slipped on her cork wedge heels and sauntered to the front door. "I'll be right back. Don't go anywhere."

"I'll try not to." Lacey reclined on the rose-chintz sofa, closing her eyes.

Tina left, and Lacey lounged, scrolling her phone. A few minutes later, a sound came from the kitchen door. Thinking maybe Tina was returning through that entrance, she walked through the kitchen, unlocked the screen, and stepped out.

Bam! Black dots connected before her eyes, and down she went.

Lacey laid on the ground, not seeing, only hearing. Shuffling. Cursing. Footsteps running. The fog in her head clouded everything. A door slammed further away.

"Lacey? I got the movie? Are you in the bathroom?"

It was Tina. Lacey opened her mouth, but a weak whisper was all that escaped. Her eyes couldn't focus, and the ground felt hard and smelled wet and dirty.

More footsteps. Looking up in a dreamy cloud, she squinted and saw a leathery, wild-haired man bending over her. He squatted by her side and smelled like body odor and seafood. She willed her arms to move away, but they wouldn't.

Suddenly, he stood. "Stay put, girl." She watched as he ran off.

Lacey turned to look, but her head throbbed, and reaching up she felt swelling on the side of her head. She attempted to sit, but the dots connected again, and she had no choice but to lay still. The screen door slammed, and she twitched.

"Oh my gosh! Lacey, what are you doing out here? What happened?" Tina screamed.

Lacey stuttered. "I don't know. I thought …" She rolled her body to the side and retched.

The wild-haired man returned.

Out of breath, Lacey choked, gasping for air. He tried to calm her, but she squirmed.

"Shhh. Shhh. I'm here, Lacey." Tina pushed back the hair from her face and looked around.

The man thrust a handkerchief toward Tina, and she wiped Lacey's mouth and chin. The soft cloth smelled surprisingly like soap. Tina pulled out her cell phone and made a call.

Why wasn't Tina scared of the stranger? Lacey wondered.

"Lacey, honey, lay still. Help is coming." Tina turned to the man and whispered, "What are you doing here? Did you see what happened?"

He shook his head. "No, ma'am. I was out for a walk, and I saw shadows running from your carport. When I came closer, I saw her lying there under the lights." He pointed to Lacey. "I came to check, but when I heard an engine, I ran back out to the street." His voice was soft.

"Shadows? Who? What? What did you see?" Tina's voice shook. "Captain Jack, it's okay. I know you wouldn't hurt her. But what did you see?"

Lacey glanced over and saw the man's eyes widened. He pulled off a tattered knit beanie. His mouth was moving, but Lacey couldn't make out his words. And a siren screamed in the distance.

Gaining and losing consciousness, Lacey heard voices. *Was that Rudy?* Strangers. She raised her arms and wanted to struggle, but her pounding head prevented it, and she heard Tina's calming voice.

"It's okay, sweetie," she cooed. "It's just the paramedics. We're taking you to the hospital. Shhh, shhh, you'll be fine."

As Lacey felt herself being lifted into a vehicle, she heard sobs. Tina's sobs. Opening her eyes, they rested on a mascara-streaked, beautiful face. All went blank.

———

By the time Melanie arrived at the local hospital, it was late. She ran through the ER barefoot, heels in her hand. Loose hair fell from her updo, and her eyes were rimmed red. She glanced at the waiting room.

Desmond moved toward her and walked with her to the check-in. "You go ahead. I'll wait here with Captain Jack." He pointed. "Tell Lacey I'm praying for her."

Melanie stared at the wild-haired man wringing a knit beanie between his fingers. Captain Jack? He was the driver of the *Fish Stalker*. What was he doing here? She stared up at Desmond.

"Mrs. Thompson, you can go back now." A nurse pointed to double doors.

Melanie ran and found Lacey's room. She fell across the girl and sobbed, but Lacey seemed soundly asleep. Tina stood by her side.

"Tina, thank you. Thank you for calling. Thank you for being there." Sobs muffled Melanie's voice.

Tina put her arms around Melanie and waited before filling her in on the details of the night. Sitting by her daughter's side, Melanie waited forever for her daughter to awaken.

"Mrs. Thompson?" A short, round man in a lab coat entered. "I'm Dr. Mackey. May I ask a few questions?"

Melanie nodded her head. Holding her daughter's hand, she never took her gaze off Lacey.

"Has your daughter had fainting spells before? Blacked out, anything like that?"

Melanie shook her head. "Do you think that's what happened?"

"We won't know until your daughter can tell us. But the assumption is she tripped or fell. She's got a nasty bump on the side of her head."

Tina had mentioned something about shadows. She looked back at Lacey and again at the doctor.

"Do you think someone could have hit her?"

He shrugged. "If that's what happened, we need to call the police."

"I'm on it, doc." Chief Bert stood at the door.

Tina patted Melanie's hand and scooted out of the room.

The doctor turned back to Melanie. "Her vitals are good. She's not dehydrated, which can cause fainting. When was her last meal?" He seemed to be ticking off a list.

Staring at the doctor, Melanie teared up. "Doctor, as far as I know, my daughter is a healthy, normal teenager. Unless there's something, I don't know."

He nodded. Maybe he thought that could be the case. "Okay, well, as soon as she wakes, I'll finish my report then. But I'll be back to check on her later."

Chief Bert walked over and patted Melanie's shoulder. "I talked to Tina. I have an officer talking to the other fellow in the lobby." He scratched his head. "Do you know the guy?"

Melanie squinted. "The fisherman?" She shivered a little. "No. I've seen him down at the pier. I think he owns that boat, the *Fish Stalker*?" Somehow, she didn't feel threatened by him anymore.

"Yeah. I got that. It seems he tried to help. At least according to your neighbor, Tina Paulson."

Lacey moaned, and her body twitched.

Taking a few steps back, the Chief let out a heavy sigh. "I'll leave you two alone now."

After he left, Melanie bowed her head and prayed for her daughter, thanking God that she was safe but begging for her to be well.

Melanie soon settled by Lacey's bedside and fell asleep. She didn't wake until the sunlight poured through the window.

"Ouch," said Lacey.

Her daughter's cry woke her, and Melanie watched a tech draw blood from Lacey's arm. Her face flooded with tears as she kissed her daughter.

"Oh, sweetie. How are you?"

"My head hurts." She smiled weakly. "Mom, you're a good sleeper. I kept waking up, and you were snoring away."

Melanie opened her eyes wide and swiped her tears. "I do not snore."

"Yes, you do. Even Pastor Brooks heard you."

"He was here?"

"Yup." She pointed to a chair. Desmond lounged with his long legs stretched out, looking uncomfortable but sound asleep.

Melanie wiped under her eyes and smoothed her hair.

"Go make yourself presentable before he wakes up," Lacey whispered.

"But Lacey, what happened?"

Lacey shook her head and frowned. "I'm not sure, and I don't want to think about it right now. Pastor Brooks prayed with me last night when you were sleeping. Go now, Mom. You're a mess. Get cleaned up before he sees you."

Melanie rolled her eyes, but a smile crossed her face, thankful that Lacey was already showing good signs of recovery.

"I mean it." Lacey fluttered her hand at the door.

Melanie cleaned up in the ladies' room. At least she was still all dressed up from the wedding. She glanced in the mirror. Her black sheath hugged her form, and the silver jewelry added just the right touch of class. She shook herself. Who even cared?

She walked into the lobby, hoping to catch Tina. Although she wasn't hopeful, seeing as it was the morning after the accident. But there she was, along with Chief Bert, Officer Blaine, and the fisherman. He was who she thought—the *Fish Stalker* guy.

"Any update on Lacey?" the chief asked.

"She's up and talking, so that's wonderful." Melanie shook her head. "But no, I haven't talked to her about anything yet."

"That's fine. All of us happened to check in this morning, just concerned for her. Officer Blaine here will write a report, and I'll get you a copy. We have no definitive answers, but we will keep a lookout for that white van."

Melanie gasped. "Do you think it was them? Did they try to …"

The chief raised a hand. "We don't want to jump to conclusions. Until Lacey talks, this guy's story is all we got." He pointed to the fisherman.

Officer Blaine looked at the disheveled man. "Thanks for your help, Justin."

The chief scratched his head. "You know this guy?"

"Yup. We went to high school together," said Officer Blaine.

Tina stepped forward. "Yes, Captain Jack. Thank you so much. I don't know what I would have done without you last night."

Melanie put out her hand. "Thank you. I'm sorry we've never met. I'm Melanie."

He shook. "Yes, ma'am. I seen you running all the time."

The chief shook his head. "Now, wait a minute. How long have I lived here, and I know nothing about this guy?" He opened a palm, pointing.

"Oh, Chief. Everyone knows Captain Jack. He lives on his boat down at the pier." Tina gave him a sideways glance. "And he always catches the yummiest lobsters!"

He narrowed his eyes. "Is it lobster season?" The chief raised both hands. "I don't want to know. We've got enough activity for one night. I don't need to go hunting down any poachers."

Officer Blaine shook his head. "It's lobster season. Just started, Chief."

The chief nodded. "Okay. He winked at Captain Jack. "Say, my wife loves lobster!"

CHAPTER 19

"Phew, lordy! How'd you beat me here?" Chief Bert removed his hat, throwing it on his desk.

Officer Blaine looked up and shrugged. "I took the statements at the hospital and wrote a preliminary report based on Captain Jack's and Mrs. Paulson's statements. Shall I file it?"

"You have to. We have little else at this point."

"What's your take, Chief?"

The chief scratched his head. "Just trying to piece all this together." He stared at Officer Blaine. "How reliable a witness is this, Captain Jack?"

"He's honest. Doesn't do drugs but has some mental imbalance issues. He was on meds in high school, but I think about the time his dad passed. He quit taking them and has been living on the docks ever since."

The chief blew out a breath. "So, not so reliable, huh?"

"Well, he didn't tell us anything definitive, but he couldn't have been that far off. Unless Lacey took a nasty fall off the porch step, someone must have hit her. Captain Jack said he saw shadows running away. Maybe Tina Paulson walked in and scared them off."

"Do you think it was a robbery in progress?"

Officer Blaine shook his head.

"Yeah, me neither. But why, Lacey? Why didn't they hurt Mrs. Pauls …" The chief's eyes widened. "Was there a vehicle around? A white van by any chance?"

"None reported. Captain Jack said he heard a vehicle is all. Saw nothing. Other than the two shadows."

"All right. Be ready to go to the hospital and take Lacey's testimony if Mrs. Thompson calls. I'm heading over to that Virginia girl's house."

"The one I patrolled last week?"

"Yes. Call the high school will you and find out if Virginia James was there today."

"What's the problem if she wasn't?"

"I have a hunch she just might be connected to something. Call me if you find anything on the white van." The chief pulled open the door, frowning at the jingling bells. "And hey, Blaine. Check out the name Will Boudreaux. It's in Thursday's report. I want to know who that guy is."

As Chief Bert drove over to Virginia's house, he shook his head. Nothing sounded right. Though unsure whether Lacey's accident and Virginia's absence were related, he had a funny feeling. He'd been in law enforcement too long to ignore a hunch.

Pulling his car in along the curb in front of the old, worn-down house, he looked around. No vehicles were in sight, and everything seemed quiet. He approached the front porch and rang the doorbell. It didn't work. As he pulled the screen door open, it fell off the hinges. Laying it aside, he rapped three times.

"Miss Hilly? It's Chief Bert. Open the door, please."

He moved to the side of the door and twisted the doorknob. Unlocked. He pushed the door opened and placed one foot in the entrance.

"Oh, man!" Grabbing his handkerchief, the chief covered his nose. He gagged, then coughed while scanning the entrance. Something wasn't right. Bypassing the living room, he followed the hallway to the kitchen. He headed that way to check the source of the decaying smell first.

"Hello? Anybody home?"

Stepping over plastic bags, food wrappers, and clothing, he shook his head. A tipped over

wastebasket lay on its side. The contents spilled out, a mixture of leftovers and unidentifiable ooze. Dirty coffee cups and a few plates piled with crusty, leftover food lay in the sink. The odor overwhelmed him, and as he walked into the living room, he covered his nose tighter.

Chief Bert perused the room and stopped near the sofa. His eyes widened at a form lying under a blanket.

"Hello? Police here. Miss Hilly? Is that you?"

He unsnapped his holster. The noise nor his words caused movement. Pulling the gun, he held it up, and with the other hand, he touched the body. He nudged, then pressed harder but finally stopped. Pulling back the worn blanket, he sighed, certain this was Miss Hilly.

He pulled out his cell. "Blaine, get over here to 25462 Oleander Drive, now. And call the coroner."

While he waited, Chief Bert put on his gloves and looked around. He spotted the cocaine and needles on the end table and searched more. A used needle lay on the ground next to the sofa. He'd seen his fill of overdosed victims, but this appeared odd. Usually, an overdose victim lay with the arm flailed out with the needle close by. At least if that was the site of injection, but she looked as if her body had been positioned comfortably on the sofa.

He left and walked up the stairs, his gun drawn. There were only two bedrooms upstairs. One room was sparse, with few clothes hanging in the closet. The bed was unmade. Cigarette butts lay in dishes and ashtrays everywhere. He walked down the hall and peeked into a bathroom. All the drawers were opened, and it looked as if a grab-and-go of toiletries exploded. The other room appeared to be a girl's room, but clothes, shoes, and accessories were strewn everywhere.

"Chief? We're here. Coroner, too," Officer Blaine yelled from downstairs.

The chief lumbered down. "That was fast. How'd I get so lucky?"

The coroner shrugged. Typically, his caseload didn't permit an immediate arrival. Chief Bert clued him in, and he instantly went to work. The chief instructed Blaine to check outside as he continued looking around.

"Chief?" Blaine called from outside.

"What's up?" he said as he exited the house.

Blaine crouched in the tall weeds covering the back lawn. "Tracks. Not fresh, but not too old. It looks like a car was parked back here."

"Can you get a make on the tires?"

"I can, but it'd be better if you got forensics out here. Shall I call them?"

The chief nodded. He stood and removed his hat, scratching his head. "Did you find anything out on Boudreaux or the van?" He doubted the answer was yes. Everything was escalating.

"He has a rental here in Bay Town."

"Let me guess, Oleander Drive." The chief pointed to the house.

"Yup. And the van is registered to an LLC. But the license is expired. I'd bet it was a phony business, and the registered address is no longer correct."

"Why am I not surprised." He patted Blaine's shoulder. "Excellent work, Blaine. Oh, and Virginia James?"

"Absent."

"I thought so." The chief returned inside to the coroner.

"What's your initial guess? And don't say accidental overdose."

The coroner shrugged. "Overdose. Accidental or otherwise, she's been dead for roughly seventy-two hours, give or take."

"Since Thursday night or Friday morning?" The chief blew out a breath. "Whoa! That's a long time."

"Yes, sir." He looked at the chief. "I'm guessing you're leaning toward foul play? In which case, I'll do toxicity. See what I can find."

The chief nodded just as Blaine walked back in. "Anything else, Chief?"

"Yeah, wait here for forensics, and help the coroner if he needs you. I'm going over to the high school."

Chief Bert walked into the old high school building and approached the front desk. "Good morning, Mrs. Crowley. Was Virginia James at school today?"

Without checking, she responded. "No, Chief. Officer Blaine called, and I told him she was absent."

"Yeah, I know. I'm just double-checking. Do you know that for sure?" Wiggling his finger at the computer, he said, "Can you check again?"

"Chief, I'm very sure. It's not that unusual for Virginia to be absent. Her Aunt Hilly does not care much that she misses school."

Principal Ladner stepped out of his office.

"Good Afternoon, Chief. Good to see you. By the way, great job playing catcher at the game on Friday. Glad you could help us out." The principal removed his glasses. "Can I help with anything?"

"Thursday evening, Virginia was with a man she called her daddy. He identified himself as her father." The chief continued a summary without the sordid commentary of the bar and Virginia's house.

Mrs. Crowley interrupted, "Chief, Virginia has no father on record and certainly no relative by the name of Boudreaux. Her aunt is the only person of legal custody—"

"Ms. Crowley, I believe that is all private information?" Principal Ladner looked at her over the top of his glasses.

She nodded and looked down.

"Well, Principal, we're all on the same team here. I could use all the information I can get," said Chief Bert.

"Yes, yes, of course," Principal Ladner stammered. "I, uh, I just wanted to make sure we followed protocol. I certainly didn't mean to hinder an investigation. Ms. Crowley, thank you for helping the Chief." Principal Ladner gave her a nod.

"Please call me if Virginia shows up tomorrow or the next day."

"Yes, Chief." Mrs. Crowley shifted her gaze from the principal to Chief Bert. "I'd be more than happy to help in any way that I can." She smiled.

"Thank you, ma'am." He tipped his hat. "And thank you, Mr. Ladner."

The chief ambled down the building's front steps and pulled out his phone to check with Officer Blaine. Chief Bert smiled as he imagined all the reports on his desk, tucked into manila folders. Blaine did everything online, but the chief always required a hard copy.

"Blaine, start a missing person report on Virginia James. I know we can't file it yet, but I want to be ready to go."

"Will do."

The chief reached his car and stopped. He thought about Virginia, then Lacey, and last, he thought about Hilly. It was easy to become calloused in his field, but since moving to Bay Town, the people in this tight-knit community meant more to him than just another case or just another overdose. He placed a hand on his car, and a chill went through him as a snap of cold wind blew through the air. He stopped and stared at the billowy gray sky. Chief Bert took off his hat and fixed his face upward.

"Lord, I'm not a praying man, but I'd like to ask a favor for Virginia. Please keep her safe, okay? I'd sure appreciate it."

CHAPTER 20

Lacey was thankful that all the routine tests were complete. Tired of the poking and prodding, she was eager to be alone in her hospital room. Although entirely alone wasn't something she wanted just yet. Pastor Brooks had spent the night and the entire morning by Melanie's and Lacey's side. She enjoyed having him there.

In the lull from doctors, nurses, and technicians, they all rested for a quiet moment. Melanie and Desmond relaxed on a bench, his legs stretched out, with his arms extended across the back of the windowsill. He sat close to Melanie.

Her eyes were closed, and her head lay back across his shoulders while they slept. Lacey cleared her throat and smiled at them. Desmond stirred a little and rubbed the stubble on his chin. He stretched, glanced over at Melanie's head on his shoulder, and his eyes grew wide.

Lacey chuckled.

He shifted a bit, removing his arm carefully from under Melanie's head.

She blinked, and her eyes went round too. Her face flushed red, and she straightened, mumbling an apology for dozing off.

He smiled back as their eyes lingered on one another.

"Thanks so much, Desmond. I don't know how we would have gotten through the night without you."

"Well, Tina and Captain Jack are your heroes. And God. With or without us, you have Him, and He got you both through this. And it will be Him that continues to do so."

Lacey stared, warmth rising from her toes to the top of her sore head. Gosh, how she liked having him in their lives right now. A permanent part would be nice, and yet, she knew that what he said was true. It was God. With or without Pastor Brooks, it was always God.

Desmond wiped the wetness from Melanie's cheek and took her hand. "Mel, I'm sorry about all this." He took a deep breath. "I know we can't help but wonder how or why this all happened, but I'm trusting that we'll get to the bottom of it. He paused again. "And I'm here for you. Anything you need. Anything at all."

Their gazes locked. It was a moment frozen in time, and Lacey felt like she was watching a romantic movie, and the screen was panning up close on their faces. But this was her mom. She wanted to scream with joy.

"Knock knock," a voice interrupted. "Blood draw."

Are you kidding me? Lacey let out an exasperated sigh. A person in blue scrubs, holding a caddy full of blood vials, walked over to Lacey. She shooed him off and whispered, "Not now."

Both Melanie and Desmond turned. They laughed and dropped hands.

He stood, shoving his hands into his pockets. "Uh, I'm going to head home. I'll let you two have some alone time."

"Can you come back?" asked Lacey.

Melanie gave her a look. "Lacey, we may be going home today."

"Well, he can come over then, right?"

Desmond's dark eyes shined as he beamed. "Sure thing."

Lacey gave him thumbs up.

Melanie and Lacey took the quiet time to pray together. That trust Desmond spoke of seemed to be there. The rest of the afternoon, the girls spent what seemed like hours just holding onto one another. They didn't talk; there would be plenty of time for that later. Finding an old black and white movie on the hospital TV's limited channels, Melanie climbed in bed with Lacey. They dozed, not really listening, just gazing at the screen.

Hours later, the doctor popped in, and much to Lacey's disappointment, he announced that he was keeping her overnight. He pulled Melanie aside, but Lacey could hear their conversation. The doctor said that there appeared to be a little swelling on her brain, and he wanted to monitor it. He seemed to assure Melanie that it wasn't too serious.

"Thank you, doctor." Melanie held the door after him. "Hey, Lacey, I'm going to get a coffee … Oh, never mind." She walked back to her daughter.

"Mom, go. I'm fine." Leaning back, Lacey closed her eyes.

Lacey didn't sleep much before Pastor Brooks popped back in.

"Hey, Lacey." He looked around. "Where's your mom?"

"She went for coffee."

He handed her a gift. "I brought you a little something."

Lacey took it and ripped open the package. Holding up a book, she read, "*One Year Book of Hymns.*"

"I wanted to give you something to help put your mind at rest. Did you know hymns are like theology set to music?"

Lacey thumbed through the book. The lyrics to a hymn were printed on one page and, on the facing page, a short biography of the author who wrote it.

"Many of those hymns were written after hardships and tragedies." Pastor Brooks stood by her bedside with his hands in his front pockets. "My wife's pastor gave me a copy, and it helped me through my roughest times when she passed away."

It was the first time Lacey had ever heard him mention his wife. She glanced at the book and placed it next to a Bible that Tina had brought. "I'll read it, but you'll have to come over and translate the thees and thous."

Pastor Brooks laughed, and Lacey drew strength from his presence. She couldn't help but think how he seemed to have played a father's protective role. Suddenly, she wanted Chris there.

After a heated argument with Stella, Chris decided to stay at a casino in Albuquerque, New Mexico. Not eager to get back to her, he enjoyed drinking with a beautiful young woman in the bar. Her long, blonde hair swung loose across her tanned back. A tight, shimmering, backless gold dress, coupled with five-inch platform heels, turned heads. As usual, Chris was the one who got the girl. He'd just met her, and they were ready to enjoy the night drinking and dancing. But a phone call intruded on his plans.

"Be right back."

He raised a finger and arched a brow, asking her to stay put. Chris blew her a kiss for extra insurance, and she tipped her head down as her large, brown eyes teased him back. He walked out of the bar into the lobby, shaking his head as he pulled out his phone, not looking at the screen. He knew who it was, and he knew he had to talk to them. For the first time in his life, he worried about his family.

Other than an unpleasant feeling, he didn't know why he had quit working for them. He made more money representing this client than any other he'd ever worked with. It was easy money, too. His brand-new BMW was evidence of that.

Chris did all the leg work, and his contented clients wanted more.

His forte was knowing what his clients were looking for and finding just the right piece of real estate. Chris was an expert in bank-owned and foreclosed properties. This was why these particular clients liked him, and the financial institutions welcomed his business. Since a short escrow was imperative to his clients, he wrote over-priced cash offers, which were eagerly accepted. His clients were more than generous with closing bonuses on top of his commission, no less. Maybe too generous. That's what tipped him off. Something didn't seem right, and even though he didn't have that strong of conscience, he'd followed his hunch on this one.

Now to get these guys off my back ... and Mel's. He decided to return their calls, settling this once and for all. They could find someone else. Before he dialed, his cell rang again, and as he glanced at it, he smiled.

"Hey, Mel, baby, what's up?"

Melanie started to speak, but the more she said, the more he heard her voice shake, and she sobbed. She gulped out words. *What was she saying?* Chris's face contorted, and his heart rate quickened. He began drilling Melanie with so many questions, she couldn't possibly answer him. With all his yelling and interrupting, she went silent, and he heard quiet sobs. Taking a deep breath, he reacted with a forceful reply.

"You know what? I'm on my way." And then, before hanging up, he changed his tone and asked, "Mel, how is she? How's my baby girl?"

Chris had never called Lacey his baby girl.

"She's fine, Chris. She's doing better than me right now."

"Hang in there, Mel," was all he could manage to say. He clicked off.

The lobby seemed to spin around him, and his heart pounded, and Chris felt something he'd not often experienced before. Guilt? Anger rose, but he had nowhere to direct it.

Anxiety built, and he couldn't brush it off. He slammed his palm against a marble pillar, and a security guard moved toward him. Chris took a deep breath, raising his hands in surrender. The guard stopped, and Chris turned around, rubbing his palm across his forehead and fixing his eyes on the bar. The music pulsed and a mirror ball light flickered from the dance floor. His head was reeling. Chris tended to act rashly when faced with emotional situations so close to his heart. Often, he gave in to escape mode, as he had many times in the past. This time was no different, and he gravitated back to the bar. Just a drink to clear his head.

By this time, the beautiful blonde had moved on. The DJ had slowed the tempo, and the room darkened as couples moved to the enticing melody. Searching the room, Chris found his date dancing intimately with a man younger than he on the crowded floor. Ordering a drink, he sat and contemplated what to do.

He felt a hot flush rise within him, and he swallowed his drink with one swig. How could this happen? How could Melanie wait so long to call? Everything happened so fast. Giving her the benefit of the doubt, he reasoned that she just forgot. *Forgot? That's a joke. I wasn't even a thought.* Chris berated himself with the guilt of being a rotten father.

Fingering the empty glass, he rapped it on the counter. He stared off through the bar into the lobby, and his eyes stopped on a family checking in. He assumed it was a family. A father, a mother, and young girls. The girls skipped and clapped as the father guided his family to the elevators. The family embraced one another lovingly as they waited.

Chris huffed loudly, and a moment later, he squared his shoulders and walked to the concierge's desk. He made arrangements to park his car in long-term parking and managed to book a red-eye flight out that evening. He'd be in Bay Town by midnight.

When his plane landed, Chris grabbed his duffle bag and strode to the curb. The smell of jet fuel mingled with the dampness of the chilly night. He shivered a little as he looked around. He'd call for an Uber, but he doubted this small town had the service. Before he could pull out his cell, a cab pulled up. Reaching for the door handle, he heard a voice behind him. Chris glanced back, and a loud, yelling woman dragging a black bag was waving her arms at him.

"Hey? Can I share the cab?"

Throwing his bag in the back seat, he opened the front door to climb in. Up to accommodating, if it didn't put him out, he turned. "Sure. Where you …" His voice trailed off.

The woman stopped short. "Chris? What are you doing here?"

Chris's shoulders dropped as he stared at Charlene, Melanie's sister. Tipping his head, he answered, "Charlene? Come on." He rolled his eyes. "I'm here the same as you. I'm still Lacey's dad, you know."

The cab driver yawned and pounded the passenger seat, motioning for his clients to get moving.

"Start your meter, buddy, and hold your horses." Chris grabbed Charlene's bag. "Get in, Charlene. Let's go."

Charlene had booked a late flight from D.C. Unlike Chris, though, she had received a call from Melanie early in the morning but couldn't get a direct flight any sooner. The information didn't sit well with Chris and put him in a worse mood than when his trip began. Charlene told him to get over it and to focus on his daughter and Melanie.

"It's not always about you, Chris," said Charlene.

He knew she was right. That was the guilt that riddled his mind. Charlene was the opposite. In a word, reliable. They both remained silent for the rest of the ride.

Arriving at the hospital, they found Lacey safe and well

taken care of. And loved. Wow, was she loved! Colorful Mylar balloons dotted the room, and candy and plush animals covered her tray. The smell of roses was in the air as vases of flowers graced the windowsill.

When they walked in, Melanie and Lacey looked up, and the tears flooded again.

"Shouldn't you be sleeping?" Charlene dropped her bags and embraced her sister.

Chris knew that Charlene was the rock that dispensed a quiet calm under challenging circumstances, not only to Lacey but also to Melanie. As feisty as Charlene was, her motherly nature kicked in, and she could be the most soothing person in times of crisis.

Chris went to Lacey, hugged her, and kissed the top of her head. He at least felt welcomed by his daughter. It was a wonderful feeling.

Everyone whispered casually about the events of the day. It was late, and Chris took care not to upset Lacey, but when Melanie said that Lacey wasn't sleeping well, he asked about sleeping aids.

Melanie explained that she was forgoing sedatives … at least for now.

It bothered Chris that he didn't have a say-so in Lacey's care. "Listen, why don't I move in with you guys just 'til Lacey's on her feet."

Melanie's eyes grew wide as saucers.

Charlene laughed out loud. "Wow! That would really help things."

Melanie shook her head and said nothing. Chris felt it spoke volumes.

The nurses assured Chris that Lacey's concussion was slight, with only minor complications. They told him she was faring well and would soon be allowed to return home. After hugs all around, Charlene coaxed Chris into buying her a bite to eat in the cafeteria.

"It's one in the morning!"

Charlene dragged him out of the room.

Stepping into the hospital cafeteria, the lack of windows accentuated the artificial light casting an even green hue—less than inviting for a dining atmosphere. Their options were slim at that time of night. Charlene grabbed a sandwich from the refrigerated section, and Chris stared at her.

"What? Too expensive for your budget?" Charlene asked.

"No. Not at all. But that's turkey you got there. Aren't you a vegetarian or something?"

Charlene dropped her shoulders and tipped her head. "Vegan. It's vegan, Chris. And yes. But I fall off the wagon when I'm stressed." Charlene grabbed a large cup and filled it with soda.

"Wow. You are off the wagon. Coke too?" Chris winked.

"Shut up, Chris."

Chris laughed and paid for her meal. The banter was fun, and Charlene got along well with Chris. He got a kick out of annoying her to no end, and she loved to comment that he had no purpose in life other than making money. But he won her over with his sanguine personality. Much like he did with most people.

As Charlene made faces over the bagged sandwich, they conversed about Lacey's incident. She also told him about her work and involvement in fighting against human trafficking.

"Yeah, Melanie told me about that." He opened his eyes wide. "Wait a minute. Is that what this is about with Lacey?"

Charlene shrugged. "Nah. Shouldn't be." But her face didn't match the body language. Firing off questions, Chris was determined to know more about Charlene's work.

She told him about her blog, and he promised to read it.

"Since when did you start reading anything besides sports?"

A fair question. Uncharacteristically, Chris marveled at the wealth of information that Charlene uncovered. When she mentioned the ring in New Orleans, he felt an uneasiness that he couldn't quite put the finger on. He thought of the constant phone calls he'd been receiving of late from his former top client. Their base of operations was in New Orleans. He shuddered at the thought that he might have an inadvertent hand in something shady. Taking it all in, his stomach knotted, and he didn't like it. Typically whenever he came close to feeling like this, he ran. But thoughts of the harm Lacey had been through made his blood boil. How could it happen to her? Why her?

"Chris? Hello? You aren't interested in all this, are you?"

Chris focused his eyes on his ex-sister-in-law and smiled a charming grin. "Well, that's my baby girl up there, ya know?"

Charlene finished her meal, and they returned to Lacey's room. Melanie lay sleeping across a bench, covered with a light blanket, and Lacey seemed to be in a deep sleep.

Chris stared at his family and whispered, "I think I'll stay."

Charlene whispered back. "I think you'll not. Come on. I'll get a cab and drop you at a hotel."

"Wait. Drop me off? Where are you staying?"

Melanie stirred, and Charlene shushed him as she answered. "Me? I'm going to Melanie's." Charlene smiled and raised a house key. "And you're not."

CHAPTER 21

Before Chris could protest, Charlene grabbed his arm and pulled him into the hallway.

"Whoa!"

Charlene almost bumped into Desmond. Raising a tray carrying two hot drinks, not from the hospital, he stepped back.

Charlene whispered, "Shhhh," and motioned him to follow.

Walking into the lobby, Desmond looked at her and said, "Charlene? Mel's sister, right?"

Charlene narrowed her eyes, then opened them wide. "Oh, yes. It's been a long time. Wow, you have an excellent memory. Do you remember all your church visitors?"

Desmond laughed and shrugged. "Just the special ones." He glanced at Chris, and his face turned red.

"Well, thanks so much for taking care of Mel and Lacey. Mel said you've been a big help."

Desmond shook his head. "Oh, no. There have been a lot of us here today. It's been a big group effort."

Chris frowned and narrowed his eyes as he stretched his body to stand a little taller.

"Well, thanks anyway. Melanie and Lacey are sleeping

now, but I could sure use a strong cup of coffee. Not that hospital junk." Charlene reached for a cup from Desmond.

Desmond extended his free hand. "I'm Desmond Brooks. Friend of Mel and Lacey's. Are you from D.C., too?"

Chris drew his lips into a thin line and straightened his shoulders. Gripping Desmond's hand, he answered, "Chris Thompson, Lacey's dad." Thrusting his head up and chin out, he added, "And Mel's husband."

Charlene choked on her drink and sputtered out, "This isn't coffee." Then glaring at Chris, she continued, "And you are not Mel's husband. Pastor, this is Mel's ex."

"Oh, sorry. It's hot chocolate," said Desmond. "For the girls."

"The girls?" Chris glared.

Both men stood a few moments with hands clasped. An awkward silence followed.

Desmond cleared his throat. "Nice to meet you, Chris. I'm sure Lacey's glad to have you here." He sounded genuine, but Chris didn't see it that way and challenged.

"Oh, and Mel's not?"

"Really? Chris. Come on," Charlene yelled.

Pointing a direct finger into Desmond's chest with a few jabs, Chris quipped, "The girls are sleeping. Best you go home, too, pal."

Charlene rolled her eyes and tugged at Chris's sleeve. "Desmond, here, is a man of God, Chris. I'm tired. Let's go."

Looking from Charlene back to Desmond, Chris squared his shoulders. "What does that even mean?"

Pulling him down the hallway, she called out to Desmond, "See you in the morning."

"What? He's coming back? Who is that guy?" Chris peppered Charlene with questions and threw up his hands at her silence.

Desmond stared after them. Tossing the other cup of cocoa in the trash, he placed his hands in his pockets and looked up as he said aloud, "Yes, God, what does this all mean?"

The doctors kept Lacey one more night, and early Tuesday morning, a young man stood in the hallway. He wrote notes, asking the names of visitors coming and going from Lacey's room. When Charlene arrived to give Melanie a rest, he approached her.

"Hey, just wondering, do you know what happened to the girl in that room?" He pointed.

Charlene narrowed her eyes. "Are you serious? Go talk to the police and leave us alone."

"And you are?" His pen poised above a notepad.

Chris, who had arrived even earlier, stepped out of Lacey's room and encountered Charlene berating the man.

"Charlene, what's up? Give the guy a break." Chris smiled.

The man jotted Charlene's name and smiled back at Chris as if to say thank you.

"Shut up, Chris. This nosey guy is a reporter. No compassion or sense of decency at all."

Throwing glaring looks at the bearded man with glasses, she added, "I bet you work for some trashy tabloid."

Again scribbling on his pad, he wrote Chris's name. The so-called reporter paid no attention to Charlene.

"Really? Hey, buddy. Leave her alone. You can read it on her blog. At least you'll know what the facts are." Chris puffed out his chest in a threatening gesture.

Smirking, the man's face lit up. "Blog? What's the name of your blog?"

"None of your business blog," Charlene yelled back.

A uniformed woman walked up. "Sir? You'll have to leave. You're causing a disturbance."

"Wouldn't want to do that." Tipping his pen to his brow, he smiled as he complied.

Automatic double doors slid apart. Perusing the parking lot, the reporter stopped and looked around as if he didn't know where the vehicle was. Panning to the far lot, he saw headlights flash off and on. Walking through the myriad of cars, he opened the door of a blue sedan.

"What'd you find out?" The driver wore a gray fedora and sunglasses.

The young man stared at the disguise and laughed. "Apparently, the daughter was attacked. I'm guessing your guys tried to take her, but it sounds like she remembers nothing. Maybe they hit her or something?"

"Idiots. They were just supposed to scare her." Boudreaux pulled off his sunglasses and pulled out his wallet. Handing the man a few large bills, he waved him out. "Go on."

"Sure. Let me know if you need me again." He waved the money and exited the car.

After spending the night at the hospital with Lacey, Melanie finally got a chance to go home and freshen up. Chris and Charlene had shown up early and shooed her home to get some sleep. *Hah! Fat chance of that.*

The unknown that happened with Lacey was unsettling, to say the least. Walking in her front door, Melanie closed it behind her and leaned against it. All strength left her, and she slumped to the floor. In the quiet of her home, she tensed at an uncertain stillness. A sense of fear and furtive unrest clouded her mind. What was happening?

The calm and tranquility she'd found in Bay Town dissipated. The haven of peace after losing her parents disappeared. A blind, unreasoning panic tried to take control. Questions clouded her mind as Melanie drew up her legs and curled herself in a ball. A silent scream escaped her lips. *Dear Jesus, help me.* Her tears fell, and in her head, she heard the words, "The steadfast love of the Lord never ceases."

Her body was wracked with pain by an invisible force. Turning toward the bay window, the golden rays of the morning sun warmed her face. "His mercies never come to an end. They are new every morning." She breathed deep and stood, finding the strength to shower and change.

The long, hot shower was just what she needed. Still wrapped in her white terry-cloth robe, she dropped onto her bed, then laid down and fell sound asleep. Thirty minutes later, her cell rang.

Startled, she fumbled to find her purse. "Hello?" Melanie answered. Not recognizing the number, she heard an unfamiliar shaky voice on the other end and asked, "Who is this, please?"

"I'm sorry, Mel. It's Carol." There was a lengthy pause. "Mel, I was just wondering if you'd found out anything more about Grady?"

Melanie was silent. *Doesn't she know what happened to Lacey? She's worried about Grady?* Maybe Carol hadn't heard.

"Anything more?" Melanie asked.

"I know you was suspicious about him, and I just wondered if you found anything else out? For sure, I mean." Carol's voice hesitated.

"I haven't had a chance. Lacey had an accident, and I've been at the hospital."

"What?" Carol gasped. "I'm so sorry. Is she all right? I better get over there."

"She's fine for now. I'll tell you about it later, but is something wrong?" Melanie pinched the bridge between her eyes.

"Grady's missing," Carol blurted. "We were supposed to head out of town for the weekend, and he went to the bank and never showed up again."

"When Carol? When was that?"

"Friday night. I waited for him all weekend, and he never showed."

"Did you call the police?"

Carol chuckled. "What for? They'd just laugh at me. It wasn't like he was really my boyfriend or anything."

Melanie didn't think her heart could hurt more, but it did. Carol's sorrow gripped her. She didn't care about Grady, but she cared about her friend.

"Carol, I'll stop by the police station and see if they saw Grady around or something." Melanie breathed deep, and her heart ached for Carol. What a horrible feeling. Rejection.

"Oh, no need. I guess I can call." Carol chuckled. "I'll suck it up and take the shame."

"No, my sister's with Lacey, and I need to talk to Chief Bert, anyway. Don't worry." She paused. "Carol. There's an answer. There always is." And hard as it was, she added, "I'll be praying for Grady. And for you, too."

"Thank you, Mel. And I'll send my good thoughts for Lacey, too."

Good thoughts aren't enough. We need lots of prayers, thought Melanie. Instead, she said, "Thank you, Carol. I'll call you later."

Melanie threw off her robe and got dressed. Driving downtown, she pulled in front of the police station, parked, and entered.

Officer Blaine looked up. "Hello, Mrs. Thompson. How's your daughter?"

"Lacey is being released today. Thank you for asking. Any news on the whole incident?"

"Sorry, ma'am. Just what we got from Captain Jack and your neighbor." He nodded. "When your daughter is up to it, we need to talk to her."

"Yes, of course. Will Chief Bert be back anytime soon?"

"Just went out to lunch, ma'am. Anything I can do for you?"

Clutching the strap of her cross-body purse, Melanie glanced around. She started to speak then halted mid-sentence. Her eyes fixed on a community bulletin board. Tacked up was a "Wanted, Person of Interest" poster. Melanie's legs wobbled a bit. The image on the poster resembled Grady.

"Ma'am? Ma'am, are you ok?" Standing, Officer Blaine started over.

Shaking her head, she spun around. Her voice shook. "This man. Do you know him?"

Officer Blaine tipped his head and gave her a sideways glance. "The question might be, do you know him?"

Melanie sat down. "Yes. Yes, I do. He was in town, but now he's gone."

Officer Blaine's picked up his pen. "Go on."

She explained all she knew about Grady and Carol. She told Officer Blaine that he was from Jackson, Mississippi, and he was the boyfriend of the mother of a young teen that got abducted from there. Normally, Melanie might throw all her accusations out there, backed by her assumptions. But she slowed herself down and tried to speak objectively. She knew the restraint she was exhibiting was not her own. She put Carol and even Grady above her judgments. It was almost supernatural, and she was thankful for it as she spoke.

"Well, I think I'll call the chief, and he'll probably pay Ms. Carol a visit real soon."

"Is there any way I could be there when he does? I mean, she's my friend, and I'd like to be there for her."

"Sure, I'll call you. Thanks, Ms. Thompson, and thanks for being forthright. It sure helps."

Melanie smiled back, but her shoulders remained slumped.

Arriving at the hospital, Melanie walked through the parking lot, appreciating the light breeze. Looking up, she smiled as Desmond approached. His greeting felt strange, and his attention seemed elsewhere. The growing closeness she'd felt with him over the past few days was missing.

"Good morning." He looked right through her. "Did you get some rest?" he asked without so much as a hug or a friendly pat.

"A little." She searched his eyes. "Hey, Desmond. Thanks for being here with Lacey. You've been a big help." She shrugged and smiled. "To both of us."

He didn't respond.

"Anyway, how about you? What time did you leave?" Melanie hoped for something. Warmth, closeness, anything.

"Late. I left late. You and Lacey were sleeping." He shifted. "I ran into Charlene and your husband in the lobby."

Melanie bristled. "Ex-husband."

Desmond nodded and shoved his hands in his front pockets. "Yes. Well, I'm sure you're both glad that Lacey's dad is back."

"Wait. Did you talk to Chris last night?" Melanie tipped her head.

"Mel ... he—"

"He nothing, Desmond. He's Lacey's father, that's all." She wanted to say more, but he wouldn't look at her.

"You know, I think he's needed right now. That family bond is something God created, and man messed up. Chris may have blown it before, but he's here now, and he wants to help."

Melanie wanted to cover her ears. She wanted to yell at him to stop. Chris was no help to anyone but himself. She peered into Desmond's eyes. Was he bowing out? A wind blew, and Melanie shivered. She just wanted Desmond's arms around her. Instead, he stepped back.

"You may not trust him now, but you can trust God. Maybe God will use Lacey's dad. Maybe it's his time." Desmond still couldn't seem to look her in the eyes.

She didn't answer, and the silence was piercing, like the look she gave him. She closed her eyes and blinked them open. He stared back at her, and his furrowed brow betrayed a struggle. He looked as if he wanted to say something but couldn't—or wouldn't—as if he was going against his own heart. Melanie felt the confusion and remained silent.

Shaking his head, he ran his fingers through his hair. "I don't know, Mel. I mean, if Chris wants to help, maybe you should let him. Everyone deserves a second chance."

Melanie's eyes grew cold, and she wanted to scream, *What about me? What about us? Don't we deserve a chance?*

"Okay. Well, thanks." She backed away and turned, leaving him standing in the parking lot without protest.

Melanie walked into Lacey's room and eyed all the bouquets. Stepping to the windowsill, she breathed deep, hoping the flowers would cheer her.

"Hey, sweetie," Tina called out. "Want a mani?" Tina sat bedside, painting Lacey's nails. Bottles of nail polish covered the utility tray.

Melanie pulled a card from a spray of flowers. "Keep trusting God." She didn't need to read the name. She knew who it was from.

Replacing the card, she turned and asked, "So where's your dad?"

"Who knows? I mean, I guess he's in the cafeteria with

Aunt Charlene. They were here earlier, and there was a shouting match in the hallway." Lacey held her hands up, admiring the glittery polish on her nails. "Oh, Tina, I love that color."

"Shouting match? Your dad and Charlene?" Melanie's purse slipped off her shoulder.

"I don't know. Wait a minute. You were still here, sleeping. It must have been last night or early this morning. You don't remember?"

"No. Not at all."

"I thought I heard Pastor Brooks's voice. You know him. Maybe he calmed everyone down?" Lacey frowned. "Or maybe I was just dreaming."

Melanie rubbed her hands over her face and felt another crack in her heart. Just then, a loud voice boomed. "Hey, there, Supergirl."

All eyes turned.

"Oh, hi, Chris … I mean, Dad. Mom was just going to look for you."

"Well, here I am, baby. What can I do for you?"

Under her breath, Mel seethed. "You've done enough." Then out loud, she added, "Nothing, Chris. Absolutely nothing."

Chris opened his eyes wide and threw up his hands. He looked at Tina. "Whaaat? What'd I do now?"

Tina waved a nail file in his direction and cooed, "Oh, honey, it's what you don't do. Now come over here. I'll give you a man's mani." Tina winked at Melanie and waved her off.

In the hallway, Melanie ran into her sister.

"I can't believe those low-life scum that call themselves journalists!" Charlene waved her arms as her voice escalated while relating the entire "reporter" incident to Melanie.

Ignoring Charlene's tirade, Melanie asked, "Char, did Desmond and Chris talk this morning?"

Charlene shook her head. "What?"

"This morning. Did Chris and Desmond speak?"

"This morning? No." Charlene squinted.

Melanie bit her lip.

"Oh, yes. I guess it was this morning, like one o'clock a.m. You were sleeping."

Melanie closed her eyes and pinched the bridge of her nose. "I figured as much."

"Listen, are you hungry? Come on, let's get some lunch downstairs."

Melanie followed Charlene through the lobby and stopped at a coffee vending machine. Charlene stared at the machine and frowned. "Uh, no."

They passed a sign pointing to the hospital chapel, and Melanie stopped again.

"Want to go in?" Charlene asked.

Staring at the red, green, and blue stained-glass panels on either side of the oak doors, Melanie stepped forward, and Charlene followed.

The small, newly-remodeled chapel had four short pews that sat in front of a plain wooden altar. A serene atrium with a few green plants rose behind it, and a colorful impressionist painting of the Garden of Gethsemane hung on one wall. On the opposite, the Resurrection of Christ. Melanie stared at one of the images. She stepped closer, and Charlene followed.

"Well, that's really comforting," whispered Charlene.

Melanie stared at the mural. "Yes. Yes, it is, isn't it?"

"I was being sarcastic. But to each his own. I'll wait outside."

Melanie's eyes fixed on *The Garden of Gethsemane.* Somehow, the suffering of Jesus while praying for deliverance brought her comfort. He knew what was coming. And yet, He still trusted God.

CHAPTER 22

L acey was finally released on Tuesday afternoon, and Melanie drove her car up to the hospital entrance. Lacey stepped out of the customary wheelchair for discharged patients and lifted her face to the bright sunshine, smiling. Melanie hugged her daughter, helping her into the front seat, and squeezed the nurse's hand before leaving.

When they arrived home, Lacey went straight to her room. Melanie didn't want to push her, but Lacey still hadn't talked about the incident. Chief Bert was pressing for her recollection, but she insisted she had none.

The spoon in Melanie's mug clinked as her sister sat across the table, sipping her coffee. Melanie continued to stir many minutes after she'd poured the cream. She stared at nothing.

"So, any thoughts on what actually happened?" Charlene asked.

"No. I can't figure it out. Lots of weird stuff going on."

"Yeah, you can say that again." Charlene glanced around the kitchen. "You got any muffins or anything? Something sweet?"

"No." She narrowed her eyes at her sister. "You know the wedding I did on Sunday? This strange guy came up to me and offered me a wedding referral."

"Well, it was a wedding. Maybe he liked your work. You're the best, sis."

"It's a huge referral. But this guy came out of nowhere. He said he was there representing friends of the bride. Anyway, he wasn't the same guy that gave me the business card last week." Melanie frowned.

"What business card? What are you talking about?" Charlene glanced at the kitchen counters. "Are you sure you have nothing sweet? Let's go get a pastry or something."

Melanie rubbed her temple. "Everything happened so fast with Lacey. I didn't have time to fill you in." She thought for a minute, not wanting to tell her sister about her financial problems. "Chris said he had a referral for me. Like months ago."

"Let me guess? It didn't come through. Surprise, surprise." Charlene rolled her eyes.

"You got that right, sort of. A week ago, Chris said he didn't have a good feeling about the client and left it at that. Wouldn't give me the name or anything, but I got an address. He's maybe the richest guy in New Orleans!" Melanie wondered if she was exaggerating. "Anyway, about thirty minutes after I spoke with Chris, a stranger walked up to me on the street and hands me a business card. It's the same address as the client that Chris had mentioned earlier, and the guy tells me to call."

Charlene shrugged. "Oh. So he did come through. It's about time."

"But he didn't. He said he knew nothing about it and told me not to call. And why was this guy in town? It's creepy, Charlene."

"Okay, so it sounds like a weird scenario, but Chris is weird. Maybe he wanted to surprise you, and this was his partner or something?"

Melanie shook her head. "No. He was pretty adamant that I not call. And then I get approached again, days later, at a wedding, I'm coordinating? The guy seemed professional, non-threatening. Still, though, he was insistent. Anyway, I said I'd call." She stared at her sister. "I thought I'd take the job, but now with Lacey and all this stuff, I'm not so sure."

Charlene sat up straight. Her eyes bored into her sister. "Melanie, do you remember the guy back in California … ?"

"Yes. I told you that. The one who came to my door asking for Chris?" Melanie shrugged. "But that was only once. Mom and Dad died, I moved out here; it never happened again."

"But now it's starting again. Well, not at your door, but at your workplace." Charlene threw her arms up. "Sis. It's Chris. It's got to be his work or something. Maybe you shouldn't call. At least not yet. Maybe, just this once, we should listen to him."

You too? Melanie rolled her eyes, thinking of how Desmond wanted her to let Chris in her life. Like give him some control or something. Like he mattered. And now her sister.

"But, sis, this job could launch my career."

"Well, it never hurts to wait. Isn't that what Dad always said? But, then again, he waited on God like you do."

"Knock-knock!" A voice, interrupting their conversation, cooed at the kitchen screen door. "Hey, girls, I bought some gourmet muffins." The screen opened, and orange, high-heeled shoes stepped in.

Charlene jumped up. "Tina! You read my mind." She held open the door, and the smell of the fresh-baked goods filled the kitchen. Tina carried in a long, rectangular box resembling something long-stemmed roses were delivered in, and Charlene reached for the container.

"Oh, girl. You're a lifesaver. I'm dying here. Melanie has no sugar." Charlene opened the box and grabbed one, mumbling through a mouthful of crumbs.

Melanie rolled her eyes.

"So, Mellie, I was thinking. Let's throw a welcome home party for Lacey." Tina raised her brows excitedly.

Melanie and Charlene stared at Tina.

Tina placed a hand on her hip. "Okay, how about a get-well party, then? Come on!"

Tina was great at entertaining, and Melanie had a gift for hospitality. She thought a party was just what she and Lacey needed.

———

Two days later, Lacey felt well enough and had jumped at the idea. Melanie was surprised at how her daughter seemed to bounce back, so the party was on in Melanie's home. Tina got everyone together, and Melanie insisted on doing all the cooking as a thank you to her friends.

Sitting in the comfy living room, the guests gathered. They were as eclectic as the mix of love seats, benches, and ottomans. Melanie brought in a few dining chairs, too, so the seating was ample.

She stepped out of the kitchen wearing a pink-and-white checked apron with a flower-patterned ruffle along the hem. If it wasn't for the jeans underneath, she was the picture of a fifties housewife.

Tina gave her a sideways glance and pointed. "Love the apron!"

Melanie smiled and clapped her hands. "Okay, everyone. We have hamburgers, cheeseburgers, potato salad, chips, watermelon, corn-on-the-cob, and English trifle with raspberries and peaches. And Lacey's yummy brownies." Melanie looked around, avoiding Desmond's gaze.

Chief Bert and Lina stood. Joe and Lyla, Tina, and Rudy followed.

"Hey, sounds like a Fourth of July picnic," bellowed Chief Bert. "God bless America. That about covers it, right, Pastor?"

Desmond laughed. "Not quite." Gazing at Melanie, he

opened his mouth but stopped. Everyone stood around, staring at one another, awkwardly.

Joe finally spoke up. "Hey, Pastor? Why don't you bless the food?"

Melanie smiled at Joe and nodded. Standing, the group formed a circle and joined hands as they bowed their heads. The warmth in the room flooded through the group.

"Father God, we are so grateful for Your loving, saving grace, especially on Lacey this week. Thank you for each person here. We ask Your blessing on each one. We ask Your blessing on this impressive spread before us, and we ask Your blessing on Melanie for preparing such a great feast. And all God's people said—"

"Amen," yelled a strange voice coming from the front porch. Everyone dropped hands and looked up. Captain Jack stood behind the screen.

Chief Bert, standing closest to the front door, opened it to let him in.

Though disheveled as ever, Captain Jack looked like he'd made an effort to tamper down his wild hair and beard. His grin spread across his face as he stood holding a large burlap bag. A wiggling burlap bag. "Fresh catch," he yelled.

Tina and Lyla screamed, both jumping behind their husbands. Melanie stood frozen, but Lacey ran over and grabbed the bag. "Thanks, Cap'n, Jack. Glad you could make it. Come on in."

Lacey took the bag and ran through the kitchen to the back door. She stopped. The white cooler sat in the carport, but she hesitated at going out.

"Hey, princess!" A voice called from the other side of the screen.

Lacey pushed open the door. "Chris!" She threw her arms around him, the bag hitting his back.

"Ouch!" He pulled back and took the bag. "What do you have in there? Baby Godzilla?" He peeked in. "Whoa! I was close, wasn't I?" Opening the cooler, he placed the bag in it.

"Did Mom invite you?"

"Invite me? To what?" He pointed inside. "I saw a crowd by the front door when I drove by, so I thought I'd slip in the back."

Lacey peeked out. "Drove by? You were just stopping to see me?" Lacey beamed. "So, where's your car?"

He yanked a thumb. "I parked it down the street. Too many in the carport here." His brows furrowed. "You having a party or something?"

Lacey stared at her dad's sad face. "Tina planned a little get together, and Mom hosted."

Chris nodded. "Ahhh. Well …" He raised a hand and ruffled his bushy, blond hair.

"So …? I thought you were headed back to California or something."

Chris grabbed Lacey. "You're kidding, right?" He hugged her tight, lifting her off the porch step. "And leave my baby girl? I don't think so!"

"Lacey? What are you doing? We're all waiting for you," a voice came from inside.

Chris and Lacey walked inside as the screen door slammed behind them.

Melanie's mouth dropped open, and she stared at her ex-husband. "Where'd you come from?"

The room went silent, and everyone stood quietly around the little kitchen, a bounty of food spread over the tables.

"Wow! What a feast." Chris walked over and gave Melanie, side-arm hug. She stiffened, and he dropped his arm. The others shifted in place with plates in hand, and Desmond looked down.

Melanie's straightened. "In case anyone missed him at the hospital, this is Chris. Lacey's father." All smiled at the introduction. "My uh, my ex." She stumbled over the words.

Chris winked, slipped an arm around her waist, and pulled her close. "Gee, thanks. Didn't know you still cared."

Melanie yanked away, releasing herself from his grip, her eyes catching Desmond's as he watched it all.

Tina reached out to Chris, touching his arm. "Welcome, Chris, glad you could make it."

"Yeah. Nothing like a party crasher, eh?" Slapping and rubbing his hands together, he called out, "Well, let's eat."

After filling their plates, most everyone took seats in the living room. With all the commotion upon Chris's arrival, they seemed to have forgotten about Captain Jack. He stood, smiling, by himself. Lacey grabbed a plate and handed it to him.

Melanie winked at her daughter and turned her attention to Captain Jack. "How do you like your burgers? I have medium and well-done."

He shrugged and took a step closer. Melanie hid her surprise at the odor coming from him.

"Any way you make 'em. Thanks." He flashed a big grin. "I was getting a little tired of crabs every day."

Chris tapped Captain Jack on his shoulder. "So, Captain Jack? How do we know you?"

Lacey broke in. "Oh, he was out walking when I ..." Melanie turned to stare at Lacey. "When I fell. When I fell off the porch."

Captain Jack piled his plate high with more food than seemed possible to fit on the plate. He stopped to speak. "Yeah, dude. I saw some guys running away. I chased them down the street but couldn't catch them."

Chris looked sideways at Melanie. "Wait a minute. Guys running? From where?"

He looked at Lacey, as did Desmond, who was still in the kitchen. Lacey's brow furrowed, and she took a few steps back.

"Listen, Lacey, why don't you take Captain Jack and join the others," said Melanie.

"Come on, Captain Jack." He followed, and Lacey asked, "So how come they call you Captain Jack?" Her voice trailed off.

"Chris, we'll fill you in later. Here, grab a plate." Melanie shoved a white platter into his stomach.

"Ouch!" He glared. "Mel, why didn't I know about this? I thought she just tripped. "He shrugged. "Like she always does."

"She doesn't always, Chris. And we'll talk later. Lacey is safe. That's all that matters right now."

"Like heck it does! Seriously, Mel? You should have told me. A chase? Come on! I had no idea Lacey's life came down to "The Fast and the Furious." Chris's voice rose.

"Chris, please," Melanie pleaded.

Desmond, who was last to get food, set his empty plate on the counter and looked up. He drew a deep breath and walked to Chris.

"Oh, look, it's the man of God." Chris searched the room. "Speaking of which, where's Charlene?"

"What are you talking about? Charlene couldn't make it." Melanie's words were directed at Chris, but her eyes rested on Desmond.

He extended a hand. "Hello again, Chris."

Melanie didn't like this one bit. Both men, together, in the same room. She couldn't trust Chris's actions, and Desmond was already retreating from her life. Her body tensed.

"I guess things were a little stressed yesterday." Chris smiled. "Nice to meet you again, Des."

Melanie rolled her eyes. He was forever shortening

people's names and taking the "oh, we've been friends forever" attitude with everyone he met, seemingly, oblivious to whether they liked it or not.

"Well, it's good to meet Lacey's dad. She's an exceptional kid." One couldn't doubt the sincerity of Desmond's words.

Melanie let out a loud sigh and couldn't take her eyes off him. He stared back.

Chris narrowed his eyes as he glanced back and forth between the two of them. "Yeah. She's a great kid." He stood up straight. "But maybe she needs her dad to take better care of her." He glared at Melanie.

Desmond took a deep breath. His eyes continued to rest on Melanie. "Everything happened so fast. "He broke his gaze and looked at Chris. "Chief Bert has the most complete information. You might ask him."

"That's a good idea." Melanie looked at Chris. "But I'll tell you everything I know. Just don't bother Lacey." Melanie ushered him toward the food.

Chris grinned and said, "Wait a minute. Pastor Brooks? So you're a priest or something, right?" He slapped his forehead. "Whew. I thought for a minute there you were Melanie's new boyfriend or something." Chris laughed loudly.

Melanie and Desmond locked eyes. Melanie broke the gaze and looked at Chris.

He narrowed his eyes. "Ohhh. I see." Chris rubbed his chin, then pointed to Desmond. "But I thought you church fathers couldn't date or marry or anything."

"Chris!" Melanie yelled and pointed to the food. "Eat! Now."

Tina peeked her head into the kitchen. "Are you guys joining us or what?"

Desmond followed Tina, as did Melanie.

Chris filled his plate and yelled, "Yes, Mom!"

Standing as far away from Chris as she could, Melanie fidgeted in a corner. She pushed her food around her plate.

The evening returned to somewhat normal, and as everyone finished, Lacey stood.

"Well, goodnight all. I'm a little tired. Thanks for coming." She smiled and waved around the room.

Everyone waved back and wished her well as Lacey retreated down the hall. The room remained quiet until Lacey's door closed, then Chris stood.

"So, what now? What's being done? This is crazy. Why my baby girl? Chief Bert, you're law enforcement. What do we do now?" asked Chris.

Chief Bert held out his hands. "We need to talk to Lacey when she's ready. Only she knows what happened. She may have been attacked. We're just not sure."

"Whaaat! Are you kidding me?" Chris spun around.

"Sit down, Chris," Melanie whispered.

"Listen, Chris, I can give you a copy of what we've reported so far. Come by the office tomorrow." Chief Bert looked around the room. "I know it often seems like enough isn't being done."

"You're darn right not enough is being done." Chris glared at the chief.

"A lot is happening around here, and we're on it." The chief blinked long.

"Chief, did you know Virginia hasn't been on the bus or at school for four days now?" Joe spoke.

Breaths drew collectively, and the room went silent.

Melanie stared at Chief Bert. Her eyes widened, and her hand covered her mouth. "Four days?" She looked at Desmond, forgetting their rift. "Desmond, you stopped by Virginia's house on Friday."

He looked at Chief Bert, who spoke first.

"Look, we have an ongoing investigation. I know Virginia hasn't been at school. Officer Blaine is filing a missing person's report on her." Taking a deep breath, he blew out and lifted his hands. "Let us do our job."

"It's not enough!" Chris yelled.

The chief stood a head taller than Chris, but it didn't seem to intimidate him.

Desmond stepped between them. "Wait a minute, Chief. Maybe we as civilians can help."

Joe breathed deep. "He's right, Chief Bert—"

"Thank you!" Chris ran a hand through his hair.

Everyone talked at once. A loud but calm voice rose above the rest.

"Community Task Force," said Desmond. "We can start a community task force." Chief Bert protested, but Desmond raised his hand. "Hear me out, Chief. If we don't hinder the ongoing, official investigation, can't we meet and take some action? Phone calls, stakeouts, ask around, things like that? Kind of pool our information?"

Chief Bert scratched his head, and his brows wrinkled. "I am a little short-staffed for all this. Four days is a long time for a girl to be missing. And with what happened to Lacey?" He shook his head. "Yes. Yes. Let's do it. The sooner, the better. How about tomorrow evening?" He looked at Desmond. "Can we meet at the church?"

Desmond shook his head. "Sorry, Friday nights are youth group, and they have stuff going on."

"Okay, I'll check the high school. I'm sure we can get a room to meet there. I'll let everyone know. You can invite whoever will come."

Chris clapped his hands. "Wow. You guys don't waste any time. What can I do? I mean, I can't make the meeting, but …"

"Of course, you can't," Melanie added quietly.

Chris dropped his shoulders and threw up his hands. "Come on, Melanie. Give me a break here."

CHAPTER 23

The rift between Melanie and Chris hushed the room.

Joe stood and offered his hand to help his wife, Lyla, from the sofa. "Well, the meeting tomorrow is a good thing, but we gots to go. Our kids prob'ly got that babysitter all tied up by now. Melanie, thanks for having us." He wrapped his huge arms around her. So did Lyla.

Chris stepped forward. "Sorry, guys. Didn't mean to be the party killer. But thanks. And hey, Chief Bert, maybe I'll stop by the station tomorrow."

He slapped the chief on the back while shaking his hand and then turned to address Lina and Lyla. His smile glistened as he winked at the women. "Have a good evening, ladies. Nice meeting you both." He leaned out and waved as they headed through the doorway.

At the same time, Tina, Rudy, and Desmond rose to leave.

Chris clapped his hands together and said, "So, I'm tucking in my baby girl. Pleasure meeting you all again." He winked and walked down the hallway to Lacey's room.

Melanie watched as Desmond's eyes followed Chris. Tina and Rudy hugged her and left, and an uneasiness continued to permeate between Melanie and Desmond.

Desmond picked up a few dishes and took them into the

kitchen. Melanie followed. Placing the dishes in the sink, Desmond turned.

"Well, thank you for dinner, Melanie. It was a great evening."

Desmond held out his hand. Reaching for it, her heart dropped. With everyone gone, and the two of them all alone, she'd hoped that his demeanor would change. It didn't. She gripped his hand. "Desmond, Chris doesn't come into play here. I mean, he's not ... We're not..." Melanie stuttered. She thought her heart would crack.

Desmond's brow furrowed as he shook his head. Their hands still locked together, he gazed into Melanie's eyes.

"It's none of my business, Melanie." With one squeeze, he let go.

Melanie's heart raced as the cold air replaced his warm grip. A wisp of hair fell across her face, and she pushed it back. Desmond turned, but before he could say goodnight, Melanie blurted, "He's not staying here. I don't want you to think...He doesn't stay here...ever."

Desmond turned. . "Like I said, Melanie. It's none of my business."

Whispering, he added, "It'd be nice if it could be."

"What did you say?" Melanie's eyes widened, hopeful that she heard him correctly.

"Nothing. But Chris, he's Lacey's dad, Melanie, and it's critical for him to be in her life now, and that means in yours, too."

He shook his head and shoved his hands in his pockets, looking away.

She wanted to scream, *Look at me!*

He did. And for a moment, it seemed nothing could break their gaze. Melanie's heart pounded, and unspoken prayers pleaded within her. She didn't even know what groanings she offered up.

"Hey, these are great!"

The couple jumped. Their heads turned to the kitchen doorway. Captain Jack's mouth was stuffed with brownies, and he held one in each hand.

Desmond slowly walked over to the disheveled fisherman.

No! She wanted to yell.

Placing a hand on his shoulder, Desmond said, "Come on, Captain Jack. Let me give you a lift home." He pointed to the kitchen door. "My car is in the carport." He looked at Melanie and shrugged. "Parking was full on the street."

"Sounds good. Let's go! Beats walking back to my boat in the dark." Grinning at Melanie, Captain Jack tipped his worn knit beanie and said, "Thank you, ma'am. Best meal I've had in a looong time." With that, he turned and followed Desmond.

The screen door slammed, and Melanie stood in the kitchen all alone. Recalling that Desmond had expressed the same sentiments at the hospital, she felt utterly rejected. *No! He can't mean it*, she thought. She knew it was foolish, but desperation led to impulsive stupidity. She ran after him.

The rain dripped, and then a downpour drenched Melanie. She stood in front of Desmond's car, oblivious to the wet and cold. The engine purred down as Desmond shifted the car into park and stepped out.

As he walked toward her, she abandoned all rational thought and rushed at him, slipping into his arms. His hands gripped her shoulders, and she saw his jaw tighten.

"What are you doing out here, Melanie?" The darkness of his eyes matched his voice.

But the minute he said her name, everything seemed to soften. The tenseness in his hands relaxed, and the warmth of his touch gave her courage.

"Desmond, please. Can't we talk?"

His hands stroked her arms. And as if he couldn't stop himself, he breathed out the words, "You are so beautiful."

Their eyes locked as the water ran down their faces in

rivulets. The pounding of their heartbeats exploded above the crashing rain, and Melanie felt dizzy drinking in the scent of Desmond. Raising his hands, he cupped her face and stroked her cheeks with his thumbs, never taking his eyes off hers. As she stared back, the space between them diminished, and she could feel the rise and fall of his chest. His body so close to hers made her light-headed. Her arms enclosed his waist. Drawing her closer, his head eased down, and hers lifted up. He covered her lips with his own. Every atom inside exploded, and in that moment Melanie knew that nothing in her life had ever felt so right.

The screen door swung open. "Melanie? Hey, Melanie, you out here?" Chris called from inside.

Desmond stepped back into the shadows, pulling Melanie with him. An icy breeze blew between them, and she shivered as he let go of her hand.

"Desmond ..." Melanie whispered. "Desmond, please."

"No, Melanie. It's not right. Not now. Maybe God has other plans."

Reaching out, she touched his fingers. "What other plans? How do you know that?"

He stepped away from her and glanced at Chris, standing under the porch light. A low, exasperated sigh escaped before he retreated to his car.

Slumping against the wall, Melanie crossed her arms and squeezed herself tight. Her eyes burned, and she couldn't tell if it was her tears or the stinging rain, but a throbbing pain seared her heart.

"There you are." Chris stepped down. He shaded his eyes at the headlights of Desmond's car backing out. He turned. "Listen, Melanie. Why don't I just spend the night? You know, just to make sure you and Lacey are okay ..."

"Go home, Chris."

"What? Come on, Lacey needs ..."

"Chris, go home. Go home now," Melanie choked out.

She pressed further into the wall, the concrete hard against her back.

Chris took a step closer. "Home, Mel? I don't have a home."

And whose fault it that, Chris?

The beating rain thrashed the streets as Desmond drove at a snail's pace along Beach Road.

"It gets raining any harder, the water be coming up over the highway," Captain Jack exclaimed. "Don't you think you should speed it up a little?"

Desmond stared straight ahead. He couldn't get his mind off Melanie. He felt like a tool leaving her standing in the carport, soaking wet. So frail, so vulnerable, so in need of God's direction. He prayed for her but found it difficult with his growing attraction to the beautiful Melanie Thompson. Her simple, sweet spirit attracted him at first, but her riveting beauty had gotten ahold of him tonight. Trying not to think about her slender, shapely body proved impossible after the evening had brought them so close. Too close, he felt as he tried to shake her out of his mind. He could still smell Melanie's sweet aroma emanating from her skin, and he felt no cold remembering the warmth of her body against his. He gritted his teeth and gripped the steering wheel tighter.

"Pastor? Hellooo?" said Captain Jack.

Desmond glanced over at his passenger. "Oh. Sorry. What's up, Captain Jack?"

"It's Justin. My name's Justin."

Desmond had met him about a year before at a church event held down at the pier. The town had donated food, clothing, and supplies and distributed them to the pier people. Many individuals, and even a handful of families, lived on their boats on the gulf. Justin was one of them, and all hailed him as Captain Jack. He'd never corrected Desmond before.

Desmond glanced over. "Well, glad to know your name, Justin. Sorry, you were saying?"

"Yeah. I'm guessing you're a little preoccupied. I'm thinking maybe it was that passionate moment with Ms. Thompson back there, eh?" He chuckled. "Whoo-hoo, there."

Desmond could feel the heat rise within. He'd hoped that the dark had shielded him and Melanie from Justin's view. Apparently not.

"Ya know, Pastor, my dad was a reverend," Captain Jack continued.

Desmond's eyes grew wide, and he glanced over once more.

"Yup, hard to believe, eh? That was a long time ago. My mom died when I was young. Pops wasn't looking to remarry real soon, but he wanted someone to be a mom to me. When he dated a little, he got a lot of flak from a few old ladies at our church."

Desmond chuckled, thinking of the senior women at his church. But it wasn't them, it was Emily. If only he'd been there for her. Maybe with his strength by her side, she could have pulled through. She'd needed him, and he wasn't there. Now, here he was thinking of another woman. Another woman with an ex-husband back on the scene. He shook his head again, hoping to clear his mind. "So, what happened?" Desmond asked.

"Heck, it was crazy, man. I could have had any number of nice moms, but my dad just gave up. It wasn't until I got older that he started getting lonely. So, he thought to try again. But I started causing trouble, and it wasn't normal teenage stuff, ya know."

Justin swirled a finger in a circle by his temple. He laughed. "When the doctors started putting me on all kinds of meds, my dad really pressed into God. He prayed about any treatment that came up. He was reading his Bible all the time, even more than just for church. I think that's the only thing that got him through. Poor Dad, he was out of money, too, because of me. But most of all, he needed a wife. He had no one to go through it all with, and he needed someone to take care of him. So when I hit my twenties, and I got my head straight ... for a little while ... I told him, 'Pops, get yourself a wife. I'll be fine.'"

The scene was almost eerie as water pelted down in sheets, and the wipers swished back and forth. An occasional crack of thunder and a flash of lightning threatened. Desmond squinted, trying to find the white lines on the highway as water sprayed out from his tires. The heater and his intriguing passenger created a pungent odor that stung his nostrils. But still, he listened, riveted to every word.

Justin stopped.

"And did he? Find a wife? I mean, were you fine?" Desmond glanced at Justin again.

His eyes were fixed straight ahead, and he sniffled a bit. Wiping his nose on his jacket sleeve, Justin whispered, "No and no." He paused. "He died, and I went nuts."

Desmond's heart felt as if it stopped. The car swerved but found its way back onto the highway. He ached to pull over, but it was too dangerous. Instead, he waited for Justin to speak.

"Pops never took care of himself. Too much stress. He missed my mom and pastoring the church, dealing with me. It was all too much. I was all he had, and I wasn't much."

"That's not true, Justin. It sounds like you cared for him as much as he did you. But you're right, I'm sure that missing your mom was an enormous part of his stress." Desmond bit his lip.

"I had a wonderful mom, ya know? Maybe too good. I think maybe Pops felt guilty when he thought about other women."

Desmond's eyes widened. He didn't know which bothered him more, the storm outside or the one gusting within.

"I guess what I'm trying to say is, if you find an honorable woman, Pastor, it's okay. Grab that jewel in the hollow of your hand. God will guide you. Just don't get all high and mighty and take the high road if you're not supposed to. It's not like you're following carnal inclinations without wisdom or restraint…at least that's what my pops might say."

Desmond coughed and cleared his throat, but before he could speak, Pier 1 appeared before them, and Justin pointed to where his boat rocked. Desmond pulled up next to the boardwalk.

"Well, Justin, I'm not sure what to say. But thanks, thanks very much. You've given me a lot to pray about." Patting Justin's arm, he added, "Hey, it's kind of wet out there. Would you like to stay at my house tonight? I have an extra room."

Justin laughed. "Good meal, good company tonight. Nah, don't think I can handle so much goodness at one time. The rain is no barrier to me. I got a warm bed in there, and my ship ain't leaking yet."

Desmond laughed. "Yeah, but your ship is rocking a lot in this storm."

"No worries, 'rock a bye baby in the treetops' …" Justin sang as he exited and slammed the door.

Desmond slid down his window. The rain splattered off his face as he called out, "So, Justin? Where'd Captain Jack come from?"

Justin turned and staggered with the sashay of a character in a pirate movie. He turned and waved, screaming, "God bless you, Pastor. God bless you real good."

Desmond smiled, and the rain slowed, and the storm calmed. Inside and out.

CHAPTER 24

Melanie, dressed for a run, walked into the kitchen and filled a water bottle with ice from the freezer. She held it to her eyes, hoping to soothe the puffiness from her restless night.

Charlene sat at the kitchen table, cell phone to her ear. "What do you mean take it down? It's my website. You can't enforce that. It's my blog. I can write whatever I darn-well please ... Fine. Do it. I'll see you in court. No, better yet, you can read about it on my blog."

Charlene clicked off her cell, almost slamming it on the table. Turning around to grab her coffee, she chuckled. "Well, at least someone's reading my blog."

"What did you stir up this time?" asked Melanie.

"Oh, I implied that the missing girl in Jackson was trafficked to New Orleans."

Melanie's swollen lids widened. *Grady!* The events from last night filled her mind, and she spun around. "Charlene! That missing girl—the mom's boyfriend? He was here in Bay Town."

"Whaaat? You didn't tell me!" Charlene's eyes widened as she stared at Melanie. "My goodness, you're a train wreck! If I didn't know better, I'd say you have a hangover. What's wrong, sis?"

Melanie breathed deep, and as she exhaled, she shook her head. "Terrible night. Anyway, with everything going on with Lacey, I forgot to tell you. Carol, the owner of Second Chances, dated a guy from Jackson, Mississippi." Melanie set down her water bottle. "He was drunk in a bar and told her he ran away after his girlfriend's daughter went missing."

Charlene stood. "Are you kidding me? Where is he? Let's go talk to him now." She started for the door.

Melanie rolled her head back. "We can't. He's missing. Carol called me and asked if Chief Bert would check on him. He's been gone since Friday night. Do you think he's guilty of something?"

"Not if he's spilling the beans to some strange woman in a bar."

"Carol is not strange." Melanie shrugged. "She's ... free-spirited."

" Oh, another one of those." Charlene rolled her eyes. "Like Chris."

Usually, Melanie would have agreed, but the mention of Chris's name brought a mixture of emotions.

"Yes, like Chris." Her shoulders drooped. "Sis? I'm wondering if maybe Chris's work has something to do with all this?"

"Yeah, we talked about that, didn't we?"

Melanie leaned back against the counter and covered her face with her hands.

Charlene walked over and hugged her. "We'll figure it out, sis. I can stay for another week. My boss is fine with me gone as long as I meet my deadlines. Let's take one crisis at a time. When can I go talk to your friend?"

"How about after my run?" Melanie hugged Charlene back and moved from the counter. Bending her knee behind her, she pulled her ankle to feel the stretch. First one leg, then the other. She turned her neck and cracked it.

Charlene watched Melanie's contortions and shivered. "So, how was the party last night?"

Melanie gave her sister a drop-dead look. "Oh, it was great. Just fine, until Chris crashed the party." She looked away.

"And?" Charlene waited.

"Well, after Lacey went to bed, Chris stirred everything up, but it turned out okay. We put together a community task force. He was inadvertently the inspiration behind it. Surprise, surprise." *The golden boy.* Melanie blew out a sigh. "Anyway, we're meeting tonight if you can make it."

"What for? What's it about?" Charlene removed her glasses.

"Everything that's been going on. Oh, wait. You didn't hear it. A girl from Lacey's school has been missing for four days now."

Goosebumps rose on Melanie's arms, and as she rubbed them, she felt selfish for stressing about Desmond all night when Virginia was in danger.

"Whaaat? Another one? And Lacey, too." Charlene's eyes widened.

"Please don't put Lacey in that group. I'm just not believing that right now." Melanie pinched the bridge between her eyes.

Charlene opened her mouth and closed it. After a while, she said, "Okay. The task force sounds good. I'll go with you. What about Chris? Is he coming?"

Melanie closed her eyes for a long blink. "Probably not. But he knows about it." She walked to the door. "I'm going to run now. Keep an eye on Lacey, okay?"

"Oh, my goodness! I forgot all about her. Is she okay? No school today?"

"Last I checked, she's fine. Sleeping in. At some point, I'm hoping she'll feel like talking. Thanks, sis."

"Hey, Mel? Did you ever call on that wedding referral?"

Melanie shook her head. "It seems like something always comes up. Maybe today." Melanie left through the front door.

The dark clouds threatened another downpour. After the storm last night, the outdoors didn't quite have that clean, after-the-rain smell. The wind whipped the gulf into a frenzy, churned up the waters, and the air smacked of strong fish and seaweed. Melanie's shoes squished as she splashed along Beach Road. Running faster than usual, she pounded the pavement as if it could erase the surreal moments of the last evening. But she didn't want it all erased. She could feel Desmond's lips on hers once again.

The half-mile marker, the marina parking lot, loomed before her. She slowed to a stop and closed her eyes. She reached up her hand and tapped her mouth. *Why God? Am I in the penalty box forever? Will I never be good enough?*

"Hey, girl. Splendid party last night. No wonder you're running late this morning, eh?"

Melanie turned in the direction of a loud voice across the street. Tina's hot pink raincoat and orange, neon polka-dot umbrella almost blinded her. Melanie stopped. Tina's ensemble made her smile.

"Nice outfit," Melanie yelled. "Love the boots." She crossed over.

Tina struck a pose in her pink and orange floral boots while standing in a puddle. She held a hand out and peeked out of her umbrella. Resting it on her shoulder, she twirled it like a pinwheel.

"Thanks! So, what's up with the gorgeous Pastor Brooks? A little chemistry last night? Hmmm?" Tina winked.

"Nothing," Melanie whispered. "Absolutely nothing." She crossed her arms and looked at the horizon.

Tina pressed her lips together, making a pretty frown. "Oh, sweetie. What's up, Mellie, honey?"

Melanie took a deep breath and sighed.

"Melanie?" Tina sang.

"It's over, Tina. Over before it began. Why did I even think he would want me?"

"Because he does. It's so obvious. The man's crazy about you. Just give it time, sweetie."

"Nope. It's hopeless. He thinks I should get back together with Chris."

"Whaaat?" Tina screamed. "I doubt that very much. You misunderstood him. Just—"

"No, I didn't, Tina. He's mentioned it more than once. He even thinks it's God's plan." Melanie raised her fingers, indicating quote marks.

"Well, we'll see about that." Tina narrowed her eyes.

"No, Tina. Say nothing. Maybe I just need to learn to trust more."

"Trust who? Not Chris. Come on."

Melanie's ponytail swished as she shook her head.

"Honey, it'll be fine. God's got this." Tina patted Melanie's shoulder and smiled.

Melanie nodded. *God's got this? He certainly does. And that's what bothers me.*

Tina blew a kiss and waved goodbye as she continued her walk.

Melanie walked, jogged, then ran. She raced, and so did her mind. Gorgeous Pastor Brooks. Yeah, the pastor who dumped her after one kiss. Was that even a kiss? How could she have chased out after him last night? What a fool.

Lamenting that their budding friendship was over, Melanie thought of what a great source of comfort Desmond had been to her. She couldn't have made it through the week without him. It felt so good to have someone looking out for her and Lacey. Since her mom and dad died, she hadn't had that in a while.

But Desmond had become more than just a source of comfort. Too soon, too fast. She'd been there before. But Chris never looked out for her, ever. He'd done nothing but cause disappointment. Melanie ran, and a deluge of water poured down. Pulling out her cell, she ducked under a covered bus stop. A car pulled up.

"Not a great day for a jog. Are you headed home?" Desmond Brooks sat in the driver's seat.

Feeling the steam rising from her skin, she gripped her cell phone. Her knight in shining armor, again. "Nope. Just waiting for the rain to stop." She looked up. No chance of that. "I'm heading to Pier 1." She pointed in the opposite direction.

Dropping his hand out the window, he glanced up. "Doesn't look like the storm will pass anytime soon. I can give you a ride." A smile spread across his face. A smile like he might give a shaggy, wet dog.

"No, thanks, Desmond. I'll wait it out." Melanie looked at her phone, avoiding what she felt was his pity.

"Oh, come on. I won't bite. I promise," he said with a chuckle.

She hated it. Shaking her head, she lifted a hand and waved him on. The rain came down harder, and with the wind, it slapped at her legs. She shivered as she glanced up at him.

He didn't move to leave but shifted the car in park and leaned toward the passenger side. "Listen, Mel. I'm sorry about last night. I shouldn't have let that happen …"

She couldn't believe he was going there and wanted to scream. Her body went rigid as she waved again. "It's fine, Desmond. It was just a moment, you know, it's gone. No worries. It's forgotten, Pastor." She lied as her stomach lurched. "Our secret's safe." She tried to laugh.

His jaw tightened. "Mel, this is all new for me, and there are a lot of circumstances that come into play ..."

"Desmond, just stop. Okay? I know, I'm divorced, and my ex is back in the picture." She narrowed her eyes. "And I guess you're right. Lacey needs him." She bit her lip. "But, you know, I need somebody, too. And if, like you said, God is at work here? Well, maybe I need to see what I saw in Chris before." She reached deep, with no intention of following up on her proposal.

It was a physical attraction with Chris when she'd first met him. But his charming ways drew her even further. Before she got pregnant, life with him was fun, exciting, and carefree. But it killed her parents that everything they taught her went out the window. They'd warned her, and they were right. It all backfired. The fleeting fantasy of romance fled, and so did Chris. She stared back at Desmond. Maybe that's all it was with Desmond. She drew false courage with the thought. Thunder cracked, and Melanie jumped with the flash of lighting over the water.

"Melanie, get in the car. It's dangerous out there." Desmond spoke forcefully.

He'd never spoken that way to her before. They'd only spent a few days together, but those days had laid a fast foundation for what she dared to hope might lead to a decent life with an honorable man. But now, she was questioning everything she'd come to believe about their future.

Her eyes hardened. She almost glared at him. "Desmond, maybe you're right. Maybe I should give Chris a chance. He may not be an Emily, but he's all I have right now." There. She said it, but a breath caught, and she could hardly believe she'd spoken those words.

Desmond turned and gripped the steering wheel, staring straight ahead. His thumbs drummed the leather, and he jammed the gear shift into drive. "Right. I'll see you at the meeting tonight."

Shocked that he actually drove off, goosebumps rose on her arms as the cold took hold of her. A long, hard swallow trapped in her throat, preventing her from catching a breath before the sobs exploded. Melanie rocked back and forth alone on the bench. *Where are You? Where are You now, God?*

Melanie burst through the kitchen door. Water dripped off her and pooled all over the black-and-white-checked linoleum floor. She pulled off her socks and shoes, threw them aside, and walked straight to the kitchen counter. Grabbing a towel and wiping her face, she then turned to her daughter.

"Where's your aunt?"

Lacey stared at her. "She had a meeting or something."

Melanie rolled her eyes. "Great. She was supposed to stay with you today." Taking a deep breath, she blew out, and her lips fluttered. "I can't count on anyone these days."

"Mom? What's wrong?" Lacey sat at the kitchen table, eyes wide.

"Nothing." She traipsed down the hall to her room. She didn't care that she was dripping. Sitting on her bed, she hit her pillow, hating that she'd let her angry feelings rule her actions and words.

Her gaze set upon her devotional book, *Pearls of Great Price* by Joni Erikson Tada. Opening to the date at hand, she read. Joni always helped her get her mind off her own selfish desires and inspired her to pray for others. Her trials still paled compared to so many others hurting around the world and in her neighborhood. Closing her eyes, she tried to pray, but the words wouldn't come.

The girls stayed in their rooms, and the quiet house smelled of cinnamon, and flickering candles grew brighter as

216 | KATHLEEN J ROBISON

the day became darker. It was difficult to distinguish between dusk setting in or the storm casting its dreary gloom.

Later, Melanie walked into the kitchen, hair damp, wearing leggings and an oversized pink sweatshirt. She heard Lacey's door open and glanced back. Lacey followed close behind.

The back door opened, and Charlene pushed through the screen door. She walked in and hung the car keys on the hook. Hanging her damp wool scarf, she turned up her nose—a mixture of sweet perfume and coffee aroma emitted from the wet fibers.

The room was quiet. "Hey! You guys are like the walking dead," Charlene called.

Lacey giggled and bounded up, hugging her aunt. She stepped back, shaking both her hands in a dripping gesture.

Charlene nodded her head. "I know. Wet out there, yeah?" She looked at Melanie, who was retrieving food from the refrigerator.

"So, what's for dinner? I'm starved."

"Salad and crab cakes. I made them myself." Lacey smiled.

"Crab cakes? Oh, okay. I guess I'm still too stressed to go back on my vegan wagon. Seafood it is." She glanced at Lacey. "Wow. I can't even get an argument from your mom."

Charlene rolled her eyes. Melanie heated up the crab cakes as Charlene chopped and tossed a salad, and Lacey set the table for the three of them. Once they all sat down, Charlene picked up her fork.

Melanie nodded at Lacey. "I'll pray," said Lacey.

Charlene paused, her mouth open and fork full of salad poised in mid-air. She smiled and bowed her head as Lacey prayed.

The conversation was light, and when they'd finished the

meal, the back screen door opened. Tina carried in a fancy, covered pottery dish.

"Hey, ladies, blueberry crisp?" She smiled, holding up the dish.

"Does she always do that?" Charlene pointed.

"Pretty much." Lacey smiled.

"Well, maybe I'll move in with you guys! Yummy. Let's dig in." Charlene rubbed her hands together and scooped up the dinner plates, clearing the table.

Lacey hugged Tina as she took the blueberry crisp, licking her lips.

"Got any ice cream, Melanie?" Charlene asked.

"I do," Tina yelled. "I'll be right back." She ran home to retrieve it.

Even Tina's bubbly presence couldn't cheer Melanie's mood. She felt as if she was grieving a loss. She tried pushing Desmond out, but he hung over her like a dream out of reach. Quietly, she got up to make some decaf, and Lacey quickly followed.

Reaching for the china dessert plates, Lacey nudged her mom. Melanie looked down at her smiling daughter. She'd been through so much, and yet, here she was smiling. A pang of guilt hit Melanie.

Clutching the dishes to her chest, Lacey stared at her aunt. Charlene narrowed her eyes. "You okay, kid?"

"This is so cool!" Lacey blurted.

Tina swept in, holding up the ice cream. "Yes, very cool."

Lacey giggled. "I love this." She circled around the room with one finger. "I feel like I'm hanging out with the cool kids in high school. Right, Mom?" Lacey's eyes widened. "Your friends are so cool."

Charlene looked at Tina and pointed. "Well, maybe her. She's the cool one." Everyone laughed, and Melanie squeezed her daughter tightly.

Charlene shrugged. "You're a weird kid. Sweet, but weird."

Lacey's eyes widened, brimming with tears.

"Oh, sweetie! You're not weird. I was just kidding." Charlene looked horrified.

Lacey shook her head and covered her face.

"Lacey, what's wrong?" Melanie enveloped her daughter in her arms.

Tears fell down Lacey's cheeks, and Charlene and Tina immediately ran over. The little circle huddled together. After a few moments, Lacey broke free and moved to sit at the table. The women lined the kitchen counter, their eyes as round as saucers.

Lacey gulped. "I think someone hit me on the porch that night." She dropped her head and sobbed.

Melanie felt her mouth drop and leaped to her daughter's side. "Lacey, we'll sort this out. You're safe with us. No one will touch you again, I promise."

The word "promise" unnerved her, and Melanie fought off tears of her own. Anger set in again, but not for her own circumstances, and her struggles faded as she battled against the tension rising within for her daughter. She stared at her sister and her friend, needing their strength. Closing her eyes, she knew it was God's strength she needed most.

"Yes, your mom is right." Charlene rushed over. "We'll get the creeps!"

Blubbering came from the direction of the kitchen counter where Tina stood sobbing. Beckoning her to join them, Tina rushed over and joined the band of women, and Melanie quietly prayed.

CHAPTER 25

"Okay. It's seven o'clock p.m. Let's get this meeting started. I thought we'd wait for the mayor, but I guess he's running late." Chief Bert shrugged.

"Figures. The mayor would run late." Charlene smirked.

The teachers' lounge emitted a pleasant aroma of strong brewing coffee. Extra chairs dotted the perimeter of the room. Still, many chose to sit on the small, comfy sofas and the eclectic, over-stuffed chairs.

Chief Bert continued. "Well, to update everyone, Melanie, do you want to speak first?"

Melanie shook her head.

"Fine. Well, everyone, Lacey thinks someone hit her last Sunday night when she stepped out onto her back porch." Chief Bert laid it out there.

A collective gasp went around the room. "Grave news, I know. But we might have a lead. Joe saw a white van and a couple of suspicious characters around town before that incident."

Melanie looked up. Her mouth hung open as she stared at the chief. "A white van almost ran Lacey and me off the road last Sunday after church."

The chief rolled his head back. "And you're just now telling me this?"

"I forgot." Her shoulders sagged.

Tina sat next to her and patted her arm. "It's okay, honey. A lot has been going on."

A green potted palm rose high in one corner, and smaller plants sat on a shelf just below a window. Generally, plants brought solace, but Melanie found none as she looked away. She glanced around the room, and her eyes rested on Desmond. He lowered his gaze.

"Okay, so Officer Blaine's been out on patrol looking for the van for the past couple of days. No luck, but he's still patrolling. Now, I'm going to throw some information at you." Chief Bert held out his hands. "Just hold your questions for now. You all know Virginia's been absent from school since Friday. That's a week now."

Heads nodded, and Chief Bert scratched his head. He took a deep breath and blew it out. "Virginia's Aunt Hilly, well, she was found dead in her home on Monday."

The shock in the room felt like a thousand volts of electricity. Melanie's mouth dropped, and she stood.

"You never told me." Even to her own ears, it sounded like an accusation. She glared at him. "That poor woman. When's the funeral? Is anybody doing anything?"

He nodded. "You had a lot going on, Mel. I didn't want to add more to your plate."

Melanie sat down, blinking hard. Tina grabbed her hand and squeezed.

"Worse yet"—the chief looked around the room, avoiding Melanie—"The coroner says she died sometime Friday night. Seventy-two hours before we found her.

"She was deceased for three days before you found her?" Principal Ladner asked quietly.

"Dead. She was dead," said Charlene.

"Yes. Since Virginia was at school on Friday, I had no cause to check over there."

Desmond raised a hand. "I checked over there after school hours on Friday. No one answered the door, but I'm sure someone was inside."

"Maybe you should have shared that information sooner." The Chief tipped back his hat. "Although, I'm not sure it would have made a difference."

Melanie felt a bit of vindication that Desmond was being reprimanded. Still, it didn't assuage the hurt she felt when seeing him.

"I don't understand," Mrs. Crowley, the school secretary, chimed in. "What does Virginia's aunt have to do with Lacey?"

"Oh, for Pete's sake. Virginia is missing, the aunt is dead, and Lacey almost gets offed." Charlene threw her hands in the air. "And to top it all off, a girl in Jackson went missing last week! Don't you people read the internet?"

Melanie glared at her sister. "Charlene …"

"All right, all right. We don't need any family squabbles. Thanks for the editorial there." The chief pointed at Charlene. "Melanie's sister has been investigating a human trafficking ring in New Orleans. I don't want to go there, but maybe Lacey and Virginia are being targeted."

Melanie closed her eyes, and when she opened them, Desmond seemed to be leaning toward her from his seat as if he wanted to comfort her. She closed her eyes again, avoiding his gaze.

"How did the aunt pass?" Principal Ladner asked.

Charlene rolled her eyes.

"Drug overdose, and I think a fellow by the name of Will Boudreaux might have had something to do with it. Just a hunch. Anybody ever heard of him or seen him? Besides me?" The chief looked around the room.

Desmond raised his hand.

"Yeah, yeah, I already know, you too," the chief said. "Anyone else?"

Melanie saw Desmond staring at her. "Did you see him, Melanie? That night at the Bayou Bar?"

The crowd chuckled, and Chief Bert laughed outright. "Well, Pastor, I was discreet about that information." The tension in the room released a little as everyone made their jokes.

"No. I didn't see him. He was standing back in the shadows of the alley." Narrowing her eyes, Melanie turned to the chief. "What did he look like?"

Desmond answered instead. "Maybe a little shorter than me. Slicked back hair. Sharp dresser." Desmond stood over six feet tall, so that still put Boudreaux as a sizable man as well.

His description matched the guy that gave her the business card on the street. The one telling her to call about Chris's referral. His voice drawled out words in a thick southern accent. The same voice in the alley. She didn't want to admit it, but she'd always had a funny feeling that he and Virginia's daddy might be the same. *That would somehow connect Chris,* she thought. Her eyes narrowed at no one in particular.

"Miz Melanie? What are you thinking?" Joe's voice boomed as he struggled to lean forward from his sinking seat on the sofa. Charlene fell against him and pushed off, trying to right herself. A few giggles arose.

"I think maybe Chris is connected. A man approached me on Main Street last week. He mentioned that Chris referred me for a wedding." Melanie rubbed her temples. "I think maybe that man was Will Boudreaux."

Chief Bert slapped a hand over his eyes. "So, where is Chris? Isn't he supposed to be here? Did you call him?"

Melanie stared back and then glanced at Desmond. She shook her head.

"He's her ex." Charlene's voice shrilled. "She doesn't keep tabs on him!"

"This is a lot of information. I'm open to some guessing here." The chief now rested his hands on his hips.

Rudy, Tina's husband, said, "Where was he from? The man on the street? Or who was he representing?"

"He didn't say. But the business card said, 'One Shell Tower Plaza.'" Melanie searched through her purse as she spoke.

Rudy blew out a breath, and his voice rose. "That's the biggest building in New Orleans. Pricey rent, too. Was there an office name or a suite number?"

Holding the card in her hand, Melanie read it. "It just says penthouse and a phone number."

"Yikes. That's a big smoking gun." All eyes turned on Rudy. "That guy up there, I don't even know his name, but the Securities Commission investigated him at least once before." He lowered his voice and looked at Melanie. "What does Chris have to do with him?"

Melanie felt lost. Guilt swept over her, and she felt her vulnerable self wanting to defend against accusations that weren't coming. "He deals in properties."

"Building acquisition and speculation for obscure clients." Charlene quipped. "It's a fancy term for commercial real estate dev—" Charlene stopped. The irritation on her face turned to alarm. "Wait a minute." She paused. "Human trafficking rings use abandoned, old commercial buildings for holding their victims before selling or transporting them."

Desmond looked around. "But Chris wouldn't deal with them." He glanced at Melanie but quickly turned his eyes on Charlene. "Would he?"

Melanie fluttered her lips. With her head down, she said, "He's a real estate broker. He handles auctions on foreclosed properties ... abandoned holdings ..." Her voice trailed off.

"Melanie, can you remember anything he might have told you about his business?" Chief Bert looked at her.

Melanie fidgeted with her fingers before she spoke. "Well,

I know that companies hire him to look for those abandoned properties. He mentioned something about bank-owned—"

Rudy cleared his throat loudly. "Chris is playing the role of the go-between guy. In this case, he finds the property and locates the owner. It's usually a bank that has foreclosed on the property. He gets all the information to his buyer. They write up a contract, and he presents the offer to the bank. Chris most likely gets his commission upon sale."

Everyone looked at Rudy, surprise all around.

Tina beamed. "Oh, didn't you know? Rudy was a big-time finance guy. A hedge-hog broker," she cooed.

A few giggles rippled around the room. Gazing adoringly at her husband, she squeezed his arm. Rudy laced his hands together and smiled while shaking his head.

"I think you mean hedge fund broker." Principal Ladner pushed his glasses up on his nose. "I have a few investments of my own."

Once again, all present turned and stared. This soft-spoken, average-looking man with thinning hair tugged on the lapels of his sport coat and nodded.

Rudy raised his eyebrows and mouthed, "Thank you."

"Okay." Charlene sighed. "Anyone else wants to confess a secret life?"

Principal Ladner raised his hand in the air.

"Really? There's more?" Chief Bert giggled.

"No, but I had a question. Kind of backtracking. What about Virginia? Are we looking for her?" Principal Ladner removed his glasses and stared at Chief Bert.

Shifting his body weight, he nodded. "Uh, yes. Well, I guess I better get it out there." He huffed and forged ahead. "Fact is, I have a hunch she's in real danger. I'm afraid this Will Boudreaux took her. I don't have enough resources to hunt for her, so we're looking for clues."

A buzz of voices broke out as well as a few gasps.

"Enough resources! The girl is being trafficked." Charlene shook her head.

"Virginia showed up at school on Friday, so there was no cause for further investigation. After Lacey's incident, when things calmed down, it turned out that Virginia hadn't shown up at school on Monday. That's when I went to the house, and we found her aunt's body still on the sofa."

The room itself seemed to shiver. Gagging sounds went round.

Melanie's heart wrenched for Hilly. She'd hoped that their last conversation had given Hilly some hope. She didn't know. *Why didn't I do more?*

Voices rose, and the chief put up his hands again. "The coroner deemed the overdose as accidental and not a homicide. Officer Blaine couldn't issue a Missing Persons with the FBI on Virginia as we had no probable cause. We couldn't prove that this Will Boudreaux wasn't her father. I tried to push through the report anyway, but they officially shut it down."

"But he's not her father," said Mrs. Crowley. More than one person shouted similar sentiments.

Charlene lost it. "Are you kidding me? What in the … oh, sorry, Pastor. Who the heck would be stupid enough to do that?"

CHAPTER 26

A loud, deep voice came from the back of the room. "That would be me."

All eyes turned, and there stood a tall, broad-shouldered, nice-looking man. His sandy, dark-blond hair, graying at the temples, complemented the sharp, tan-colored suit he wore. Though very distinguished looking, he loosened his paisley tie and unbuttoned his collar.

Chief Bert walked from the front of the classroom and shook his hand.

The man addressed the group with a soothing southern drawl. "Hello, everyone. I'm Mayor John Taylor. Please call me John. And yes, you may address your disappointment"— He nodded in Charlene's direction with no apparent animosity but exuding authority.—"and your agitation toward me."

His charming smile seemed to disarm all but Charlene. He straightened. "Unfortunately, that is the official protocol that we must follow."

"Official? Are you seriously going to go there, Mayor?" Charlene glared.

Joe Cunningham squeezed Charlene's arm with his large hand and whispered, "Give the man a chance, Ms. Charlene."

"Yes, ma'am, and officially, I have to go there."

A sly smile from the mayor seemed directed at Charlene, but he made eye contact with each person in the room. "But this is not an 'official' meeting, am I correct?"

Each task force member smiled back, one-by-one, each one except Charlene.

"And that's why I'm here." Mayor Taylor continued, "Principal Ladner, may I suggest you file a truancy report on Virginia Jones? Coming from the high school, it should get this ball rolling. This is how we can then involve Social Services, who I'm sure can then file a missing person report upon their initial evaluation." Mayor Taylor paused, perusing the group.

"I'd be happy to, Mayor. Do I send the report straight to you so we can shortcut to find Virginia?" He paused. "Before … it's too late?" Principal Ladner raised his eyebrows.

"You can't send it to him. This is an unofficial meeting, and Mayor Taylor, uh John, is telling you unofficially to officially file a report from the school." Charlene rolled her eyes.

Nodding his head in her direction, with a glint in his eye, the mayor added, "Yes, thank you, ma'am, and you are?"

"Charlene Chadwick. Melanie Thompson's sister. It was my niece that was almost offed this week."

"Quit saying that!" Melanie flushed. "She's from Washington, D. C., Mayor. My sister is an activist with the Gosford Institute. She's deeply passionate in her fight against her causes."

"You don't need to defend me, Melanie. And they're not my causes."

"And that's why we're all here, Ms. Chadwick," said the Mayor.

"It's Charlene, John."

Chief Bert swiped his hand across his brow. The silence was thick, but Tina's giggles broke the tension in the room.

"Okay," Chief Bert began, "Let's get back to Virginia …"

"If she's still alive," Charlene added under her breath.

All eyes locked on Charlene, and heads shook in disbelief.

Desmond straightened. "She's still alive. We haven't given up hope."

Melanie heard that forceful voice again. This time it calmed her but also made her heart ache all the more.

Chief Bert took charge. "Principal Ladner, you file that truancy report. Give Charlene a copy of it, and maybe she can act as your secretary on this. I'm sure she'll be able to get some action on it."

Principal Ladner gave a sideways glance at Charlene, then shifted his eyes back to Mayor Taylor. It appeared that Charlene saw the exchange.

"Oh, I get it. I'm not from around these here parts, eh? That's it, right?"

Melanie's heart quickened as she watched her sister getting worked up again and was thankful when Mayor Taylor ignored her question but directed her diplomatically.

"Ms. Chadwick, just be sure to mention my name. You have my full jurisdiction on this. I think with your expertise, we may get somewhere." He winked and flashed that handsome smile.

Charlene shook her head as if not amused. Glancing back, Chief Bert waited as Principal Ladner gave a weak thumbs up. The mayor walked over and sat on the sinking sofa, lowering his lengthy body right next to Charlene. Her slight frame fell in his direction, and once again, she struggled to sit up. He smiled, but she appeared oblivious. Melanie chuckled at the odd pairing on the couch and welcomed the light moment.

Bert continued, "Okay, so back to the real estate business. Who's going to check out the real estate thing?"

Rudy raised a hand as he spoke up. "I will."

Tina pointed to him, mouthing, "That's my man."

Rudy and Tina smiled at one another, and Melanie gazed

adoringly at the couple. She glanced over at Desmond but quickly dropped her eyes. Resignation and loss.

"Okay, so, Melanie, you've got to get a hold of Chris. He might be the key here."

Melanie almost laughed. "Sure," she replied, "I'll try him tonight."

Pastor Brooks ran his fingers through his hair and spoke up. "I hate to be blunt here, but what might be the connection between Lacey's incident and Chris's involvement with the real estate stuff?"

"You think Chris had something to do with Lacey's incident?" Melanie's eyes narrowed.

"Melanie honey, Pastor Brooks is just concerned like the rest of us," said Tina.

Charlene piped in. "Wow. For a man of the cloth, you sure know how to sugar coat it."

"Charlene, be quiet." Melanie shot a look at her sister.

"He's got a point. There's so much going on, I might as well spill the rest of it." Chief Bert rubbed the back of his neck as the room went quiet. "Last week, when the girl from Jackson High went missing, a person of interest was being sought ..."

Melanie opened her eyes wide and tipped her head. She'd given the chief the information about Grady on Monday. Thinking of Carol, she pleaded with her eyes. Hoping he wouldn't bring Carol into this.

He continued. "Turns out he was right here in Bay Town ..."

A force of air rushed out as everyone gasped.

"Doing what?" a voice called out.

Glancing at Melanie, Chief Bert continued. "Doesn't much matter. He skipped town on Friday night."

Everyone talked at once, but Bert raised his hands. "We're still checking into it. So Pastor Brooks is right. We need to check into all connections. We also need to keep our priorities in order. Right now, that means protecting Lacey and Melanie, finding Virginia, and locating Chris. We'll let the FBI handle the human trafficking stuff if that turns out to be what this is."

Most everyone nodded, and Joe clapped his hands. "Hey, my Lyla is waiting at home for me. Let's wrap this up. Tell me what I can do?"

"Okay," Bert answered. "Well, the rest of you keep an eye out for that white van. Joe, can you do a drive-by at Melanie's house every night? I can only patrol so much." Nodding at Mayor Taylor, he added, "Unofficially, of course."

"Look," Mayor Taylor responded, "I know that sometimes the bureaucracy frustrates people, and sometimes rightfully so. But when that frustration motivates dutiful citizens like yourselves, and the community gets involved, well, that's a wonderful outcome. Be careful and mindful of the law and stay connected. Please run everything by Chief Bert here, and give him an account of all you do so he can keep tabs—a paper trail of sorts. Fair enough?"

"You know, I think it might be a good idea right now to seek some wise direction," Desmond spoke up.

Bert replied, "You're right, Pastor. Mayor John, you got time tomorrow—"

"We needs to pray," Joe interrupted.

"What?" a few voices, not in unison, said aloud.

"I think the direction that Pastor Brooks is talking 'bout is God. We needs to pray," Joe said, nodding at Desmond. "Pastor?"

One by one, heads bowed around the room. Some even grasped hands, and Desmond prayed. He gave thanks for all present and asked for God's guidance, protection, and intervention on all the events at hand. As he finished, a unison "Amen" broke the hushed, solemn moment.

Some of the tender-hearted sniffled, many hugged, but Melanie clenched her fists. Still thinking about Chris and the accusations that he might be involved with Lacey's attack, her eyes widened as she watched Desmond approach. She stepped to her sister's side turning her back on him.

Charlene stood, as did Mayor Taylor, and before she could speak, he said in his deep, soothing drawl, "Hey, Ms. Thompson...excuse me, I mean Miss Charlene. Thanks for going easy on me tonight. I sure appreciate it."

He extended his hand, and she shook it firmly. "Wait 'til next time." Charlene smiled as she pointed a finger at him.

Melanie noticed that the Mayor held onto Charlene's hand a little longer than a natural handshake.

As he let go, he flashed a last grin and turned. "Hey, Chief. Call me tomorrow, will ya?" gesturing a phone call with his hands as he spoke. Turning back to the sisters, he said, "Ms. Melanie, we'll sort this out. You have my word." He nodded and left.

"Okay, everyone, thanks for coming. Keep in touch." The chief's voice bellowed as he helped Principal Ladner straighten up.

Melanie turned to join her friends and caught Desmond staring at her. They stood ten feet apart, but it felt like a football field. Was it just her, or did he feel a pull too? She longed for the closeness they'd almost had.

Stop it, she told herself.

Desmond helped the men rearrange the room and turned to look at Melanie. She nodded and walked quietly down the corridor, alone.

CHAPTER 27

Saturday morning after the task force meeting, Desmond woke long before dawn, feeling unsettled. He hadn't slept well, so he went straight to his Bible and read and prayed. He asked God for direction as he thought about the events taking place in his little town. After a while, he went to the computer and researched human trafficking. At one point, he stopped. The vulgarity and horrific content seared his conscience, yet he knew God was calling him to action.

When the sun finally broke through the trees, he made a pot of coffee and sat out on his porch, watching the sunrise. Chirping twittered about as branches snapped in the trees. He watched them fall, and birds of all varieties flitted in and out of the yard. The October blue skies held such promise. Yet the rising sun and the beauty before him paled as darkness shrouded his mind and enveloped his heart.

He thought about Virginia and where she might be, of the danger she was in. Recalling the task force discussions, he thought of New Orleans. Lots of abandoned buildings in New Orleans. Was she there? And Chris. What was his connection?

Desmond couldn't wait. He clenched his fists. Virginia had to be found, along with other innocent victims. He paced the floor. And Lacey? She needed to feel safe. His pulse quickened as his thoughts went to Melanie. *She needs peace.* He stopped, and his shoulders slumped as he resigned that the only way to comfort her was to be there for her, with her. But he couldn't do that. Thoughts of Emily twisted his heart. He hadn't been there for her either.

But this was different. Desmond shook his head and set his jaw. He felt that Chris would become what she and Lacey needed. That was Chris's role now. *God, raise him up.*

Taking a deep breath, the smell of fresh coffee filled him with memories of Melanie again. The coffee shop. The hospital visit and the closeness between them he'd felt with her by his side that day. A strange bittersweet sensation took over as he remembered that he hadn't felt joy like that since Emily. Standing, he shoved his hands in his pockets and walked inside.

Desmond pulled his cell from his pocket and dialed. "Hey, Charlene, this is Desmond. Uh, Pastor Brooks?"

"Good morning, and why are you calling me so early?"

"Oh, I'm sorry. I just had some thoughts from the meeting last night and wanted to follow up. Do you happen to have Chris's cell number?"

"Chris?" Charlene chuckled. "Sure. I'll text it to you. Go for it."

"Thanks, Charlene. I appreciate it. Oh, and could you not tell Mel? I mean, keep it quiet for now?"

"Mum's the word. But you have to promise to clue me in."

"It's a deal. Thanks, Charlene."

Desmond got dressed. Though convicted to work on his sermon instead, he followed the gnawing of the unfinished business. *Lord, I'm trusting you.* He dialed Chris's number.

"Yeah. Leave a message." Chris's recording was short and abrupt.

"Chris. This is Desmond, Pastor Brooks? Can you call me? It's about Lacey. Thanks."

Desmond dressed and drove to the church office, deciding

to wait for Chris's call there. Walking into his office, he dropped onto the couch and picked up his Bible. As he studied, he tried to take notes but stared at a blank page. Finally, he stood, stretched, and walked to his desk. He looked at Emily's framed photograph perched on the corner. Taking a deep breath, he closed his eyes.

Well, Em, who would have thought, huh? Not sure where this is all going to lead, but I have to do it. For the first time since Emily's death, looking at her photograph didn't bring the confidence he normally felt when indecision clouded his thoughts. She was now so far removed from all the events during this part of his lifetime.

Leaning back, he closed his eyes for a few seconds, then he glanced down at his calendar. There, tucked in between the months, was Melanie's Quaint Affairs brochure. Her smiling, gentle face stared back at him. He propped an elbow on the desk and raised a fisted hand to his chin, and glanced between the two pictures. *A little help here?*

His cell buzzed, and looking at the screen, he grabbed it. "Hi, Chris, thanks for returning my call."

"Yeah, well, a call from the man of God. It must be important. What's up?"

"We had our task force meeting last night. And I thought we could use your help."

Silence.

"Chris? You there?"

"Yeah. Listen, Des, what I'm going to tell you needs to be quiet. I've been torn on what to do. I'm thinking I could use your help. What do you guys call it? Your direction or guidance."

Desmond chuckled. "Not mine, but, yeah, I guess that's right."

Chris explained how, since Lacey's incident, he had done some private investigation work of his own. He gave Desmond some history of his work; how some of his real estate dealings had taken him to New Orleans in the past year. All this human trafficking business raised his concerns over what he previously thought was a little suspicious. Still, he knew they were legal in representation by lawyers and the industry, but his skin crawled at the possibility of a connection. He had let it go at the time, not being one to get too involved, particularly when he was getting paid well, and his concerns were just a hunch.

Chris's voice took on a more serious tone as he continued the story. "You know, it all started at the beginning of the year. A client called and asked me to find some abandoned properties in New Orleans. Said he got my name from some other client that I'd worked with in LA before. Investors."

"Were they shady, too?"

"Who said they were shady?" Chris sounded annoyed. "But, you know, I'm not sure." He paused. "Anyway, I found a few and showed them two properties in an area struck by the last big hurricane. Mostly drug dealers and homeless people hung out on the streets there." Chris took a deep breath and blew it out. "It was weird. They told me to write the offers. That quick." A snap of fingers came through the line. "They offered to pay way too much. I mean way too much. So, of course, the deals went through almost immediately, and I got a hefty commission. They even gave me a ridiculously high bonus from the two deals."

A sick feeling rumbled in Desmond's gut as Chris continued. He stood and walked to the window where the white clouds were swirling by. While Chris talked, Desmond prayed.

"I was feeling funny about what could go down. I mean, I had no idea, but I'd never felt like that before, so I started asking questions." Chris's voice took on a more serious, hushed tone. "I asked about the use of the properties and would they want to flip them, just fishing, you know. My hunch was a drug ring, and I wanted nothing to do with it."

"Well, I'm glad to hear that." Desmond winced, wishing he hadn't said that.

"Geez, give me a little credit, Pastor. Anyway, I told them in so many words to get lost. A couple of weeks later, they asked me to write offers in other cities for the same type of properties. No questions asked, I was told. The money was hard to pass up, but I declined anyway."

Desmond smiled, thinking, *Well, at least he's got a conscience.*

"When I refused to write the offers, they threatened me. I mean his lawyer or whatever did. I met the big guy once or twice, but I mostly worked with a go-between. So, I told them there were plenty of other realtors who could help them out, but they said something about me already being on the inside."

Desmond rubbed his temple. The thought of Melanie and Lacey being in danger because of Chris gave rise to a headache.

"Anyway, I told them their threats didn't scare me, and I cut my ties."

"When? When did you cut your ties?" Desmond asked.

"A couple months ago, but they kept calling. The last week or two, I started ignoring their calls."

Desmond didn't like the coincidence of Lacey's incident and Melanie's encounter with a stranger.

Chris continued. "So, after talking with Charlene, I started feeling like I needed to do something. She told me about how she was working on this human trafficking thing, and I thought, 'Could my daughter have been a victim?' So, then it got personal. I mean, they hurt my baby girl."

What about Melanie? Desmond wanted to ask.

"So, Pastor, I thought, you know, I have to do something, and I was trying to formulate a plan on what to do next, but I'm just not sure what to do? If it was those creeps, I work for that went after Lacey, well, what if they came again? What if it was Melanie next?"

Desmond's voice caught in his throat, but he said, "Chris, did you hear about the men that contacted Melanie? They used your name."

"Yeah, she told me something. I told her to forget it. We got in a fight."

"Yes, well, Charlene said another guy did too."

"Who? What did he look like? What kind of car did he drive?" Chris was yelling now.

"The first guy was a little shorter than me. Had slicked back hair and drove a blue Lincoln?"

"Nope. It doesn't sound familiar. No one I ever worked with before. What about the other guy?"

"I don't know. He approached her at a wedding."

"Are you kidding me? If it's them, I have to get over there and see if she's ok. Is she ok? Who's with her? If they hurt my girls, I'll kill 'em."

Desmond winced at both the word "kill" and the words "my girls." But Chris was right. *They are his girls.*

"Well, we won't let that happen, Chris. Joe is monitoring their house, and Charlene is here for a while. They're well taken care of. How about we take a trip down to New Orleans? We can check out those properties you closed."

"What are you looking for, Des?"

Desmond took a breath. "I'm looking for a girl from our town that went missing. Maybe she's in one of those properties. What do you say? Let's give it a try?"

"What? Who? Wait. You and me?" Chris chuckled. "Sure, pal. Why not? Butch Cassidy and Sundance, right?"

"Yeah, right?" Desmond laughed. "Wait a minute, who's who?"

"Who cares. We're both jumping off the cliff here. Meet me at the Bourbon Orleans at three o'clock."

"Sure thing." Desmond clicked off and looked at his watch. He had some time to work on his sermon and, more importantly, time to pray.

CHAPTER 28

I t was late Saturday afternoon at Melanie's house, and the girl's still lounged in their pajamas. Melanie didn't even get up to run. Pouring a cup of coffee, she leaned against the kitchen counter and thought about the task force meeting the previous night. She slouched, thinking of Hilly. Without next of kin, who would bury her? Her stomach felt sour just thinking about the poor woman. And Virginia. Where was she? Melanie closed her eyes. She'd been praying all night but couldn't seem to find peace. Too anxious. Too much to process.

She walked into the living room where her sister and daughter sat snuggled together, watching an old black and white movie. Smiling, she turned and pulled out her phone, called Chris, and waited. It went to voicemail. She blew out a loud, audible sigh.

"Let me guess? Chris didn't answer?" Charlene called out.

"Maybe you should try him. He's not answering my calls." She thought of her harsh words to him after the party. The last time she'd seen him. *Go home, Chris.*

"Shhhh!" Lacey put a finger to her lips.

Melanie waved her sister to the kitchen and walked to the counter.

"You two have a lover's spat or something?" Charlene chuckled and screamed as a dishrag landed atop her head.

"Serves you right." As Melanie left, her cell rang.

"Give him my love!" Charlene called out as Melanie walked down the hall.

She answered the call. "Oh, hey, Chief. What's up?"

Melanie listened as Chief Bert asked her to come down to the station. He said it was about Grady and Carol. Melanie made arrangements for Tina to sit with Lacey, and she took Charlene with her to the station.

Bells jingled as they walked into the police station. Charlene pointed and laughed, but Chief Bert didn't. He stood at his desk, his brow furrowed.

"What's up, Chief?" asked Melanie.

He stared at the women. "Well, you know how I wanted to question Carol about her boyfriend?" He glanced at the poster on the wall.

"You, too?" Charlene pointed. "I need to get some answers about the Jackson case."

"Well, you can't now. I got a phone call from the Pascagoula Police Station. A man that matched that description"—he pointed—"came up dead near the bus terminal in Pascagoula."

Melanie felt behind her and ran a hand along the top of the visitor bench. She dropped down. Charlene stepped forward.

"No! What the heck is going on in your town?" Charlene sounded accusatory.

"Technically, it wasn't in our town. But they found a bus ticket originating from here in the dead guy's pocket." The chief shook his head.

The poster was the one that Melanie identified as Grady,

Carol's boyfriend. The Pascagoula authorities called Bay Town Police because of the bus ticket. But the ID in his wallet said Grayson Mitchell, not Grady. It was a viable nickname. The cause of death was attributed to hit-and-run, vehicular manslaughter.

"What got me riled is the video retrieved from the city's street camera. It showed a blue car barreling down the alley. Heck, the victim flew through the air like a rag doll." Chief Bert flung his arms up high and shook his head. "He didn't stand a chance."

Melanie closed her eyes and cringed.

"And the vehicle never even stopped. The Pascagoula Police said it looked like it was a late model Lincoln, but it was moving so quickly, I couldn't tell. Even the license plate on the video was a blur, and freeze-framing and enlarging couldn't confirm identification."

"Boudreaux," Melanie whispered and stared at the Chief. "Doesn't he drive a blue Lincoln?"

"He did that night at the bar. That's why I called you. The FBI will want to talk to Miss Carol now, too."

Oh, poor Carol. "Chief, we have to go tell her first."

"After what you told me about this guy and the missing Jackson girl, I already alerted the FBI. But what's the connection with Boudreaux? Why was he after Grady?" Placing his hands on his hips, he nodded. "If it was him."

"And how did they know each other?" Melanie tipped her head.

"The Jackson girl! It had to be why Boudreaux offed him." Charlene stared wide-eyed.

"Charlene, the poor man was murdered." Grady creeped her out, but it was God's compassion gripping her heart for him now.

Chief Bert rapped his knuckles on his desk, looking deep in thought. "Bingo!" He sat up straight. "Last Friday afternoon I talked to Boudreaux outside the bus station in town." His face hardened. "And he had his eyes pegged on Miz Carol's shop."

The bench felt hard beneath her, but Melanie felt her body sinking. The connection. Here it was—the missing girl in Jackson, Hilly's death, Virginia's disappearance, Grady's death. And Boudreaux was the thread that bound them. He had to be the trafficker. Melanie's eyes teared. Was Lacey next? She stared at the poster. And what about Chris? Was he in danger, too?

Melanie thought about her insistence with the high-profile wedding of the One Shell Tower Plaza client. She rubbed her temples. Chris had warned her. For once, he'd shown caution and concern, and all she wanted was to ignore it.

"We need to go talk to your friend now," Chief Bert said, interrupting her thoughts.

———

Pulling her car in front of Second Chances, Melanie stepped onto the sidewalk, but Charlene hesitated.

"Hey, sis? I think I'll wait in the car. Maybe now's not the time for my questions." She hugged her sister and turned.

As the chief and Melanie walked into the shop, chimes rang out, and Carol walked from around the cash register. "Hey there …" She stopped and stood with her hands on her hips. Her lips pursed together in a straight line. "He got arrested, didn't he?" Carol slapped the counter. "Gosh darn it all. I am so stupid. Why do I always fall for the losers?" She brushed the long wisps of wavy hair away from her face and blew out a breath of disgust. "Ya know—"

"Carol, stop." Melanie placed her hand on Carol's arm. "I'm afraid it's worse than that."

Carol gulped, and the gravity of Melanie's words seemed

to grip her. She shrugged off Melanie's hand and raised her own to her mouth. Shaking her head, she whispered, "No."

"Miz, Carol. I'm sorry, but I need to ask a few questions. A man matching the description of your ..." Chief Bert looked at Melanie.

In hushed tones, Melanie asked, "Carol, did Grady go by any other name?"

Carol nodded. With head down, she whispered, "Grayson. Grayson Mitchell."

"Carol, I'm sorry ..."

Shaking her head, she turned her back. "Oh, I didn't know him that well." Carol's voice cracked. "I mean, I only met him at a bar." Forcing a laugh, she waved her hands, then spoke in a whisper. "Don't tell me. I don't want to know. I'm used to picking up my pieces, and I'll just do it again."

She stood to walk but crumpled, and Chief Bert and Melanie caught her. A single sob emitted from her throat. Their arms tangled in the fringe of her shawl and her long red hair, but no one moved.

Finally, Carol regained her footing and stood straight. "Chief, can I come down to the station when I'm ready. Maybe not today, but tomorrow?" She waved them off and stepped toward the back of her store.

"Sure thing, Miz Carol. Take your time." He tipped his hat and turned to leave.

"Mel?" Carol called over her shoulder.

"Yes, Carol?"

"I'm sorry. I'm sorry if Grady." Carol gulped. "If he had anything to do with—"

"Carol. Let's not worry about that right now," said Melanie softly.

"Well, I ... I really messed it up big time, didn't I?" Carol sniffled and wiped her nose. "Mel, I think maybe I'll take you up on that church invite. That is if you'll have me?" Her head turned slightly, and her fingers wiped a tear.

The abruptness of the request took Melanie by surprise, and a sheepish grin crept upon her lips. But a bittersweet sorrow lighted on her soul as she wondered why it came to this.

"Of course, Carol. Why Lacey will be so excited, we'll pick you up next week."

Melanie thought of Hilly and missed opportunities. "Carol, there is a Ladies Bible Study at the Church midweek. Would you like to go to that with me?"

"Ladies? Nah, don't think I'm ready for that yet." Carol's back straightened. "Well, go on now. Go take care of Lacey and tell her I said hey."

As they left the shop, Chief Bert mentioned the FBI again. Melanie nodded, and an overwhelming rush washed over her. She knew what was coming.

"They'll want to talk to Chris. And you too."

Melanie swallowed hard. "I know. Let me know when."

"Have you gotten in touch with him? Chris?"

"No. He hasn't answered my call." Her chest felt like a weighted bar rested there. "I'll try again." Melanie blurted out before the chief left, "Chief, do you think Boudreaux killed Hilly?"

"I don't think it was an accidental overdose."

"Do you think he took Virginia?"

"Yes, ma'am. I do."

Melanie pressed her lips together and shook her head. "He's a despicable man." Her hands shook.

"Now, Melanie. You don't need to get worked up. Remember, we're on it, but it's the weekend, and we can't do much until Monday. You just got to trust us." He turned to leave then called out, "And pray. We can always use that."

Trust. There it was again. She scooted into her car and rested her head on the steering wheel. Her sister's hand stroked her back.

"I'm sorry, sis. Hey, I can skip New Orleans. I can take care of that anytime." Charlene waved a hand.

Melanie shook her head and mumbled, "No. You go. I'll be fine." Through stinging eyes, she smiled. "Besides, you might find something out that will help."

CHAPTER 29

"Listen, sis, I can do this interview on the phone."

"No, Charlene. Your work is important." Melanie glanced back at Second Chances. "Especially now. We have to find out what's going on."

"We? Are you crazy, Mel? You can't fight these guys." Charlene gripped her sister's shoulder. "This isn't like you. Don't you leave things like this to God or something?"

Melanie smiled, and her eyes softened. "I will if you will?"

Charlene let out an exasperated growl. "Oh, all right. You win. I'm going to New Orleans. I'll see you in the morning."

"Seriously? You can't even ..."

"You go to God or pray or whatever. I'll be fine." Charlene waved her off.

She often ignored comments like that from her sister. Faith and religion weren't subjects they discussed, not since the death of their parents. Still, Melanie's sorrow indicator went up whenever Charlene spoke like that.

Charlene called an Uber and left for New Orleans, while Melanie sat in her car staring at Carol's shop. Feeling a vise-like grip on her heart, she ached for her friend. Anger exploded as she thought of the blue car that hit Grady. It had to be Boudreaux. She had never really met the guy, but she hated him. He preyed on weak people. Virginia? Where was she? And Hilly. Melanie breathed deep and blew out. Her lips fluttered, and her body shuddered. Hitting the steering wheel, she lowered her hand and started the engine.

Fifteen minutes later, she arrived at Oleander Drive and idled in front of Hilly's house. Her skin prickled. The place looked as sad and miserable as Hilly's wretched life had been. A screen door lay on the front porch, and the front door had caution tape across it. She stared.

"That's all? Ugly yellow caution tape marking the end of life?" An empty cold shivered over her.

Melanie drove back to Main Street, to Max's florist shop. She would order the biggest bouquet she could afford and place it on Hilly's front porch. And not the funeral serene white, but bright reds, oranges, and vibrant yellows. She didn't know where Hilly stood with her faith, but she knew Hilly had heard the message. Melanie put her hope that somewhere, sometime, Hilly had cried out to God. And if she had, Melanie was certain the Lord Almighty heard her plea.

As she pulled into a parking space in front of The Pink Rosette, she spotted an older couple strolling down the sidewalk, headed in her direction. A white-haired woman hung on the heavy-set man's arm. Looking back at the florist shop window, she smiled at the wedding display. But a light switched in her brain, and her eyes widened as she glanced at the approaching couple. It was Mr. Woodley, the banker. Melanie had never called him to confirm that she got the wedding contract for One Shell Tower Plaza. She shivered. The one that would hold off the foreclosure of her home. With everything happening, she had forgotten all about that.

Ducking down in her seat, she hoped he wouldn't see her and stop. If he asked her how the referral was coming with One Shell Tower Plaza, she'd have to lie again. She dug through her purse, looking for the business card. Pulling it out, she tapped the number. She grabbed her cell, making another rash move.

"Penthouse. How may I help you?"

Penthouse? That was how they answered? Impressed but confused, she asked, "Is this the One Shell Tower Plaza penthouse?" *Of course, it is. Stupid.*

"Yes, it is." A low, female voice spoke. "Who is calling, please?"

"Hi. This is Melanie Thompson. I'm from ..."

"Quaint Affairs. Yes, Mrs. Thompson. We were expecting your call a few days ago. It's good to hear from you. Please hold."

Classical music played, and Melanie smiled. Pachelbel's *Canon in D.* Her favorite wedding music. And the favorite of every other hopeless romantic. Scrunching her face, she wondered how the secretary, or whoever she was, knew her business.

"Mrs. Thompson, I've been instructed to book you for an appointment with the bride on Monday. Is that acceptable?"

Melanie pulled her phone away from her ear and pressed the speaker icon. Her brows furrowed as if she was facing the woman in person. "Well, I'd like to get some details first." Like the bride's name?

She heard a faint chuckle. "We're quite busy here at the moment, but the bride is the one you should talk to, and she'll be able to answer all your questions on Monday."

Melanie paused, trying to make out a faint conversation in the background. She couldn't. "But, I don't ..."

"Mrs. Thompson, how is your daughter doing? We heard she took a nasty fall."

Melanie gasped and stared at the phone. Her stomach knotted, and her skin grew hot. If they knew about Lacey, it involved Chris. She practically whispered. "How did you know about ..."

"Oh, we care about our employees."

"But I'm not your employee."

Another chuckle. "Of course. Not yet. But your husband is. Mr. Thompson."

"But he doesn't. He doesn't work for you anymore."

A pause. More voices. "Is that what he told you?"

Oh, Lord, I need calm here. Melanie thought she should end it, but her mind raced with the task force meeting. Old, abandoned hotels, empty buildings. Obscure real estate dealings. Her pulse quickened, and the calm didn't come.

"You know, maybe I'm mistaken. I mean, he told me about the last closing on the one in New Orleans. It was... on...uh ..." Melanie waited, hoping they'd take the bait. No answer. "Oh, I can't remember where. But you know, he told me he found another one down there, but I thought he had another buyer for it. Another client." Melanie winced. A pain sliced her heart at the lies, but she went on justifying a necessary indiscretion. "Anyway, thank you. My daughter is doing well. She fell and..."

"Was the property he found in the Lower Ninth?" A voice spoke, and it sounded as if she was repeating someone else's words. "And who is this other client?"

"The Lower Ninth? Yes, I think so. Yes, that's what he said. I think it was near the other one." Melanie found a grocery receipt and crinkled it over the phone. "Let me see. I'll see if I can find the address...Hmmm...Is this it? Nope ..."

"Jourdan Avenue?" It was a statement posed as a question.

Melanie scrolled her phone to the Notes app and tapped *Jourdan Ave, Lower 9th.* Her heart rate rose. "Yes. Yes, I think so."

She had to get out of this. But one more thing was bugging her. Boudreaux. What was his involvement? Courage waned but hate for him and fear for her own daughter spurred her on.

Her mind sprang into action. Rolling down her window,

she yelled at no one. "Hey! Good to see you. Let me finish this call. I'll join you in a second."

Two women walking the street looked around. They pointed to themselves, smiled, then waved. Melanie chuckled. *Tourists*, she thought, as she resumed her conversation.

"Listen, I have to run. But Monday is good. Just text me the time and place. Oh, wait, is Mr. Boudreaux there?" Silence. "I'd like to thank him for passing your card on to me." She waited. Silence again. Melanie pushed. "May I speak to him, please?"

Melanie heard a prolonged breath intake, and the female voice spoke. "Mr. Boudreaux is unavailable." Click.

Melanie threw her phone on the passenger seat and stared. Her hands shook. Now she knew.

Virginia was missing. That was the first thing and finding her was the top priority right now. *Chief Bert.* She should start there. *No.* If she did that, he'd have to go through all the red tape, and there was no time. Chris wasn't dependable, and Desmond didn't want to help. A pinch hurt her heart, but shaking it off, she formulated a plan. New Orleans was an hour away, but if she did call the chief, at least he could get the ball rolling.

"Hey, Chief. Melanie here. I think I have a lead on where Virginia might be." She took deep, cleansing breaths.

There was a long pause. "Melanie, where are you?"

"I'm in town." She tried to calm her shaking voice.

"Make sure you stay in town." He spoke forcefully. "I don't know how you got a lead but give it to me, and I'll call it in to the New Orleans Police. We can hope for a drive-by, but they probably won't do anything since I have no report of criminal activity."

"Seriously?" Melanie's voice rose.

It didn't seem to faze the chief. "And how did you come about this information?"

"It's a long story. I'll tell you later."

"You better. That station down there is a busy precinct, but I'll give you the Sexual Assault Division number. Maybe you can get somewhere with them."

"Me? Can't you call them?" She sounded desperate even to her own ears.

"I could, but a woman calling might get further."

"You're right. Give me the number." Melanie's anxiousness weighed heavy.

After finishing her call with Chief Bert, she called the number he gave her and got nowhere. The detective took her report and told her that most of the area was under low surveillance. Still, they had detected no suspicious activity. Petty crime, break-ins, and even prostitution were right under their noses. They were looking for more prominent kingpins. They needed concrete proof.

She called Chris. Waiting for him to answer again, she stared out her window. Blue skies. What a change. The storms both inside and out had lingered for so long, she didn't know how to process the warmth the day offered to promise. *What promises?* Her thoughts were interrupted.

"Hey, babe! What's up?" Chris's cheery voice irritated her initially, but she relaxed, feeling a little humbled that he never held a grudge. Even after her last biting words.

"Hey, Chris." She took a shallow breath and blew out. "We missed you at the task force meeting last night."

She'd never heard him at a loss for words, but his response sounded measured. "You missed me?"

Melanie winced. "Well, we all did. Lots of stuff came out. Listen. I don't have much time, but you don't happen to have the address of the properties you closed recently in New Orleans, do you?"

"Oh, I get it. You missed me for my input. And no, Mel. I don't know what you want with those addresses, but I'm not giving them to you."

"Well, I was just going to pass them on to Chief Bert. So

he could investigate." The lies were beginning to strangle her conscience, pushing out thoughts of God. *He might stop me,* she thought.

"I can call the chief myself."

Melanie fluttered her lips. "Okay, you do that. I have to go." She didn't have the time or energy to argue.

"Love you, babe!"

"Yeah, sure."

Melanie clicked off and sat, contemplating a plan. She wanted to pray, but the only words she uttered were, *I'm sorry.* Going against her better judgment, she started her engine, intending to drive to New Orleans, but stopped. *Lacey. I have to call her.* She hit the number.

"Hey, Lacey. Listen, I've got some work to take care of. Are you okay with Tina?"

Melanie waited while Lacey checked.

"Okay, great. I'll be home after dinner tonight. Put in a frozen pizza. Tina will love you for it! Bye. I love you, sweetheart."

Driving out of Bay Town, Melanie hopped on the expressway and arrived a little over an hour later with plenty of daylight left. New Orleans bustled, and she drove through the French Quarter, passing the Hotel Mont Leon. Fond memories of staying there with her dad when she was a little girl filled her mind. She shook her head. No time for warm fuzzies now.

She thought about every detail of the phone call with the One Shell Tower Plaza. *Mr. Boudreaux is unavailable.* What did that mean? Did he take Virginia and leave? Did he have more girls? And Jourdan Avenue. Where was that?

The Lower Ninth was the hardest hit district after the last big hurricane. It was also on the New Orleans tour registry of places to visit.

The tour agencies were a dime a dozen. Bicycle tours, double-decker bus tours, and shady little beat-up cars had "Lower 9th Tours" painted across them. She strolled the sidewalk to where the private cars were parked. Inquiring about the tours' prices, the newer model cars were too pricey, so she settled on an older model. Much older. A classic but clean and beautifully restored. Pulling out her wallet, she booked it.

"Does the tour go to Jourdan Avenue?" Melanie asked.

The driver peered at her in the rearview mirror and narrowed his eyes. "Nope." His black dreads hung in his face as he turned. "Why do you want to go there?"

Melanie ignored the question. "Can we skip the rest of the tour and just show me around there instead?"

He hesitated but shrugged. "Sure. But it's just a bunch of torn up hotels and stuff. Jourdan Avenue is an old, abandoned business district. Wasn't much before, and it ain't nothing now." He turned and asked again. "Why do you want to go there?"

"Just doing some research." She clenched her hands tightly in her lap.

"Your money, lady." He didn't drive immediately but instead held up his cell so that both he and she were on the camera screen. "Smile!" He snapped a selfie of both of them.

Rubbing her arm, she felt the hairs rise. Something was odd, but before she could ask, he laughed.

"Souvenir photo. Give me your number, and I'll text it." His grin was more of a sneer.

"No, thanks." She leaned back as far as she could into the back seat. "Can we just get going?"

He seemed not to listen, and with his head down, she thought she heard the clicking of his cell.

It wasn't a lengthy drive, but Melanie cringed at the urban ruins along the way. Some newer pre-fab houses sprung up between the torn-up foundations of former homes in the neighborhood.

The driver passed some apparent peddlers lining the side of the road. They seemed to be selling souvenirs and trinkets. She noticed a teenager up ahead sitting in a bright-green, metal, folding chair. What looked like jewelry sparkled in the sun in front of her. The girl's arms were crossed, and short, slim legs stretched out before her. A colorful, printed turban framed her serene face. It was quite a contrast to the plain white tee-shirt and ripped blue jeans, much like Virginia wore. She couldn't be much older than Lacey. In a split second, Melanie yelled, "Stop!"

When the driver slowed and stopped, the girl didn't flinch, and the stern expression on her face remained stoic.

Looking at her watch, Melanie reasoned she had a few extra minutes. Especially since she really had no plan but to check out Jourdan Avenue, hoping she'd see Virginia—hoping by some miracle to help her. But this girl, though not resembling Virginia, tugged at Melanie's heart, too.

"That's just junk," the driver called back.

Melanie stepped out.

The wire-wrapped, beaded jewelry sparkled in the sunlight. A tattered black cloth draped the rusty TV tray that held the trinkets. The girl gave Melanie a hard stare.

Fingering the pieces, Melanie asked, "Did you make these yourself?"

The girl nodded but didn't smile. Her arms were loosely crossed over her chest.

"They're lovely." Melanie admired the silver earrings and bracelets. She picked out two pieces and handed the girl a twenty-dollar bill.

One brow raised.

"Oh, I'm sorry. Is that not enough?" Not waiting for an answer, Melanie pulled out another twenty.

The girl pursed her lips like a whistle but made no sound. Raising one eyebrow, she said, "I don't have change for that."

Melanie noticed her perfectly manicured nails. She

glanced down. The toenails matched, but the worn sandals had mud caked on the bottoms. "Oh, well. Keep the change. I…"

The girl stuffed the bills into her shirt before Melanie could finish.

"Do you have a business card or something? I have a friend that owns a shop in Bay Town. She'd sell them there. Your work is pretty impressive."

The driver honked, and the girl peered around Melanie. She raised a finger in a lewd gesture toward the driver. Melanie shuddered, and the man laughed.

Pulling out one of her cards, Melanie handed it to the girl. "Here, take my card and call me if you want to sell more."

The girl made no move to take the card, so Melanie laid it down. "Well, thank you." She extended a hand. "I'm Melanie."

Raising her head high, the woman jutted her chin up. "Verona."

"Well, it's nice meeting you, Verona. You're an incredibly talented young lady."

Melanie slid into the car as the tour driver continued past more devastation. She'd seen pictures, but they did nothing to wrench her heart like this. All her experience in New Orleans had been in scoping out the iconic hotels and plush venues for weddings. She turned to look back for the girl, but she was already out of view. Sorrow tugged again. *Oh, Lord, please protect her.*

As the driver flew past the streets, she couldn't make out the name markers.

"Hey, you're taking me to Jourdan Avenue, right?"

The man shook his head. "Sure, if you say so." Finally, he turned onto a street with taller buildings. They looked like they might have been old hotels or restaurants. She pulled out her phone and held it up, trying to snap pictures.

"Hey, what are you doing?" The driver stared at her in the rearview mirror.

What an odd question.

"I mean, these ain't worth nothing. I can take you to some really nasty parts." He grinned.

Melanie shivered as he drove a little too quickly. "Slow down, please."

Glancing up, she thought she saw someone in an upstairs window of a two-story building. A broken sign, propped on the ground, read, HOTEL.

"Can you slow down, please?"

The driver shifted to a crawl.

"Okay, here. Stop."

Melanie jerked forward as the driver stomped on the brake.

She snapped a few pictures, but the man in the upstairs window had already disappeared. She took more photos of the driveway where the back of a blue car peeked out of the side breeze-way. Her eyes widened, and her heart beat a little faster. She looked in the rearview mirror, and the driver's dark face stared back at her.

"Everything, okay, ma'am?"

She got an eerie feeling and texted the picture of the blue car to the chief immediately.

Just then, a man in a suit walked out of the building, and Melanie's breath caught in her throat. He was large in height and build. A small sigh escaped. It wasn't Boudreaux. The relief was short-lived as she recognized that it was the man who approached her at the wedding. The one who told her to call One Shell Tower Plaza. His eyes fixed on the car as he walked closer.

"Go. Go now!" she said to the driver.

"What? I thought you wanted to take pictures." He glanced away as he shifted into park.

She heard a click and looked at her door. The driver had

locked her in. *How could that be in an old vehicle?* The man outside walked toward her, and she scrambled across the wide backseat to the opposite door. Her fingers fumbled with the lock. No luck. She yanked at the door handle.

"Open it, right now!" Melanie yelled.

"If you say so."

The locks clicked again, and the man outside reached for the handle. Melanie yanked hers and pushed the door. Falling out of the car, she kicked off her clogs and ran. She didn't know where to, she just ran.

"Antoine!" The man's voice boomed behind her. "Get her!"

As she ran, the private tour car reversed, swung around, and followed her. The other man made chase but was no match for Melanie's stride. Her pounding heart drove her on as she pumped her arms. The gravel and dirt made her run difficult, but she maneuvered as best she could. The car was close, and she felt the flying dust and heat of the engine gaining on her. She feared he would slam her body against a building.

A break between the structures appeared, and Melanie ducked down an alley too narrow for the car to follow. Looking back, she stumbled and screamed. The debris tearing up her feet stopped her, and before she could stand, the driver had jumped from his car. Melanie sprung forward, and turning down another lane, she saw a black sedan blocking the exit. Another alley, and she turned. She wanted to stop but couldn't. Rounding yet another corner, she screamed.

The large man from the hotel faced her. Laughing, he reached out. She stumbled backward, and he grabbed at her, catching her blouse. When she continued scrambling back-ward, the thin fabric tore in his hands, and he lost his grip. Catching herself, she ran hard in the opposite direction, watching for the other driver. Making a quick turn, she raced toward the parked black car and scooted around it.

Finding another alley, she kept darting in and out of buildings, but didn't stop to look, didn't stop to catch her breath. When she heard no more footsteps, she curved down a wide alley. It opened to a street with nothing but piles and piles of debris. Everything looked the same. Suddenly another turn took her onto a paved, wide asphalt street. Pumping her arms and legs, her long strides carried her a considerable distance. Before she knew it, she was back at the corner where she'd bought the jewelry. Melanie saw the girl walking down the street.

"Help! Please!" Melanie yelled, running toward her.

The girl picked up her pace, but the chair and TV tray slowed her down. She looked back over her shoulder.

"Verona! Please, help me!"

Melanie stopped, bent over, and rested her hands on her knees, trying to catch her breath. She looked up, and Verona had dropped her goods and was yelling and pointing.

Melanie, still hunched, raised her head just as her tour driver's car screeched to a halt, almost hitting her. Before she could gain her balance, she fell hard on the rubble. The tour guide jumped out and grabbed her and threw her in the car.

CHAPTER 30

I t was late afternoon before Desmond arrived in New Orleans. His eyes widened as he entered the iconic Bourbon Orleans Hotel in the heart of the French Quarter. The aura of a decade's rich history still permeated the recent multimillion-dollar renovation.

A colossal crystal chandelier glistened above the lobby floor. As Desmond stared upward, he brushed against fronds reaching from green cascade palms. Guests mingled about, some relaxing on the plush, burgundy velvet chairs and couches placed about the breathtaking lobby. An eclectic mix of luxurious fabrics hung from the tops of floor-to-ceiling windows and lavish furnishings intertwined with fields of tapestry rugs that ran the length of the lobby and beyond. The upscale décor presented itself far above anything Desmond had ever seen or experienced before.

"Hey, Des. I just checked in. Do you want a room?" Chris slapped him on the back. "I'm not paying, though."

Desmond spun around. "Yeah, right. But why here?" Desmond raised a brow. "I thought this was just a meeting place. I didn't know you checked in."

"Why not?" Chris laughed, then explained that the implied threats he received spooked him, so he thought this

part of town might be an excellent place to hide if needed. He figured crowds of affluent tourists were a suitable cover.

"I know. I know. Maybe I might be over-imagining the danger, but it's a good excuse to stay here, right?" Chris laughed, clapping his hands together.

Desmond shrugged and noticed Chris's attire. Donning a smart-looking Panama hat with black trim and flashy Ray-Bans, he looked like a wealthy out-of-towner. His classy pale-yellow Hawaiian shirt and tan slacks seemed to fit the bill. Casual brown leather loafers with no socks completed the look.

Desmond pulled down his sunglasses and grabbed a folded baseball hat from his back pocket.

They walked out and asked the bellman to hail a cab.

"Hey, did you talk to Mel, by any chance?" asked Chris.

Desmond breathed deep. "Not since yesterday. Why?" Desmond recalled leaving Melanie in the rain at the bus stop.

"Oh, nothing. She called and wanted something." Chris shrugged. "I kind of blew her off."

Desmond stared at Chris with hard eyes. "You shouldn't treat her like that. She doesn't deserve that." He hated that he judged Chris, but he couldn't seem to help it right now. "I don't want to tell you your business, but you have a special family with Mel and Lacey. With Mel's parents gone, it's taken them a while to start a new life here and find some happiness again. Now, with all this happening, they could sure use family support."

"Family?" Chris put a hand on his chest. "But I thought maybe ..." He pointed at Desmond. "I thought you were weaseling in?"

Desmond's mouth drew a taut line and he drew a deep breath and sighed. "Listen, if it's something you've thought about lately, maybe God is nudging you in that direction. It doesn't matter what's happened in the past. If you want a second chance, God is all about that. That's all I'm saying.

Don't do it just for fun or for kicks. They need stability. Their world's been rocked."

Chris rolled his head back and closed his eyes. He pocketed his hands and drew his shoulders back. For once, Chris was silent.

Desmond's heart sunk with the conflict raging inside himself. He shook it off. "So, what's the plan?"

"The plan? I thought you wanted to go check out the properties I sold?"

"Just checking. So we're headed where?"

"To a dump called, The Lower Ninth." Chris shrugged.

They caught a cab to the Lower Ninth, just three miles away from the Quarter. Time stood still, and renovation and reconstruction had not caught up. As the taxi approached their destination, Chris instructed their driver to drop them at the top of the street and return to a specific address in thirty minutes. The driver was reluctant, but Chris promised to compensate. It was getting late, and Chris knew too well this wasn't the place to be after dark.

They looked out of place at first glance, but a band of bicycle tourists rode by gawking at the abandoned structures. It eased Desmond some until Chris stopped.

"Here's one of the properties."

The building had new windows and new framed double front doors, but it lacked fresh paint and décor. Desmond questioned the hotel's current use, and a sickening surge rose in his gut. He prayed as he stared.

"Time to rock-n-roll!" Chris pulled out his cell phone and struck silly poses. He appeared to be taking selfies with the hotel in the background—lots of them.

A squatty but broad-chested dark man with long, wavy hair exited the hotel. "Hey, man! What the heck are you doing out here?" His wide, flat nose dwarfed his small eyes that were squinting in the sun.

Desmond placed himself between Chris and the man, his Navy Seal instincts on high alert.

Chris flashed a smile. "Excuse me? Oh, hey, I heard there was a new cafe that opened with great barbecue. Someone said it was in one of these hotels?"

Desmond marveled at how fast Chris could make up a story.

"It ain't here, man. Now move on."

"Say, isn't this a hotel? I mean, it says hotel on the sign there." Chris pointed to the jagged marquee resting against the dirty building and chuckled.

The imposing man clenched his fists and narrowed his eyes. "Yeah. So what? You telling me you wanna book a room?" He took steps toward Chris.

Desmond clenched a fist.

"Yeah, I don't think so." Chris laughed and raised his hands in surrender. "Hey, we're just curious, you know, about all this renovation and reconstruction going on. It seems like your place hasn't made much progress." He laughed again. It wasn't reciprocated.

The man lunged at Chris. Desmond moved in, placing a hand on his shoulder, and the man glared at him. Before he could react, a voice spoke.

"Hey, Antoine." The man's greeting drawled from the hotel entrance, stopping all action. He wore a light-gray suit with a fashionable tie and expensive-looking shoes. Lighting a cigarette, he breathed deep, then tossed the match at Chris's feet.

Desmond's eyes widened behind his sunglasses. He released the man called Antoine and pulled down his baseball cap, hoping his disguise would hide him.

"What's the problem here? This ain't how we treat our guests. Be nice, Antoine." He tried to look at Desmond's face, but Desmond looked down. The man extended a hand to

Chris. "The name's Bodine. Bill Bodine, at your service. And your name, sir?"

Chris smiled. "Tommy. Tommy Bahama."

"You're joking, right?"

Desmond would have laughed if not for the danger in front of him. He'd recognized Bill Bodine. That slow southern speech, his slicked-back hair, and that flashy smile were all too familiar.

"And you are?" He stared at Desmond.

Desmond lowered his voice and growled. "We're just tourists. Apparently, we're lost." Pulling at Chris' sleeve, he continued, "Come on, man. I told you we were in the wrong place. Let's go." Desmond took steps to leave.

Chris frowned and held out his hand, stopping Desmond. The man in the suit stared.

"Hold on, bro. Listen, Mr. Bodine, my brother, might be anxious to leave, but I'm representing a non-profit foundation that"s looking to give out some funds—a grant. You know, to help with the renovation down here."

Antoine narrowed his eyes. "You said you was looking for barbecue." His biceps bulged as his short arms hung by his sides.

"Well, that, too. It is lunchtime, isn't it?" Chris attempted a smile. "But seriously, if you'd like, I can look inside, take a few photos, and present it to our board of directors?"

Bill Bodine let out a long puff of smoke.

Chris coughed.

Bodine laughed. "Yeah, right."

A movement at the double-door entrance caught Desmond's eye. A scantily dressed teen stepped out. She wobbled on high heels and pushed back her platinum blonde curls that were falling across her brow. She was apparently drunk or drugged. Desmond's body went rigid. He took a few steps toward the young woman but stopped himself.

Bodine turned. "Git, girl. Back inside." He turned back, addressing Chris. "This foundation. What's the name?"

"Uh, the name? Well, I represent many—" Chris stuttered.

"The name?" Bodine narrowed his eyes.

"The Chadwick Foundation," Chris blurted out.

Desmond's mouth hung open, and he glared at Chris. Good one. That was Charlene's surname.

"They're always looking for down-and-out businesses to support. And by the looks of things, you guys need it." Chris rattled on. "Get this place fixed up, and it could boost the economy down here. Create a lot of jobs and opportunities for the locals. Lots of tourists out there, you know, always looking for a good bargain." Chris sounded a bit too frantic.

"Uncle Will, can I have a cigarette, please?" The girl's slurred voice interrupted.

All eyes spun around to the girl leaning on the concrete planter just outside the entrance. Desmond caught it. Uncle Will, she'd said. It took all the self-control he had not to grab her and run. He said a silent prayer and faced the girl. He removed his sunglasses, hoping she'd connect with him. Hoping he might catch a plea for help. She glanced at him but showed no expression at all and turned her eyes back toward Bodine.

"Shut up, girl. I said, go to your room. We're doing business here."

With pouting lips, she turned away but stopped to lean on the planter once more.

Chris backed up, and Bodine faced him, giving Antoine a sideways nod. Both advanced on him.

Antoine grabbed Chris's arms and twisted them behind his back. Desmond saw an opportunity and bolted after the girl, who was now struggling to walk inside.

"Matt!" Bodine's voice bellowed. "Git down here now!"

Desmond reached the girl and lifted her while she kicked

him with no force at all. He threw her frail body over his shoulder and made a run for it.

"Matt!" bellowed Bodine again.

A man emerged from the hotel, making chase after Desmond. He hooked Desmond's leg with his foot causing him to stumble. The girl fell from his shoulder as he toppled forward and screamed as she hit the ground. Matt lunged at Desmond. They rolled over the driveway, exchanging hard punches. The girl stood, but the men fell toward her, and Matt landed a blow against her jaw that was clearly meant for Desmond. She went down again, this time out cold. Matt threw another punch, sending Desmond sprawling.

Antoine held onto Chris's arms, who tried to wiggle free. With each struggle, Antoine tightened his grip, and Chris grimaced in pain.

Bodine glanced at the brawl in the courtyard. "Matt, take care of him!" he screamed as he dug through Chris's pockets, pulling out a wallet.

Suddenly, a loud horn honked from the street in front of the hotel. Desmond scrambled to stand and ran at Matt, full force, throwing him against the concrete planter. He slumped, his eyes, glazed. Desmond picked up the girl and ran for the taxi. He held her tightly and shoved Antoine as he passed.

Antoine tripped, releasing his grip on Chris. As he fell backward, he slammed his head on the driveway and lay stunned.

Chris fell forward, his body striking Bodine, and the wallet flew in the air. Bodine reached for it, but at the same time, Chris grabbed Bodine's suit pocket and drew back a fist. His clenched hand dropped Bodine to the cracked concrete. Shaking his hurt hand, Chris scooped up his wallet and ran for the taxi door.

He yelled over his shoulder, "Sorry, guys. Don't think the foundation can help you out." He passed Desmond, and opening the rear door, he jumped in.

Antoine wobbled to a standing position, shook his head, and stumbled after them.

Desmond reached the taxi and threw the girl in the back-seat as Chris yanked at her arms. Desmond attempted to climb in, but Antoine caught him and heaved him back. Kicking the door closed just before Antoine threw him to the ground, Desmond yelled.

"Go! Go! Go now!"

Chris yelled from inside the car, but Desmond waved him off as the taxi driver peeled out of the driveway.

Antoine kicked Desmond's body strategically, incapacitating him, then his huge arms pummeled Desmond's body.

Bodine wobbled to standing and wiped his cut lip. "Stop! Antoine, now!"

Desmond lay barely conscious and didn't move.

Antoine turned toward Bodine. "Are you crazy, man? They're witnesses! And that guy's got, Ginny."

"Shut up. Just shut up," Bodine yelled back. "She ain't gonna talk. She's too stupid and strung out."

The other man was just stirring, and Bodine pulled him up with one hand. "Matt, get up. Get the girls ready. We're transporting now."

Pulling out his phone, he made a call. "Mr. Black, we got a problem down here." He walked to his car and laid the cell phone on his hood with the speaker-mode on. He pulled a clean white handkerchief from his pocket and patted his swollen lip, smearing blood.

Desmond's consciousness was coming and going. *Bodine? It's got to be Boudreaux.* He struggled to listen but could only hear Bodine's side of the conversation.

Boudreaux spewed a stream of expletives. "It's a big problem. I'm moving the girls now. I need to get out of this place."

Boudreaux went silent. He spun around and kicked the tire.

"I don't care about the other group of girls. Take them

someplace else. Send the van now. I'm taking them to the docks tonight." After ending the call, he slipped it into his pocket.

Desmond tried to focus on Boudreaux's face, but all went black.

CHAPTER 31

The taxi sped down the potholed blacktop streets. The boarded-up houses and trash-hewn lots whizzed by, and Chris argued with himself. Not knowing what to do, he stared at the girl lying in the back seat, wondering if she was still alive. He watched and waited. Finally, he saw a slight movement of her body rising and falling. Who was she? He recalled Bodine calling her Ginny, but why did Desmond take her? Chris heaved a heavy sigh. *He's a better man than me.*

"Hey, man, I'm calling the cops." The driver fumbled with his phone. "What about that girl? We taking her to the hospital or what?"

Chris stared as the taxi driver spoke, but his mind wasn't processing.

"My phone died. You better call the cops now." The driver sounded frantic.

Chris pounded the back of the seat. Helpless frustration gripped hold.

"Hey! Knock it off," said the taxi driver.

Totally lost, Chris couldn't think. He'd never had to take care of anyone, much less an unconscious teenager. He needed help. "Sorry, man. Just give me a sec," he said.

"We don't have a sec. Just call the cops. If I didn't think we were being followed, I'd stop now. And what about your friend? You can't just leave him."

Chris blocked out the questions. His mind didn't know where to go, and he glanced upward. He thought he knew but couldn't make himself go there. God wouldn't listen to him, anyway. He pulled out his cell and dialed Melanie. It went to voicemail.

"Come on, Mel? I need help. Pick up, please!"

He saw a notification and looked at the number. It was a missed call from Charlene. Why did she call? Melanie. It had to be. He hit redial.

"Hey, Charlene. Is Mel there?"

"Chris? Everyone's been trying to reach you since last night. Listen, we need some info—"

"Melanie. Is she there?" Chris interrupted.

"No, I think she's home with Lacey."

Chris hung up and hit Lacey's number.

"Hey, Lacey. This is Chr ... This is Dad. Can you pick up?" He waited.

"Dad? Are you in town? Everyone thought you skipped out after the party," said Lacey sounding out of breath.

"No. Lacey, let me talk to your mom. She's not answering her phone."

"She's not here. She went somewhere with Aunt Charlene this afternoon and hasn't been back."

A sweat broke out, and Chris swiped his forehead. He hoped Melanie was on her way home. "Lacey, you're not alone, are you?"

Silence. When Chris heard Tina's voice laughing in the background, he blew out a breath.

"No, Tina's here. We're watching a movie." Another pause. "What's wrong, Dad?"

Chris held back a choke. His throat felt dry and parched as he rasped, "Nothing, princess. We're good. Let me speak to Tina, okay?"

"Sure, I'll go get her."

Chris touched Ginny. She felt clammy and a little cold, but she was breathing. He saw her shiver. Struggling to hold the phone to his ear, he removed his shirt and covered her.

"Whoa! Whoa there, man. Keep your clothes on," the driver called back.

"The girl's freezing! Listen, is there a hospital in Bay Town?" Chris asked.

"Bay Town? That's a good 45 minutes away from here."

"I'll pay you double if you can make it in thirty minutes."

The engine roared as the car veered onto Highway 10.

"Hey, Chris. What's up?" Tina answered.

"I need you to call Chief Bert. I'm giving you a lot of information, so if you can record this, do it. But don't let Lacey know. When I'm done, send the recording to the chief."

"Chris, you're scaring me," Tina whispered.

"Yeah, well, you're nowhere near as scared as I am." Chris relayed the harrowing incidents of the last hour, and when he finished, he heard Tina whimpering.

"Suck it up, Tina. Make the call." He hung up.

Tina immediately called Chief Bert. She sent the recording, and he jumped on it. Officer Blaine typed the transcript and faxed it to the precinct in New Orleans. Chief Bert followed up with a phone call and found that they were sending a squad of cars over to his relief.

"Chief? What about the FBI?" Blaine asked.

The chief shook his head. "Those guys move so slow, they need concrete proof for ..." He stopped, and his eyes widened. He pulled out his cell to call Chris and noticed a missed text notification from earlier. It was Melanie. Opening it, he froze. "Blaine, what was the address of that hotel Chris was at?"

Blaine shifted through papers. "I know it was Jourdan Avenue. I'm checking." He flipped through the reports.

Her photograph depicted a rundown hotel, and when he zoomed in, his eyes widened. A blue sedan was parked in the driveway. The only message Melanie typed was "Jourdan Avenue." He dialed her number, but the phone recording said the number couldn't be reached. He tried again—same response. Chief Bert didn't like the hunch growing inside. He dialed Chris's number.

"Where you at? Is Melanie with you?"

"Who is this?" Chris asked.

"Chief Bert."

"I'm hoping Mel's on her way home. What's up?"

The Chief knew he had to handle the initial danger, and right now, Melanie's whereabouts were just a hunch.

"So you left Desmond at some hotel?"

"I didn't leave him." Chris choked. "They grabbed him. But yeah, he's at a hotel on Jourdan Avenue in the Lower Ninth."

Melanie! A sweat broke out thinking of the pictures she had sent, but he said nothing about it to Chris. He hoped that she was long gone from Jourdan Avenue.

"Do you have any pictures of the hotel?"

"Yes. I do."

"Send them and send me a photograph of that girl you got with you, too."

"Okay, but what about Melanie?"

"Nothing." *I hope.* "Do you know the name of the girl you got with you?"

"Bodine called her Ginny."

The chief blew out an exasperated sigh and waited anxiously for the pictures.

Meanwhile, Chief Bert studied the photograph that Melanie had sent. He scratched his head. What was she doing there? When his phone buzzed, his pulse quickened as the picture of the girl appeared. He squinted. It looked like Virginia, curled up and sleeping. When he received the hotel pictures, he gasped. It was the same place that Melanie had photographed. He texted Chris back.

I THINK YOU GOT VIRGINIA. SHE'S OUR BAY TOWN'S MISSING GIRL. GOOD JOB, CHRIS. I'LL MEET YOU AT THE HOSPITAL.

He typed nothing about Melanie.

"Blaine, scan these photos and email the report to the FBI."

Chief Bert called the FBI and waited while they retrieved the scanned pictures and report. It was what they needed to move into action. The chief clicked off and turned to Blaine. "Meet Chris at the hospital. I'm heading to New Orleans." He raised a hand. "Wait. Blaine, I need you to check on the whereabouts of Melanie Thompson. Call everybody you know."

Chief Bert grabbed a copy of the report from the printer and looked it over. The chief's mind raced. How could things escalate so fast? And now Desmond and Melanie, too? Taking a deep breath, he choked a little. *I'm coming, Pastor. I'm coming.*

The chief removed his hat and looked up. "I don't know if You're listening to me. But Your man is in trouble. And we all could use Your help, please?"

Virginia was so drugged that she slept the entire ride. Chris touched the swelling on her jaw, and he winced. When they arrived at the small hospital in Bay Town, she was admitted immediately. Officer Blaine was waiting outside, and Chris joined him

"Where's the chief?" Chris asked. "We have to go back and get Desmond."

Officer Blaine followed. "He's on it, sir. Mr. Thompson, have you seen or heard from Melanie Thompson?"

"Officer, do you have a car here …" Chris's eyes widened. "Wait. What do you mean? The Chief asked the same thing. Why is everyone asking?"

"We're trying to locate her." Officer Blaine pulled out his phone and scrolled. He showed the screen to Chris. "She sent the chief this picture earlier this afternoon. He just got it tonight."

Chris's eyes widened, and he slumped.

Officer Blaine reached out to steady him. "Sir?"

Chris's eyes pooled. "They've got her. I know they do. They got Desmond, too."

"Who's got her, sir?"

He grabbed Blaine. "Come on. Take me there."

"I can't do that, sir. My orders are to stay here with Miss Virginia. The chief is on his way to this place. He's got it covered."

"You don't understand! These guys will kill her." He stopped. "Desmond." He stared at Blaine again. "Maybe Desmond can get them out. Come on. I gotta get there."

"Orders, sir. Why don't you wait with me? When the chief calls, maybe I can take you there."

Chris threw a fist in the air. He felt his cell buzz and answered it.

"Yeah?"

"Chris, where's my sister?"

"Charlene? We don't know." Chris almost whispered.

"Everyone's looking for her. Lacey called, you called. I even got a call from the Bay Town Police." Charlene's voice escalated over the phone.

"Yeah, I know. They're looking for Mel now. Listen, a lot is going down right now. Where you at?"

Charlene was on her way back to Bay Town, and Chris told her he'd fill her in when she arrived at the hospital.

Desmond struggled as he awoke. His hands, feet, and mouth were taped. He blinked a few times trying to adjust his eyes, but it made no difference. Everything was black, and he quickly realized he was in the trunk of a car. The air suffocating, but something warm and soft rested up against his back. He smelled a floral scent, then nudged what he was sure was a body. No response.

His fingers worked at the tape on his hands that were restrained behind his back. As he did, he inadvertently poked the soft flesh repeatedly. The body next to him writhed and a muffled scream emitted. It was kneeing him but causing little harm compared to what he was already feeling. When it subsided, a garbled plea cried out.

The voice. It was Melanie! Desmond thrashed his head, trying to speak out her name. The duct tape was so tight, his voice caught in his throat. He prayed, *Lord, let her know it's me.* He forced his mind not to ask questions but to get into escape mode.

A garbled, affirming sound came from behind him, and he only hoped she knew it was him. Wiggling his fingers, they caught hold of hands, and she gripped his fingers tightly. He squeezed, trying to assure her. Feeling that her hands were bound like his, his strong fingers set to work, peeling off strips of tape. The process was slow, but when her hands were free, Melanie wriggled to flip around and face his back. She peeled the tape off her mouth, and a gasp accompanied what sounded like a forceful intake of air.

The sweet voice whispered, "Desmond? Is that you?"

She pressed close to him, and he felt her struggle to reach her hand around his face. Slowly, she pulled the tape off his mouth. He felt her head drop against his back, and as she cried, wetness seeped into his shoulder blades.

He breathed deep. "Yes, Melanie, it's me." Then speaking more forcefully, he whispered. "Free my hands."

When she did, he shifted, but he was too large to flip around like her, so as they both faced toward the front of the opening, he whispered, "God's got us, Melanie. He'll get us out." There was not a speck of light, but hope soared within, and he felt Melanie's nod.

He searched around for tools, but when he heard voices and footsteps on gravel, Melanie's body flinched, and he instructed her to be still.

"Drive them to the back roads on Highway 10. Sink the car in the river." The voice faded, and one set of footsteps retreated but stopped. "And check the trunk before you go."

"They're fine. That's why I drive this classic. Lots of trunk space, but no escape latch." The voice laughed.

Desmond heard a cell ring from outside.

"Hello, New Orleans Tours here?"

Melanie's body stiffened, then flinched again. Desmond wished to comfort her, but anything he did now would endanger them more. He waited.

"I can book you in tomorrow morning. Sure. Nine a.m. it is. Thanks for calling New Orleans Tours. Have a good evening."

As a click sounded, the trunk raised, and Desmond immediately thrust his legs out, kicking with taped ankles. He hit the driver square in the groin. Falling to the ground, he writhed and moaned, giving Desmond enough time to remove the tape from his ankles. Desmond lifted Melanie from the trunk, and as he set her down, she did the same.

The driver rolled to his knees and raised his head. He tried to yell but could only manage a groan. Desmond reached to pick him up, but the driver grabbed Desmond's shirt, pulling him down. The driver rolled on top of him, sat up, and pointed a gun at Desmond's head.

Thud! The man fell forward. His limp body flopped on

top of Desmond, and Melanie stood holding a large rock between both hands. She dropped it and stared wide-eyed.

Desmond pushed the driver off and checked the man's pulse. He nodded at Melanie, hoping to assure her without words that he was alive. Hoisting him, Desmond threw him into the trunk of the car and closed the trunk lid.

Grabbing Melanie's hand, he gripped it tightly and pulled her toward the sound of sirens. They stopped. Two men appeared from the hotel's back entrance, dragging a line of girls roped together. Their mouths were taped shut, but their terrorized fears muffled out. Desmond pulled Melanie into a close-by hedge.

He counted eight girls and pushed Melanie further back behind the hedge. She winced as blood trickled down her arm from the broken branches, but still, he motioned for her to stay put.

He ran across the roadway as the last girl passed and yanked hard on her rope. She fell and like dominos, so did the others, one-by-one. They went down close to the building. Sorrowful pleas that sounded much like bleating sheep came from the pile of girls as the men whispered harsh threats. Desmond hid in the shadows as the men berated the girls and labored to lift them. He leaped out from the bushes and punched the first man who went sprawling into the alley. He kicked the second who fell into the girls. They surrounded him and began kicking. Desmond turned to see the first man wobble to standing in the middle of the street. He pulled a gun, aiming at Desmond.

An engine roared down the alleyway, and all eyes turned to the sound. Headlights flared, and Desmond rolled to the side. The man with the gun stared as a blue car barreled into him. His body flew into the air and continued recklessly down the road. The girls huddled together, and the second man scrambled to his feet and ran away.

Melanie came out from the shadows and ran to the girls.

"You're safe. We'll take care of you." She enveloped as many of them as she could within her arms.

She stared at Desmond and whispered, "What now?"

Desmond put a finger to his lips. "Shhh. I'm not sure we're safe yet Stay here."

CHAPTER 32

D esmond crouched as he crept around the back of the hotel to the side parking lot. The noise was deafening as he stared at the scene before him. Red and blue lights were flashing in all directions. Floodlights highlighted the drizzle of rain descending on the array of squad cars, swat teams, and unmarked vehicles. The scene looked like a bank robbery heist stand-off. Desmond walked out. His knowledge of official procedures guided him. He knew the drill. With his arms raised high, he inched out slowly. Spotlights flooded him, and instructions yelled from a megaphone. Slowly, he bent a knee, his body wracked with pain that he hadn't felt until now.

He lay on the ground, face down, and moved his arms and legs to a spread-eagle position. Wet asphalt stung his nostrils as he breathed the mixture of oil and dirt. Gravel dug into his beaten face, and patches of skin cracked from the caked-in dried blood. The beating he'd taken from Antoine late in the afternoon took its full effect. Recollection of the ordeal flooded his brain, and he fought to remain lucid while thinking. *I'm trusting you, God. Take care of Melanie. Just keep her safe.*

Footsteps sounded, and he saw and heard the boots of men surrounding him. A foot dug around his body. His ears perked when he heard shuffling accompanied by cries and muffled sobs. It was bittersweet music to his ears.

"All secure!" yelled the SWAT-team member standing closest to his head.

In the distance, Desmond heard a booming shout that overrode every other sound.

"Hold on there! Chief of Police, Bay Town, Mississippi, here. I know this man. He's a Minister. He isn't a perp."

Desmond raised his head and saw Chief Bert pushing through the barricades yelling at the man with the megaphone.

A jab flicked Desmond's neck. "Keep your head down."

As he lowered his head again, he saw the point of a rifle.

The officer with the megaphone spoke again. "Stand down, men. I repeat. Stand down! Pastor Brooks, stand slowly, keep your hands in the air, and then place them on your head. Remain there until you are approached and given further instructions."

Desmond complied once more. He wanted to turn and see if Melanie was safe, but the men surrounding him held fast to their guns, aimed at his slowly rising body.

The chief ran to Desmond. A broad smile broke across his face, and he extended a hand. They shook, and the chief turned to the SWAT team. "Go on. I got this."

The SWAT team leader signaled for the rest of the men to join the sentry guarding the group of girls huddled behind them.

The chief grabbed Desmond's shoulders.

Desmond winced and tried to smile.

"Man, am I glad to see you." The chief looked around and pulled off his hat. He drew an intense breath. "Hey, Pastor. We're missing Melanie."

It hurt, but a smile formed, and Desmond turned, nodding in the direction of the crying girls who were being attended to by the Swat Team. Melanie emerged from the group, and when Desmond's eyes found hers, she smiled and took a step. Guns clicked. She froze.

Chief Bert stepped forward he threw his hands in the air. "You were all told to stand down!" His voice boomed, and the guns lowered.

Melanie ran to them and melted into Chief Bert's comforting arms. Desmond stared at her, one eye almost swollen shut.

She gaped when she saw him in the harsh lights. "Desmond? What happened to you?"

She left the chief's arms and reached out to touch Desmond's battered face as her tears fell.

The chief drew his shoulders back. "Oh, man, you need help, buddy! Paramedics!" he yelled as he waved. It wasn't necessary. They were rushing forward to help the terrified girls. Controlled mayhem of hysterics huddled in the parking lot.

Melanie hugged Desmond, burying her head in his chest. A groan escaped, and he didn't know if it was the pain of broken ribs or his broken heart.

A paramedic stood by, and the chief looked at him. "What's wrong with you? Can't you see the man needs help? Geeze!"

"Looks like he's getting all the help he needs." The paramedic winked at Melanie.

She let go and stepped back.

Desmond tried to breathe, but it hurt too much. Not wanting to feel what he was feeling for Melanie, he stared at the chief. "Don't you have work to do here?"

"Not me. Not my jurisdiction. But I can take you two into custody if you want?" He chuckled and patted the paramedic. "Take good care of him, will you?"

An hour flew by, and after the chief had filled Melanie and Desmond in, Melanie's adrenalin subsided. Knowing Lacey was safe, she expressed her desire to see Virginia. The chief agreed to take them to her. Desmond refused a ride to a New Orleans ER but promised to get care in Bay Town.

When Melanie scooted into the squad car's back seat, Desmond seemed to avoid sitting next to her. He slid into the front seat instead. Before Chief Bert started the engine, Desmond turned and looked at Melanie.

"Hey, how about we pray?"

Melanie nodded, and Chief Bert removed his hat and smiled. "Yeah, you know I think the guy up there is listening." He pointed.

"Well, Lord, we thank You, and we give You all the glory for our safety. Take care of these girls. Restore their lives. Make them full with a new life in You."

"Amen! And Hallelujah!" the chief yelled and started his engine. "Good words, Pastor. Good words."

Melanie stared at Desmond as he laid his head back and didn't say another word.

Once they got to Bay Town, Melanie and Desmond encountered Chris outside, pacing. The chief stayed behind, fielding calls in the squad car.

Chris ran toward Melanie. He embraced her and lifted her off the ground. As she slid out of his arms, their faces met, and he gently brushed her lips. Momentarily, she lost herself in memories of too long ago. Chris released her and stared. The shock showing in his face matched how she felt.

"Whoa. Sorry about that, Mel." They both took a step back. "I'm just so glad you're okay." He reached out and stroked her head. A smile crossed his face.

She winced and touched where his hand rested. "Ouch."

"You're not okay!" Chris yelled. "Doctor! I need a doctor..."

Melanie removed his hand. "I'm fine, Chris."

"But Lacey and I have been worried sick about you. Where in the heck did you disappear to?"

Melanie's thoughts shot to Desmond, and she glanced back at him. He leaned against a massive column at the hospital entrance. She didn't know what she read in his eyes. Regret? Sorrow? Loss? His gaze dropped to the ground, and he shoved his hands in his pockets, wincing.

Melanie shook her head and turned to stare back at Chris. Her brows furrowed. "Lacey? She knows about this?"

Chris nodded his head. "You were missing, Mel. She asked if she could be with me." He smiled. "Me. She even called me Dad."

The grin looked like the Cheshire cat in *Alice in Wonderland*. Melanie closed her eyes, and her heart reflected the look she saw in Desmond's eyes.

"Mom!" Lacey came running from the lobby. Tina and Charlene followed.

Melanie threw out her arms, and the girls all hugged and cried and talked at once. Arm in arm, they walked toward the hospital but stopped at the double doors.

"Wait!" Lacey yelled and turned.

Melanie looked back as Lacey ran to Chris. Wrapping her arms around his neck, she hugged him tight. He stared back at Melanie and smiled again.

"I love you, Dad." Lacey kissed Chris's cheek and let go. Turning, she saw Desmond and gasped and walked slowly toward him. Tears fell again from Lacey's eyes, and Melanie watched as Desmond looked away, sinking down onto the concrete bench next to them. Melanie gulped, holding back her own deluge.

"You need help." Lacey lifted a hand to touch his face, but he drew back.

He shook his head, and a slight scrunch of his lips indicated a smile attempt.

"You're my hero," Lacey whispered. "Thank you, Pastor

Brooks. Thanks for saving my mom." She took his hand. "Come on. I'll take you to the ER."

"I'll make it." He looked at Melanie.

Her tears dropped, and she bit her lip hard. Their eyes locked, and the surreal silence that embraced just them lasted but a few seconds before he broke it.

"Go on, Lacey. Take your mom to see Virginia." Desmond nodded.

Lacey hugged him again and ran back to her mom, dragging her into the hospital. As Melanie turned, her last look lingered in her mind. Chris with his silly grin, and Desmond with his battered body ... and heart.

Chris spun around. He looked at Desmond and shrugged his shoulders. "Well, that was awkward." Running a hand through his hair, he breathed deep and pulled out his cell. "I'm going to head back." He tapped in a few numbers. "Why waste a good suite?"

Desmond stared. "Chris, give her time. She's been through a lot."

Chris narrowed his eyes. "Yeah, with you. Right? I mean, you rescued her, but I got her into this mess to begin with." He shook his head.

The chief walked up. "Hey, don't take all the credit, Chris. Women are bull-headed, ya know. Always doing their own thing."

Desmond stared at Chris. "You weren't responsible for all this. Nothing you did was illegal. You didn't know these guys. And if it weren't for your cooperation today, we'd have never saved those girls."

Chief Bert slapped Chris on the back. "The man's right. You're the hero, man! You got Virginia out, and you got proof for the FBI. Dude, we couldn't have done it without you."

Chris frowned and shook his head, but slowly a smile crept on his face. He glanced at the hospital. "Hey, you think you could tell that to Melanie?"

Desmond nodded. "I think she might be figuring it out." The words tasted like vinegar. He looked at Chief Bert. "Yeah, maybe you could lay it on a little thick for the guy." Desmond took a deep breath and tried to laugh, but it hurt. Inside and out.

That seemed to lighten Chris's load as he pointed two hands at Desmond like he was shooting guns. "Okay, there, Sundance!"

The chief looked between them. "Oh, Butch and Sundance. I get it!" He scratched his head. "But doesn't Sundance get the girl?"

Chris threw up his arms. "Oh, come on, now! Give Butch a chance." Waving a hand in the air, Chris smiled. "Well, my Uber's here, and I have a grand hotel suite waiting for me. I'll see you … when I see you, I guess."

"Yeah, don't leave town, though. We've got a lot of paper-work to fill out." The chief swiped a hand across his forehead. "Not looking forward to that. Especially since we didn't get any of the big guys."

"Whaaat?" Chris wrinkled his face.

"Well, not yet. Blaine called me." Chief Bert rested his hands on his hips, shaking his head. "They arrested some guys who aren't talking. No surprise there. But they seem to be just the muscle."

Chris looked at Desmond. "Hopefully, one's the guy that beat the pulp out of you." Chris pummeled his arms in the air, then halted. "Hey, Des, I'm really sorry …"

Desmond raised a hand. "You got Virginia out of there. That was the most important thing." He turned to the chief. "What about that Bodine … or Boudreaux, if that was him?"

"We got tracers on a blue Lincoln. I think we'll get him.

But there's someone a lot bigger than him in all this." He looked at Chris.

"The FBI will need your help. That One Shell Tower Plaza penthouse keeps coming up."

Chris nodded. "Yup, no problem. I'll tell them everything I know. Just keep my girls safe." He nodded at Desmond.

Taking a deep breath, Desmond blinked. "Well, maybe you should do that now."

Chris smiled. "You know, buddy? I'm thinking about it."

Chris took an Uber back to the Bourbon Hotel in New Orleans. He was flying high on the victory, and he wanted to enjoy a luxury celebration in the high-class establishment. Stepping into his plush suite, he called room service for a steak dinner with all the trimmings, then jumped in the shower.

The opaqueness of the steam-filled room with lavender scents filled the air with a serene quietness. The pulsating stream from the hot shower calmed Chris's nerves as he tried to remember and recall all that he'd seen and heard. Bill Bodine, Antoine, Virginia. The poor young thing. How did she get there? And she was Lacey's friend, no less. He shuddered, thinking that could have been Lacey. He tried to banish the thought from his mind, but if it weren't for Desmond, Virginia would still be there. He hated to admit it, but he liked the guy a lot.

He's everything I'm not, Chris thought.

Desmond had pretty much given his blessing for Chris to make a move on Melanie. Feeling uncharacteristically unsure of himself, Chris tried to remember something Desmond said, something about God being about second chances.

He stepped out of the shower and wrapped himself in a thick terry robe. He was thankful that he'd checked into the Bourbon. Extravagant as it was, it helped him blot out the

hotel's dark ugliness that was almost the site of his and Desmond's demise.

And Melanie? He still didn't know what she'd been doing down there. He shuddered, thinking about how his work had endangered his family. Guilt set in as he thought about how he was the one that closed the deal on that place.

Thinking about his selfish lifestyle, it was as if a day of reckoning was at hand. Picking up his cell, he dialed Melanie's number. He waited. *Come on, Mel, pick up.*

He took a deep breath as the call went to voicemail. Chris said things to Melanie that he'd never ever said before. He didn't know where they came from, but he left his heart in the message.

A knock at the door jarred him, and he remembered his steak dinner. Rubbing a towel over his wet hair, he threw it on the bed and tightened the belt of the terry cloth robe. He opened the door, and there stood a tall, beautiful blonde. Thick blonde curls fell to her the waist of her concierge's uniform. She smiled sweetly.

"Room service, sir."

CHAPTER 33

C licking and pressure releasing sounds hummed and buzzed. Melanie stared at Virginia's sweet face. Even with a few bruises and abrasions, she was still beautiful. *Thank You, God,* prayed Melanie.

Her prayers didn't stop there. She asked for God's intervention in Virginia's life. She poured out a heart of praise for all that God had done. Then Desmond popped into her head. Her prayers stopped, and taking a deep breath, she asked for God's wisdom with Chris and Desmond.

A nurse walked in. "I'll be checking her vitals in a few minutes. Are you planning on staying the night? I can bring a blanket."

"No. I won't be too long. But I left my contact number at the nurses' station. Could you call me as soon as she wakes? Anytime, day or night?"

The nurse smiled. "You bet."

Everyone else had left. Tina had taken Charlene and Lacey home, and Melanie felt secure. At least for now. She'd silenced her phone while she sat with Virginia, but now she pulled it out. A missed call from Chris. She smiled, sat down, and hit voicemail.

"Hey, Mel. Chris here. Well, I guess you knew that.

Anyway, I was hoping to talk to you. Guess we've been playing phone tag. Listen… Geeze, uh, I really wish you'd pick up. This isn't making things very easy for me. But here goes. I was thinking, Mel. I want back in your and Lacey's lives. I mean, I just want to be Lacey's dad. And … I'd like to try being your hus—well, being a family again. I mean for real. Whew, I said it. Anyway, I'm ready for the commitment, and I'm ready to make a lot of changes… and I mean a lot. Heck, I'm even ready to try church with you guys. Anyway, think about it, ok? And don't say anything to Lacey. If you decide we can do this, I want to be there to tell her together. Anyway, how about it? Give me another chance, will ya? Thanks, Mel … I love you, baby."

Melanie laid the phone down. Cupping her chin in her palm, she stared. *Give me another chance?* Did he really ask that of her? Was God asking that of her? Why? This couldn't be happening. She stood just as the nurse walked back in. Melanie nodded and slipped out.

A soft swishing sound filled the hallway. With every pass of the janitor's mop, the smell of disinfectant washed over her. Just as the floor became sterile, so did her heart toward Chris. *How dare he!*

As she turned down the hallway to the lobby, Desmond approached from the opposite direction, and Melanie's cold heart immediately warmed at the sight of him.

His head hung down as he limped.

Melanie picked up her pace. "Desmond? How are you…?"

Looking up, he nodded. "I'm fine, Mel."

"Oh, my goodness." Her eyes widened. "You're not going home, are you?"

Bandages covered his black-and-blue, battered brow, cheek, and chin. The exterior wounds were all clearly visible, but Melanie felt the scars of his heart. Something was there. She knew it.

"Yes. They did some scans and x-rays but let me go as long as I promised to see the doctor on Monday." His lips twitched into a slight smile. "Got church in a couple hours, you know."

Melanie stepped forward. "No, Desmond, you can't." She reached out to touch his brow.

He yanked his head back and diverted his eyes to the diffused fluorescent lighting overhead. He shook his head. "I'm fine," he repeated.

Biting her lip, she stared for a moment. "Desmond, I just listened to a message from Chris."

He closed his eyes and nodded. "Good."

Melanie pulled her shoulders back. "Good? You don't even know what he said."

"Well, I'm sure he meant well with whatever he said. You know, Mel, he's got promise. He's not a bad guy."

"Really? Desmond, he doesn't even know God. He's so far from …"

"You don't know that, Melanie. Give him a chance."

She froze. "What did you say to him?" Melanie whispered and felt like she'd been tag-teamed. "Just like that? You save my life after he endangers it, and now …" Her voice rose.

"Stop, Melanie." Desmond's dark eyes deepened. "We don't know what God is doing here. What I do know is that God is a forgiving God, and if there's any chance of you two reconciling …" His glare softened, and he closed his eyes. "Mel …"

Melanie nodded and backed away. *Desmond's not feeling right. They must have given him pain meds,* she thought.

"Desmond, you know, I think you need to get home. Let's call a cab." She moved to take his arm, and he pulled it away.

"No, Mel. Officer Blaine is on patrol, and he's out there waiting for me. Thanks."

He turned to leave, and she let him walk steps ahead of

her. She placed a finger on her lip and tapped. When he stopped, her heart leaped.

"Virginia?" he asked.

Melanie felt guilty for her disappointment. "She's good. Resting quietly. She's going to need a lot of help."

"Well, we'll be there for her."

Melanie searched his face, looking for something. For anything. His eyes steered clear of hers, and her heart beat faster. Despite the chilly hospital air, heat rose within her. This couldn't be the end. She wouldn't let it. Chris wouldn't win!

Desmond blew out a big breath and nodded. "Bye, Mel." He limped away, head down.

Bye? Not see you at church? Not even see you later? But bye?

He turned again. "Hey, Mel? I'll be praying for you. God will guide you and get you through this. I know you know that. Trust Him."

As much as she wanted to chase after him, to shake some sense into him, she let him go. *He'll be better tomorrow. We'll talk later.*

CHAPTER 34

Sunday afternoon, Melanie awoke to a dream-like hush in her house. The smell of fresh coffee filled the air, even late in the day. The girls had missed church, sleeping in, instead. Walking to her front porch, Melanie stepped outside. The hush was there, too. The sun peeked between the clouds, and orange hues bounced off the gulf waters.

Melanie gripped her mug with both hands and took a sip. Smiling, she thought of her dad. The gulf exuded peace and serenity, two reasons he loved it there. Her brows furrowed, and she looked up. *Oh, Daddy, I'm glad you weren't here for all this.* She closed her eyes and thought of the broken bliss of Bay Town.

Her cell rang again. Calls had poured in all morning. The success of the sting operation in New Orleans and the story of Virginia's rescue caused a joyful excitement in town, and a celebration was scheduled. Everyone was meeting at the Bay Town Community Church in the Community Hall.

There was no getting around it. Her hesitation came in not knowing what seeing Desmond again might prompt her to do. She needed to pray, but she wasn't sure how to give this up. How to give him up. If that's what God wanted.

But Melanie had to attend. Tina hailed her the hero, too,

claiming the photographs she sent secured the proof for the FBI to act quickly.

Later, she chuckled as she stood in front of her closet. Anxiety brewed but soon burned to anger. Anger that all of this happened, affecting so many women. And anger for being forced into a position where she didn't see a way out. She didn't even know if Chris was sincere, but whether or not he was, she didn't want him. She wanted Desmond. And now that was practically impossible. Either way she looked at it, Chris was here to stay in Lacey's life, for sure. Melanie sighed and got dressed.

Arriving at the church, Charlene and Lacey rushed in ahead, and Melanie walked in slowly. The room smelled delightful. It was inherent that the celebration was a potluck, and everyone brought a favorite dish to share.

"Hey, friend!" Tina hugged Melanie. "Come on, look at that spread." Tina pointed to the food table. "You know, Big Joe had made his famous bourbon Boston baked beans, and Lyla, her to-die-for mac-n-cheese. And even better, her chocolate praline pecan pie! Oh, and Lina brought homemade salsa and chips."

Melanie's eyes swept the room. "Is Chief Bert here?"

"No, but Lina said he'll be here soon."

Tina pulled Melanie away from the door, waving at Principal Ladner, Mrs. Crowley, and many others. Someone called for Tina's help, and she left Melanie by the potluck table. There were more platters of food than people, but when Melanie spotted Desmond, she didn't care who brought what.

Melanie watched him struggling to set up additional chairs. He didn't need to. There were plenty all about the room, and she couldn't help but imagine his avoidance again, especially when his gaze caught hers from across the room. He turned in the other direction and walked into the kitchen, but he was immediately shoved out. Bethie Cooke and some other older ladies chattered that he was in the way. Melanie chuckled and turned at the sound of the music. She tried to enjoy the celebration. *Give him time*, she thought, but she was afraid of an uneasiness brewing within. The desperation that might drive her to do something foolish.

A flash of color caught her attention, and she looked at the entrance. Her eyes widened, and she strode over. "Carol!" She embraced her friend, and for the first time, Melanie thought Carol seemed at a loss for words. "Hey, Carol. I'm so glad you came."

"I'm just leaving." Carol pulled her colorful silk shawl snuggly around her.

"What? We're just getting started." Melanie held her hand but frowned.

Carol squeezed it and let go. "I've been here for about ten minutes." She looked around. "That's a stretch for me."

"Come on. Let me introduce you."

Carol shook her head and took a step back. "You gave me a chance, and I'm taking it. But I'm taking it slow." Carol brushed back some long, red strands of hair behind her ear and chuckled. "I'll be at church soon enough." She left before Melanie could protest.

Two young men from the worship team brought their guitars and played some praise songs. To everyone's delight, they even strummed a few pop songs. Some smaller children began dancing, and a few of the older folks joined in, too. Tina grabbed Rudy, and they glided and twirled across the entire room.

Melanie laughed, hearing Charlene yell, "And I thought your church couldn't dance." As she grabbed Lacey, they spun around the floor.

"Hey, Aunt Charlene, have you heard from my dad yet?" Lacey called out as they danced by Melanie.

Her heart lurched, and her palms dampened. A beating from her chest palpitated so hard, she feared someone would hear it. She wasn't ready for Chris. Not yet. Before Charlene

CHAPTER 35

Three Months Later
  Gripping the book, Lacey pressed it against her chest. She knocked.

"Come in." Desmond stood. "Hey, Lacey. Good to see you."

Lacey took a seat across from his desk. She was beginning to like being in his church office. It felt safe. She laid the book in her lap and stared as she smoothed her hand over it. Somehow it reminded her of Chris. Though, he didn't give it to her. The fact was, she had no special mementos from him. But this devotional book of hymns that Pastor Brooks had given her in the hospital months ago helped. She always brought it with her for her appointments.

This morning was an unusually early session. Desmond had other appointments, and this wasn't her scheduled day. But Lacey was thankful he could see her as it had been a rough night. She was worried about her mom, but Chris, her dad, haunted her dreams. She didn't know where he was. In heaven, or ... It was a horrible thought, but she just didn't know.

Yeah, he was flaky, but he'd changed since her life had been in danger. It seemed like he sort of grew up or something. Maybe he turned his life over to God? She sure hoped so. It was like he'd cared about someone other than himself for a change, and Lacey knew that someone was her.

That's what hurts the most. Her dad finally cared about her, but now he was gone. She'd never let herself go there before. It was so much easier when she regarded him as just a fun guy that popped into her life once a year. A dad that made life a blast whenever he came to visit, nothing more. But then he was there for her when the incident happened, and she liked it. She wanted more. But as quickly as he had blazed into her life, like a giant party bus, it was like he drove off into the sunset, and she was left gazing after an empty horizon. There was a hurt brewing that hadn't been there before.

"Lacey … Hey, Lacey … you in there?" Desmond tapped his pen on his desk and looked at her.

"What? Oh, sorry." Lacey hadn't shared with anyone her concerns regarding her dad. She wasn't sure she was ready to. "Zoning off, I guess."

"Want to share what about?"

His smile could make any person forget their troubles. Well, almost any person.

Lacey sat up straight, slipped her feet back into her canvas shoes, and looked around the office as if something sparked her interest. She stopped panning the room when she came to the photo wall. She pushed her hands into the pockets of her overalls, got up, and walked over. Framed photos of people from all different countries looked back. Some were smiling, crying, laughing, some were being baptized, and many hugged Desmond Brooks.

She chuckled to herself. What a difference. Pastor Brooks lived his life serving others, whereas Chris always lived for himself. Until he didn't.

Lacey spun around and took her hands out of her pockets. Grinning, she clapped her hands together. "Hey, I am starving. That green smoothie I had this morning has way worn off.

could answer, Lacey's friend Allie cut in and grabbed Lacey as they attempted the latest dance moves. It released some of Melanie's anxiety, watching them perform so poorly. She laughed.

The mood was joyful, happy, and positive.

She thought of Chris and sighed, but when her gaze caught Desmond, her shoulders dropped. *I can't let him go. He doesn't want it this way.*

Melanie rushed forward. His back was to her, but it didn't stop her, and just as she approached, he turned with more chairs in hand.

"I think there are enough chairs, Desmond." She forced a chuckle hoping to lighten his mood.

His eyes seemed to focus on her hair. It hung over her shoulders, and she'd wished she'd curled it and applied a tad more makeup. Pressing her lips together, she felt the light gloss smear a little. She lifted a finger to swipe it, and he stared at her every move.

Melanie even thought she saw him shiver a bit. Neither spoke, and she smoothed down the front of her dress and tightened the sash around her waist. She felt the hem flutter just above her knee. The wedged taupe sandals made her stand a little taller than average. A little more statuesque. She felt like her shoes gave her strength and courage. She wobbled on them a bit but was reminded that she should trust God for whatever was about to happen. She was hopeful.

"Desmond?"

"Hey, Mel." He squinted at her from his one unswollen eye and sighed. "You look beautiful." The words rushed out as if he couldn't stop himself. He took a breath. "So, hear from Chris? Is he coming tonight?" He rambled. "Of course, he is. I just wonder what's taking him so long. Bert, too? Maybe I should go call the chief's office—"

"Desmond. Can we talk? Please?"

One eye blinked, then he looked away. "We already did."

"No, Desmond. You talked. But I know you were exhausted. It was late. I'm surprised you're even here." Melanie squinted. "Did you even preach today?" She struggled to control the quiver in her voice.

"I said all I needed to say." He leaned the chairs against a wall. "I mean unless you and Chris need some counseling or something." He frowned. "You know what, I can't do that. I'll find someone for you."

Melanie wanted to slap him. "What counseling? Who said anything about counseling? I haven't heard from Chris since he left the message on my cell. For all I know, he's changed his mind and is on his way to California by now."

At first, Desmond stared at her wide-eyed. But soon, he narrowed his eyes, and Melanie watched as he straightened. His chest seemed to tense, and the tendons in his neck stiffened. His jaw jutted out, and Melanie feared the resolve she saw growing in him.

"Mel, don't make this harder than it is. If you value it, my opinion is that God's shown you clearly the right path for you and Lacey. The family is essential to God. He created it. I wish I could—"

Cheers and applause interrupted Desmond's words. Melanie huffed at the intrusion, and Desmond had already turned to look.

Chief Bert walked in. His usual jovial self appeared subdued. As the applause diminished, the room quieted, prompting his response.

"Thank you. Thank you. We all did it, didn't we? Some of the guys are in custody. The girls are safe—"

More clapping, along with a few shrill whistles, echoed around the room. Chief Bert raised his hands. "But we still got a long, hard job to do." Everyone's rejoicing slowly faded, and Bert seemed to peruse the room. "But for tonight, we can celebrate a job well done by everyone." He smiled weakly and clapped.

"And give the good Lord thanks," yelled Big Joe as he lumbered over to give his friend a big bear hug. Everyone gathered around and followed suit. Chief Bert broke away and walked to Melanie.

"Hey, Bert?" She wondered why he appeared so somber.

Lacey ran over, and the three caught up together, with Desmond close behind.

"Chief Bert? Where's Chris? Where's my dad?" Lacey tipped her head, her eyes round.

Bert held his hat in his hand and looked down. He wouldn't look at Lacey, who continued staring back at him.

"Chief, where's my dad?" she repeated.

Chief Bert wiped his face and pursed his lips. He nodded toward Desmond, who immediately came close by Melanie and Lacey's side.

"He's hurt, isn't he?" Lacey went white. "Isn't he? Can I go see him?" She switched her gaze back and forth between her mom and the chief.

Melanie stared at Bert, who in turn nodded at Desmond. She caught the exchange and wondered what it meant.

"Hey, why don't we go into the church where it's quieter." Desmond seemed to shift into pastor mode.

He ushered them to the doors just beyond the community room. They stepped into the dim tranquility of the sanctuary, and Bert motioned for the girls to sit in the pews. Lacey protested, but Melanie pulled her in.

Bert spoke in almost a whisper. "Lacey, Melanie, Chris ... well, he, he's gone ..."

Melanie interrupted. "Gone? You mean like back to California?" Her eyes widened.

Desmond pressed a hand on Melanie's shoulder.

Bert continued. "No, Mel." He glanced at Lacey but returned his gaze on Melanie while his voice cracked. "The New Orleans police responded to a call at the Bourbon Orleans Hotel this morning." Chief Bert cleared his throat

and paused. "Chris was found ... they found him ..." Drawing a breath, he whispered, "Dead in his hotel room." He shook his head. "An investigation is going on right now." Bert swiped his eyes.

Melanie's mouth dropped, and she shot a look at Desmond. Pleading with her eyes, they expressed her helplessness. She spun around to look at Bert, and the tears splashed.

Lacey screamed, she sobbed, and her body shook. Melanie dropped her head on Lacey's. Their sorrow filled the beautiful stained-glass sanctuary, shattering the serene quiet.

Lacey, didn't move. He waited, then asked, "What's up, Lacey?" He turned in his seat toward her.

She pursed her lips and then fluttered them.

He laughed. "Your mom always does that."

Lacey turned to him and smiled. He turned bright red again, and she laughed. "Yes, she does." Her mood turned somber again. "I have awful dreams about my dad."

He paused for a few moments. "Your mom expresses a quiet faith, and your dad saw it. You know he did because he joked about it a lot, right?" Desmond raised an eyebrow. "He wouldn't joke about it if it didn't make an impression on him."

Lacey shrugged and glanced at him. "You think so?"

"I'm sure of it. Only God knows a man's heart. Remember the thief on the cross at Christ's death? That man's life was not one of faith, but his confession at the end was." Desmond reached out and touched her shoulder. "Cling to that, Lacey. Maybe your dad made that confession. He definitely heard the truth." Desmond smiled. "And you, young lady, live your life so that no one ever has to doubt where you stand."

Reaching over, she hugged him.

"Anything else? You got me for …" He looked at his watch. "Another 30 minutes."

Tapping a finger to her lips, she raised her eyebrows. "You know, Pastor Brooks, I like going to church. I never want to miss a Sunday. It's like I know what praise and worship are all about now."

She smiled at him as he took a deep breath and looked up.

"Well, that's music to a pastor's heart." He thumped his chest.

"I just wish my mom was into her faith again."

Desmond cleared his throat. "Me too, Lacey. Keep praying for her. I do every day."

"Yeah. It's so weird. Everything seems okay now. Sort of."

Can we go get a donut?" She gave a sideways glance at Pastor Brooks.

Still sitting behind his desk, his brows furrowed, and he looked at his watch. Usually, his counseling sessions lasted an hour.

He nodded. "Okay, a donut it is." He stood and tidied up the papers on his desk.

Lacey looked surprised. "Really?"

"Yes, I could use a donut myself. How about we go to Donut Heaven?" He paused for a minute, and then he and Lacey both burst out laughing. She envisioned a giant donut in the clouds hovering above the pearly gates.

"Don't you mean Donut Haven?" Lacey giggled. "Although Mom might not have such a problem with a donut from heaven."

"Yes, right. I think Mel." He turned red. "I mean, I think your mom would have a problem with any donut."

Lacey's smile faded. "Yeah. Not anymore. I don't think she cares much about anything these days."

"Give her time, Lacey. She's dealing with a lot, too." He breathed deep. "Okay, Let's go. I've got almost an hour to kill." He grabbed his keys as he put an arm around her shoulder, leading her out the door.

Lacey was learning to overcome her fears and anxieties from all the turmoil. Each week she couldn't wait for her sessions with Pastor Brooks. He encouraged her to dig into God's word, and it worked. The sessions with him brought her peace, and he always pointed her to Jesus. He was her rock, and she often felt like she couldn't go on without his help.

Her faith had strengthened at the loss of her father. But it was the question of Chris's salvation that brought on some real, newfound anxiety. She knew he didn't go to church, not that that was a death sentence, but she didn't remember him ever mentioning faith except to tease her mom.

As Desmond pulled into the Donut Haven and parked,

Can we go get a donut?" She gave a sideways glance at Pastor Brooks.

Still sitting behind his desk, his brows furrowed, and he looked at his watch. Usually, his counseling sessions lasted an hour.

He nodded. "Okay, a donut it is." He stood and tidied up the papers on his desk.

Lacey looked surprised. "Really?"

"Yes, I could use a donut myself. How about we go to Donut Heaven?" He paused for a minute, and then he and Lacey both burst out laughing. She envisioned a giant donut in the clouds hovering above the pearly gates.

"Don't you mean Donut Haven?" Lacey giggled. "Although Mom might not have such a problem with a donut from heaven."

"Yes, right. I think Mel." He turned red. "I mean, I think your mom would have a problem with any donut."

Lacey's smile faded. "Yeah. Not anymore. I don't think she cares much about anything these days."

"Give her time, Lacey. She's dealing with a lot, too." He breathed deep. "Okay, Let's go. I've got almost an hour to kill." He grabbed his keys as he put an arm around her shoulder, leading her out the door.

Lacey was learning to overcome her fears and anxieties from all the turmoil. Each week she couldn't wait for her sessions with Pastor Brooks. He encouraged her to dig into God's word, and it worked. The sessions with him brought her peace, and he always pointed her to Jesus. He was her rock, and she often felt like she couldn't go on without his help.

Her faith had strengthened at the loss of her father. But it was the question of Chris's salvation that brought on some real, newfound anxiety. She knew he didn't go to church, not that that was a death sentence, but she didn't remember him ever mentioning faith except to tease her mom.

As Desmond pulled into the Donut Haven and parked,

Lacey, didn't move. He waited, then asked, "What's up, Lacey?" He turned in his seat toward her.

She pursed her lips and then fluttered them.

He laughed. "Your mom always does that."

Lacey turned to him and smiled. He turned bright red again, and she laughed. "Yes, she does." Her mood turned somber again. "I have awful dreams about my dad."

He paused for a few moments. "Your mom expresses a quiet faith, and your dad saw it. You know he did because he joked about it a lot, right?" Desmond raised an eyebrow. "He wouldn't joke about it if it didn't make an impression on him."

Lacey shrugged and glanced at him. "You think so?"

"I'm sure of it. Only God knows a man's heart. Remember the thief on the cross at Christ's death? That man's life was not one of faith, but his confession at the end was." Desmond reached out and touched her shoulder. "Cling to that, Lacey. Maybe your dad made that confession. He definitely heard the truth." Desmond smiled. "And you, young lady, live your life so that no one ever has to doubt where you stand."

Reaching over, she hugged him.

"Anything else? You got me for …" He looked at his watch. "Another 30 minutes."

Tapping a finger to her lips, she raised her eyebrows. "You know, Pastor Brooks, I like going to church. I never want to miss a Sunday. It's like I know what praise and worship are all about now."

She smiled at him as he took a deep breath and looked up.

"Well, that's music to a pastor's heart." He thumped his chest.

"I just wish my mom was into her faith again."

Desmond cleared his throat. "Me too, Lacey. Keep praying for her. I do every day."

"Yeah. It's so weird. Everything seems okay now. Sort of."

Lacey scrunched her face. "Did you know? Mom was about to lose the house and business before all this?"

His eyes widened. "I had no idea. Your mom never said a word. Are you guys okay? Do you need anything?"

"Are you kidding? My dad left us a ton of money! He had a life insurance policy."

"I wondered about the substantial tithe check ..." He looked down. "Never mind."

"I guess she never told anyone. I overheard my mom tell my aunt after everything settled. Did you know my dad had a will, too? It shocked Aunt Charlene. She said it was a guilt thing after my accident. Anyway, Mom yelled at Charlene for thinking that. But he took care of us."

Desmond smiled. "I didn't know him long, but I liked your dad. I'm glad to hear this."

"Yeah, we're doing great. Mom even has Dad's fancy car now." She dropped her eyes. "But she never drives it."

"Trust, Lacey. Your mom loves God. She'll come back."

Nodding, she sat up straight. "And then there's Virginia. I keep inviting her to church when I visit her at the group home, but she's not interested. She still says it's boring."

"Ouch." Pastor Brooks winced as if his ribs hadn't healed.

Lacey hit his arm. "Yeah, but I go to her group Bible study, and she seems to be understanding some of it, so that's a good thing." Brushing back some loose strands of hair, she smiled at Desmond. "What about you, Pastor? How are you doing?"

Staring at her, he nodded. "Well, God is good, Lacey."

She rolled her eyes. "Well, that's a safe answer. I'll remember that one."

Desmond laughed. "Okay." He pointed to her. "But it's true, He is always good. But I struggle, too. I haven't experienced anything like that since ... well, in an awfully long time."

"You mean since you were in the Navy Seals. You never talk about that. Why?" Lacey pressed.

His brows furrowed, and he was slow to speak. "It wasn't the job, Lacey. It was me. I defended my country, but I let my family down. My wife."

"But she forgave you, right? And God has."

Smiling back at her, Desmond shook his head. "Look who's counseling who now." He laughed. "But yes, and thanks for reminding me of that. I forget it way too often. My wife, Emily, never held a grudge."

Lacey smiled back. "That's what my mom always said about my dad." She punched his arm again. "So quit feeling guilty. Now, let's go get that donut!"

Desmond dropped Lacey off and headed back to the church office. Dropping his keys on his desk, he sat down and propped his feet up. A calm and peace rested in his soul and spirit. The sessions that he and Lacey had together brought him great joy. And today was significant.

Opening a drawer, he pulled out Melanie's shop's brochure. He drew a deep breath. Mel. What about her? He was at a loss, not knowing how to help her. Or if he should. He shook his head as he thought of Chris.

Having never spoken directly with Chris about faith, Desmond regretted it. Thankful for the words he did express, he still wished he'd been bolder. Truth be told, Desmond's desire for Melanie compounded the remorse.

He wanted to be the one in her and Lacey's life. The longing for that paralyzed him. It still did, causing him to stay away from Melanie. He couldn't help feeling responsible, like he was the root of her trials of late. She needed someone, but it couldn't be him. Not now. He closed his eyes. *Or could it be?*

As he held Melanie's brochure in his hand, he glanced at

Emily's photograph. He used to cling to the memories of his life with Emily. The memories sustained him, gave him purpose. And he felt ashamed when they weren't enough anymore. He even got angry at himself that the sweet reminiscences of her wouldn't satisfy his own desires even now.

He breathed deep. And yet ...

Through this whole ordeal, he'd never once thought about Emily. Not once. It was all about Melanie. He sighed and closed his eyes, praying. He prayed, not knowing how or what to pray. As he groaned unuttered words, the pain in his heart slowly dissipated, and a bittersweet feeling remained. *Emily?* He opened his eyes and stared once again at her photograph. She smiled back, and he saw a smile of assurance, of hope. Hope for his future. A new future. He nodded and whispered, "Thanks, Em."

THE END

Melanie pounded down Beach Road. Lately, she pushed herself to run faster, harder, and longer. She was preparing to run the 5-10K fundraiser to fight against human trafficking in New Orleans. But everyone knew it was her way of coping. She had been avoiding friends and neighbors, and they were thoughtful in giving her time to heal. Still, she laid awake nights—thoughts of Chris and his last phone call haunting her.

Struggling with anger and guilt, her quiet times were few as she avoided time alone with God. She was angry at Chris for imposing himself into her life again, and she felt guilty about it. And then Desmond. He never fought for her heart. He just gave her up. But ultimately, Melanie felt ashamed whenever she admitted to herself that she thought God had failed her. That he withheld true happiness from her.

Reaching the turnaround point of her run, Pier 1, she saw Captain Jack. He waved, and, for some reason, he made her smile. She jogged to his pier.

"Hey, Miz Melanie." Captain Jack removed his knit beanie and smoothed down his wild mane.

It reminded her of Chris, and her smile faded.

"Are ya goin' to the church party tonight?" He grinned,

and Melanie always marveled at how his flashy, white teeth popped against his leathery, tanned face.

She shrugged. "No, I don't think so." She frowned. "Why is the church having a party?" Why was Captain Jack asking her about her church? A twitch gripped her heart. He was more in touch than she was.

Captain Jack waved his arms wide. "Whaaat? It's the post-holiday party. Ya know, the New Year!"

"New Year has come and gone." Melanie crossed her arms. She hadn't celebrated the holiday besides watching an old movie with Lacey and drinking sparkling cider at midnight.

"Oh, no, ma'am. It's January. The New Year's just beginning." He gave her a sideways glance. "God's got glorious plans. You better grab 'em and follow the course."

"Sure." She jogged in place. "I have to go. Have fun at the party."

"Miz Melanie?"

She stopped.

"I'm really sorry about all that happened to you a couple months back. It's hard to come back from stuff like that. But the sooner you face it, the sooner you'll figure out what God wants for you." He spoke slowly, his southern drawl accentuated.

Melanie's mouth gaped. "Wants for me. I'm not sure He cares anymore." She wasn't often blunt with acquaintances, but this guy was intruding.

"Oh, ma'am. You need to talk to Pastor Brooks."

Her body temp went from lukewarm to boiling. She clenched and released her fists. Staring at the horizon, her eyes narrowed, and she shook her head.

"Whatever happened? I mean, I was there when you guys had that passionate moment in the driveway. Whoo-whee! I told Pastor Brooks that night, if you were the one, he should go for it. I think you guys got something."

Melanie couldn't believe that he was speaking to her this way. This guy had no filter. She knew he struggled with some issues, but this was no excuse, and she wanted to lay into him for reminding her of that night. Bulldozing those memories out of her mind every day tore up her heart. Memories that brought more pain than passion. She spun around to face him.

"Well, it's gone now." She crossed her arms. Her nails dug into her skin.

"Why?"

The wind blew so hard, escaped strands flew from her loose ponytail and fluttered around her face. "Why, what?"

"Why's it gone? He loves you. You love him …"

She glared. "You don't know what you're talking about. You're crazy!" Melanie gasped, wishing she could take back those words.

He threw his head back and laughed so hard he coughed and sputtered. "Well, that's a real shocker. But ya see, crazy people see things normal people don't. I seen something kinda magical in you guys that night. Ya know, Pastor drove me home after, and we talked. He was a struggling man, and I'm guessing he still is. He's been down here a few times. We talk, ya know?" He laughed again. "I guess you could say I'm his counselor. Anyway, I always ask him about you."

Melanie covered her eyes. She'd shut Desmond out when Chris died, and she'd shut God out that night, too. Lowering her hands away from her face, she stared at the bushy-haired man before her.

"He acts just like you do now when I bring you up—something inside you two points to guilty. The difference is, he's humble about it. And you're not. It seems you're angry and a bit prideful, ma'am."

Melanie stood up straight. She had nothing to be prideful about. How could he say that about her? He was getting a rise

out of her, and the angrier she got, the more indignant she
became.

Captain Jack put up both hands, palms toward her. "I may
not know much, but if Pastor Brooks makes a move, you
better go for it."

"He's not going to ..."

"He will if you open the door. Be humble, ma'am. Be
humble." He waved her off. "Go on now. This will cost you,
you know?" He laughed again.

She seethed inside, wishing he'd stop his incessant laughter. Still, he had her puzzled, and he seemed to know it.

"Counseling! How about you pay me for dinner sometime? When you find out I'm right?"

Shaking her head, Melanie turned and jogged away. His
laughter rang in her ears as she pounded home, sprinting the
last mile.

"Knock, knock. Hey? Anybody home?" Charlene yelled while
standing at the front door to Melanie's cottage. She had taken
an Uber from the airport and was hoping to surprise Lacey
and Melanie. Turning around, she saw Tina bent over her
flower beds with a hose in hand.

"Hi, Tina." Charlene waved.

"Hey, girl."

"Where is everyone?"

"Oh, Mel's out for a run, I'm sure. That's all she ever does
anymore." Tina pushed her lips out, pouting.

"Yeah. She's still pretty traumatized. When I call, I can't
even get her to argue with me anymore. Not even about
God."

Tina's brows furrowed. "Why would you do that?"

"It's a long story. But I've come a long way. I just can't
share it with her right now."

"Maybe you should? Maybe it will bring her around. Anyway, I'm glad you're here. We have to do something."

"We'll give it our best shot. Where's Lacey?"

"I have no idea. That girl is so busy. It's like she's going to live life and not let anything pass her by." Tina waved her arms in the air, spraying the hose water everywhere.

"Whoa, there. It's a little too cool in the season to be playing in the sprinklers."

Tina giggled. "Oops." She turned off the faucet. "So, what brings you back in town? Please, no more espionage stuff."

"What do you mean? It's only been three months." Charlene laughed.

She had gone back to D.C. to do more investigating. Her blog had covered a grand expose on the raid in New Orleans. Boudreaux was in jail, and the news was abuzz in helping to implicate him in the big ring. But she knew someone bigger was at fault.

For now, though, it was time to reconnect with the girls. Lacey had told her about the church event, and she used it as an excuse to check up on Melanie.

"So, this is just a fun trip?" Tina raised her brows.

"That and I'm concerned about my sis. She talks in fragmented sentences. Like she's given up on life or something."

"You got that right." Tina turned and held a finger to her lips.

Just then, Melanie ran up, dripping with sweat and panting hard. Wearing shorts and a tank, she stared at her sister.

Charlene shivered. "Are you crazy, sis? It's winter, you know."

Melanie smiled and gave her sister a big hug. With her hands on her hips, she panted. "It's good to see you, too. Why didn't you call?"

"Oh, I just wanted to surprise you."

Melanie waved at Tina but turned before Tina could wave back.

Tina's shoulders drooped, and Charlene gave her a consoling smile. Wiping water droplets off her clothes and arms, she shook off her hands and followed Melanie.

"Want to order some Chinese? I have nothing ready for dinner," Melanie said over her shoulder.

"Chinese? Are you kidding me? When did you start ordering Chinese takeout?"

Melanie gave Charlene a look and walked inside, holding the door for her sister. "I'm showering. Make yourself at home." She trudged down the hallway to her bedroom.

"Gee, thanks."

Bringing in her luggage, she looked around. Melanie's warm and welcoming touches were missing. No fresh flowers, no holiday décor, and no candles or potpourri anywhere.

"Wow. She is off," Charlene said out loud.

"Who's off?" came a voice from outside.

"Hey, Lacey. Where'd you come from?" Charlene grabbed her niece and gave her a big hug.

"Oh, I was with Pastor Brooks. Then we went to see Virginia. He just dropped me off."

Charlene looked puzzled. "What? And he didn't come in?"

Lacey shook her head. "No, he had another counseling appointment. After mine and Virginia's, I mean."

Lacey smiled and hugged her aunt again. "I'm glad you're here. Mom needs you. I don't know what to do. Nobody does. I keep asking Pastor Brooks to help, and he says, 'Give her time.' It's like he avoids her."

"Well, he might just be part of the problem … you think?" Charlene looked sideways at Lacey.

"Yeah, I think I know what you mean. She won't even talk to him when she goes to church. Which isn't even every week anymore. I thought there was something between them, but if there ever was, it's gone now. Ever since my dad died." Lacey lowered her eyes and leaned back on the kitchen counter. "But I've been praying. Just for God's will, you know? I don't know how else to pray for my mom. You know, I used to wish she and Pastor Brooks would get together, but now I just want her to be happy again."

"Don't we all? Hey, what's up for tonight?" Charlene raised her eyebrows.

"Baking night! Let's make some pies," Lacey yelled. "It's been ages."

"Huh? Come again?"

"Yeah. Remember? Tomorrow's the church post-holiday party, and Mom hasn't made a thing."

"Right. But explain to me. What's a post-holiday party?" Charlene wrinkled her face.

"Oh, you know. Everyone is so busy over the holidays with family and parties that, after Christmas, it's nice to have a get together for no reason!"

Charlene let out a sigh. "Okay. Well, come on, get your mom's keys and let's get to the store. You make the pies. I'll make my famous Cranberry Apple Cake."

The morning of the proposed church party arrived, but all the coaxing in the world couldn't get Melanie to agree to attend it. She thought it was ridiculous. And after Captain Jack's assault, she struggled even more with blocking Desmond out of her mind and life.

Melanie poured a cup of coffee and sat at the kitchen table. She stared at some pies on the counter.

Charlene walked in and pointed. "So, hey, you want some pie?" She gave Melanie an enticing glance.

"When did you make those?"

"What do you mean when did I make those? Lacey and I

baked all afternoon yesterday. They're for the post-holiday party!"

"Hmmm. Have fun." Melanie sipped her coffee.

Charlene slammed a fist on the table. Melanie jumped.

"Enough. Enough of this mourning or pouting or whatever. You didn't even mope this long after Mom and Dad died."

Melanie glared. "How dare you? How dare you ..."

"They were my parents too. So, yes, I dare. But you have to face this, sis. I don't know what you're dealing with. I didn't know you cared this much about Chris ..."

Melanie stood, her slight frame shaking. She'd become even thinner after these past three months. Biting her lip, they flushed white as she took steps to leave the kitchen.

Charlene grabbed her arm. "Uh, uh. You're not going anywhere."

Melanie looked at the hand gripping her arm and then stared at her sister.

"You have a great life, Melanie. I know what happened was horrible. I know it seems like you've had to deal with too much in a short time. But so have I. I lost my parents, too. And I've dealt with the loss of my husband years before that. And now, I'm dealing with the loss of my sister." Charlene's eyes held a reservoir of tears.

Charlene never cried. Melanie looked at her sister, her brows furrowed. "What are you talking about?"

"You're not here anymore, Melanie. My loving, sweet sister. The opposite of me. The woman of faith ..."

Melanie let off a low chuckle. "And since when did you ever care about faith, Char?"

"Now, Melanie. Right now." Charlene let go of her sister's arm. She wiped at tears before they fell. "For the first time since Mom and Dad died, I've been praying. I asked God to bring you back." Charlene choked and sat down, covering her face. "I hate that you do this to me!"

Charlene watched Melanie's eyes widen. She opened her mouth, but shut it.

"That's why I came, Melanie. I came to tell you I'm back with God. I needed Him, and He was there. He never left me. I left Him. Just like you have. Whatever it is, you need to give it up. Lacey needs you, I need you, and I don't know who else does. But you need God." Charlene stood and wiped her face on her sleeve. She stomped her foot loudly. "Melanie, we are going to that party, whether you like it or not. It means the world to Lacey, and if I have to …"

"I'll go," Melanie whispered.

"What?"

Melanie nodded. "I'll go." Standing slowly, she retreated to her room.

Entering the community room at church, Melanie froze. The room looked much the same as the last time she'd been there, the night they were told of Chris's death. Overwhelmed, she turned and closed her eyes. She crossed her arms tightly across her shaking body. She couldn't breathe. The darkness of the memories from the months before flooded her mind. They would never go away, and she recalled the shock of the news that night once more.

"Mom? It's all right, Mom." Lacey stood in front of her.

But being in the room was all too reminiscent, and she turned to leave. Before she could take a step, everyone was so excited to see her, and they crowded around. One by one, they hugged her, and one by one, she softened at each touch. Each word. Each look. Her friends, the community, and the church expressed their joy at seeing her again. Sentiments of "Welcome back" and "We missed you" besieged her. Some people just smiled, but many grabbed her hands and blurted out things they thought she'd like to hear about their own lives—everything she'd missed.

Not only the warmth of those around her but the smells of delicious food filling the air helped to change her spirits. The scent of fresh roasted turkey wafted throughout the hall and almost overpowered the eclectic mix of traditional and new dishes. There was nothing like a church potluck to grip a person's heart and stomach.

She'd neglected so much these last few months—Thanksgiving, Christmas. They'd all whizzed by. And worst of all, she'd ignored God. And yet, here He was. She saw Him in Lacey, who glowed and lit up the room. She heard Him in the band singing praises, and she felt Him with each touch from her friends.

Melanie melted into the joy that seeped into her heart. She'd known that hiding was the wrong thing to do. But she couldn't break out of it. Feeling all the love and warmth emitting from everyone finally gave her the courage she needed. It was time to step out. It was time to come back. The anger and confusion had had their way. It was time to trust God again.

Tina skipped over and winked.

Melanie smiled.

Tina squealed and hugged her. Choking a little, she whispered, "Welcome back, old friend."

Melanie squeezed her friend's hands, but the squeeze turned to a death grip. Her smile disappeared as her eyes widened.

Tina turned.

Desmond was making a beeline to Melanie.

"I don't think I'm ready for this," Melanie whispered, trying to turn.

Tina squeezed her shoulders tightly, hiding behind her until Desmond stopped in front of them.

"Hey, Pastor Brooks." Tina peeked around Melanie. "Listen, you two, I brought some unhealthy heat-and-serve buns.

You know, those deliciously white, squishy ones in the foil tray? They're in the kitchen. In the oven. Go. Go get them out for me. Please?"

Tina pushed them both toward the kitchen. Rushing ahead, she shooed everyone out of the way and let the floppy doors close behind them.

Melanie stood frozen, and Desmond rocked back on his heels, his hands shoved in his front pockets. His smile looked more like twitching lips. Taking a few steps, he stopped in front of her and stared into her eyes. Melanie squirmed.

It seemed like he was seeing her for the first time. She glanced down, tugged at the plain white sweater, the sleeves hanging past her palms, and felt the cuffed jeans rub her ankles. She felt Desmond's gaze sinking into her.

He touched her hand. "I'm so sorry, Mel."

Melanie's eyes covered every inch of his face. It had been so long. Her gaze took in his deep, dark eyes, and she wanted to touch his soft, wavy hair. Dark stubble covered his cheeks and chin, doing nothing to hide the tense jaw revealing anguish—anguish that seemed to express her own deeply embedded hurt. The grief that she had refused to give up.

"Sorry? Sorry about what, Desmond?"

"About everything." He huffed. "About not being there for you. About Chris. About … us." His gaze was intense.

"Us?" Melanie's brow furrowed. "Is there an us?" She choked on the words.

Gripping her arms around herself, she said, "Desmond, I feel so guilty. You were right. I should have told Chris, yes. But I didn't want Chris. I wanted …" She dropped her eyes. "But then he was gone before I could say anything, and I'm not sure what I would have said. And Lacey. She didn't even know. I feel awful. If he had lived, I don't know that I would have taken him back. I'm a horrible person." She choked.

Desmond lifted a hand to her chin and raised her face. He gazed into her eyes. "No, Mel. I shouldn't have told you what

to do. You never asked for my advice." Looking sorrowfully, he said, "That was your decision to make, and I should have trusted God to guide you. Melanie, will you forgive me?"

Confusion choked her voice. "Forgive you? I should be asking you that." She raised her hands and covered her face. "And God, I need to ask God." Her voice broke.

Pulling her hands away, Desmond looked intently at her. His eyes shone. "He's forgiven you, Mel. Right now. He knows your heart." Suddenly, he chuckled. "You know what? Everything's changed, Mel. All our guilt? Yours and mine? All this guilt we've been living with? It's crippling. It crippled us. That's not what God wants. He is a God of forgiveness. Mel, we can't look back. We need to move ahead. He wants us to seek Him. That's what He asks of us."

Desmond smiled, and Melanie's heart lurched. If a face could shine forth hope, his could, and at that moment, God's promise shone in him.

He fixed his eyes on hers and gripped both of her shaking hands. The pounding of her heart resonated so loudly, she thought her ears would burst. Desmond raised her hands to his lips. He kissed one, then the other. Melanie made no move to stop him as he guided her arms around his neck. He pulled her tight against his chest and lowered his head, gently brushing her lips. Pulling back, he stared into her eyes, and once more, even more deeply, he kissed her.

CRASH!

A shriek came from the kitchen entrance, and there stood old Bethie Cooke, mouth hanging open, staring at Desmond and Melanie's embrace. Everyone came running and crowded the open double doorway.

Melanie's eyes widened, and she tried to pull back, but Desmond held her tight.

Lacey pushed her way through the crowd. "Hallelujah!" She clapped and pumped a fist in the air. "Yes!" she yelled.

Pulling only slightly apart, Desmond and Melanie laughed

as their foreheads pressed together. Everyone continued to gawk.

Another senior member, Sally Trotman, yelled, "What's the matter with you, Bethie Cooke? Haven't you ever seen a pastor kiss before? He's not a priest, for Pete's sake. Come on, everyone, leave 'em alone. It's about time."

In the kitchen's quietness, Desmond stepped back, and with a straight face, he pushed her an arm's length away and dropped his hands.

Melanie's eyes opened wide, and her lips quivered. Her insides gave way to a rising panic. She smoothed down her sweater for no reason and lowered her eyes.

"What now, Desmond?" she whispered.

Desmond lifted her chin and stared.

"You know, we gave quite a shock to Bethie Cooke and the congregation just now."

Melanie's shoulders dropped. *Here we go again.*

"How about we really give them something to talk about? he winked. "I know of a quiet little coffee shop where we can be alone." He nodded in the exit's direction. "Join me, Mel?"

Melanie hit him playfully. "Lead the way, Pastor Brooks."

AFTERWORD

"Mom wrote a book, and it has no bad language, no sex, and no graphic violence, but it's about human trafficking."

I homeschooled my eight children, and they all attended a conservative Christian university. My husband is a pastor. So, when I started writing Shattered Guilt, the quote above was the running joke in the family. Although the subject matter is not a joke, they were correct. God gave me the words to depict a passionate stance against sin, a pure romance, and horrific tragedy…hopefully, all without offending my readers.

I started the story with Melanie and her daughter Lacey, and my relationship with my youngest daughter. I love the mother-daughter bond, but Melanie's past mistakes linger in the back of her mind, and she somehow thinks herself not worthy of a lot of things. The theme of guilt runs throughout this book in both the lives of those trafficked and those not. When young girls are targeted for human trafficking, Melanie lays aside the self-imposed shame of her past and fights to save those who will suffer far worse feelings of guilt and shame, for which they had no control.

My heart breaks for those whose lives are paralyzed by their pasts. While writing Shattered Guilt, I didn't realize the connection between Melanie's guilt and the victims of trafficking who would also suffer similar feelings, through no fault of their own. All of us carry baggage, and if it's something that needed confession and repentance, and we've done that, it's a done deal. We shouldn't let the past petrify us from living a life of fullness in Christ. Melanie and even Pastor Desmond come to realize this in their lives. We need to be the best that God desires for us to be, and to be effective in His work, we must experience his love and forgiveness.

Years ago, when I was first writing the rough draft of this novel, human trafficking was finally getting recognition in the world, and the horrors of who was being trafficked were shocking. That's what gripped my heart, and I was embarrassed that I didn't have a clue about the scope of this morally reprehensible practice. Enslavement of human beings by another has been on this earth forever, and that's why awareness and action are so important today. In addition, there are so many facets as to how one becomes a victim in this tragedy. I now try never to assume how someone's life takes the path it does, but I only care that they find a way to hear God's voice calling them. Every Christian story is about God's love.

Although I love writing a suspense story, I love creating my characters too. I hope you'll enjoy getting to know the people of Bay Town as much as I enjoyed writing about them. I look forward to sharing more about these endearing characters and the trials they face. Please come back and visit the charming community of Bay Town, in the continuing series.

If God has put a burden on your heart for those trapped in human trafficking, I'd like to urge you to seek out a Christian ministry, there are a few, that need prayer and financial support for our fight against this evil. I encourage you to pursue how you can help. Most importantly, continue to pray and love your family members, children, grandchildren, and greats, if you have them. Our world is not our home, and sin abounds, but living a life that exemplifies the heart of Christ through prayer, the Word, and your actions is the first defense against all sin. God bless you, and thanks for reading.

ACKNOWLEDGMENTS

I started this writing journey in 2012 and couldn't be more blessed with positive encouragement every step of the way. Expressing my appreciation adequately for the many who have helped me is practically impossible. But here goes. To my son **Jonathan Robison**, who read the first draft of my first book, Shattered Guilt. You were much more merciful to me than I was when I homeschooled you. Not only were you graciously encouraging, but you introduced me to the craft of writing. Your guidance in suggesting books, and videos to improve my skills, and hone my craft, was like you holding my hand again, only you were leading and I am forever grateful.

To my sister **Margaret Bacon Schulze**, an author and journalist, who also read my first draft. Thank you for being extremely gracious in your critique. Your advice for joining a critique group was seriously life-changing in furthering my journey in becoming an author. Thanks for your example and love for the written word. I still remember waiting for each page you typed, so I could read your stories almost faster than you typed them. You are a talented wordsmith, and I so enjoy your stories.

To my dear friend, **Joy Hartley**, who refused to give me negative criticism of my first draft and was so faithful to finish and praise my meager early works. Thank you for taking time from your busy life to read that hot mess.

To my sons **Daniel Robison** and **Jonathan**, who challenged me to do NaNoWriMo. I'd never heard of National Novel Writing Month, and although the first year I didn't reach 50,000 words, I beat you both with a meager count. It was because of your challenge that I went on to finish Shattered Guilt the following year. I loved the adventure of writing with you, albeit online, in California, Washington, and Japan. Because of you two, April, July, and November Nano months are my most productive in writing new novels and finishing manuscripts.

To **Foothill Ranch Library Support and Critique Group,** California. It was as if I were blind, and then I could see. To our moderator, **Skye Pratt Epperson** and **Stella Carruth,** Facilitator and Branch Manager. Your loving critiques and shared expertise have propelled our group to a level of writing I didn't think I could achieve. Your time, teaching, and support are unequaled in any such group, of that, I am sure. I have learned so much from you and our entire eclectic, talented group of writers. The love we have for one another is like a faithful weekly family gathering. I love you all.

To **Cathleen Armstrong, Susan K. Beatty, and Nancy Brashear.** I wish I had space to chronicle God's divine meeting for me with you, Cathleen. Little did I know that when we met at RWA, Orange County (Romance Writers of America), that would lead me on a journey to join **Serious Scribblers**. Ladies, your godly inspiration, critique, and editing have made me a much better writer. After all the red lettering required in my first draft, I'm shocked you invited me to join the group years ago. You are each so talented and accomplished. It's an incredible honor to be sisters in ink, but more esteemed, as sisters-in-Christ.

After I met with Cathleen, it was a chain reaction. Thank

you, **ACFW, American Christian Fiction Writer's group of Orange County.** I have learned much from the presentations, not to mention each individual who spurred me on in my journey. A special thanks to **Rebecca Luellen Miller,** my first professional editor. Your patience, and loving advice to a green novice like me, expanded the scope of my learning. Thank you for your patience. To **Carol Alwood,** who traded manuscripts with me for critiquing. I could never have done what you've done for me. Thank you, friend. You are one talented lady. And all those at OC ACFW, you are family.

And from ACFW, the explosion happened! Literally, because **Sandy Womack Barela (Celebrate Lit Publishing)** and **Chautona Havig,** author/mentor, you two are like crashing atoms. The energy, the love, and the commitment you pour out to me (and many others) bring me to tears. You both are like a fiery lava flow pushing me to the finish line but making sure I do it right and for the right reasons. Your love for Jesus outshines everything within and without the world of writing, and your continual reminder to me of why I write and to whom I write for revives my joy every day. Thank you for taking a chance on me. I'm truly humbled for the opportunity to be a Celebrate Lit Publishing author.

There are so many others. To **all my family** for their comical support and encouragement and for sharing my books with your friends. As well to the numerous friends who did the same. To **Heather Halverson**, who first recognized me as a writer before I did. Just your mention of putting my book (not even finished at the time) in the university library at APU encouraged me more than you'll ever know. You and your family are a sweet reminder of the love of Christ. To **Val Bishop,** my crafty sister who reads and edits faster than anyone I know. Thank you for taking the time and lots of it to help and encourage me.

To my readers, my **FB friends, and family**, and especially to my **2021 Street Team**. Thank you, ladies, and gents, for getting the word out on FB, reading my bloopers, and sticking with me.

And to the one who shares this journey with me, my husband, **Bruce.** Thanks for your encouragement and patience in listening to hours and hours of me reading aloud. And for going to meetings with me, as well your patience when I left you home alone. Thank you for loving me and driving me forward, even if it was because you were hoping to retire on my earnings! Your love, and laughter, makes this life worth living, and your amazing mind blows me away. You spur me on to love and good works. God gave me a wonderful gift when he gave me you. Thanks for sticking with me all these years, sweetheart.

And most importantly to the **Father of all creation**, who put the stories in my head. Lord, God Almighty, I pray that the words in these pages inspire us to surrender and live our lives for you alone. **All for your glory, Jesus.**

ABOUT THE AUTHOR

Kathleen J. Robison is an Okinawan-American. Born in Okinawa, raised in California, Florida, Mississippi, and Singapore. Her travels are the inspirational settings for her stories. She and her Pastor husband have eight adult children. Seven are married, blessing them with fourteen grandchildren and counting. The diversity of their 31 family members provide the inspiration for more lively characters than can be imagined. Her husband grew up in the streets of Los Angeles raised by a single working mom, and that life provides fodder for many of the conflicts of her characters.

Tackling difficult life's trials with God's strength are the central theme of Kathleen's stories. She hopes to inspire her readers to trust God and with His strength, weather through and rise above trials and tragedies. If you like suspenseful stories with a thread of romance, you will enjoy Kathleen's Bay Town Series!

f facebook.com/kathleenjrobisonauthor

⊙ instagram.com/kathleenjrobison

BB bookbub.com/profile/3794692396